# Learning
## to
# Kill

# Learning to Kill

## STORIES

# Ed McBain

AN OTTO PENZLER BOOK
HARCOURT, INC.
Orlando   Austin   New York
San Diego   Toronto   London

Requests for permission to make copies of any part of the work
should be submitted online at www.harcourt.com/contact
or mailed to the following address:
Permissions Department, Harcourt, Inc.,
6277 Sea Harbor Drive, Orlando, Florida 32887-6777.

www.HarcourtBooks.com

Library of Congress Cataloging-in-Publication Data
McBain, Ed, 1926–2005
Learning to kill: stories/Ed McBain. — 1st ed.
p. cm.
"An Otto Penzler Book."
Includes bibliographical references.
1. Detective and mystery stories, American.   I. Title.
PS3515.U585L43   2006
813'.54—dc22       2005027059
ISBN-13: 978-0-15-101222-0   ISBN-10: 0-15-101222-9

Text set in Electra
Designed by Cathy Riggs

Printed in the United States of America

First edition
A C E G I K J H F D B

This is for my wife, Dragica —
who wasn't there then,
but who is always here for me now.

# Contents

# Contents

# Introduction

**A**ll of the stories in this collection were written between 1952 and 1957. During part of that time, I was working at the Scott Meredith Literary Agency, earning forty dollars a week at first (and later forty-five dollars a week) as "Executive Editor," an exalted title that meant I handled the agency's "commissionable" clients—among whom were Arthur C. Clarke, Lester del Rey, P. G. Wodehouse, John Jakes, Poul Anderson, Frank Kane, Helen Neilsen, Richard Prather, Steve Frazee, and a great many other well-known (at the time) mystery, science fiction, and Western writers.

The agency also handled wannabe writers who'd never been published and who paid a fee to have their manuscripts read and analyzed. If one of the agency's fee readers thought a manuscript had possibilities, he passed it on to me. Occasionally, we sent one of these out to market. But for the most part, I was working with professional writers who were regularly selling their manuscripts to book and magazine publishers all over New York City.

I had stumbled upon this job quite by accident.

At Hunter College, I was an English major (an English "concentrator," as it's now called) and my minors were dramatics and education. The dramatics minor was for fun. The education minor was for insurance. I already knew in college that I wanted to be a writer, but I did not think I'd set the world on fire the minute I stepped out on my own, and I figured a teaching license would help support me while I wrote the Great American Novel. It did indeed support me for a total of seventeen days. Like millions of other World War II veterans, I was graduated in June of 1950, and that fall I began teaching with a so-called emergency license at Bronx Vocational High School. I despised the job, and I quit after I got my first paycheck.

Jobs were scarce in that fall of 1950.

I took a nighttime job with the Automobile Club, answering calls from motorists in distress, and then I found a daytime job with a company called Regal Lobster on West 72nd Street, another job entailing phone calls, this time to restaurants asking if they'd "like a quote this morning on some live Maine lobsters." I had meanwhile decided that the only way to become a published writer was to get a job with either a book publisher or a magazine, and so I prepared a catchy résumé and sent it out hither and yon. By the winter of 1951, I'd had no responses.

It must have been in February that I saw a blind ad in the *New York Times*'s Help Wanted columns. It read something like this:

**EDITOR**
No experience necessary. Must be familiar with book and magazine markets. Reply to box number...

Well, I didn't have much experience with book markets, but I'd read a lot of books. And during my two years in the

Navy, and my four years in college, I'd sent dozens of short stories to nearly every magazine in existence, so I was certainly familiar with magazine markets. In fact, the walls of the bathroom in the apartment I shared with my then-wife and my firstborn son, on North Brother Island in the middle of the East River, were papered entirely with rejection slips. Besides, the ad said "No experience necessary," didn't it?

So I wrote a witty letter, and sent it off to the indicated box number, and a week or so later I picked up the phone at Regal Lobster, and my wife was on the other end, and she told me she'd got a call from a man named Steve Marlowe who said he wanted to interview me regarding my letter about the editorial position. On my lunch hour that day, I took the subway downtown, walked crosstown to Forty-seventh Street and Fifth Avenue, entered 580 Fifth, took the elevator up to the eighteenth floor, walked down the hall to room 1806, and there on the upper glass panel of the door were lettered the words:

SCOTT MEREDITH
LITERARY AGENCY

My hand was on the doorknob.
I thought, A *literary agency?*
Who the hell wants to become a literary agent?
I almost turned away from that door.
I almost walked away from the greatest opportunity life would ever offer me.
Instead, I turned that doorknob, and I opened that door, and stepped into a small waiting room. There was a closed glass panel on the right-hand wall. There was a little push button set on a ledge before the panel. I pressed the button. The

panel slid open. I told a pretty blonde receptionist who I was, and she asked me to take a seat, please, and the glass panel slid shut again. I sat on a sofa on the opposite wall. In a few minutes, a man of about my age—I had just turned twenty-four in October of 1950—came out, shook my hand, introduced himself as Steve Marlowe, told me he was the current Executive Editor at the agency, advised me that they'd been impressed by my letter, and asked if I would mind taking a written test. I said I would be happy to.

He led me into the inner office where there were half a dozen desks with young men behind them, all of them either reading or typing, and then he showed me to an empty desk with a typewriter on it and a chair behind it. He gave me a manuscript titled "Rattlesnake Cave" and asked me to read it and to write a letter to the author, telling him why I thought the story was either salable or not salable. He said I had fifteen minutes. I looked at my watch and began reading.

The story was absolutely terrible.

I later learned that it had been written by Lester del Rey, one of the pre-eminent science fiction writers of the day, and that it was deliberately awful. I didn't know that at the time. I merely wrote a letter telling the supposed real author exactly what I thought of the story.

Steve Marlowe collected the letter when I'd finished it, asked me to wait outside again, and came out some twenty minutes later to tell me he'd showed the letter to Scott, and that they would like to hire me for a two-month trial period. He told me I would be handling the agency's professional clients, and that Scott himself would be my immediate superior. He told me the job paid forty dollars a week. He told me I would be replacing him as Executive Editor.

# Introduction

I have to tell you, I was singularly unimpressed.

The office looked shabby and small, the salary was less than I was earning at Regal Lobster, and a literary agency did not seem the stepping stone I had in mind for a burgeoning literary career.

I said, "Why are *you* leaving the job?"

He said, "Because I'm making so much money selling my own stuff that it doesn't pay to stay here anymore."

My ears shot up.

"When do I start?" I asked.

I did not bring in a batch of my own short stories until the two-month trial period was over, and I was sure the job was truly mine. I gave them to Scott on a Friday afternoon, just before quitting time, and he promised to read them over the weekend. On Monday morning, after he'd read all the mail, he buzzed me into his office. As was our usual working routine, we discussed responses to the various letters from our clients, and he handed me the stack of manuscripts we'd received from them that day, and then he said, "Now, your stories," and slid my precious tales from where he had them neatly stacked on one side of his desk.

"This one, burn," he said, and moved it aside, and picked up another one, and said, "This one, too," and placed it on top of the first one, and then picked up the third story.

"This one, I think we can salvage," he said. "I'll tell you how to rewrite it," and moved it aside into what I hoped would become a growing pile.

"This one, I think I can sell," he said. My heart leaped. I looked at the title. It was called "Welcome, Martians."

"This one, burn," he said.

"This one…"

Of the dozen or so stories I'd showed him, only "Welcome, Martians" met with his approval. He sold it at once to an editor named Bob Lowndes at a pulp magazine called *Science-Fiction Quarterly*. I got a quarter of a cent a word for it. Scott took his 10 percent commission.

I was a writer.

And I had an agent.

I left the agency in May of 1953 because — like Stephen Marlowe before me — I had begun selling so many of my own stories that it was unprofitable for me to stay there any longer. "Welcome, Martians" is not included in this collection, nor are any of the other science fiction, adventure, or Western stories I wrote while learning my craft at the agency, or while honing it later on. All of the stories in this collection are crime stories. Of the twenty-five stories represented here, you will find only one that I wrote in 1952. That's because most of the stories I wrote when I first began working for the agency were as lousy as "Rattlesnake Cave" — though not deliberately so.

Nine of the following stories were published in 1953, six in 1954, five in 1955, two in 1956, and another two in 1957. All but five of them were first published in a detective magazine called *Manhunt*. None of them appeared under the Ed McBain byline. They were written as either Evan Hunter (which in 1952 became my legal name) or as Richard Marsten (a pseudonym derived from the first names of my three sons, Richard, Mark, and Ted) or as Hunt Collins (from my alma mater). But over, lo, these many years, McBain has become the name most closely associated with matters criminal — and this collection, after all, is about learning to write crime fiction.

As you will soon discover, in those early years I was trying my hand at every type of crime story. By the time I wrote the first of the 87th Precinct novels, all of the elements were already in place. Here were the kids in trouble and the women in jeopardy, here were the private eyes and the gangs. Here were the loose cannons and the innocent bystanders. And here, too, were the cops and robbers.

Ed McBain made his debut in May of 1956.

By then, I felt I knew how to write a crime story.

Here's how I learned to do it.

# KIDS

*This story first appeared in* Manhunt. *The editor of the magazine was someone named John McCloud. No one knew who John McCloud was. The poem parody we recited was "I wandered lonely as McCloud." Well, John McCloud was Scott Meredith. It was very good to be working for the man who was editing the hottest detective magazine of the day; in 1953 alone, fourteen of my stories appeared in* Manhunt *under the Marsten, Hunter, or Collins bylines. This one was published in 1955, under the Evan Hunter byline, which by that time had been my legal name for almost three years.*

# First Offense

HE SAT IN THE POLICE VAN WITH THE COLLAR OF HIS leather jacket turned up, the bright silver studs sharp against the otherwise unrelieved black. He was seventeen years old, and he wore his hair in a high black crown. He carried his head high and erect because he knew he had a good profile, and he carried his mouth like a switch knife, ready to spring open at the slightest provocation. His hands were thrust deep into his jacket pockets, and his gray eyes reflected the walls of the van. There was excitement in his eyes, too, an almost holiday excitement. He tried to tell himself he was in trouble, but he couldn't quite believe it. His gradual descent to disbelief had been a spiral that had spun dizzily through the range of his emotions. Terror when the cop's flash had picked him out; blind panic when he'd started to run; rebellion when the cop's firm hand had closed around the leather sleeve of his jacket; sullen resignation when the cop had thrown him into the RMP car; and then cocky stubbornness when they'd booked him at the local precinct.

The desk sergeant had looked him over curiously, with a strange aloofness in his Irish eyes.

"What's the matter, Fatty?" he'd asked.

5

The sergeant stared at him implacably. "Put him away for the night," the sergeant said.

He'd slept overnight in the precinct cell block, and he'd awakened with this strange excitement pulsing through his narrow body, and it was the excitement that had caused his disbelief. Trouble, hell! He'd been in trouble before, but it had never felt like this. This was different. This was a ball, man. This was like being initiated into a secret society someplace. His contempt for the police had grown when they refused him the opportunity to shave after breakfast. He was only seventeen, but he had a fairly decent beard, and a man should be allowed to shave in the morning, what the hell! But even the beard had somehow lent to the unreality of the situation, made him appear — in his own eyes — somehow more desperate, more sinister-looking. He knew he was in trouble, but the trouble was glamorous, and he surrounded it with the gossamer lie of make-believe. He was living the storybook legend. He was big time now. They'd caught him and booked him, and he should have been scared but he was excited instead.

There was one other person in the van with him, a guy who'd spent the night in the cell block, too. The guy was an obvious bum, and his breath stank of cheap wine, but he was better than nobody to talk to.

"Hey!" he said.

The bum looked up. "You talking to me?"

"Yeah. Where we going?"

"The lineup, kid," the bum said. "This your first offense?"

"This's the first time I got caught," he answered cockily.

"All felonies go to the lineup," the bum told him. "And also some special types of misdemeanors. You commit a felony?"

"Yeah," he said, hoping he sounded nonchalant. What'd they have this bum in for anyway? Sleeping on a park bench?

"Well, that's why you're goin' to the lineup. They have guys from every detective squad in the city there, to look you over. So they'll remember you next time. They put you on a stage, and they read off the offense, and the Chief of Detectives starts firing questions at you. What's your name, kid?"

"What's it to you?"

"Don't get smart, punk, or I'll break your arm," the bum said.

He looked at the bum curiously. He was a pretty big guy, with a heavy growth of beard, and powerful shoulders. "My name's Stevie," he said.

"I'm Jim Skinner," the bum said. "When somebody's trying to give you advice, don't go hip on him..."

"Yeah, well, what's your advice?" he asked, not wanting to back down completely.

"When they get you up there, you don't have to answer anything. They'll throw questions but you don't have to answer. Did you make a statement at the scene?"

"No," he answered.

"Good. Then don't make no statement now, either. They can't force you to. Just keep your mouth shut, and don't tell them nothing."

"I ain't afraid. They know all about it anyway," Stevie said.

The bum shrugged and gathered around him the sullen pearls of his scattered wisdom. Stevie sat in the van whistling, listening to the accompanying hum of the tires, hearing the secret hum of his blood beneath the other louder sound. He sat at the core of a self-imposed importance, basking in its warm glow, whistling contentedly, secretly happy. Beside him, Skinner leaned back against the wall of the van.

When they arrived at the Center Street Headquarters, they put them in detention cells, awaiting the lineup which began at nine. At ten minutes to nine they led him out of his cell, and the cop who'd arrested him originally took him into the special prisoners' elevator.

"How's it feel being an elevator boy?" he asked the cop.

The cop didn't answer him. They went upstairs to the big room where the lineup was being held. A detective in front of them was pinning on his shield so he could get past the cop at the desk. They crossed the large gymnasium-like compartment, walking past the men sitting in folded chairs before the stage.

"Get a nice turnout, don't you?" Stevie said.

"You ever tried vaudeville?" the cop answered.

The blinds in the room had not been drawn yet, and Stevie could see everything clearly. The stage itself with the permanently fixed microphone hanging from a narrow metal tube above; the height markers—four feet, five feet, six feet— behind the mike on the wide white wall. The men in the seats, he knew, were all detectives and his sense of importance suddenly flared again when he realized these bulls had come from all over the city just to look at him. Behind the bulls was a raised platform with a sort of lecturer's stand on it. A microphone rested on the stand, and a chair was behind it, and he assumed this was where the Chief bull would sit. There were uniformed cops stationed here and there around the room, and there was one man in civilian clothing who sat at a desk in front of the stage.

"Who's that?" Stevie asked the cop.

"Police stenographer," the cop answered. "He's going to take down your words for posterity."

They walked behind the stage, and Stevie watched as other felony offenders from all over the city joined them. There was one woman, but all the rest were men, and he studied their faces carefully, hoping to pick up some tricks from them, hoping to learn the subtlety of their expressions. They didn't look like much. He was better-looking than all of them, and the knowledge pleased him. He'd be the star of this little shindig. The cop who'd been with him moved over to talk to a big broad who was obviously a policewoman. Stevie looked around, spotted Skinner, and walked over to him.

"What happens now?" he asked.

"They're gonna pull the shades in a few minutes," Skinner said. "Then they'll turn on the spots and start the lineup. The spots won't blind you, but you won't be able to see the faces of any of the bulls out there."

"Who wants to see them mugs?" Stevie asked.

Skinner shrugged. "When your case is called, your arresting officer goes back and stands near the Chief of Detectives, just in case the Chief needs more dope from him. The Chief'll read off your name and the borough where you was pinched. A number'll follow the borough. Like he'll say 'Manhattan one' or 'Manhattan two.' That's just the number of the case from that borough. You're first, you get number one, you follow?"

"Yeah," Stevie said.

"He'll tell the bulls what they got you on, and then he'll say either 'Statement' or 'No statement.' If you made a statement, chances are he won't ask many questions 'cause he won't want you to contradict anything damaging you already said. If there's no statement, he'll fire questions like a machine gun. But you don't have to answer nothing."

"Then what?"

"When he's through, you go downstairs to get mugged and printed. Then they take you over to the Criminal Courts Building for arraignment."

"They're gonna take my picture, huh?" Stevie asked.

"Yeah."

"You think there'll be reporters here?"

"Huh?"

"Reporters."

"Oh. Maybe. All the wire services hang out in a room across the street from where the vans pulled up. They got their own police radio in there, and they get the straight dope as soon as it's happening, in case they want to roll with it. There may be some reporters." Skinner paused. "Why? What'd you do?"

"It ain't so much what I done," Stevie said. "I was just wonderin' if we'd make the papers."

Skinner stared at him curiously. "You're all charged up, ain't you, Stevie?"

"Hell, no. Don't you think I know I'm in trouble?"

"Maybe you don't know just how much trouble," Skinner said.

"What the hell are you talking about?"

"This ain't as exciting as you think, kid. Take my word for it."

"Sure, you know all about it."

"I been around a little," Skinner said drily.

"Sure, on park benches all over the country. I know I'm in trouble, don't worry."

"You kill anybody?"

"No," Stevie said.

"Assault?"

Stevie didn't answer.

"Whatever you done," Skinner advised, "and no matter how long you been doin' it before they caught you, make like it's your first time. Tell them you done it and then say you don't know why you done it, but you'll never do it again. It might help you, kid. You might get off with a suspended sentence."

"Yeah?"

"Sure. And then keep your nose clean afterwards, and you'll be okay."

"Keep my nose clean! Don't make me laugh, pal."

Skinner clutched Stevie's arm in a tight grip. "Kid, don't be a damn fool. If you can get out, get out now! I coulda got out a hundred times, and I'm still with it, and it's no picnic. Get out before you get started."

Stevie shook off Skinner's hand. "Come on, willya?" he said, annoyed.

"Knock it off there," the cop said. "We're ready to start."

"Take a look at your neighbors, kid," Skinner whispered. "Take a hard look. And then get out of it while you still can."

Stevie grimaced and turned away from Skinner. Skinner whirled him around to face him again, and there was a pleading desperation on the unshaven face, a mute reaching in the red-rimmed eyes before he spoke again. "Kid," he said, "listen to me. Take my advice. I've been…"

"Knock it off!" the cop warned again.

He was suddenly aware of the fact that the shades had been drawn and the room was dim. It was very quiet out there, and he hoped they would take him first. The excitement had risen to an almost fever pitch inside him, and he couldn't wait to get on that stage. What the hell was Skinner talking about anyway? "Take a look at your neighbors, kid." The poor jerk probably had a wet brain. What the hell did the police bother with old drunks for, anyway?

A uniformed cop led one of the men from behind the stage, and Stevie moved a little to his left, so that he could see the stage, hoping none of the cops would shove him back where he wouldn't have a good view. His cop and the police-woman were still talking, paying no attention to him. He smiled, unaware that the smile developed as a smirk, and watched the first man mounting the steps to the stage. The man's eyes were very small, and he kept blinking them, blinking them. He was bald at the back of his head, and he was wearing a Navy peacoat and dark tweed trousers, and his eyes were red-rimmed and sleepy-looking. He reached to the five-foot-six-inches marker on the wall behind him, and he stared out at the bulls, blinking.

"Assisi," the Chief of Detectives said, "Augustus, Manhattan one. Thirty-three years old. Picked up in a bar on Forty-third and Broadway, carrying a .45 Colt automatic. No statement. How about it, Gus?"

"How about what?" Assisi asked.

"Were you carrying a gun?"

"Yes, I was carrying a gun." Assisi seemed to realize his shoulders were slumped. He pulled them back suddenly, standing erect.

"Where, Gus?"

"In my pocket."

"What were you doing with the gun, Gus?"

"I was just carrying it."

"Why?"

"Listen, I'm not going to answer any questions," Assisi said. "You're gonna put me through a third degree. I ain't answering nothing. I want a lawyer."

"You'll get plenty opportunity to have a lawyer," the Chief of Detectives said. "And nobody's giving you a third degree. We just want to know what you were doing with a gun. You know that's against the law, don't you?"

"I've got a permit for the gun," Assisi said.

"We checked with Pistol Permits, and they say no. This is a Navy gun, isn't it?"

"Yeah."

"What?"

"I said yeah, it's a Navy gun."

"What were you doing with it? Why were you carrying it around?"

"I like guns."

"Why?"

"Why what? Why do I like guns? Because..."

"Why were you carrying it around?"

"I don't know."

"Well, you must have a reason for carrying a loaded .45. The gun was loaded, wasn't it?"

"Yeah, it was loaded."

"You have any other guns?"

"No."

"We found a .38 in your room. How about that one?"

"It's no good."

"What?"

"The .38."

"What do you mean, no good?"

"The firing mechanism is busted."

"You want a gun that works, is that it?"

"I didn't say that."

"You said the .38's no good because it won't fire, didn't you?"

"Well, what good's a gun that won't fire?"

"Why do you need a gun that fires?"

"I was just carrying it. I didn't shoot anybody, did I?"

"No, you didn't. Were you planning on shooting somebody?"

"Sure," Assisi said. "That's just what I was planning."

"Who?"

"I don't know," Assisi said sarcastically. "Anybody. The first guy I saw, all right? Everybody, all right? I was planning on wholesale murder."

"Not murder, maybe, but a little larceny, huh?"

"Murder," Assisi insisted, in his stride now. "I was just going to shoot up the whole town. Okay? You happy now?"

"Where'd you get the gun?"

"From the Navy."

"Where?"

"From my ship."

"It's a stolen gun?"

"No, I found it."

"You stole government property, is that it?"

"I found it."

"When'd you get out of the Navy?"

"Three months ago."

"You worked since?"

"No."

"Where were you discharged?"

"Pensacola."

"Is that where you stole the gun?"

"I didn't steal it."

"Why'd you leave the Navy?"

Assisi hesitated for a long time.

"Why'd you leave the Navy?" the Chief of Detectives asked again.

"They kicked me out!" Assisi snapped.

"Why?"

"I was undesirable!" he shouted.

"Why?"

Assisi did not answer.

"Why?" There was silence in the darkened room.

Stevie watched Assisi's face, the twitching mouth, the blinking eyelids.

"Next case," the Chief of Detectives said.

Stevie watched as Assisi walked across the stage and down the steps on the other side, where the uniformed cop met him. He'd handled himself well, Assisi had. They'd rattled him a little at the end there, but on the whole he'd done a good job. So the guy was lugging a gun around. So what? He was right, wasn't he? He didn't shoot nobody, so what was all the fuss about? Cops! They had nothing else to do, they went around hauling in guys who were carrying guns. Poor bastard was a veteran, too; that was really rubbing it in. But he did a good job up there, even though he was nervous, you could see he was very nervous.

A man and a woman walked past him and onto the stage. The man was very tall, topping the six-foot marker. The woman was shorter, a bleached blonde turning to fat.

"They picked them up together," Skinner whispered. "So they show them together. They figure a pair'll always work as a pair, usually."

"How'd you like that Assisi?" Stevie whispered back. "He really had them bulls on the run, didn't he?" Skinner didn't answer.

The Chief of Detectives cleared his throat. "MacGregor, Peter, aged forty-five, and Anderson, Marcia, aged forty-two, Bronx one. Got them in a parked car on the Grand Concourse. Backseat of the car was loaded with goods, including luggage, a typewriter, a portable sewing machine, and a fur coat. No statements. What about all that stuff, Pete?"

"It's mine."

"The fur coat, too?"

"No, that's Marcia's."

"You're not married, are you?"

"No."

"Living together?"

"Well, you know," Pete said.

"What about the stuff?" the Chief of Detectives said again.

"I told you," Pete said. "It's ours."

"What was it doing in the car?"

"Oh. Well, we were…uh…" The man paused for a long time. "We were going on a trip."

"Where to?"

"Where? Oh. To…uh…"

Again he paused, frowning, and Stevie smiled, thinking what a clown this guy was. This guy was better than a sideshow at Coney. This guy couldn't tell a lie without having to think about it for an hour. And the dumpy broad with him was a hot sketch, too. This act alone was worth the price of admission.

"Uh…" Pete said, still fumbling for words. "Oh…we were going to…uh…Denver."

"What for?"

"Oh, just a little pleasure trip, you know," he said, attempting a smile.

"How much money were you carrying when we picked you up?"

"Forty dollars."

"You were going to Denver on forty dollars?"

"Well, it was fifty dollars. Yeah, it was more like fifty dollars."

"Come on, Pete, what were you doing with all that stuff in the car?"

"I told you. We were taking a trip."

"With a sewing machine, huh? You do a lot of sewing, Pete?"

"Marcia does."

"That right, Marcia?"

The blonde spoke in a high, reedy voice. "Yeah, I do a lot of sewing."

"That fur coat, Marcia. Is it yours?"

"Sure."

"It has the initials G. D. on the lining. Those aren't your initials, are they, Marcia?"

"No."

"Whose are they?"

"Search me. We bought that coat in a hockshop."

"Where?"

"Myrtle Avenue, Brooklyn. You know where that is?"

"Yes, I know where it is. What about that luggage? It had initials on it, too. And they weren't yours or Pete's. How about it?"

"We got that in a hockshop, too."

"And the typewriter?"

"That's Pete's."

"Are you a typist, Pete?"

"Well, I fool around a little, you know."

"We're going to check all this stuff against our stolen goods list. You know that, don't you?"

"We got all that stuff in hockshops," Pete said. "If it's stolen, we don't know nothing about it."

"Were you going to Denver with him, Marcia?"

"Oh sure."

"When did you both decide to go? A few minutes ago?"

"We decided last week sometime."

"Were you going to Denver by way of the Grand Concourse?"

"Huh?" Pete said.

"Your car was parked on the Grand Concourse. What were you doing there with a carload of stolen goods?"

"It wasn't stolen," Pete said.

"We were on our way to Yonkers," the woman said.

"I thought you were going to Denver."

"Yeah, but we had to get the car fixed first. There was something wrong with the…" She paused, turning to Pete. "What was it, Pete? That thing that was wrong?"

Pete waited a long time before answering. "Uh…the… uh…the flywheel, yeah. There's a garage up in Yonkers fixes them good, we heard. Flywheels, I mean."

"If you were going to Yonkers, why were you parked on the Concourse?"

"Well, we were having an argument."

"What kind of an argument?"

"Not an argument, really. Just a discussion, sort of."

"About what?"

"About what to eat."

"What!"

"About what to eat. I wanted to eat Chink's, but Marcia wanted a glass of milk and a piece of pie. So we were trying to decide whether we should go to the Chink's or the cafeteria. That's why we were parked on the Concourse."

"We found a wallet in your coat, Pete. It wasn't yours, was it?"

"No."

"Whose was it?"

"I don't know." He paused, then added hastily, "There wasn't no money in it."

"No, but there was identification. A Mr. Simon Granger. Where'd you get it, Pete?"

"I found it in the subway. There wasn't no money in it."

"Did you find all that other stuff in the subway, too?"

"No, sir, I bought that." He paused. "I was going to return the wallet, but I forgot to stick it in the mail."

"Too busy planning for the Denver trip, huh?"

"Yeah, I guess so."

"When's the last time you earned an honest dollar, Pete?"

Pete grinned. "Oh, about two, three years ago. I guess."

"Here're their records," the Chief of Detectives said. "Marcia, 1938, Sullivan Law; 1939, Concealing Birth of Issue; 1940, Possession of Narcotics — you still on the stuff, Marcia?"

"No."

"1942, Dis Cond; 1943, Narcotics again; 1947 — you had enough, Marcia?"

Marcia didn't answer.

"Pete," the Chief of Detectives said, "1940, Attempted Rape; 1941, Selective Service Act; 1942, Dis Cond; 1943, Attempted Burglary; 1945, Living on Proceeds of Prostitution; 1947, Assault and Battery, did two years at Ossining."

"I never done no time," Pete said.

"According to this, you did."

"I never done no time," he insisted.

"1950," the Chief of Detectives went on, "Carnal Abuse of a Child." He paused. "Want to tell us about that one, Pete?"

"I…uh…" Pete swallowed. "I got nothing to say."

"You're ashamed of some things, that it?"

Pete didn't answer.

"Get them out of here," the Chief of Detectives said.

"See how long he kept them up there?" Skinner whispered. "He knows what they are, wants every bull in the city to recognize them if they…"

"Come on," a detective said, taking Skinner's arm.

Stevie watched as Skinner climbed the steps to the stage. Those two had really been something, all right. And just looking at them, you'd never know they were such operators. You'd never know they…

"Skinner, James, Manhattan two. Aged fifty-one. Threw a garbage can through the plate-glass window of a clothing shop on Third Avenue. Arresting officer found him inside the shop with a bundle of overcoats. No statement. That right, James?"

"I don't remember," Skinner said.

"Is it, or isn't it?"

"All I remember is waking up in jail this morning."

"You don't remember throwing that ash can through the window?"

"No, sir."

"You don't remember taking those overcoats?"

"No, sir."

"Well, you must have done it, don't you think? The off-duty detective found you inside the store with the coats in your arms."

"I got only his word for that, sir."

"Well, his word is pretty good. Especially since he found you inside the store with your arms full of merchandise."

"I don't remember, sir."

"You've been here before, haven't you?"

"I don't remember, sir."

"What do you do for a living, James?"

"I'm unemployed, sir."

"When's the last time you worked?"

"I don't remember, sir."

"You don't remember much of anything, do you?"

"I have a poor memory, sir."

"Maybe the record has a better memory than you, James," the Chief of Detectives said.

"Maybe so, sir. I couldn't say."

"I hardly know where to start, James. You haven't been exactly an ideal citizen."

"Haven't I, sir?"

"Here's as good a place as any. 1948, Assault and Robbery; 1949, Indecent Exposure; 1951, Burglary; 1952, Assault and Robbery again. You're quite a guy, aren't you, James?"

"If you say so, sir."

"I say so. Now how about that store?"

"I don't remember anything about a store, sir."

"Why'd you break into it?"

"I don't remember breaking into any store, sir."

"Hey, what's this?" the Chief of Detectives said suddenly.

"Sir?"

"Maybe we should've started back a little further, huh, James? Here, on your record. 1938, convicted of First-degree Murder, sentenced to execution."

The assembled bulls began murmuring among themselves. Stevie leaned forward eagerly, anxious to get a better look at this bum who'd offered him advice.

"What happened there, James?"

"What happened where, sir?"

"You were sentenced to death? How come you're still with us?"

"The case was appealed."

"And never retried?"

"No, sir."

"You're pretty lucky, aren't you?"

"I'm pretty *unlucky*, sir, if you ask me."

"Is that right? You cheat the chair, and you call that unlucky. Well, the law won't slip up this time."

"I don't know anything about law, sir."

"You don't, huh?"

"No, sir. I only know that if you want to get a police station into action, all you have to do is buy a cheap bottle of wine and drink it quiet, minding your own business."

"And that's what you did, huh, James?"

"That's what I did, sir."

"And you don't remember breaking into that store?"

"I don't remember anything."

"All right, next case."

Skinner turned his head slowly, and his eyes met Stevie's squarely. Again there was the same mute pleading in his eyes, and then he turned his head away and shuffled off the stage and down the steps into the darkness.

The cop's hand closed around Stevie's biceps. For an instant he didn't know what was happening, and then he realized his case was the next one. He shook off the cop's hand, squared his shoulders, lifted his head, and began climbing the steps.

He felt taller all at once. He felt like an actor coming on after his cue. There was an aura of unreality about the stage and the darkened room beyond it, the bulls sitting in that room.

The Chief of Detectives was reading off the information about him, but he didn't hear it. He kept looking at the lights, which were not really so bright, they didn't blind him at all. Didn't they have brighter lights? Couldn't they put more lights on him, so they could see him when he told his story?

He tried to make out the faces of the detectives, but he couldn't see them clearly, and he was aware of the Chief of Detective's voice droning on and on, but he didn't hear what the man was saying, he heard only the hum of his voice. He glanced over his shoulder, trying to see how tall he was against the markers, and then he stood erect, his shoulders back, moving closer to the hanging microphone, wanting to be sure his voice was heard when he began speaking.

"...no statement," the Chief of Detectives concluded. There was a long pause, and Stevie waited, holding his breath. "This your first offense, Steve?" the Chief of Detectives asked.

"Don't you know?" Stevie answered.

"I'm asking you."

"Yeah, it's my first offense."

"You want to tell us all about it?"

"There's nothing to tell. You know the whole story, anyway."

"Sure, but do you?"

"What are you talking about?"

"Tell us the story, Steve."

"What're ya makin' a big federal case out of a lousy stickup for? Ain't you got nothing better to do with your time?"

"We've got plenty of time, Steve."

"Well, I'm in a hurry."

"You're not going anyplace, kid. Tell us about it."

"What's there to tell? There was a candy store stuck up, that's all."

"Did you stick it up?"

"That's for me to know and you to find out."

"We know you did."

"Then don't ask me stupid questions."

"Why'd you do it?"

"I ran out of butts."

"Come on, kid."

"I done it 'cause I wanted to."

"Why?"

"Look, you caught me cold, so let's get this over with, huh? What're ya wastin' time with me for?"

"We want to hear what you've got to say. Why'd you pick this particular candy store?"

"I just picked it. I put slips in a hat and picked this one out."

"You didn't really, did you, Steve?"

"No, I didn't really. I picked it 'cause there's an old crumb who runs it, and I figured it was a pushover."

"What time did you enter the store, Steve?"

"The old guy told you all this already, didn't he? Look, I know I'm up here so you can get a good look at me. All right, take your good look, and let's get it over with."

"What time, Steve?"

"I don't have to tell you nothing."

"Except that we know it already."

"Then why do you want to hear it again? Ten o'clock, all right? How does that fit?"

"A little early, isn't it?"

"How's eleven? Try that one for size."

"Let's make it twelve, and we'll be closer."

"Make it whatever you want to," Stevie said, pleased with the way he was handling this. They knew all about it, anyway, so he might as well have himself a ball, show them they couldn't shove him around.

"You went into the store at twelve, is that right?"

"If you say so, Chief."

"Did you have a gun?"

"No."

"What, then?"

"Nothing."

"Nothing at all?"

"Just me. I scared him with a dirty look, that's all."

"You had a switch knife, didn't you?"

"You found one on me, so why ask?"

"Did you use the knife?"

"No."

"You didn't tell the old man to open the cash register or you'd cut him up? Isn't that what you said?"

"I didn't make a tape recording of what I said."

"But you did threaten him with the knife. You did force him to open the cash register, holding the knife on him."

"I suppose so."

"How much money did you get?"

"You've got the dough. Why don't you count it?"

"We already have. Twelve dollars, is that right?"

"I didn't get a chance to count it. The Law showed."

"When did the Law show?"

"When I was leaving. Ask the cop who pinched me. He knows when."

"Something happened before you left, though."

"Nothing happened. I cleaned out the register and then blew. Period."

"Your knife had blood on it."

"Yeah? I was cleaning chickens last night."

"You stabbed the owner of that store, didn't you?"

"Me? I never stabbed nobody in my whole life."

"Why'd you stab him?"

"I didn't."

"Where'd you stab him?"

"I didn't stab him."

"Did he start yelling?"

"I don't know what you're talking about."

"You stabbed him, Steve. We know you did."

"You're full of crap."

"Don't get smart, Steve."

"Ain't you had your look yet? What the hell more do you want?"

"We want you to tell us why you stabbed the owner of that store."

"And I told you I didn't stab him."

"He was taken to the hospital last night with six knife wounds in his chest and abdomen. Now how about that, Steve?"

"Save your questioning for the Detective Squad Room. I ain't saying another word."

"You had your money. Why'd you stab him?"

Stevie did not answer.

"Were you afraid?"

"Afraid of what?" Stevie answered defiantly.

"I don't know. Afraid he'd tell who held him up? Afraid he'd start yelling? What were you afraid of, kid?"

"I wasn't afraid of nothing. I told the old crumb to keep his mouth shut. He shoulda listened to me."

"He didn't keep his mouth shut?"

"Ask him."

"I'm asking you!"

"No, he didn't keep his mouth shut. He started yelling. Right after I'd cleaned out the drawer. The damn jerk, for a lousy twelve bucks he starts yelling."

"What'd you do?"

"I told him to shut up."

"And he didn't."

"No. he didn't. So I hit him, and he still kept yelling. So I gave him the knife."

"Six times?"

"I don't know how many times. I just gave it to him. He shouldn't have yelled. You ask him if I did any harm to him before that. Go ahead, ask him. He'll tell you. I didn't even touch the crumb before he started yelling. Go to the hospital and ask him if I touched him. Go ahead, ask him."

"We can't, Steve."

"Wh…"

"He died this morning."

"He…"

For a moment, Stevie could not think clearly. Died? Is that what he'd said? The room was curiously still now. It had been silently attentive before, but this was something else, something different, and the stillness suddenly chilled him, and he looked down at his shoes.

"I…I didn't mean him to pass away," he mumbled.

The police stenographer looked up. "To what?"

"To pass away," a uniformed cop repeated, whispering.

"What?" the stenographer asked again.

"He didn't mean him to pass away!" the cop shouted.

The cop's voice echoed in the silent room. The stenographer bent his head and began scribbling in his pad.

"Next case," the Chief of Detectives said.

Stevie walked off the stage, his mind curiously blank, his feet strangely leaden. He followed the cop to the door, and then walked with him to the elevator. They were both silent as the doors closed.

"You picked an important one for your first one," the cop said.

"He shouldn't have died on me," Stevie answered.

"You shouldn't have stabbed him," the cop said.

He tried to remember what Skinner had said to him before the lineup, but the noise of the elevator was loud in his ears, and he couldn't think clearly. He could only remember the word "neighbors" as the elevator dropped to the basement to join them.

*In this story—which first appeared in* Manhunt *in 1953, under the Evan Hunter byline—there's a detective named Marelli and another one named Willis and yet another one named Ed. Is it just coincidence that I chose the pseudonym Ed McBain for the series of cop novels I would begin writing a few years later? Is it further coincidence that two of the continuing characters in the 87th Precinct novels are named Carella and Willis? I don't know. Maybe "Kid Kill" should properly belong in the Cops and Robbers section of this book. But when I wrote it back in 1953, I didn't think of it as the first cop story I'd ever written in my life. I just thought of it as a story about a kid.*

# Kid Kill

IT WAS JUST A ROUTINE CALL. I REMEMBER I WAS SITTING around with Ed, talking about a movie we'd both seen, when Marelli walked in, a sheet of paper in his hand.

"You want to take this, Art?"

I looked up, pulled a face, and said, "Who stabbed who now?"

"This is an easy one," Marelli said. He smoothed his mustache in an unconscious gesture, and added, "Accidental shooting."

"Then why bother Homicide?"

"Accidental shooting resulting in death."

I got up, hitched up my trousers, and sighed. "They always pick the coldest goddamn days of the year to play with war souvenirs." I looked at the frost edging the windows and then turned back to Marelli. "It *was* a war souvenir, wasn't it?"

"Luger," Marelli said. "Nine millimeter. The man on the beat checked it."

"Was it registered?"

"You tell me."

"Stupid characters," I said. "You'd think the law wasn't there for their own protection." I sighed again and looked over to where Ed was trying to make himself look small. "Come on, Ed, time to work."

Ed shuffled to his feet. He was a big man with bright red hair, and a nose broken by an escaped con back in '45. It happened that the con was a little runt, about five feet high in his Adler elevators, and Ed had taken a lot of ribbing about that broken nose—even though we all knew the con had used a lead pipe.

"Trouble with you, Marelli," he said in his deep voice, "you take your job too seriously."

Marelli looked shocked. "Is it my fault some kid accidentally plugs his brother?"

"What?" I said. I had taken my overcoat from the peg and was shrugging into it now. "What was that, Marelli?"

"It was a kid," Marelli said. "Ten years old. He was showing his younger brother the Luger when it went off. Hell, you know these things."

I pulled my muffler tight around my neck, and then buttoned my coat. "This is just a waste of time," I said. "Why do the police always have to horn in on personal tragedies?"

Marelli paused near the desk, dropping the paper with the information on it. "Every killing is a personal tragedy for someone," he said. I stared at him as he walked to the door, waved, and went out.

"Pearls from a flatfoot," Ed said. "Come on, let's get this over with."

It was bitter cold, the kind of cold that attacks your ears and your hands, and makes you want to huddle around a potbelly stove. Ed pulled the Mercury up behind the white-topped squad car, and we climbed out, losing the warmth of the car heater. The beat man was standing near a white picket fence that ran around the small house. His uniform collar was pulled high onto the back of his neck and his eyes and nose were running. He looked as cold as I felt.

Ed and I walked over to him and he saluted and then began slapping his gloved hands together.

"I been waitin' for you, sir," he said. "My name's Connerly. I put in the call."

"Detective Sergeant Willis," I said. "This is my partner, Ed Daley."

"Hiya," Ed said.

"Hell of a thing, ain't it, sir?"

"Sounds routine to me," Ed said. "Kid showing off a war trophy, bang! His little brother is dead. Happens every damned day of the week."

"Sure, sir, but I mean…"

"Family inside?" I asked.

"Just the mother, sir. That's what makes it more of a tragedy, you see."

"What's that?" I asked.

"Well, sir, she's a widow. Three sons. The oldest one was killed in the last war. He's the one sent the Luger home. Now this. Well, sir, you know what I mean."

"Let's get inside," I said.

Connerly led us to the front door, and rapped on it with a gloved hand. Ed stole a glance at me, and I knew he didn't relish this particular picnic any more than I did.

The door opened quickly, and a small woman with dark

blue eyes looked out at us. She might have been pretty once, but that was a long time ago, and all the beauty had fled from her, leaving her tired and defeated.

"Mrs. Owens, this is Detective Sergeant Willis and his partner," Connerly said.

Mrs. Owens nodded faintly.

"May we come in, ma'am?" I asked.

She seemed to remember her manners all at once. "Yes, please," she said. "Please do." Her voice was stronger than her body looked, and I wondered if she was really as old as she seemed. A widow, one son killed in the war. Death can sometimes do that to a person. Leave them more withered than the corpse.

"We're sorry to bother you, ma'am," I said, feeling foolish as hell, the way I always did in a situation like this. "The law requires us to make a routine check, however, and..."

"That's quite all right, Mr. Willis." She moved quickly to the couch and straightened the doilies. "Sit down, won't you?"

"Thank you, ma'am." I sat down with Ed on my right. Connerly stood near the radiator, his hands behind his back.

Ed took out his pad, and cleared his throat. I took that as my cue and said, "Can you tell us exactly what happened, ma'am."

"Well, I...I don't really know, exactly. You see, I was in the kitchen baking. This is Wednesday, and I usually bake on Wednesdays. The boys..." She hesitated, bit her lip. "The boys like pie, and I try to bake one at least once a week."

"Yes, ma'am."

"I...I was putting the pie into the oven when I heard this...this noise from the attic. I knew the boys were up there playing so I didn't think anything of it."

"What are the boys' names, ma'am?"

"Jeffrey. He's my oldest. And…and…"

"Yes, ma'am."

"Ronald."

"Was Ronald the boy who was shot, ma'am?"

She didn't answer. She simply nodded. I got up and walked to the upright piano, where there were four photos in silver frames. One was of an older man, obviously the dead Mr. Owens. A second was of a young man in an Army uniform, crossed infantry rifles on his lapels. The other two were of the younger boys.

Mrs. Owens blew her nose in a small handkerchief and looked up.

"Which one is Jeffrey?" I asked.

"The…the blond boy."

I looked at the photo. He seemed like a nice kid, with a pleasant smile and his mother's dark eyes.

"Is he in the house?"

"Yes. He's upstairs in his room."

"I'd like to talk to him, ma'am."

"All right."

"If you don't mind, I'd like to see the attic first."

She seemed about to refuse, and then she nodded. "Certainly."

"You needn't come up, Mrs. Owens," Ed said. "The patrolman can show us the way."

"Thank you," she said.

We followed Connerly up the steps, and he whispered, "See what I mean? Jesus, this is a rotten business."

"Well, what're you gonna do?" Ed philosophized.

---

35

The attic had been fixed as a playroom, with plasterboard walls and ceiling. An electric train layout covered one half of the room. On the other side of the room, young Ronald Owens lay covered with a sheet. I walked over, lifted the sheet, and looked down at the boy. He resembled the older Jeffrey a great deal, except that his hair was brown. He had the same dark eyes, though, staring up at me now, sightless. There was a neat hole between his eyes, and his face was an ugly mixture of blood and powder burns. I lowered the sheet.

"Where's the gun?" I asked Connerly.

"Right here, sir."

He fished into his pocket and produced the Luger, wrapped carefully in his handkerchief. I opened the handkerchief and stared at the German gun.

"Did you break it open, Connerly?"

"Why, no, sir. A patrolman isn't allowed to..."

"If you broke it open, you'll save me the trouble."

Connerly looked abashed. "Yes, sir, I did."

"Any shells in it?"

"No, sir."

"Not even in the firing chamber?"

"No, sir."

"One bullet, then. That's strange."

"What's so strange about it?" Ed wanted to know.

"A Luger's magazine fed, that's all," I said. "Eight slugs in a clip. Strange to find only one." I shrugged, handing the pistol back to Connerly. "Let's see what else is around here."

We started rummaging around the attic, not really looking for anything in particular. I think I was just postponing the talk I had to have with the young kid who'd shot his own brother.

"Bunch of books," Ed said.

"Mmmmm?"

"Yeah. Few old newspapers."

"Here's something," Connerly said.

"What've you got?"

"Looks like a box of clips, sir."

"Yeah? For the Luger?"

"Looks that way, sir."

I walked over to where Connerly was standing, and took the box from the shelf. He had carefully refrained from touching it. The box was covered with a fine layer of dust. There were two clips in the open box, and they, too, were covered with dust. I lifted one of the clips out, running my eyes over the cartridges. Eight. The second clip had only seven cartridges in it.

"Only seven here," I said.

"Yeah," Connerly said, nodding. "That's where the bullet came from, all right."

"Anything else there, Ed?" I asked, turning to where he was kneeling over another box on the floor.

"Just these loose newspaper clippings. Nothing really... hey!"

"What've you got?"

"This's strange as hell," Ed said.

"What? What's so strange?"

He got to his feet and walked over to me, holding a clipping in his big hand. "Take a look at this, Art."

The clipping had been scissored from one of the tabloids. It was simply the story of a boy and a girl who'd been playing in their backyard. Playing with a Colt .45 that was a war souvenir. The .45 had gone off, blowing half the girl's head away.

There was a picture of the boy in tears, and a story of the fatal accident.

"Some coincidence, huh, Art?"

"Yeah," I said. "Some coincidence."

I put the box of Luger magazines back on the shelf.

"I think we'd better talk to the kid now," I said.

We left the attic, Connerly whispering something about the way fate sometimes works. He called Mrs. Owens, and she came up to lead us to the boy's room on the second floor of the house.

She rapped on the door and softly called, "Jeffrey?"

I could hear sobbing beyond the door, and then a muffled, "Yes?"

"Some gentlemen would like to talk to you," she said.

The sobbing stopped, and I heard the sound of bare feet padding to the door. The door opened and Jeffrey stood there, drying his face. He was thinner than the photograph had shown him, with bright blue eyes and narrow lips. His hair hung over his forehead in unruly strands, and there were tear streaks under his eyes and down his cheeks.

"You're policemen, aren't you?" he said.

"Yes, son."

"We just want to ask a few questions," Ed said.

"Come in."

We walked into the room. There were two beds in it, one on either side of the large window. There was one dresser, and I imagined the two boys shared this. Toys were packed neatly in a carton on one side of the room. A high school pennant and several college pennants decorated the walls, and a model airplane hung from the ceiling.

Mrs. Owens started into the room, and Ed said gently, "If we can talk to him alone..."

Her hand went to her mouth, and she said, "Oh. Oh, all right."

Jeffrey walked to his bed and sat on it, one leg tucked under him. He stared out the window, not looking at us.

"Want to tell us how it happened, son?"

"It was just an accident," he said. "I didn't mean to do it, honest."

"We know," Ed said. "We just want to know how it happened."

"Well, we were upstairs playing with the trains, and then we got sort of tired. We started kidding around, and then I found Perry's...that's my older brother who was killed in the war...I found Perry's Luger and we started foolin' around with that."

"Is that the first time you saw the gun, son?"

"No, no." He turned to look me full in the face. "Perry sent it home a long time ago. Before he was killed, even. One of his buddies brought it to us."

"Uh-huh. Go on, son."

"Well, then we found the bullets in the box..."

"You didn't know the bullets were there before this?"

"No." Again, Jeffrey stared at me. "No, we just found them today."

"Did you know where the gun was?"

"Well...yes."

"You said you found it, though. You didn't mean that, did you, son?"

"Well, I knew it was in the attic someplace because that's where Mom put it. I didn't know just where until I found it today."

"Oh, I see. Go on, please."

Ed looked at me curiously, and then turned his interest back to the boy.

"We found the bullets, and I took a cartridge from one of the magazines, just to fool around. I stuck it in the gun and then all at once the gun went off...and...and...Ronnie... Ronnie..."

The kid turned his face away, then threw himself onto the pillow.

"I didn't mean to do it," he said. "Honest, honest. The gun just went off. It just did. I loved my brother. I loved my brother. Now there's just me and Mom, just the two of us. I didn't want it to happen. I didn't."

"Sure, son," I said. I walked to the bed and sat down beside him. "You liked your brother a lot. I know. I have a brother, too."

Ed gave me another curious look, but I continued to pat the kid's shoulder.

"Yes," Jeffrey said, "I did like him. I liked Perry, too, and he was killed. And now...now this. Now there's just me and Mom. They're all gone. Dad, and Perry, and...and...Ronnie. Now we're all alone." He started bawling again. "It's my fault," he said. "If I hadn't wanted to play with that old gun..."

"It's not your fault," I said. "Accidents happen. They happen all the time. No one could possibly blame you for it."

His tears ebbed slowly, and he finally sat up again. "You know it's not my fault, don't you?" he asked solemnly.

"Yes," I said. "We know."

He tried to smile, but failed. "It was just an accident," he said again.

"Sure," I said. I picked myself off the bed and said, "Let's go, Ed. Nothing more for us here."

At the door, I turned to look at Jeffrey once more. He seemed immensely relieved, and he smiled when I winked at him. The smile was still on his mouth and in his eyes when we left him.


It was cold in the Merc, even with the heater going.

We drove in silence for a long time, and finally Ed asked, "All right, what was all that business about?"

"What business?"

"First of all, that brother routine. You know damn well you're a lousy, spoiled, only child."

"Sure," I said. "I just wanted to hear the kid tell me how much he loved his brothers."

"That's another thing. Why the hell did you cross-examine the kid? Jesus, he had enough trouble without your…"

"I was just wondering about a few things," I said. "That's all."

"What kind of things?"

"Well, the newspaper clipping about the little boy who accidentally killed that girl, for one. Now why do you suppose any kid would save a clipping like that?"

"Hell," Ed said, "you know how kids are. It probably caught his fancy, that's all."

"Probably. Maybe the Luger magazine caught his fancy, too."

"What do you mean?"

"The kid said he found those magazines for the first time today. He said he took a cartridge from one of the clips and stuck it into the gun. Tell me how he managed to handle a dust-covered magazine without smearing any of the dust."

Ed looked at me.

"He didn't, Ed, that's the answer. He took that bullet from the clip a long time ago. Long enough ago for the box and the magazine to acquire a new coat of dust. This was no spur-of-the-moment job. No, sir, not at all."

"What the hell are you trying to say?" Ed asked. "You mean the kid did this on purpose? You mean he actually *killed* his brother? *Murdered* him?"

"Just him and Mom now, Ed. Just the two of them. No more Dad, no more big brother, and now no more little brother." I shook my head and stared at my own breath as it clouded the windshield. "But just take it to a judge. Just take the whole fantastic thing to a judge and see how fast he kicks you out of court."

Ed glanced at me quickly, and then turned his eyes back to the road.

"We'll have to watch that kid," I said, "maybe get him some psychiatric care. I hate to think what would happen if he suddenly builds up a dislike for his mother."

I didn't say anything after that, but it was a cold ride back to the station.

Damned cold.

*I grew up as Salvatore Lombino, on 120th Street between First and Second avenues, in New York City's East Harlem. My grandfather had a tailor shop on First Avenue. We grandsons and granddaughters of Italian, Irish, Jewish, and German immigrants lighted celebratory bonfires in the streets on election night, and sometimes roasted potatoes over smaller fires in vacant lots. We roller-skated in the streets. We played marbles—or "immies," as we used to call them—in the curbside gutters. We played stickball and Johnny-on-a-Pony and Ring-a-Leevio. It was a good street with good people on it. In all of my twelve years on that street, I never met any kid like the lead character in this story.*

*"See Him Die" was first published in* Manhunt *in July of 1955 under the Evan Hunter byline. By then, I was using my new (hey, only three years old!) name on virtually everything I wrote; the movie version of* The Blackboard Jungle *had been released in February of that year, and the novel was now a multimillion-copy bestseller in paperback (which it hadn't been in hardcover) and so Evan Hunter was now somewhat well-known.*

*I was busy finishing my second Evan Hunter novel, almost prophetically titled* Second Ending *(it later sold only 16,000 copies, most of them bought by my mother) when Herb Alexander, the editor in chief of Pocket Books, called Scott Meredith. What happened was that Scott had submitted to Pocket an as-yet-unpurchased Hunt Collins novel titled* Cut

Me In, *and despite the pseudonym, Herb had recognized the style. He called Scott to ask, "Is this our friend Hunter?" Surprised to learn that I also wrote mysteries, eager to find a successor to the aging Erle Stanley Gardner, he explored with Scott—and later with me—the possibility of my writing a continuing series of novels. By then, I was convinced that cops were the only legitimate people to investigate crimes. Herb didn't buy* Cut Me In, *but he gave me a contract to write three cop novels. Thus were Ed McBain and the 87th Precinct born.*

*"See Him Die"—in a greatly changed and expanded version—was later retitled* See Them Die, *and published in 1960 as the thirteenth novel in the 87th Precinct series.*

# See Him Die

WHEN YOU'RE THE HEAD MAN, YOU'RE SUPPOSED TO GET the rumble first. Then you feed it to the other kids, and you read off the music, and if they don't like it that's their hard luck. They can take off with or without busted heads.

So that's why I was sore when Aiello comes to me and starts making like a kid with an inside wire. He's standing in a doorway, with his jacket collar up around his nose, and first off I think he's got some weed on him. Then I see he ain't fixing to gather a stone, but he's got this weird light in his eyes anyway.

"What're you doing, A," I said.

Aiello looked over his shoulder as if the bulls were after him. He takes my arm and pulls me into the doorway and says, "Danny, I got something hot."

"What?" I said. "Your head?"

"Danny, what I mean, this is something."

"So tell it."

"Harry Manzetti," he said. He said it in a kind of a hoarse whisper, and I looked at him funny, and I figured maybe he'd just hit the pipe after all.

"What about him?"

"He's here."

"What do you mean, here? Where here?"

"In the neighborhood."

"You're full of it," I told him.

"I swear to God, Danny. I seen him."

"Where?"

"I was going up to Louise's. You know Louise?"

"I know Louise."

"She lives on the seventh floor. I spot this guy up ahead of me, and he's walking with a limp and right off I start thinking of the guys in the neighborhood who limp, and all I come up with is Carl. And then I remember Harry."

"There must be a million guys who limp."

"Sure, but name me another one, dad. Anyway, I get a look at his face. It was Harry."

"How'd you see his face?"

"He went up the seventh floor, too. I was knocking on Louise's door, and this guy with the limp goes down the end of the hall and sticks a key in the latch. Then he remembers I'm behind him, and he turns to cop a look, and that's when I see his face. It was Harry, all right."

"What'd you do?"

"Nothing. I turned away fast so he wouldn't see I spotted him. Man, that cat's wanted in more states…"

"You tell Louise this?"

"No."

"You sure?"

"Dad, I'm sure." Aiello looked at me peculiar, and then he turned his eyes away.

"Who'd you tell, A?"

"Nobody. Danny, I swear it on my mother's eyes. You the first one I'm talking to."

"How'd he look?" I said.

"Harry? Oh, fine. He looked fine, Danny."

"Whyn't you tell me sooner?"

"I just now seen you!" Aiello complained.

"Whyn't you look for me?"

"I don't know. I was busy."

"Doing what? Standing in a doorway?"

"I was..." Aiello paused. "I was looking for you. I figured you'd come by."

"How'd you figure that?"

"Well, I figured once the word leaked, you'd be around."

"How'd the word leak if you're the only one knows it?"

"Well, I figured..."

Aiello stopped talking, and I stopped listening. We both heard it at the same time, the high scream of a squad car siren.

"Cops," I said.

And then we heard another siren, and then the whole damn block was being busted up all at once, sirens screaming down on it from all the side streets.


In fifteen minutes, every damn cop in the city was on our block. They put up their barricades, and they hung around behind their cars while they figured what to do. I spotted Donlevy in the bunch, too, strutting around like a big wheel. He had me in once because some jerk from the Blooded Royals took a slug from a zip gun, and he figured it was one of my boys who done it, and he tried to hang it on me. I told Donlevy where he could hang his phony rap, and I also told him he better not walk alone on our block after dark or he'd be using his shield for a funeral emblem. He kicked me in the butt, and told me I was the one better watch out, so I spit at his feet and called him a name my old man always uses, and Donlevy wasn't hip to it so he didn't get too sore, even though he knew I was cursing.

So he was there, too, making like a big wheel, with his tin pinned to his coat so that everybody could know he was a cop. All the bulls were wearing their tin outside, so you could tell them from the people who were just watching. There were a lot of people in the streets now, and the cops kept shoving them back behind the barricades which they'd set up in front of the building where Harry was. It didn't take an Einstein to figure that somebody'd blown the whistle on Harry and that the bulls were ready to try for a pinch. Only thing, I figured, they didn't know whether he was heeled or not, and so they were making their strategy behind their cars, afraid to show their stupid faces in case he *was* heeled. I'd already sent Aiello for the boys, and I hung around on the outside of the crowd now because I didn't want Donlevy to spot me and start getting wise. Also, there were a lot of bulls all over the place, and outside of the tin you couldn't tell the bulls from the people without a scorecard, and nobody was selling scorecards. So when a bull's back was turned and the tin couldn't be seen, he looked just like anybody else, and Christ knows which bull had spotted me somewhere doing something or other, and I didn't want to take chances until all the boys were with me.

There was a lot of uniformed brass around the cars, too, and they all talked it up, figuring who was going to be the first to die, in case Harry was carrying a gun. Harry was born and

raised right in this neighborhood, and all the kids knew him
from when he used to be king of the hill. And Harry was always heeled, even in those days, either with brass knucks or a
switch knife or a razor or a zip gun, and later on he had a .38
he showed the guys. That was just before he lammed out—
the time he knocked off that crumb from uptown. I remember once when Harry cut up a guy so bad, the guy couldn't
walk. I swear. I mean it. He didn't only use the knife on the
guy's face. He used it all over so the guy couldn't walk later,
that guy was sorry he tangled with a customer like Harry, all
right. They only come like Harry once in a while, and when
you got a Harry in your neighborhood, you know it, man. You
know it, and you try to live up to the rep, you dig me? You got
a guy like Harry around, well hell, man, you can't run the
neighborhood like a tea party. You got certain standards and
ideals, I guess you would call them. So we was all kind of sorry
when Harry had to take off like that, but of course he was getting all kinds of heat by that time, not only from the locals who
was after him for that crumb uptown, but also he was getting
G-heat because the word was he transported some broads into
Connecticut for the purpose of being illegal, leastways that's
the way they read it off on him at the lineup, and I know a guy
who was at the lineup personally that time, so this is straight
from the horse's mouth.

But if those cops were wondering whether or not Harry
was heeled, I could have saved them a lot of trouble if they
wanted to ask me. I could tell them Harry was not only heeled
but that he was probably heeled to his eyeballs, and that if they
expected to just walk in and put the muscle on him, they had
another guess coming, or maybe two or three. It didn't make
one hell of a big difference anyhow, because the cops looked

as if they took along their whole damn arsenal just to pry Harry out of that seventh-floor apartment.

The streets were really packed now with people and cops and reporters and the emergency cop truck, and I expected pretty soon we would have President Eisenhower there to dedicate a stone or something. I began to wonder where the hell the boys were because the rooftops were getting lined pretty fast, and if the cops and Harry were going to shoot this thing out, I wanted to watch him pick them off. And unless we got a good spot on the roof, things would be rugged. I was ready to go looking for Aiello when he comes back with Ferdy and Beef.

Ferdy is a guy about my height and build, except he's got straight black hair and brown eyes, and my hair is a little curly and my eyes are not brown really, they're amber — that's what Marie says, and she ought to know, dad. I been going with Marie since we was both thirteen, and that makes it close to three years now, so she knows the color of my eyes, all right.

"This the straight dope?" Ferdy asked. Ferdy used to be on H, but we broke him of it 'cause there's no room in our bunch for a hophead. We broke him by locking him in a cellar for about two weeks. His own mother didn't even know where he was. We used to go down there and give him food every day, but that was all. He could cry his butt off, and we wouldn't so much as give him a stick of M. Nothing till he kicked the heroin monkey. And he kicked it, dad. He kicked it clear out the window. It was painful to watch the poor guy, but it was for his own good, so we let him claw and scream all he wanted to, but he didn't get out of that cellar. Pot is okay, 'cause it don't give you the habit, but anybody wants to hang around me, he don't have no needle marks in his arm. He can bust a joint anytime he likes, but show me a spoon, and show me a guy's bowing to the White God, and I break his butt for him, that's the truth, that shows you the kind of guy I am.

"Harry's up there," I told Ferdy.

"How you like that?" Beef said. Beef must weigh about two thousand pounds in his bare feet. He don't talk English so good because he just come over from the old country, and he ain't yet learned the ropes. But he's a big one, and a good man to have in the bunch, especially when there's times you can't use hardware, like when the bulls is on a purity drive or something. We get those every now and then, but they don't mean nothing, especially if you know how to sit them out, and we got lots of patience on our street.

"What took you guys so long?" I said.

"A only just reached us," Ferdy said.

"A's turnin' into a real slowball," I said. "Look at them goddamn rooftops. How we gonna watch this now?"

The boys looked up and seen the crowd.

"We shove in," Beef said.

"Shove this," I told him. "There's grown-ups up there. You start shoving with all them bulls in the street, and they'll shove you into the Tombs."

"What about Tessie?" Ferdy said.

"What about her?"

"Her pad's right across the way. We stomp in there, dad, and we got ringside seats."

"Her folks," I said sourly.

"They both out earning bread," Ferdy said.

"You sure?"

"Dad, Tessie and me's like *that*," Ferdy said, crossing two fingers.

So we lit out for Tessie's pad.

She didn't answer the door till we told her who we was.

Even then, she wasn't too keen on the idea. She played cat and mouse with Ferdy, and he's honeying her up, come on doll, open the door, and all that kind of crap until I tell her to open it or I'll bust the goddamn thing right off the hinges. She begins to whimper she ain't dressed then, so I told her to throw something on because if that door ain't open in three flat I'm going to bust it open.

She opened the door then, and she was wearing a sweater and skirt, and I said, "You're a fast dresser, huh?" and she nodded, and I wanted to paste her in the mouth for lying to me in the first place. If there's one thing I can't stand, it's anybody who lies.

We go over to the windows and throw them open, and Tessie says, "What's all the noise about?" and Ferdy tells her Harry's in the apartment across the way and maybe we'll see some lead soon. Tessie gets the jitters. She's a pretty enough broad, only I don't go for her because Marie and I are that way, but you can bet Marie wouldn't get all excited and shaking because there might be some gunplay. Tessie wants to clear out, but Ferdy throws her down on the couch and she sits there shaking as if she's got pneumonia or something. Beef goes over and locks the door, and then we all pile onto the windowsills.

It's pretty good because we can see the apartment where Harry's holed up, right across the alleyway and only one floor down. And we can also see the street on the other side where the bulls are mulling around. I can make out Donlevy's strut from up there, and I feel like dropping a flowerpot on his head, but I figure I'll bide my time because maybe Harry's got something better for that lousy bull.

It's pretty quiet in the street now. The bulls are just about decided on their strategy, and the crowd is hushed up, waiting for something to happen. We don't see any life coming from the apartment where Harry's cooped, but that don't mean nothing.

"What they doing?" Beef says, and I shrug.

Then, all of a sudden, we hear the loudspeaker down below.

"All right, Manzetti. Are you coming out?"

A big silence fell on the street. It was quiet before, but this is something you can almost reach out and touch.

"Manzetti?" the loudspeaker called. "Can you hear us? We want you to come out. We're giving you thirty seconds to come out."

"They kidding?" I said. "Thirty seconds? Who they think he is? Jesse Owens?"

"He ain't going out anyway, and they know it," Ferdy said.

Then, just as if Harry was trying to prove Ferdy's point, he opens up from the window below us. It looks like he's got a carbine, but it's hard to tell because all we can see is the barrel. We can't see his head or nothing, just the barrel, and just these shots that come spilling like orange paint out of the window.

"He got one!" Beef yells from the other window.

"Where, where?" I yelled back, and I ran over to where

Beef was standing, and I shoved him aside and copped a look, and sure as hell one of the bulls is laying in the street, and the other bulls are crowding around him, and running to their cars to get the ambulance because by now they figure they're gonna need it.

"Son of a bitch!" I say. "Can that Harry shoot!"

"All right," the loudspeaker says, "we're coming in, Manzetti."

"Come on, you rotten bastards!" Harry yells back. "I'm waiting."

"Three cops moving down there," Ferdy says.

I look, but I can only see two of them, and they're going in the front door. "Two," I say.

"No, Donlevy's cuttin' through the alley."

I ran over to Ferdy's window, and sure enough Donlevy is playing the gumshoe, sneaking through the alley and pulling down the fire-escape ladder and starting to climb up.

"He's a dead duck," I said.

"Don't be so sure," Aiello answered, and there's this gleam in his eyes as if he's enjoying all this with a secret charge. "They may try to talk Harry away from the fire escape."

"Yeah," I said slow. "That's right, ain't it?"

"I want to get out of here," Tessie said. "He might shoot up here."

"Relax," Ferdy told her, and then to make sure she relaxed, he sat down on the couch and pulled her down in his lap.

"Come on," she said, "everybody's here."

"They only the boys," Ferdy said, and he starts mushing her up. You can hear a pin drop in the street down there. Everybody on the rooftops is quiet, too.

"What do you think..." Beef starts, and I give him a shot

in the arm to shut him up. From inside the building across the way, and through Harry's open window, I can hear one of the cops talking. At the same time, while they're pulling Harry over to the door of the apartment, Donlevy's climbing up that fire escape. He's up to the fourth floor now, and going quiet like a cat.

"How about it, Manzetti?" the cop in the hallway yells, and we can hear it plain as day through Harry's open window.

"Come and get me!" Harry yells back.

"Come on out. Throw your gun in the hallway."

"Screw you, cop!"

"How many guns you got, Manzetti?"

"Come in and count them!"

"Two?"

"*Fifty*-two," Harry yells back, and that one really busts me up. I stop laughing long enough to see Donlevy reaching the fifth floor, and making the turn in the ladder, going up to the sixth.

"He's gonna plug Harry in the back," I whisper.

In the hallway, the bull yells, "This is only the beginning, Manzetti. We haven't started playing yet."

"Your friend in the street don't think so," Harry answered. "Ask him if we started or not. Ask him how that slug felt."

Donlevy is almost on the seventh floor now. He steps onto the fire escape as if he's walking on eggs, and I can see the Detective's Special in his fist. I hate that punk with every bone in my body. I almost spit out the window at him, and then he's flattening himself against the side of the building and moving up to Harry's window, a step at a time, while the bull in the hallway is talking, talking, and Harry is answering him. Donlevy gets down on his knees, and he's got that gun in his right hand, and he's ready to step up to the window and start blasting.

That's when I started yelling.


"The window, Harry! The window!"

Donlevy looks up for a second, and I can see the surprised look on his face, but then he begins to back off, but he's too late. The slugs come ripping out of the window, five in a row, as if Harry's got a machine gun in his mitts. Donlevy grabs for his face, and then the gun flies out of his hand, and then he clutches at his stomach, and then he spins around and he's painted with red. He stumbles forward to the fire escape, and then he crumbles over the railing and it looks as if he's going to hang there for a second. The crowds on the rooftops are cheering their heads off by now, and then Donlevy goes all the way over, and Harry is still blasting through that window, pumping slugs into Donlevy's body, and then Donlevy is on his way down, and the cheers get cut off like magic, and there's just this god-awful hush as he begins his drop, and then a lady in the street starts to scream, and everybody's screaming all at once.

"He got him!" I said, and my eyes are bright in my head because I'm happier than hell.

"He got Donlevy!"

"Two down," Beef said.

"They'll get him," Aiello said, and he's got a worried look in his eyes now.

"You sound like you want that," I tell him.

"Who, me?"

"No, the man in the moon. Who you think, who?"

"I don't want them to get Harry."

"Then stop praying."

"I ain't praying, Danny."

"There ain't a bull alive can take Harry," I inform him.

"You can say that again," Ferdy says from the couch. Tessie ain't saying nothing anymore. She figures she might as well play ball or Ferdy will get nasty, and she knows Ferdy's got a switchblade knife in his pocket.

A phone starts ringing somewhere across the alleyway. It's the only sound you can hear on the block, just that phone ringing, and then Harry's head pops up at the window for just a second, and he waves up, not looking at us, not looking at anybody, just looking up sort of, and he yells, "Thanks," and then his head disappears.

"You saved his life, Danny," Ferdy said.

"And he appreciates it, dad," I answered.

"Sure, but what're they gonna throw at him next?" Aiello says, and from the tone of his voice I figure like he wants them to throw a Sherman tank at him.

"Look, meatball," I tell him, "just keep your mouth shut. You talk too much, anyway."

"Well, what the hell. Harry ain't nothing to me," Aiello said.

"Hey," Ferdy said, "you think the bulls are gonna come up here and get us?"

"What the hell for? They don't know who yelled. It could have been anybody on the roof."

"Yeah," Ferdy said, and he kisses Tessie and Tessie gets up and straightens her skirt, and I got to admit Ferdy knows how to pick them, but she still don't compare to Marie. She goes in the other room, and Ferdy winks and follows her, and I figure we lost a good man for the proceedings. Well, what the hell. There's just me and Beef and Aiello in the room now, and we're watching through the window, and it suddenly dawns on me what Aiello said.

"What do you mean, Harry ain't nothing to you?"

"He ain't," Aiello said.

"A," I told him, "you're looking for a cracked head."

"I ain't looking for nothing. What the hell, he's a killer. He's wanted everywhere."

"So what?"

"So that don't make him my brother, that's all. I never killed nobody."

"He's from the neighborhood," I said, and I tried to put a warning in my voice, but Aiello didn't catch it.

"So it's not my fault the neighborhood stinks."

"Stinks!" I walked away from the window and over to Aiello. "Who said it stinks?"

"Well, it ain't Fifth Avenue."

"That don't mean it stinks."

"Well, a guy like Harry..."

"What about Harry?"

"He...well...he don't help us none."

"Help us with who? What're you talkin' about?"

"Help us with nobody! He stinks just the way the neighborhood..."

I was ready to bust him one, when the shooting began again outside.

I rushed over to the window. The shooting was all coming from the streets, with Harry not returning the fire. It seemed like every cop in the world was firing up at that window. The people on the roofs were all ducking because they didn't want to pick up no stray lead. I poked my head out because we were on the other side of the alleyway.

"You see him?" Beef asked.

"No. He's playing it cool."

"A man shouldn't walk around free after he kills people," Aiello said.

"Shut your mouth, A," I told him.

"Well, it's the truth."

"Shut up, you dumb crumb. What the hell do you know about it?"

"I know it ain't right. Who'll he kill next? Suppose he kills your own mother?"

"What's he want to kill my old lady for? You're talking like a man with a paper..."

"I'm only saying. A guy like Harry, he stinks up the whole works."

"I'll talk to you later, jerk," I said. "I want to watch this."

The cops were throwing tear gas now. Two of the shells hit the brick wall of the building, and bounced off, and went flying down to the street again. They fired two more, and one of them hung on the sill as if it was going in, and then dropped. The fourth one went in the window, and out it came again, and I whispered, "That's the boy, Harry," and then another one came up and sailed right into the window, and I guess Harry couldn't get to it that time because the cops in the hallway started a barrage.

There were fire trucks down there now, and hoses were wrapped all over the street, and I wondered if they were going to try burning Harry out. The gas was coming out his window and sailing up the alleyway, and I got a whiff of the apple blossoms myself, that's what it smells like, and it smelled good, but I knew Harry was inside that apartment and hardly able to see. He come over to the window and tried to suck in some air, but the boys in the street kept up the barrage, trying to get him, and I felt sorrier'n hell for the poor guy.

He started firing then and throwing things out the window, chairs, and a lamp, and an electric iron, and the cops held off for just a few secs, and Harry copped some air, but not enough because they were shooting more tear gas shells up there, and they were also firing, and you could tell they had some tommies in the crowd because no .38 ever fired like that, and no carbine ever did either. I was wishing I had a gun of my own because I wanted to help Harry, and I felt as if my hands were tied, but what the hell could I do? I just kept sweating it out, and Harry wasn't firing through the window anymore, and then all of a sudden everything in the street stopped and everything inside the apartment was still.

"Manzetti!" the cop in the hallway yelled.

Harry coughed and said, "What?"

"You coming out?"

"I killed a cop," Harry yelled back.

"Come on out, Manzetti!"

"I killed a cop!" Harry yelled, and he sounded as if he was crying from the gas those bastards had fed him. "I killed a cop, I killed a cop," he kept saying over and over again.

"You only wounded him," the cop yelled, and I shouted, "He's lying, Harry."

"Get me a priest," Harry yelled.

"Why he wants a priest?" Beef asked.

"It's a trick," I said. "He wants a shield."

"No dice," the cop answered. "Come on, Manzetti, throw your weapons out."

"Get me a priest."

"Come on, Manzetti."

"No!" he screamed. "You lousy punk, no!"

"Manzetti..."

"Get me a priest," Harry shouted. "I'm scared I'll...get me a priest."

"What'd he say?" I said to Beef.

"I didn't catch," Beef said, and then the firing started again. It must have gone on for about ten minutes, and then all of a sudden, just the way it started, that's the way it stopped again.

"They got him," Aiello said.

"Bull," I answered.

I kept watching the street. It was beginning to get dark now, and the cops were turning on their spots and playing them up at Harry's window. There wasn't a sound coming from the apartment.

"They got him," Aiello said again.

"You need straightening, you jerk," I told him.

The streetlights came on, and after about a half hour a few more cops went into the building.

"Harry!" I yelled from the window.

There was no answer.

"Harry!"

Then we heard the shots in the hallway, and then quiet again, and then the sound of a door being busted, and then that goddamn telephone someplace in the building began ringing again.

About ten minutes later, they carried Harry out on a stretcher.

Dead.

We hung around the streets late that night. There'd been a big fuss when they carried Harry out, everybody yelling and shouting from the rooftops, as if this was the Roman arena or something. They didn't realize what a guy Harry was, and what a tough fight he'd put up.

"They got him, all right," Ferdy said, "but it wasn't easy."

"He took two of them with him," I said.

"A guy like Harry, it pains you to see him go," Ferdy said.

"Yeah," I answered.

We were an quiet for a little while.

"Where's A?" Beef asked.

"I don't know," I told him. "The hell with that little jerk anyway."

"He got an inside wire, all right," Ferdy said. "He was the first cat to tumble to this."

"Yeah," I said. I was thinking about the look on Donlevy's face when those slugs ripped him up.

"How'd he tip to it, anyway?"

"He spotted Harry in the hall. Going up to Louise."

"Oh." Ferdy was quiet for a while. "Harry see him?"

"Yeah."

"He should have been more careful."

"A guy like Harry, he got lots of things on his mind. You think he's gonna worry about a snot nose like A?"

"No, but what I mean...somebody blew the whistle on him."

"Sure, but that don't…" I cut myself dead. "Hey!" I said.

"What?"

"Aiello."

"Aiello what?"

"I'll bet he done it! Why, I'll bet that little crumb done it!"

"Tipped the cops to Harry, you mean?"

"Sure! Who else? Why, that little…"

"Now, hold it, Danny. Now don't jump to…"

"Who else knew it?"

"Anybody could have spotted Harry."

"Sure, except nobody did." I waited a minute, thinking, and then I said, "Come on."

We began combing the neighborhood.

We went down to the poolroom, and we combed the bowling alley, and then we hit the rooftops, but Aiello was no place around. We checked the dance in the church basement, and we checked the Y, but there was still no sign of him.

"Maybe he's home," Ferdy said.

"Don't be a jerk."

"It's worth a try."

"Okay," I said.

We went to the building where Aiello lived. In the hallway, Beef said, "Somebody here."

"Shut up," Ferdy said. We went up to Aiello's apartment and knocked on the door.

"Who is it?" he answered.

"Me," I said. "Danny."

"What do you want, Danny?"

"I want in. Open up."

"I'm in bed."

"Then get out of bed."

"I'm not feeling so hot, Danny."

"Come on, we got some pot."

"I don't feel like none."

"This is good stuff."

"I ain't interested, Danny."

"Open up, you jerk," I told him. "You want the Law to know we're holding?"

"Danny, I..."

"Open up!" I began pounding on the door and I knew that'd get him out of bed, if that's where he was, because his folks are a quiet type who don't like trouble with the neighbors.

In a few seconds, Aiello opened the door.

I smiled at him and said, "Hello, A."

We all went inside. "Your people home?"

"They went visiting."

"Oh, visiting, huh? Very nice."

"Yeah."

"Like you was doing with Louise this afternoon, huh?"

"Yeah, I suppose," Aiello said.

"When you spotted Harry."

"Yeah."

"And then what'd you do?"

"I told you."

"You went into Louise's apartment, that right?"

"Yes, I..." Aiello paused, as if he was trying to remember what he'd told me before. "No, I didn't go in. I went down in the street to look for you."

"You like this gang, A?"

"Yeah, it's good," Aiello said.

"Then why you lying to me?"

"I ain't lying."

"You know you wasn't looking for me."

"I was."

"Look, tell me the truth. I'm a fair guy. What do I care if you done something you shouldn't have."

"I didn't do nothing I shouldn't have," Aiello said.

"Well, you did do something then, huh?"

"Nothing."

"Come on, A, what'd you do?"

"Nothing."

"I mean, after you left Louise?"

"I went to look for you."

"And before you found me?"

"Nothing."

"Did you blow the whistle on Harry?"

"Hell no!"

"You did, didn't you? Look, he's dead, what do I care what you done or didn't do? I ain't the Law."

"I didn't turn him in."

"Come on, A."

"He deserved what he got. But I didn't turn him in."

"He deserved it, huh?"

"Yeah. He was rotten. Anybody rotten like Harry..."

"Shut up!"

"...should have the whistle..."

"Shut up, I said!" I slapped him across the mouth. "Did you?"

He dummied up.

"Answer me!"

"No."

I slapped him again. "Answer me!"

"No."

"You did, you punk! You called the cops on Harry, and now he's dead, and you ain't fit to lick his boots!"

"He was a killer!" Aiello yelled. "That's why I called them. He was no good. No damn good. He was a stink in the neigh…"

But I wasn't listening no more.

We fixed Mr. Aiello, all right.

Just the way Harry would have liked it.

# WOMEN
# IN JEOPARDY

When I was twelve, and the family moved to the Bronx, my commute to school was a short one because we lived on 217th Street between Barnes and Bronxwood avenues, right across the street from Olinville Junior High School. Later, I would walk the ten blocks every weekday morning to Evander Childs High School on Gun Hill Road. But when I won a scholarship to the Art Students League and was later accepted as an art student at Cooper Union, subways and elevated trains from the Bronx to Manhattan became a routine part of my life. It was inevitable, I suppose, that a native New Yorker would one day write a story set in a subway car. This one was published in Manhunt in September of 1953. It carried the Hunt Collins byline.

# The Molested

SHE WAS SHOVED INTO THE SUBWAY CAR AT GRAND CENtral. It was July, and the passengers reeked of sweat and after-office beers. She wore a loose silk dress, buttoned high on the throat, and she wished for a moment that she had worn something lower cut. The overhead fans in the cars were going but the air hung over the packed passengers like a damp clinging blanket.

She was packed in tightly, with a stout woman standing next to her on her right, a tall thin man on her left, and a pair of broad shoulders in front of her. The fat woman was wearing cheap perfume, and the aroma assailed her nostrils, caused her senses to revolt. The thin man on her left held a thinly folded copy of the *New York Times*. He sported a black mustache under his curving nose. The nose was buried in the newspaper, and she glanced at the paper and then took her eyes away from the headlines.

There was a slight movement behind her. She leaned forward. The broad shoulders in front of her shoved back indignantly. Whoever was behind her moved again, and she felt a knee pressing into the backs of her own knees.

She moved again, away from the pressure of the knee, and then she tried to look over her shoulder, turning slightly to her left. Her elbow brushed the *Times*, and the thin man lifted the paper gingerly, shook it as if it were crawling with ants, and then went back to his reading.

The knee was suddenly removed.

She thought, *No, I didn't mean you should…*

She was suddenly aware of something warm touching the back of her leg. She almost leaped forward because the touch had surprised her with its abruptness. Her silk dress was thin, and she wore no girdle. She felt the warmth spread until it formed the firm outline of fingers touching her flesh.

A tremor of excitement traveled the length of her body, spreading from the warmth on her leg. She moved again, and the stout woman on her right shot her an angry glance, but the hand was taken from her leg.

The excitement in her ebbed.

She stood stock-still, wondering when it would start again. She almost didn't breathe.

It seemed as if there would be no more. She moved her leg impatiently, but the excitement that had flared within her was dead, and now she felt only the oppressive heat of the train. The car jogged along, and she cursed her foolishness in trying the subway to begin with. She thought of the thousands of girls who rode home every night and then the heat overwhelmed her again, and she was sorry for herself once more.

The train rounded a curve, and she lost her balance. She lurched backward, felt the smooth, gentle hands close on her, then release her instantly as she righted herself.

The train pulled into 86th Street, and the door slid open. She was pushed onto the platform, and shoved past the man and woman who had been standing behind her in the train. The man was short and squat, and he wore a battered panama. His hands were thin, with long fingers that clung innocently to the lapels of his suit. She looked at the tall girl, and the girl's eyes met hers sympathetically. She smiled quickly, darting her eyes away, and the girl smiled. The embarking passengers rushed by her, and suddenly everyone on the platform was scrambling to get into the car again. She stepped in quickly, moving deliberately in front of the tall girl, and away from the man. He pushed into the car behind her, and she felt the girl shoved rudely against her, too. She heard the door close behind them, and she sucked in a deep breath as the heat descended again.

She knew what was going to happen, and she waited expectantly. The excitement was mounting in her again, and she found herself wishing desperately for the warmth. When it came she almost sighed aloud. The hands were gentle, as before, as she knew they had to be. They touched her, and then held tight. She shivered and the hands moved slowly, deliberately. For a moment there was sudden doubt in her mind, and then she put the doubt aside and thought only of the moving hands, the deliberate pressure of the hands.

They became more insistent, strangely so, strongly so. A perplexed frown creased her brow, and the doubt returned, and she was almost tempted to turn and look. But that was absurd...that was...

The hands continued, moving feverishly, and suddenly she realized there was wild strength in the fingers. She looked down in panic. This wasn't...couldn't be...

The hand she saw was covered with hair.

Long slender fingers, but dark masculine hair.

"I thought…" she murmured, and then she began screaming.

When the train pulled into 125th Street, she was still screaming. The tall girl who'd also been standing behind her left the car with the other passengers, all shaking their heads.

The policeman held the short, squat man firmly.

"He was molesting me!" she told the policeman. "A man. A *man*!" And then, because he was looking at her so strangely, she added, "This man, Officer."

*This story carried the Richard Marsten byline when it was first published in* Manhunt *in February of 1953. As a twist on a* Woman in Jeopardy *yarn, it combines an exotic locale with a sort of action-adventure hero and a true bandito-style villain. It is an absolute coincidence that the bad guy in this story is called Carrera whereas the good guy in the 87th Precinct series, three years later, would be called Carella.*

*I promise.*

# Carrera's Woman

THE MEXICAN SKY HUNG OVER OUR HEADS LIKE A PALE blue circus tent. We crouched behind the rocks, and we each held .45s in our fists. We were high in the Sierra Madres, and the rocks were jagged and sharp, high outcroppings untouched by erosive waters. Between us was a stretch of pebble-strewn flatland and a solid wall of hatred that seemed alive in the heat of the sun. We were just about even, but not quite.

The guy behind the other .45 had ten thousand dollars that belonged to me.

I had something that belonged to him.

His woman.

She lay beside me now, flat on her belly, her hands and her feet bound. She was slim and browned from the sun. Her legs were long and sleek where her skirt ended. Her head was twisted away from me, her hair as black as her boyfriend's heart.

"Carrera!" I shouted.

"I hear you, *señor*," he answered.

His voice was as big as he was. I thought of his paunch, and I thought of the ten G's in the money belt pressed tight against his sweaty flesh. I'd worked hard for that money. I'd sweated in the Tampico oil fields for more than three years, socking it away a little at a time, letting it pile up for the day I could kiss Mexico good-bye.

"Look, Carrera," I said, "I'm giving you one last chance."

"Save your breath, *señor*," he called back.

"You'd better save yours, you bastard," I shouted. "You'd better save it because pretty soon you're not going to have any."

"Perhaps," he answered.

I couldn't see him because his head was pulled down below the rocks. But I knew he was grinning.

"I want that ten thousand," I shouted.

He laughed aloud this time.

"Ah, but that is where the difficulty lies," he said. "*I* want it, too."

"Look, Carrera, I'm through playing around," I told him. "If you're not out of there in five minutes, I'm going to put a hole in your sweetie's head." I paused, wondering if he'd heard me. "You got that, Carrera? Five minutes."

He waited again before answering.

"You had better shoot her now, *señor*. You are not getting this money."

The girl began laughing.

"What's so damn funny?" I asked her.

"You will never outwait Carrera," she said. Her voice was as low and as deep as her laugh. "Carrera is a very patient man."

"I can be patient, too, sister," I said. "I patiently saved that ten thousand bucks for three years, and no tinhorn crook is going to step in and swipe it."

"You underestimate Carrera," she said.

"No, baby, I've got Carrera pegged to a tee. He's a small-time punk. Back in the States, he'd be shaking pennies out of gum machines. He probably steals tortillas from blind old ladies down here."

"You underestimate him," she repeated.

I shook my head. "This is Carrera's big killing—or so he thinks. That ten thousand is his key to the big time. Only it belongs to me, and it's coming back to me."

"If you were smart," she said, "you would leave. You would pack up and go, my friend. And you wouldn't stop to look back."

"I'm not smart."

"I know. So you'll stay here, and Carrera will kill you. Or I will kill you. Either way, you will be dead, and your money will be gone, anyway." She paused. A faint smile tugged at the corners of her mouth. "It is better that you lose only your money."

I glanced at my watch.

"Carrera has about two minutes, honey."

"And after that?"

"It's up to him," I said. As if to check, I shouted, "You like your girlfriends dead, Carrera?"

"Ten thousand dollars will buy a lot of girlfriends," he called back.

I looked down at her.

"Did you hear your boyfriend?" I asked.

"I heard."

"He doesn't seem to give a damn whether I shoot you or not."

She shrugged. "It is not that," she said. "He simply knows that you will not kill me."

"Don't be too surprised, baby."

The smile flitted across her face again, was gone almost before it started. "You will not kill me," she said.

I didn't answer her. I kept looking at my watch until the time was up. Nothing came from Carrera. Not another word.

"Now what?" she asked.

"What's your name?"

She didn't answer.

I shrugged. "Suit yourself," I said.

"My name is Linda," she said.

"Make yourself comfortable, Linda," I told her. "We're going to be here for quite some time."

I meant that. I still hadn't figured out how I was going to get my money from Carrera, but I knew damn well I was staying here until I *did* get it. Crossing the open dirt patch would have been suicide. But at the same time, Carrera couldn't cross it, either. Not unless he wanted a slug through his fat face. I thought of that, and I began to wish he would try to get across the clearing. Nothing would have pleased me more than to have his nose resting on the sight at the end of my gun muzzle.

Ten thousand bucks! Ten thousand, hard-earned American dollars. How had Carrera found out about it? Had I talked too much? Hell, it was general knowledge that I was putting away a nest egg to take back to the States. Carrera had probably been watching me for a long time, planning his larceny from a distance, waiting until I was ready to shove off for home.

"It's getting dark," Linda said.

I lifted my eyes to the sky.

The sun was dipping low over the horizon, splashing the sky with brilliant reds and oranges. The peaks of the mountains glowed brilliantly as the dying rays lingered in crevices and hollows. A crescent moon hung palely against the deepening wash of night, sharing the sky with the sinking sun.

And suddenly it was black.

There was no transition, no dusk, no violets or purples. The sun was simply swallowed up, and stars appeared against the blackness. A stiff breeze worked its way down from the caps of the mountains, spreading cold where there had once been intolerable heat.

"You'd better get some sleep," I said.

"And you?"

"With that pig across the way? I'll stay awake, thanks."

She grinned. "Carrera will sleep. You can bet on that."

"I wish I could bet on that. I'd go right over and make sure he never woke up."

"Oh my," she mocked, "such a tough one."

I said nothing.

"I don't even know your name," she said.

"Jeff," I told her. "Jeff MacCauley."

She rolled over, trying to make herself comfortable. It wasn't easy with her hands and feet bound. She settled for her left side, her arms behind her, her legs together.

"Well," she said, *"buenos noches,* Jeff."

I didn't answer.

I was watching the rocks across the clearing. Carrera may have planned on sleeping the night, but I wasn't counting on it.


She woke up about two A.M. She pushed herself to a sitting position and stared into the darkness.

"Jeff," she whispered. Her accent made my name sound like "Jaif." I pulled the .45 from my waistband and walked over to her.

"What is it?"

"My hands. They're…I can't feel anything. I think the blood has stopped."

I knelt down beside her and reached for her hands. The strap didn't seem too tight. "You'll be all right," I said.

"But…they feel numb. It's like…like there is nothing below my wrists, Jeff."

Her voice broke, and I wondered if she were telling the truth. I held the .45 in my right hand and tugged at the strap with my left. I loosened it, and she pulled her hands free and began massaging the wrists, breathing deeply.

"That's much better," she said.

I kept the .45 pointed at her. She looked at the open muzzle and sighed, as if she were being patient with a precocious little boy. She leaned back on her arms then, tilting her head to the sky, her black hair streaming down her back.

It's a beautiful night," she said.

"Yeah."

"Just look at the moon, Jeff."

I glanced up at the moon, taking my eyes off her for a second.

That was all the time she needed.

She sprang with the speed of a mountain lion, pushing herself up with her bound feet, her fingernails raking down the length of my arm, clawing at my gun hand. I yanked the gun back and she dove at me again, the nails slashing across my face. She threw herself onto my chest, her hands seeking the wrist of my gun hand, tightening there, the nails digging deep into my flesh. I rolled over, slapping the muzzle of the .45 against her shoulder.

She fell backward and then pushed herself up from the ground, murder in her eyes. She hopped forward, and I backed away from her. She kept hopping, her feet close together, the material from her skirt keeping her in check. And then she toppled forward, and she would have kissed the ground if I hadn't caught her in my arms.

She kissed me instead.

Or I kissed her.

It was hard to tell which. She was falling, and I reached for her, and she was suddenly in my arms. There was a question in her eyes for a single instant, and then the question seemed to haze over. She closed her eyes and lifted her mouth to mine.

Sunlight spilled over the twisted ground, pushing at the shadows, chasing the night.

She was still in my arms when I woke up. I stared down at her, not wanting to move, afraid to wake her.

And then her eyes popped open suddenly, and a sleepy smile tilted the corners of her mouth.

"Good morning," she said.

"Hello."

She yawned, stretching her arms over her head. She took a deep breath and then smiled, and I looked deep into her eyes, trying to read whatever was hidden in their brown depths.

"Your boyfriend," I said. "Carrera."

"He's not my boyfriend."

Her face was serious, so serious that it startled me.

"No?"

"No."

"He's still got my ten thousand," I said.

"I know."

"I want it back."

"I know."

"I want you to help me get it."

She was silent for a long while.

When she spoke, her voice was a whisper.

"Why?"

"Why? Holy Jesus, that's ten thousand bucks! You know how much work I did to get that money?"

"Why not forget it?

"Forget it? No."

"Carrera will kill you. I know him. Would you rather be dead without your money . . . or would you rather be alive without it? Alive and . . . with me?"

"If you help me, we can have both," I said.

She considered this for a moment and then asked, "What do you want me to do?"

"You'll help?"

"What do you want me to do?"

"I want to set a trap for him."

"What kind of a trap?"

"Will you help?"

She moved closer to me and buried her head against my shoulder.

"I'll do whatever you say," she said.

———

We crouched behind the rocks, our heads close together. The sun bore down ferociously, baking the earth, spreading heat over the surface of the land. The sky was streaked with spidery white clouds that trailed across a wide wash of blue. It was the Mexico of the picture books, bright and clear, warm, alive, and it should have been pulsating with the throb of laughter and music, wine and song, fiesta.

Instead, a funeral was being planned.

Carrera's.

There was a sheer wall behind him, rising like a giant tombstone for some hundred feet, terminating there in a jumble of twisted branches and fallen rock. A few feet in front of the wall was the outcropping behind which Carrera squatted with his .45 and my ten G's.

My watch read 12:40.

Linda screamed.

"Shut up!" I shouted.

"José!" she bellowed, her head turned toward where Carrera lay crouched behind the rocks. There was no sound from across the clearing. I wondered if he was listening.

"Hey!" I yelled. And then, "Let go the gun!"

I pointed the .45 over my head and fired two quick shots. I screamed as loud as I could, and then I dropped my voice into a trailing moan, and at last fell silent.

It was quiet for a long time.

Linda and I crouched behind the rocks, waiting, looking at each other, the sweat pouring from our bodies. There was still no sound from the other side of the clearing.

And then, softly, cautiously, in a whisper that reached across the pebble-strewn clearing and climbed the rock barrier, Carrera called, "Linda?"

I put my finger to my lips.

"Linda?" he called again.

I nodded this time, and she answered, "It's all right, José. It's all right."

Carrera was quiet again. I could picture him behind his rock barrier, his ears straining, his fat face flushed.

"The American?" he called.

"He is dead," Linda answered.

"Tell him to come over," I prompted.

She hesitated for a moment and then said, "Come here, José. Come."

I waited, my chest heaving, the .45 heavy in my hand.

"Throw out the American's gun," Carrera said. His voice was cold and calculating. He wasn't buying it. He suspected a trick, and he wanted to make sure I wasn't forcing his woman to play along with me.

"Give me the gun," Linda whispered.

"What for? What good would that...?"

"I'll stand up. When he sees me with the gun, he will no longer suspect. Give it to me."

"Throw out the gun, Linda," Carrera called again.

"Quick," she said, "give me the gun."

I hesitated for a moment, and then I passed the gun to her, holding it by the barrel, fitting the stock into her fingers.

She took the gun gently, and then pointed it at my belly. A small smile tilted the corners of her mouth as she stood up. My eyes popped wide in astonishment.

"It's all right now, José," she called. "I've got his gun."

"*Bueno*," Carrera said, and I could hear the smile in his voice. I'd been suckered, taken like a schoolboy, hook, line, and sinker.

"So that's the way it is," I said.

"That's the way it is, *señor*," she answered. The gun didn't waver. It kept pointing at my belt buckle.

"And it's *señor* now," I added. "Last night, it was Jeff."

"Last night was last night," she said. "Now is now."

Across the clearing, I could hear Carrera's feet scraping against the rocks as he clambered to a standing position. Linda heard the sound, too. Her eyes flicked briefly to the right and then snapped back.

"I'm surprised," I said. I kept my voice low, a bare whisper that only she could hear. From the corner of my eye, I watched Carrera's progress.

"You should learn to expect surprises, *señor*," she answered.

"I thought last night meant a little more than..."

I stopped and shook my head.

She was interested. I could see the way her brows pulled together slightly, a small V appearing between them.

"Never mind," I said. "We'll just forget it."

"What is there to forget?" she asked.

She wanted me to go on. She tried to keep her voice light but there was something behind her question, an uncertain probing. Carrera was halfway across the clearing now. I saw the .45 in his pudgy fist and I began to sweat more heavily. I had to hurry.

"There's you to forget," I said. "You and last night."

"Oh, stop it," she said. "Last night meant nothing. Not to you, not to me."

"It meant everything to me," I said, and took a step closer to her.

"That's too bad," she said. "I'm Carrera's woman."

He was no more than fifty feet away now. I could feel the

sun on my shoulders and head, could hear the steady crunch of his feet against the pebbles.

"Is that who you want?" I asked.

"Yes," she said.

"Look at him, Linda," I said, my voice a husky whisper now. "Take a look at the fat slobbering pig you're doing this for."

"Don't," she said.

"Take a look at your boyfriend!" I said. "Is that who you really want?"

"He's not my boyfriend," she said.

He was almost upon us. I could see his features plainly, could see the sweat dripping off his forehead. I took another step toward Linda.

"He's my husband," she said.

She lowered the .45 for an instant, and that was when I sprang. I didn't bother with preliminaries. I brought back my fist and hit her hard, just as the gun went off into the ground. She was screaming when my fist caught her, but she stopped instantly, dropping the gun, crumpling against the ground.

Carrera was running toward us now.

I picked up the gun and fired at once. He wasn't hard to hit. Something that big never is. I fired two shots that sprouted on his shoulder like red blossoms across his white cotton shirt. He clutched at the blossoms as if he wanted to pick them for a bouquet, and then he changed his mind and dropped the gun, and fell forward onto his face.

I looked over my shoulder at Linda. She was still sprawled on the ground. I climbed over the rocks and walked to where Carrera was lying, breathing hard, bleeding. I rolled him over and unfastened the money belt. Carefully, slowly, I counted the money. It was all there, ten thousand bucks worth. I picked up his .45 and tucked it in my waistband. Overhead, the vultures were already beginning a slow spiral.

I walked back to the rocks, the .45 cocked in my right hand.

She was just sitting up when I got there. Her knees were raised, her skirt pulled back over them. She brushed a lock of hair away from her face, looked up at me.

Her voice caught in her throat.

"Carrera?" she asked.

"He's hurt bad," I said. "But he isn't dead."

She nodded, stared at the ground for a moment. She got to her feet then, dusted off her skirt, glanced up at the vultures.

"Do you have the money?" she asked.

"I have the money."

"Did you mean what you said about last night?" she asked.

"Yes," I said.

"Then let's go," she said, and nodded.

"Just what I plan to do," I said. "Alone."

A puzzled look crossed her face.

"You're Carrera's woman," I said. "Remember? Go back to him."

I turned away from her then, and started walking down the twisting path, the sky a brilliant blue above, except where the vultures hung against it, circling.

*I*n 1955, when I began writing the first of the 87th Precinct novels, I thought it would be a good idea to make Steve Carella's girlfriend (and later wife) a deaf mute who would get into all sorts of trouble because she could neither hear nor speak. The ultimate Woman in Jeopardy, so to speak. Over the years, Teddy Carella has developed into a strong and independent woman and no one in his right mind would ever consider her vulnerable — but that was the notion back then. Perhaps I'd forgotten that in that very same year, 1955, a magazine called Real published a story titled "The Big Scream" by Evan Hunter. It follows under my original derogatory title, which I like much better.

# Dummy

THE GULLS WERE MAKING A HELL OF A RACKET OUT OVER the bay, mostly because the boats were coming back and they all had fairly good hauls. Falco was standing knee-deep in the stink of mackerel when the blonde walked down the dock and stood looking out over the water. He didn't notice her at first because he was busy with the fish, and then he looked up and she was standing there silhouetted against the reddish-gold sky, with her hair blowing back loose over her shoulders.

There was a strong wind that day. It molded the silk dress against her, outlining her body. He was holding a mackerel in his big, hair-covered hands, and his fingers tightened unconsciously on the cold fish, and his mouth fell open, and he kept looking at the girl.

She didn't seem to notice him at all. She just kept staring out over the water, and Falco kept watching her, his palms beginning to sweat, a funny kind of warmth starting at the pit of his stomach and spreading up to his throat where it almost choked him. The wind kept pressing the dress to her body, and he studied every curve of her, thanking the wind because she might have been standing there without a stitch on. Her long blonde hair kept dancing around her shoulders, rising and falling, almost as if it had a life of its own. She had an oval face with high cheekbones burned dark from the sun, and he could see the startling blue of her eyes even from where he stood.

The gulls kept screaming out there, and Donato's boat pulled up to the dock, and then DiAngelo, the kid he had working for him, threw the lines over and hopped ashore.

"Ho, Falco!" Donato yelled. "You in early today?"

"Nice catch today," Falco yelled back, but he did not take his eyes from the girl. An upcurrent of wind caught the hem of her dress, flapped it back wildly over the long curve of her leg. She didn't seem to notice the wind for a moment, and then she reached down and spread her dress flat again, as if she were spreading a tablecloth. Falco wet his lips, and tightened his hands. He had never seen anything like this girl before, had never felt this way before, either. He heard boots clomping on the wooden dock but he didn't pay any attention to them until he heard Donato's voice again.

"Ho, Falco! Wake up, hah, boy?"

He looked up as Donato jumped into his boat, and then he said, "You do all right today?"

"Every day should be like this one, Falco. Then I retire a rich man. When the fish run like—"

He stopped because he saw that Falco wasn't listening to him, and then his eyes followed Falco's to where the blonde stood on the dock. He appraised her silently, and then he said, "Nice, hah, Falco?"

Falco didn't answer. His eyes were riveted to the blonde's body, and there was a tight, grim set to his mouth.

"That's Panza's daughter," Donato said.

# Dummy

"Whose?"

"Panza. You know Panza?"

"The fat one? Panza? With the crooked teeth and the mustache? You're kidding me."

"No, no, this is his daughter. Truly, a silk purse from a sow's ear."

Falco nodded and wet his lips. Panza's daughter. He couldn't believe it. Why, Panza was a slob. And this girl…no, it couldn't be.

"But a sow's ear is always a sow's ear," Donato said sadly.

"What do you mean?" Falco asked.

"A dummy," Donato said.

"A what?"

"A dummy. She doesn't speak, Falco. There is something wrong with her tongue. She doesn't speak."

"But she hears?"

"Ah, yes, she hears. But there is no voice there, Falco. Nothing. A dummy, truly."

"That's too bad," Falco said slowly. "What's she doing here?"

Donato shrugged. "To meet the old man, perhaps. I've seen her once or twice already."

Falco wet his lips. "I've never seen her," he said.

"And you like what you see, hah, boy?" Donato said, and chuckled heartily. "Why don't you go talk to her, Falco? Go ahead. You're young, boy, and your arms are strong. Go talk to her. Who knows?"

"No, I couldn't," Falco said.

"Faint heart…"

"No, no, it isn't that," Falco said.

"Then what?"

"I...I would tremble. I don't think I'd be able to...control myself. She is very beautiful."

The wind lifted her skirt again. This time she did not notice it at all because Panza's red boat was pulling up to the dock. She ran to the edge of the dock, and her legs flashed in the deepening dusk, and Falco watched those legs, with his palms sweating again. Panza came out of the boat and embraced his daughter, slobbering a kiss onto her with his fat mouth and his dripping mustache. She hugged him tightly. Falco watched. Panza said something to her, and she nodded mutely in answer, her lips not moving. And then she and Panza walked away from the boat and down the dock, and past Falco's boat full of mackerel. And Falco watched her as she walked by, and wet his lips again, and kept watching her until she was out of sight, and even then the picture of her was still in his mind.

She came to the dock two, sometimes three, times a week. He learned from the others that her mother was dead, and that she did modeling, a job where she did not need her voice, only her body. She was always dressed like a queen, always with clothes that showed the firmness of her body. She lived alone with Panza, they told him, though she could easily have afforded a high-class apartment uptown. She preferred to look after old Panza in the shack where he lived near the docks.

The voice, they said, was something psychological, and this Falco could not understand. They said it had happened to her when she was a little girl, something that paralyzed her throat muscles, something with a stumblebum who had come down to the docks shortly after her mother had died, and found the young girl alone. The doctors could do nothing for this voice of hers that was missing, it was all psychological, all part of this something that had happened to her long ago.

But he didn't care about her voice.

He watched her whenever she came to the dock.

Always, he watched.

And then one day, he came in very early because he knew it was a day she would be on the dock and she was there as always, sitting on a crate near the loading platform, her legs crossed with the sun flashing on them, the skirt pulled back over her knees. Her head was thrown back with the blonde hair trailing over her shoulders. She sucked in a deep breath, and he watched and thought suddenly, *Why, she knows I'm here. She knows I'm watching her.*

He dried his hands on a rag and climbed up out of the boat and onto the rotted, wooden planking of the dock. He walked over to her, and she did not look at him. She kept looking out over the water as if he were not there at all.

He cleared his throat and made a small sound, but she showed no indication of having heard him, and he wondered about her ears, because sometimes dummies could not hear, but everyone said her ears were all right.

He cleared his throat again and then said, "Are you waiting for your father?"

She turned then and looked at him. Her eyes were very cold, her mouth was unsmiling. She did not answer, not by voice which she could not, and not by any movement of her head.

"Are you . . . are you waiting for your father?" he asked again.

This time her eyes met his squarely, and her mouth curled

into obvious distaste. He had seen that look before. He had seen it on the women in the marketplace the times he had gone down to the fish stand his brother operated. It was a look that said, "You are a fish peddler," and this girl, this Panza's daughter, did not need any voice when she could cast looks like that one.

He began to feel warm again, but a different kind of warmth this time. He felt blood rise to his face, and when the girl turned her back to him and lifted one knee, cupping that knee with her clasping hands, he stood there like an idiot for a moment longer, and then he turned and walked slowly back to his boat, thinking, *I've been a fool. She's a model. I've been a fool.*

But he could not take his eyes from her.

And later that afternoon, before the other boats returned, she lifted her skirt as she sat where he could not miss seeing her and she straightened the seams of her stockings, running her long tapering fingers up over her legs, and then fastening the garters. He watched her and the old flame roared higher inside him, and then he saw her smile a superior smile and drop the skirt suddenly and walk to the edge of the dock where the descending sun splashed through the thin dress she wore and showed him the full silhouette of her body.

When Panza's boat came in, she embraced her father as always, and then they walked past Falco's boat, and he may have imagined it, but he thought she swung her hips with more abandon when she passed above him, and he listened to the click of her high heels on the dock, and his hands longed for the touch of her flesh.

He tried to speak to her only once again. She was wearing slacks this time, and a tight, full sweater. She walked deliberately to his boat where he was mending his nets, an excuse he'd given himself for coming in early. She stood above him, her hands on her hips, looking down at him. And finally he looked up and said, "Good afternoon."

She continued looking at him, her hands on her hips.

"What do you want of me?" he asked then, and she did not answer.

"Do you want to torment me? Is that what you want?"

She smiled that superior smile again, the smile one gives to an idiot child.

"Don't play with me!" he shouted. "Do you hear me? Don't play with Falco!"

She threw her head back and opened her mouth, and he knew she was laughing, but no sound came from her lips and he understood then the full extent of her voicelessness, and his eyes narrowed a little.

He went back to mending his nets, and she walked away from him, her head still thrown back in that silent mocking attitude of laughter, her blonde hair glinting in the sun.

He went out alone in his boat the next day.

He went out alone, and he talked aloud to the water, because the water would listen and not repeat. Sitting in the stern shortly after dusk, water lapping at the wooden sides of the boat, the sun edging the waterline far off on the horizon, he told the water of his plan.

"I must have this one," he said. "Can you understand the way I feel?"

The sea said nothing. The sea had listened to men before, and the story Falco told was an old one. The sea only lapped gently at the sides of the boat.

"She's a witch, I know that," he said. "She's truly a witch. But she's *here*," he said, and hit his heart with his clenched fist, "and she's also in my mind, and I won't rest until I have her. I see her at night, when I sleep. She's always there with those long legs of hers, and I see her straightening her stockings until I want to scream aloud. And sometimes I do scream aloud, and I wake myself, and she's there even when I'm awake, in the darkness, with her body there before me all the time. She knows what she's doing. She's a witch, and so she knows. But she's also a dummy."

He stared into the black depths of the water, calm and serene, the sun dappling it with oranges and reds and yellows.

"She's a dummy," he said. "There's no voice there, none whatever. Not even to laugh. And if there's no voice to laugh with, can there be a voice to scream with? No. No, she has a body, and she flaunts the body for the taking, but if the body were taken, could she protest the taking?"

He kept staring into the water, the oranges and yellows and reds vanishing now, leaving only a deep blackness that reflected his own face darkly.

"She stays in the shack when she doesn't model," he said, whispering now even though he was alone. "She stays there and she tidies things for that fat slob of a father, Panza, upon whom she showers kisses every night, against whom she presses her young body. For me, she wiggles and she teases, and she says 'Come, come, Falco' with her eyes and legs, but her mouth mocks because Falco is only a fisherman.

"She says, 'Come, come, Falco, come try to take me, Falco,' but she doesn't think she will be taken. She doesn't know she will be taken by me, Falco, nor will she scream for help, by God, because there is no voice in that lovely throat of hers, no voice at all."

And so he talked while waves rolled beneath the wooden bottom of the boat, and the stars appeared in the sky overhead, hard and unblinking.

He waited until all the fishermen were gone the next day. He had told them he had a bad cold and should not be out on the water. Donato laughed at him, calling him a fake fisherman, a fisherman who would not go out because of a cold. But he waited until they were all gone, waited until Panza's sleek red boat had joined the rest of the fleet, and then he stood on the dock until he could no longer make out the crafts heading for sea.

He went back to his boat, and he propped up a mirror in the cabin, and he combed his hair and brushed his teeth, and then he washed his hands. He left the boat and walked down the dock, past the loading platform, over the railroad tracks where the refrigerated cars were loading fish, and then out past the big hatchery, and over toward the shacks dotting the harbor's edge. He knew which shack was Panza's, and he knew the girl was home today when he saw the smoke coming from the metal stovepipe in its roof. He felt no fear. His palms were dry. He felt extremely calm because he knew just what he was going to do, and he knew there was no way he could be stopped.

He walked up the cinder path leading to the shack and then he knocked on the door, and did not wait for an answer. He shoved the door open and stepped into the small room.

It was almost as if she'd been waiting for him.

She was standing by the woodstove when he came in. Her eyes opened slightly wider in recognition. A smile came onto her face.

"Hello," he said.

His heart was beginning to pound now, not through fear, but because he was near her, and whenever he was near her there was a fever in his blood.

She said nothing. She looked at him with that strange smile on her face, a haughty smile, a smile that told him she knew he would eventually come here to her. She moved away from the woodstove, walked to a dresser on one wall of the shack, opened a purse there and removed a package of cigarettes from it. She shook one cigarette loose and hung it on her mouth, and then she moved closer to Falco and handed him the book of matches.

He struck a match, watching her eyes all the time, watching the smile on her mouth. She blew out a cloud of smoke and then went to stand near the dresser and the open purse, putting the cigarettes down behind her. She crossed her arms and Falco's breath caught in his throat.

"Why are you doing this to me?" he asked.

She kept looking at him steadily.

"I'm going to have you!" he shouted. "Do you understand me? Can you hear that, or are you deaf also? I've taken too much from you, too much, and now it's your turn, do you hear me? Do you hear me?"

He reached for her, and she did not scream, nor did she protest. She didn't even seem frightened. Her eyes remained calm and the smile stayed on her full mouth. He took her in his arms, and she leaned back on the dresser with one arm to support herself.

He buried his mouth in her throat, and smelled the deep perfume of her, and he murmured helplessly, "I could love you, you dummy, I could really love you."

He took his mouth from her throat then, and he saw her hand close on the small pistol in her purse. He tried to move away but her hand came up fast, and he felt the muzzle of the gun between the second and third ribs on his left side, and then he heard the explosion. The bullet tore him free from her, and his eyes opened wide in shock, because he had not thought a dummy would have a gun, had not thought a pretty dummy like this one — who could not scream if attacked — would protect herself in some other way.

He staggered back, his hands covering the blood that spurted from his chest. He looked at her face, and the coldness was still there in her eyes, a coldness he could not understand. He moved his lips, but no sound came from his mouth, and he felt his legs weakening under him, and he kept staring at her face, and the coldness there, and he realized suddenly that the coldness was not there for him but for the other man a long time ago, the man who had stolen her voice.

His eyes glazed over, and he dropped to the floor, and then he made a crawling, painful reach for her, his big blood-stained hand outstretched. The girl backed away, and the muscles of her throat quivered, and her lips trembled, and then a surprised, awed look came into her eyes.

His hand dropped. He saw her only dimly now, but he heard the scream burst from her mouth, a high, penetrating scream, shrilling into the shack. And then the scream changed to something exultant, something wild in its ecstasy, and it rose higher and higher, louder and louder, assailing his ears until he died.

# PRIVATE EYES

Starting with its very first issue in January of 1953, and continuing through July of 1954, Manhunt published seven stories featuring an alcoholic former private eye named Matt Cordell. All of these stories carried the Evan Hunter byline. Cordell was my stab at creating a private eye character who was something different for his time. It amuses me when some reviewers call the 87th Precinct novels "hard-boiled." I think of them as bittersweet, lyrical, even sometimes sentimental. But hard-boiled? You want hard-boiled, try the Matt Cordell stories. The one that follows was published in July of 1953, and is the tamest of the lot. In fact, Cordell is almost likable in this story, a trait not often attributed to him.

# Good and Dead

HE WAS A SMALL MAN, SMALL IN STATURE AND SMALL IN social significance. Another bum, another wino, another panhandler. A nobody.

But he was Joey, and we'd shared the warmth of many a doorway together, tilted the remains of countless bottles of smoke together, worked the Bowery from end to end like partners, like friends.

He was Joey, but he was dead.

He was tattered in death, as he had been when alive. His clothes were baggy and ill-fitting, rumpled with the creases of park benches and cold pavements, stinking with the sweat of summer's heat, crawling with the lice that were the legged jewels of the poor.

"Shall we get the cops, Matt?" someone asked.

I nodded and kept looking down at Joey and at the bright stain of blood on the side of his head, the matted hair soggy and dirt encrusted where the bullet had entered.

Cooper Square, and the statue of Peter Cooper looked down with bronze aloofness, hemmed in by a grilled fence, surrounded by empty park benches. Cooper Square, and a summer night as black as a raven's wing, sprinkled with a dazzle of stars that Joey would never see again.

I felt empty.

"Why'd anyone want to kill a bum, Matt?" one of the winos asked.

"I don't know," I said.

Across the street, the squat structure that was Cooper Union fought with the Third Avenue El for dominance of the sky. A boy and a girl hugged the shadows of the building, walking their way slowly toward the small park and the cluster of winos. There was a mild breeze on the air, a summer breeze that touched the skin with delicate feminine hands. There was a hum on the air, too, the hum of voices on fire escapes, of people crowding the streets, of the day dying as Joey had died.

And over the hum came the wail of a siren, and the winos faded back into the anonymity of the Bowery, blending with the shadows, merging with the pavements and the ancient buildings, turning their backs on the law.

I turned my back, too. I walked away slowly as the siren got louder. I didn't turn for another look. I didn't want another look.


Chink was waiting for me outside the flophouse I'd called home for close to three months.

He was standing in the shadows, and I'd have missed him if he hadn't whispered, "Matt?"

I stopped and peered into the darkened doorway. "Who's that?"

"Me. Chink."

"What is it?"

"You got a minute, Matt?"

"I've got a lifetime. What is it?"

"Joey."

"What about him?"

"You were friends, no?"

I stared into the darkness, trying to see Chink's face. It was rumored that he came originally from Shanghai and that he could speak twelve Chinese dialects. It was also rumored that he'd been a big man in China before he came to the States, that he'd come here because of a woman who'd two-timed him in the old country. That gave us a common bond.

"You were friends, weren't you, Matt?"

"We were friends. So?"

"You know what happened?"

"I know he was killed."

"Do you know why?"

"No." I stepped into the doorway. There was the sickish smell of opium about Chink, overpowering in the small hall-way. "Do you?"

"No."

"Then why the hell are you wasting my time?"

"I got an idea, Matt."

"I'm listening."

"Are you interested?"

"What the hell are you driving at, Chink? Spit it out."

"Joey. I think he was killed for some reason."

"That's brilliant, Chink. That's real..."

"I mean, I don't think this was just an ordinary mug-and-slug, you follow? This was a setup kill."

"How do you figure?"

"I think Joey saw too much."

"Go smoke your pipe, Chink," I said. I started to shove past him. "Joey was usually too drunk to see his own hand in front of…"

"Harry Tse," Chink said.

It sounded like Harry Shoe. "Who's Harry Shoe?"

"He was killed the other night, Matt. You heard about it, didn't you?"

"No."

"They thought it was a tong job. Harry was big in his own tong."

"What is this, Fu Manchu?"

"Don't joke, Matt."

"Okay, Chink, no jokes. What makes you think they tie?"

"Something Joey said when I told him about Harry."

"When was this?"

"Yesterday. He said, 'So *that's* who it was.'"

"That doesn't mean a damned thing, Chink."

"Or it could mean a lot."

"Stop being inscrutable. So it means a lot, or it means nothing. Who gives a rat's backside?"

"I thought Joey was your friend."

"He was. He's dead now. What do you want me to do? The cops are already on it."

"You used to be a shamus."

"Used to be, is right. No more. Joey's dead. The cops'll get his killer."

"You think so? They're already spreading talk he fell and cracked his head that way even though there's a bullet hole in him. They say he was drunk. You think they're gonna give a damn about one bum more or less?"

"But you do, huh, Chink? You give a damn?"

"I do."

"Why? What difference does it make to you?"

"Joey was good to me." His voice trailed off. "He was good to me, Matt." There was a catch in his voice, as if he were awed by the idea of *anybody* being good to him.

"The good die young," I said. "Let me by, Chink. I need some sleep."

"You're...you're not going to do anything about it?"

"I guess not. Maybe. I don't know. I'll think about it. Good night, Chink."

I started up the stairs and Chink yelled, "He was your friend, too, Matt. Just remember that. Just remember it."

"Sure," I said.

It took me a long time to forget it.

I still hadn't forgotten by the time I fell asleep.


The morning was hot and sticky. My shirt stuck to my back and my skin was feverish and gummy, and I wanted to crawl out of it like a snake. I dug up a bottle of wine, taking four drinks before one would stay down. I faced the morning then, blinking at the fiery sun, wishing for a beach, or a mountain lake, or even a breeze. There was none. There was only the El, rusted and gaunt, and the baking pavements. I started walking, heading for Chinatown because things can look different in the blaze of a new day.

I found Chink. He was lying on a pad, and there was opium in his eyes and the slack tilt of his mouth.

He looked up at me sleepily, and then grinned blandly. "Hello, Matt."

"This Harry Shoe," I said.

"Harry Tse."

"Yeah. Any survivors?"

"His wife. Lotus Tse. Why, Matt? You going to do something? You going to get Joey's killer?"

"Where is she? Tse's wife."

"On Mott Street. Here, Matt, I'll give you the address." He reached behind him for a brush, dipped it into a pot of ink, and scrawled an address on a brown piece of paper. "Tell her I sent you, Matt. Tell her Charlie Loo sent you."

"Is that your name?"

He nodded.

"All right, Charlie. I'll see you."

"Good luck, Matt."

"Thanks."


I knocked on the door and waited, and then I knocked again.

"Who is it?"

The voice had a singsong lilt, like a mild breeze rustling through a willow tree. It brought pictures of an ancient China, a land of delicate birds and eggshell skies, colorful kimonos and speckled white stallions.

"I'm a friend of Charlie Loo," I said to the closed door.

"Moment."

I waited a few more minutes, and when the door opened, I was glad I had. She was small, with shiny black hair that tumbled to her shoulders, framing an oval face. Her eyes tilted sadly, brown as strong coffee, fringed with soot-black lashes. She had a wide mouth, and she wore a silk blouse and a skirt that hugged her small, curving hips. "Yes, please?"

"May I come in?"

"All right." The singsong made it sound like a question. She stepped aside, and I walked into the apartment, through a pair of beaded drapes, into a living room that was cool with the shade of the building that crowded close to the open window.

"My name is Matt Cordell," I said.

"You are a friend of Charlie's?"

"Yes."

"I see. Sit down, Mr. Cordell."

"Thank you." I slumped` into an easy chair, clasped my hands over my knees. "Your husband, Mrs. Tse. What do you know about his death?"

Her eyes widened a little, but her face remained expressionless otherwise. "Is that why you are here?"

"Yes."

She shrugged her narrow shoulders. "He...was killed. Is there more to say?"

"How?"

"A knife."

"When?"

"Tuesday night."

"Today is Friday," I said, thinking aloud.

"Is it?" she asked. There was such a desperate note in her voice that I looked up suddenly. She was not watching me. She was staring through the open window at the brick wall of the opposite building.

"Do you have any idea who did it?"

"The tong, they say. I don't know."

"You don't think it was a tong?"

"No. No, I don't think so. I...I don't know what to think."

"What did your husband do?"

"Export-import. His business was good. He was a good man, my husband. A good man."

"Any enemies?"

"No. No, I don't know of any."

"Did he seem worried about anything?"

"No. He was happy."

I took a deep breath. "Well, is there anything you can tell me? Anything that might help in..."

She shook her head, dangerously close to tears. "You... you do not understand, Mr. Cordell. Harry was a happy man. There was nothing. No reason. No...reason to kill him. No reason."

I waited a moment before asking the next question. "Was he ever away from home? I mean, any outside friends? A club? Bowling team? Band? Anything like that?"

"Yes."

"What?"

"A club. He went on Mondays. He was well liked."

"What's the name of the club?"

"Chinese Neighborhood Club, Incorporated, I think. Yes. It's on Mulberry Street. I don't know the address."

"I'll find it," I said, rising. "Thank you, Mrs. Tse. I appreciate your help."

"Are you looking for Harry's murderer, Mr. Cordell?"

"I think so."

"Find him," she said simply.


The Chinese Neighborhood Club, Inc., announced itself to the sidewalk by means of a red and black lettered sign swinging on the moist summer breeze. A narrow entranceway huddled beneath the sign, and two Chinese stood alongside the open doorway, talking softly, their panamas tilted back on their heads. They glanced at me as I started up the long narrow stairway.

The stairwell was dark. I followed the creaking steps, stopping at a landing halfway up. There were more steps leading to another landing, but I decided I'd try the door on this landing first. I didn't bother to knock. I took the knob, twisted it, and the door opened.

The room was almost unfurnished. There was a long curtained closet on one wall, and an easy chair just inside the doorway. A long table ran down the center of the room. A man was seated at the table. A stringed instrument rested on the table before him, looking very much like a small harp. The man had the withered parchment face of a Chinese mandarin. He held two sticks with felted tips in his hands. A small boy with jet-black hair stood alongside the table. They both looked up as I came into the room.

"Yes?" the old man asked.

"I'm looking for friends of Harry Tse."

"Okay," the old man said. He whispered something to the boy, and the kid tossed me a darting glance, and then went out the door through which I'd entered. The door closed behind him and I sat in the easy chair while the old man began hitting the strings of his instrument with the two felted sticks. The music was Old China. It twanged on the air in discordant cacophony, strangely fascinating, harsh on the ears, but somehow soothing. It droned on monotonously, small staccato bursts that vibrated the strings, set the air humming.

The sticks stopped, and the old man looked up.

"You *who?*" he asked.

"Matt Cordell."

"Yes. Mmm, yes."

He went back to his instrument. The room was silent except for the twanging of the strings. I closed my eyes and listened, remembering a time when Trina and I first discovered the wonder of Chinatown, found it for our very own. That had been a happy time, our marriage as bright and as new as the day outside. That was before I found her in Garth's arms, before I smashed in his face with the butt of my .45. The police went easy on me. Trina and Garth dropped charges, but it was still assault with a deadly weapon, and the police yanked my license, and Matt Cordell drifted to the Bowery along with the other derelicts. Trina and Garth? Mexico, the stories said, for a quick divorce. Leaving behind them a guy who didn't give a damn anymore.

I listened to the music, and I thought of the liquor I'd consumed since then, the bottles of sour wine, the smoke, the canned heat. I thought of the flophouses, and the hallways, and the park benches and the gutters and the stink and filth of the Bowery. A pretty picture, Matt Cordell. A real pretty picture.

Like Joey.

Only Joey was dead, really dead. I was only close to it.

The music stopped. There was the bare room again, and the old man, and the broken memories.

"Is someone coming to talk to me?" I asked.

"You go up," the old man said. "Upstairs. You go. Someone talk to you."

"Thanks," I said, and went into the hallway, wondering why the old man had sent the kid up ahead of me. Probably a natural distrust of Westerners. Whoever was up there had been warned that an outsider was in the house. I climbed the steps, and found another doorway at the landing.

I opened the door.

The room was filled with smoke. There were at least a dozen round tables in the room, and each table was crowded with seated Chinese. There was a small wooden railing that separated the large room from a small office with a desk. A picture of Chiang Kai-shek hung on one wall. A fat man sat at the desk with his back to me. The kid who'd been downstairs was standing alongside him. I turned my back to the railing and the desk, and looked into the room. A few of the men looked up, but most went on with what I supposed were their games.

The place was a bedlam of noise. Each man sitting at the tables held a stack of tiles before him. As far as I could gather, the play went in a clockwise motion, with each player lifting a tile and banging it down on the table as he shouted something in Chinese. I tried to get the gist of the game, but it was too complicated. Every now and then, one man would raise a pointed stick and push markers across wires hanging over the tables, like the markers in a poolroom. A window stretched across the far end of the room, and one group of men at a table near the window were the quietest in the room. They were playing cards, and from a distance, it looked like good old-fashioned poker.

I turned away from them and stared at the back of the man seated at the desk. I cleared my throat.

He swung his chair around, grinning broadly, exposing a yellow gold tooth in the front of his mouth.

"Hello, hello," he said.

I gestured over my shoulder with my head. "What's that? Mah-jongg?"

He peered around as if he hadn't seen the wholesale gaming. "Chinese game," he said.

"Thanks," I said. "Did Harry Tse play it?"

"Harry? No, Harry play poker. Far table. You know Harry?"

"Not exactly."

The Chinese shook his head, and the wattles under his chin flapped. "Harry dead."

"I know."

"Yes. Dead." He shook his head again.

"Was he here last Monday night?"

"Oh sure. He here every Monday."

"Did he play poker?"

"Oh sure. He always play. Harry good guy."

"Who played with him?"

"Hmm?"

"Last Monday? Who was he playing with?"

"Why?"

"He was killed. Maybe one of his friends did it. Who did he play with?"

The fat Chinese stood up abruptly and looked at the far table. He nodded his head then. "Same ones. Always play poker. Only ones." He pointed at the far table. "They play with Harry."

"Thanks. Mind if I ask them a few questions?"

The fat Chinese shrugged. I went across the room past the mah-jongg tables and over to the poker game. Four men were seated at the table. None of them looked up when I stopped alongside it.

I cleared my throat.

A thin man with short black hair and a clean-shaven face looked up curiously. His eyes were slanted, his skin pulled tight at the corners. He held his cards before him in a wide fan.

"My name's Cordell," I said to him. "I understand Harry Tse was playing cards here the night before he was killed."

"Yes?" the thin man asked.

"Are you the spokesman for the group?"

"I'll do. What's on your mind?"

"Who won Monday night?" The thin man thought this over. He shrugged and turned to another player. "Who won, Tommy?"

Tommy was a husky boy with wide jowls. He shrugged, too. "I don't remember, Lun."

"That your name?" I asked the first guy.

"That's right. Lun Ching."

"Who won, Lun Ching?"

"I don't remember."

"Did Harry win?"

"I don't think so."

"Yes or no?"

"No."

"Are you sure?"

Lun Ching stared at me. "Are you from the police?"

"No."

He nodded his head imperceptibly. "Harry didn't win. That's enough for you." He turned back to his cards, fished two from the fan, and said to a player across the table, "Two cards."

The dealer threw two cards onto the table, and Lun Ching reached for them. I reached at the same time, clamping my fingers onto his wrist.

"I'm not through yet, Lun."

He shook his hand free, and shoved his chair back. "You better get the hell out of here, Mac," he said.

"Matt," I corrected. "I want to know who won here Monday night. You going to tell me?"

"What difference does it make?"

"I want to know."

Lun Ching gestured impatiently with his head. "Tommy won."

I turned to the husky-jowled Chinese. "Did you?"

"Yes."

"How much?"

"A few bucks."

"Did Harry lose?"

"Yes."

"How much?"

"I don't know. Two, three dollars."

"Who else won?"

"What?"

"You said you'd won a few bucks, Tommy. You also said Harry lost about three bucks. What did the rest of you do?"

Lun Ching stood up. "We broke even. Does that answer you?"

"Maybe," I said. I turned and started across the room. Over my shoulder, I said, "I might come back."

Someone from the table whispered, "Don't hurry."

The fat Chinese looked up when I stopped at the desk behind the wooden railing.

"I don't think I caught your name," I said.

"Wong. Sam Wong."

"Mr. Wong, did Harry leave here alone on Monday night?"

# Good and Dead

"Yes, he did."

"Did he say where he was going? Did he have to meet anyone?"

"No. He didn't say. I think he go home."

"I see."

Sam Wong looked at me curiously. "Harry no killed Monday night," he said, his voice puzzled. "Harry killed Tuesday night."

"I know," I said. "That's what's bothering me."

None of it fit.

I was banging my head against a stone wall, and I didn't like the feeling. It wasn't like the old days when someone shoved a fat retainer under my nose, held it out like a carrot to a rabbit, challenged me to find a missing husband or squelch a bit of blackmail.

There was no retainer now. There was only the thought of Joey lying dead in that small park, Joey about whom I knew practically nothing. We shared a big thirst, that was all, and we'd done our damnedest to quench it. I thought of the last bottle I'd shared with him. We'd sat on the corner of my flophouse cot a few days back, drinking the fifth of Imperial, forgetting the heated streets outside, forgetting everything but the driving desire to get blind stinking drunk.

Now Joey was dead, and Charlie had suggested a tie-in between that and the death of Harry Tse, a man I didn't know at all. A sensible man would have called it a day. A sensible man would have said, "All right, you stupid bastard, your first idea was wrong. Harry Tse didn't win any money, and that's not

123

why he was killed. There was another reason, and it wasn't a cheating wife because her love is stamped all over her face. So give it up and go rustle a bottle of smoke, give it up and forget it."

I'd stopped being sensible a long time ago.

I'd stopped the night I took Garth's face apart.

I shook my head and bummed a dime from the next guy who passed. That bought me a glass of beer, and that cleared my head a little, and I was ready to play shamus again even though it was too hot to be playing anything.

I started walking through Chinatown, looking for an idea. I passed windows crammed with herbs and roots, crammed with fish and spice and fowl. I passed windows brimming with sandals and kimonos and jade and beads and boxes and figurines and fans. I passed newsstands displaying Chinese periodicals and newspapers. I passed restaurants, upstairs, downstairs, level with the street. I passed all these in a miasma of heat that clung to the narrow streets like a living thing.

And no idea came.

The heat stifled thought. It crawled around the open throat of my shirt, stained my armpits, spread sweat across my back muscles. It was too hot to walk, and too hot to think, and too damned hot to do anything but sidle up to a beer glass beaded with cold drops.

But I had to think, so I forced the heat out of my mind and I tried to remember what Mrs. Tse had told me about her husband, Harry.

*Export-import.*

I stopped in the nearest candy store, waded through two dozen Tses in the phone book, and finally located his business address, right in the center of Chinatown where I'd hoped it would be. I sighed against the heat, wiped the sweat from my forehead, and headed for his office.

It was upstairs. A small unimportant office with an important-looking title on the door: HARRY TSE: EXPORTS-IMPORTS. I tried the knob, half expecting the office to be closed. The door opened, and I found myself in a small reception room. A desk hugged the wall, and a Chinese girl hugged the desk. She stopped typing when I came in, her sloe eyes frankly appraising me.

She was dressed like any girl you'd see in the subway. She was small, the way most Chinese women are, but there was nothing slight or delicate about her. She wore no makeup other than a splash of lipstick across her full mouth.

"My name is Matt Cordell," I said.

"Yes?" she said. "How may I help you, sir?"

"Mrs. Tse sent me," I lied. "What do you know about her husband?"

"You're investigating his murder?"

"More or less," I said.

She looked at me dubiously and then she shrugged, and her eyes met mine frankly and levelly.

"I don't know anything about his murder," she said.

"What about his habits?"

"What about them?"

"Do you know where he was going on the night he was killed?"

"Yes. One of his clients lives on West Seventy-second Street. I think he was going there. In fact, I'm sure he was."

"How do you know that?"

"He told me he was walking up to Fourteenth to catch the uptown subway there. He never reached it. He was stabbed outside Cooper Union."

"Where Joey was killed," I said.

"Who? Oh yes, Joey. Charlie Loo's friend."

"You knew Joey?"

"No, I didn't know Joey," she said. "But Charlie told me what he said."

"What do you mean?"

"About seeing somebody."

"Is *that* what Joey said?"

"Well, not exactly."

"What *did* he say, exactly?"

"He said, 'So *that's* who it was.'"

"And that's what Charlie told you, is that it?"

"Yes. So I figured there might be some connection. To Mr. Tse getting stabbed."

"I see."

"So I passed it on to Mrs. Tse. She said she was going to look up Charlie and get him to point out this Joey person to her. She said she wanted to ask him what he'd seen."

"When was this? That you told Mrs. Tse?"

"Yesterday, I think. I don't really remember. There's been so damned much confusion around here…"

She shook her head.

"You've been very helpful," I said.

"Yeah," she said, and went back to her typing.


I'd been walking for two blocks before I realized I was being followed. I quickened my pace, hurried down narrow twisting streets, ducked into an alley, and sprinted for the other end. My followers knew Chinatown better than I did. Lun Ching and his pal Tommy were waiting for me at the other end of the alley.

"You son of a bitch," Lun shouted.

The sap in his hand went up over his head and came down on the side of my neck, knocking me flat against one wall of the alley. I grabbed at the bricks for support, but the sap went up and down again, and this time it peeled back a half inch of flesh from my cheek.

"You're going to the morgue, you bastard," Lun said. He brought back the sap again, swung it at my head. I fell to my knees and Tommy kicked me quickly and expertly. Lun bent over me, the sap a sledgehammer now, up and down, hitting me everywhere, on my shoulders, my face, my upraised hands and arms.

"Break up the card game, will you? Come acting tough, huh?"

And always the sap, up and down, viciously pounding me closer and closer to the cement until my head was touching it and Tommy's kick to my temple made everything go black.


The brick wall was a mile high. It stretched out above me and leaned dangerously against the sky. I watched it, wondering when it would fall, and after a while I realized it wasn't going to fall at all.

I stumbled to my knees then and touched the raw pain that was my face. I ached everywhere, and I ached more when I remembered Tommy and Lun. But I wasn't angry at them. They'd given me a hell of a beating, but they'd also given me an idea, and it was an idea any stupid bastard should have got all by himself. So I filed them away under unfinished business and stumbled my way out of the alley.

Lun Ching had said I was going to the morgue, and he was right.


It was cool inside the morgue.

I thanked the respite from the heat and followed the attendant down the long, gloomy corridor.

"This is it," he said. He pulled out the drawer and I looked down into Joey's lifeless face, at the flabby whiskey-sodden features that even death could not hide.

"That's him," I said.

"Sure, I know it's him," the attendant answered, his voice echoing off the windowless walls.

"I was wondering about his personal effects," I said.

"You a relative?"

"No. I don't think he had any relatives. I was his friend."

The attendant considered this.

"Not a hell of a lot there," he said at last. "Sent all of it up to Homicide because they're still investigating this. Got a list, though, and I can tell you what was on him."

"I'd appreciate that."

"Sure. No trouble at all." I followed him to a desk at the end of the corridor. He sat down and picked up a clipboard, and then began flipping the pages. "Let's see. Yeah, here he is, Joseph H. Gunder."

I hadn't even known Joey's last name. The anonymity of the Bowery is almost complete.

"Yeah, he didn't have much," the attendant said. "Want me to read this off?"

"Yes, please."

"A dollar bill, and thirty-five cents in change. Want that broken down?"

"No, that's fine."

"Okay, let's see. Handkerchief, switchblade knife, pint of Carstairs, almost empty, some rubber bands, package of Camels, two butts in it. Wallet with identification. That's it."

"A pint of Carstairs?"

I was thinking of the fifth of Imperial Joey had brought to me and how we'd killed it.

"Yep, that's right."

"And...a switchblade knife?"

"Yeah."

"And money, too?"

"Say, you want me to repeat the whole damn list?"

"No, that's fine. Thanks." I paused. "Did they decide what killed him?"

"Sure. Hole in the head. Want to see him again?"

"No. I meant, what caliber pistol?"

".22. Why?"

"Just curious. I'll be going."

"Drop in again sometime," he said.

I walked out into bright sunshine. For me, the beginning was in the morgue, after all, and I owed Lun Ching a debt. But the end was somewhere else, and I headed there now.

The door opened when I knocked and gave my name.

"I'm sorry," I said. "I just came across something."

"That's all right."

"May I come in?"

"Certainly."

I followed her into the living room again, and I sat down in the same easy chair. I didn't look at the floor or my clasped hands this time. I looked directly at her.

"Ever walk through the Bowery, Mrs. Tse?"

Her eyes were still troubled. "Yes?" she said.

"Often?"

"I know the neighborhood."

"Do you own a gun, Mrs. Tse?"

She hesitated. "Why…yes. Yes, I do."

"A .22 maybe?"

She hesitated again, for a long time. She sighed deeply then and lifted her eyes to mine. There was no expression on her face, and her tone was flat.

"You know," she said.

"I know."

She nodded.

"He deserved what he got," she said.

"Joey?"

"Yes. Joey. He was your friend, wasn't he?"

"My drinking companion, Mrs. Tse. A man doesn't get to know much about anyone in the Bowery. Nor about what makes them tick."

"How did you know? How did you know I…killed him?"

"A few things. A bottle of Imperial, for one. When Joey brought it to me, I never thought to ask where he'd got the money for it. That kind of money doesn't come easy to a bum. When I saw his stuff at the morgue, there was another pint there, and more money. I knew then that Joey had hit it rich recently and his switchblade knife told me how."

"Harry was stabbed," she said tonelessly.

"Sure. Joey didn't even know who his victim was. When Charlie mentioned it to him, Joey was probably drunk. He said, 'So *that's* who it was,' without even thinking. Charlie thought Joey had only *seen* your husband's murderer. He didn't know Joey *was* the murderer."

"And me? How did you come to me?"

"A guess, and a little figuring. A .22 is a woman's gun."

"I have a permit," she said. "I go through the Bowery often. Harry thought...he thought I should have one."

"What happened, Mrs. Tse? Do you want to tell me?"

"All right," she said, and paused. "Charlie pointed out your...friend to me. Joey. I followed him to Cooper Square. I asked him what he'd meant by 'So *that's* who it was.' He got terribly frightened. He said he hadn't meant to kill Harry. I think he was drunk, I don't know. He said he'd asked Harry for a dime and Harry refused. He pulled a knife and when Harry started to yell, he stabbed him. For a...a dime. He stabbed him for a dime."

"He got more than just a dime, Mrs. Tse."

"I couldn't believe it, Mr. Cordell."

She still couldn't.

"For a *dime!*" she said again, and shook her head. "I took the gun from my purse and shot him. I shot him only once. Just once. Because he'd stabbed Harry, you see."

"Yes, I understand."

"So I shot him," she repeated. Her voice was very small now. "Will you take me to the police?" she asked.

"No," I said.

"But..."

I got to my feet.

"Mrs. Tse," I said, "we've never even met."

I walked to the door, leaving her alone in the living room that faced a blank wall, leaving her alone because once upon a time I'd lost someone I loved, and I knew exactly how it felt.

It was hot in the street.

But it was hotter where Joey was.

*This story was first published as "Ticket to Death" in the September 1954 issue of* Argosy. *It carried the Evan Hunter byline. I wrote it while I was still living in a development house in Hicksville, Long Island. I know this because the guy next door was a commercial airline pilot who provided much of the flight information in the story. "Death Flight"—my original title, and the one I'm using here—was an early shot at a more conventional p.i. story than the Matt Cordells. I later decided cops were the only people who had any right to be sticking their noses in murder investigations.*

# Death Flight

Squak Mountain was cold at this time of the year.

The wind groaned around Davis, and the trees trembled bare limbs, and even at this distance he could hear the low rumble of planes letting down at Boeing and Renton. He found the tree about a half mile east of the summit. The DC-4 had struck the tree and then continued flying. He looked at the jagged, splintered wood and then his eyes covered the surrounding terrain. Parts of the DC-4 were scattered all over the ridge in a fifteen-hundred-foot radius. He saw the upper portion of the plane's vertical fin, the number-two propeller, and a major portion of the rudder. He examined these very briefly, and then he began walking toward the canyon into which the plane had finally dropped.

Davis turned his head sharply once, thinking he'd heard a sound. He stood stock-still, listening, but the only sounds that came to him were the sullen moan of the wind and the muted hum of aircraft in the distant sky.

He continued walking. When he found the plane, it made him a little sick. The Civil Aeronautics Board report had told him that the plane was demolished by fire. The crash was what had obviously caused the real demolition. But the report had only been typed words. He saw "impact" now, and "causing fire," and even though the plane had been moved by the investigating board, he could imagine something of what had happened. It had been in nearly vertical position when it struck the ground, and the engines and cockpit had bedded deep in soft, muddy loam. Wreckage had been scattered like shrapnel from a hand grenade burst, and fire had consumed most of the plane, leaving a ghostlike skeleton that confronted him mutely. He stood looking at it for a time, then made his way down to the charred ruins.

The landing gear was fully retracted, as the report had said. The wing flaps were in the twenty-five-degree down position.

He studied these briefly and then climbed up to the cockpit. The plane still stank of scorched skin and blistered paint. When he entered the cockpit, he was faced with complete havoc. It was impossible to obtain a control setting or an instrument reading from the demolished instrument panel. The seats were twisted and tangled. Metal jutted into the cockpit and cabin at grotesque angles. The windshield had shattered into a million jagged shards.

He shook his head and continued looking through the plane, the stench becoming more overpowering. He was silently grateful that he had not been here when the bodies were still in the plane, and he still wondered what he was doing here anyway, even now.

He knew that the report had proved indication of an explosion prior to the crash. There had been no structural failure or malfunctioning of the aircraft itself. The explosion had occurred in the cabin, and the remnants of the bomb had shown it to be a homemade job. He'd learned all this in the past few days, with the cooperation of the CAB. He also knew that the Federal Bureau of Investigation and the military police were investigating the accident, and the knowledge had convinced him that this was not a job for him. Yet here he was.

Five people had been killed. Three pilots, the stewardess, and Janet Carruthers, the married daughter of his client, George Ellison. It could not have been a pleasant death.

Davis climbed out of the plane and started toward the ridge. The sun was high on the mountain, and it cast a feeble, pale yellow tint on the white pine and spruce. There was a hard gray winter sky overhead. He walked swiftly, with his head bent against the wind.

When the shots came, they were hard and brittle, shattering the stillness as effectively as twin-mortar explosions.

He dropped to the ground, wriggling sideways toward a high outcropping of quartz. The echo of the shots hung on the air and then the wind carried it toward the canyon and he waited and listened, with his own breathing the loudest sound on the mountain.

I'm out of my league, he thought. I'm way out of my league. I'm just a small-time detective, and this is something big...

The third shot came abruptly.

It came from some high-powered rifle, and he heard the sharp *twang* of the bullet when it struck the quartz and ricocheted into the trees. He pressed his cheek to the ground, and he kept very still, and he could feel the hammering of his heart against the hard earth. His hands trembled and he waited for the next shot.

The next shot never came.

He waited for a half hour, and then he bundled his coat

and thrust it up over the rock, hoping to draw fire if the sniper was still with him. He waited for several minutes after that, and then he backed away from the rock on his belly, not venturing to get to his feet until he was well into the trees.

Slowly, he made his way down the mountain.


"You say you want to know more about the accident?" Arthur Porchek said. "I thought it was all covered in the CAB report."

"It was," Davis said. "I'm checking further. I'm trying to find out who set that bomb."

Porchek drew in on his cigarette, and leaned against the wall. The busy hum of radios in Seattle Approach Control was loud around them. "I've only told this story a dozen times already," he said.

"I'd appreciate it if you could tell it once more," Davis said.

"Well," Porchek said heavily, "it was about 2036 or so…" He paused. "All our time is based on a twenty-four-hour clock, like the Army."

"Go ahead."

"The flight had been cleared to maintain seven thousand feet. When they contacted us, we told them to make a standard range approach to Boeing Field and requested that they report leaving each thousand-foot level during the descent. That's standard, you know."

"Were you doing all the talking to the plane?" Davis asked.

"Yes."

"All right, what happened?"

"First I gave them the weather."

"And what was that?"

Porchek shrugged, a man weary of repeating information over and over again. "Boeing Field," he said by rote. "Eighteen hundred scattered, twenty-two hundred overcast, eight miles, wind south-southeast, gusts to thirty, altimeter twenty-nine, twenty-five. Seattle-Tacoma, measured nineteen hundred broken, with thirty-one hundred overcast."

"Did the flight acknowledge?"

"Yes, it did. And it reported leaving seven thousand feet at 2040. About two minutes later, it reported being over the outer markers and leaving the six-thousand-foot level."

"Go on," Davis said.

"Well, it didn't report leaving five thousand and then at 2045, it reported leaving four thousand feet. I acknowledged this and told them what to do. I said, 'If you're not VFR by the time you reach the range you can shuttle on the northwest course at two thousand feet. It's possible you'll break out in the vicinity of Boeing Field for a south landing.'"

"What's VFR?" Davis asked, once again feeling his inadequacy to cope with the job.

"Visual Flight Rules. You see, it was overcast at twenty-two hundred feet. The flight was on instruments above that. They've got to report to us whether they're on IFR or VFR."

"I see. What happened next?"

"The aircraft reported at 2050 that it was leaving three thousand feet, and I told them they were to contact Boeing Tower on 118.3 for landing instructions. They acknowledged with 'Roger,' and that's the last I heard of them."

"Did you hear the explosion?"

"I heard something, but I figured it for static. Ground witnesses heard it, though."

"But everything was normal and routine before the explosion, that right?"

Porchek nodded his head emphatically. "Yes, sir. A routine letdown."

"Almost," Davis said.


He called George Ellison from a pay phone. When the old man came on the line, Davis said, "This is Milt Davis, Mr. Ellison."

Ellison's voice sounded gruff and heavy, even over the phone. "Hello, Davis," he said. "How are you doing?"

"I'll be honest with you, Mr. Ellison. I'd like out."

"Why?" He could feel the old man's hackles rising.

"Because the FBI and the MPs are already on this one. They'll crack it for you, and it'll probably turn out to be some nut with a grudge against the government. Either that, or a plain case of sabotage. This really doesn't call for a private investigation."

"Look, Davis," Ellison said, "I'll decide whether this calls for..."

"All right, you'll decide. I'm just trying to be frank with you. This kind of stuff is way out of my line. I'm used to trailing wayward husbands, or skip-tracing, or an occasional bodyguard stint. When you drag in bombed planes, I'm in over my head."

"I heard you were a good man," Ellison said. "You stick with it. I'm satisfied you'll do a good job."

"Whatever you say," Davis said, and sighed. "Incidentally, did you tell anyone you'd hired me?"

"Yes, I did. As a matter of fact..."

"Who'd you tell?"

"Several of my employees. The word got to a local re-porter somehow, though, and he came to my home yesterday. I gave him the story. I didn't think it would do any harm."

"Has it reached print yet?"

"Yes," Ellison said. "It was in this morning's paper. A small item. Why?"

"I was shot at today, Mr. Ellison. At the scene of the crash. Three times."

There was a dead silence on the line.

Then Ellison said, "I'm sorry, Davis, I should have realized."

It was a hard thing for a man like Ellison to say.

"That's all right," Davis assured him. "They missed."

"Do you think — do you think whoever set the bomb shot at you?"

"Possibly. I'm not going to start worrying about it now."

Ellison digested this and then said, "Where are you going now, Davis?"

"To visit your son-in-law, Nicholas Carruthers. I'll call in again."

"Fine, Davis."

Davis hung up, jotting down the cost of the call, and then made reservations on the next plane to Burbank.


Nicholas Carruthers was chief pilot of Intercoastal Airways's Burbank Division. The fatal flight had been made in two seg-ments; the first from Burbank to San Francisco, and the sec-ond from Frisco to Seattle. The DC-4 was supposed to let down at Boeing, with Seattle-Tacoma designated as an alter-nate field. It was a simple ferry flight, and the plane was to pick

up military personnel in Seattle, in accordance with the company's contract with the Department of National Defense.

Quite curiously, Carruthers had been along on the
Burbank-to-Frisco segment of the hop, as company observer.
He'd disembarked at Frisco and his wife, Janet, had boarded
the plane there as a nonrevenue passenger. She was bound for
a cabin up in Washington, or so old man Ellison had told
Davis. He'd also said that Janet had been looking forward to
the trip for a long time.

When Davis found Captain Nicholas Carruthers in the
airport restaurant, he was sitting with a blonde in a black cocktail dress, and he had his arm around her waist. They lifted
their martini glasses and clinked them together, the girl laughing. Davis studied the pair from the doorway and reflected that
the case was turning into something he knew a little more
about.

He hesitated inside the doorway for just a moment and
then walked directly to the bar, taking the stool on Carruthers's left. He waited until Carruthers had drained his glass
and then he said, "Captain Carruthers?"

Carruthers turned abruptly, a frown distorting his features.
He was a man of thirty-eight or so, with prematurely graying
temples and sharp gray eyes. He had thin lips and a thin
straight nose that divided his face like an immaculate stone
wall. He wore civilian clothing.

"Yes," he said curtly.

"Milton Davis. Your father-in-law hired me to look into
the DC-4 accident," Davis said, and showed his identification.
"I wonder if I might ask you a few questions?"

Carruthers hesitated, and then glanced at the blonde, apparently realizing the situation was slightly compromising. The blonde leaned over, pressing her breasts against the bar top, looking past Carruthers to Davis.

"Take a walk, Beth," Carruthers said.

The blonde drained her martini glass, pouted, lifted her purse from the bar, and slid off the stool. Davis watched the exaggerated swing of her hips across the room and then said, "I'm sorry if..."

"Ask your questions," Carruthers said.

Davis studied him for a moment. "All right, Captain," he said mildly. "I understand you were aboard the crashed DC-4 on the flight segment from Burbank to San Francisco. Is that right?"

"That's right," Carruthers said. "I was aboard as observer."

"Did you notice anything out of the ordinary on the trip?"

"If you mean did I see anyone with a goddamn bomb, no."

"I didn't—"

"And if you're referring to the false alarm, Mr. Whatever-the-Hell-Your-Name-Is, you can just start asking your questions straight. You know all about the false alarm."

"Why don't you tell me about it all over again," Davis said.

"Sure," Carruthers said testily. "Shortly after takeoff from Burbank, we observed a fire-warning signal in the cockpit. From the number-three engine."

"I'm listening," Davis said.

"As it turned out, it was a false warning. When we got to Frisco, the mechanics there checked and found no evidence of a fire having occurred. Mason told the mechanics—"

"Who's Mason?"

"Pilot in command." A little of Carruthers's anger seemed

to be wearing off. "He told the mechanics he was satisfied from the inspection that no danger of fire was present. He did not delay the flight."

"Were *you* satisfied with the inspection?" Davis asked.

"It was Mason's command."

"Yes, but your wife boarded the plane in Frisco. Were you satisfied there was no danger of fire?"

"Yes, I was."

"Did your wife seem worried about it?" Davis asked.

"I didn't get a chance to talk to Janet in Frisco," Carruthers said.

Davis was silent for a moment. Then he asked, "How come?"

"I had to take another pilot up almost the moment I arrived."

"I don't understand."

"For a hood test. I had to check him out. I'm chief pilot, you know. That's one of my jobs."

"And there wasn't even enough time to stop and say hello to your wife?"

"No. We were a little ahead of schedule. Janet wasn't there when we landed."

"I see."

"I hung around while the mechanics checked the fire-warning system and Janet still hadn't arrived. This other pilot was waiting to go up. I left."

"Then you didn't see your wife at all," Davis said.

"Well, that's not what I meant. I meant I didn't speak to her. When we were taxiing for takeoff, I saw her come onto the field."

"Alone?"

"No," Carruthers said. "She was with a man."

"Do you know who he was?"

"No. They were rather far from me, and I was in a moving ship. I recognized Janet's red hair immediately, of course, but I couldn't make out the man with her. I waved, but I guess she didn't see me."

"She didn't wave back?"

"No. She went directly to the DC-4. The man helped her aboard, and then the plane was behind us and I couldn't see any more."

"What do you mean, helped her aboard?"

"Took her elbow, you know. Helped her up the ladder."

"I see. Was she carrying luggage?"

"A suitcase, yes. She was bound for our cabin, you know."

"Yes," Davis said. "I understand she was on a company pass. What does that mean exactly, Captain?"

"We ride for a buck and a half," Carruthers said. "Normally, any pilot applies to his chief pilot for written permission for his wife to ride and then presents the permission at the ticket window. He then pays one-fifty for the ticket. Since I'm chief pilot, I simply got the ticket for Janet when she told me she was going up to the cabin."

"Did you know all the pilots on the ship?"

"I knew one of them. Mason. The other two were new on the route. That's why I was along as observer."

"Did you know Mason socially?"

"No. Just business."

"And the stewardess?"

"Yes, I knew her. Business, of course."

"Of course," Davis said, remembering the blonde in the cocktail dress. He stood up and moved his jacket cuff off his wristwatch. "Well, I've got to catch a plane, Captain. Thanks for your help."

"Not at all," Carruthers said. "When you report in to Dad, give him my regards, won't you?"

"I'll do that," Davis said.


He bought $25,000 worth of insurance for fifty cents from one of the machines in the waiting room, and then boarded his return plane at about five minutes before takeoff. He browsed through the magazine he'd picked up at the newsstand, and when the fat fellow plopped down into the seat beside him, he just glanced up and then turned back to his magazine again. The plane left the ground and began climbing, and Davis looked back through the window and saw the field drop away below him.

"First time flying?" the fellow asked.

Davis looked up from the magazine into a pair of smiling green eyes. The eyes were embedded deep in soft, ruddy flesh. The man owned a nose like the handle of a machete, and a mouth with thick, blubbery lips. He wore an orange sports shirt against which the color of his complexion seemed even more fiery.

"No," Davis said. "I've been off the ground before."

"Always gives me a thrill," the man said. "No matter how many times I do it." He chuckled and added, "An airplane ride is just like a woman. Lots of ups and downs, and not always too smooth—but guaranteed to keep a man up in the air."

Davis smiled politely, and the fat man chuckled a bit more and then thrust a beefy hand at him. "MacGregor," he said. "Charlie or Chuck or just plain Mac, if you like."

Davis took his hand and said, "Milt Davis."

"Glad to know you, Milt," MacGregor said. "You down here on business?"

"Yes," he said briefly.

"Me, too," MacGregor said. "Business mostly." He grinned slyly. "Course, what the wife don't know won't hurt her, eh?"

"I'm not married," Davis told him.

"A wonderful institution," MacGregor said. He laughed aloud, and then added, "But who likes being in an institution?"

Davis hoped he hadn't winced. He wondered if he was to be treated to MacGregor's full repertoire of worn-out gags before the trip was over. To discourage any further attempts at misdirected wit, he turned back to the magazine as politely as he could, smiling once to let MacGregor know he wasn't being purposely rude.

"Go right ahead," MacGregor said genially. "Don't mind me."

That was easy, Davis thought. If it lasts.

He was surprised that it did last. MacGregor stretched out on the seat beside him, closing his eyes. He did not speak again until the plane was ten minutes out of San Francisco.

"Let's walk to the john, eh, Milt?" he said.

Davis lifted his head and smiled. "Thanks, but—"

"This is a .38 here under my overcoat, Milt," MacGregor said softly.

For a second, Davis thought it was another of the fat man's tired jokes. He turned to look at MacGregor's lap. The overcoat was folded over his chunky left arm, and Davis could barely see the blunt muzzle of a pistol poking from beneath the folds.

He lifted his eyebrows a little. "What are you going to do

after you shoot me, MacGregor?" he asked. "Vanish into thin air?"

MacGregor smiled. "Now who mentioned anything about shooting, Milt? Eh? Let's go back, shall we, boy?"

Davis rose and moved past MacGregor into the aisle. MacGregor stood up behind him, the coat over his arm, the gun completely hidden now. Together, they began walking toward the rear of the plane, past the food buffet on their right, and past the twin facing seats behind the buffet. An emergency window was set in the cabin wall there, and Davis sighed in relief when he saw that the seats were occupied.

When they reached the men's room, MacGregor flipped open the door and nudged Davis inside. Then he crowded in behind him, putting his wide back to the door. He reached up with one heavy fist, rammed Davis against the sink, and then ran his free hand over Davis's body.

"Well," he said pleasantly. "No gun."

"My name is Davis, not Spade," Davis told him.

MacGregor lifted the .38, pointing it at Davis's throat. "All right, Miltie, now give a listen," he said. "I want you to forget all about that crashed DC-4. I want you to forget there are even such things as airplanes, Miltie. Now, I know you're a smart boy, and so I'm not even going to mark you up, Miltie. I could mark you up nice with the sight and butt of this thing." He gestured with the .38 in his hand. "I'm not going to do that. Not now. I'm just telling you, nice like, to lay off. Just lay off and go back to skip-tracing, Miltie boy, or you're going to get hurt. Next time, I'm not going to be so considerate."

"Look..." Davis started.

"So let's not have a next time, Miltie. Let's call it off now.

You give your client a ring and tell him you're dropping it, Miltie boy. Have you got that?"

Davis didn't answer.

"Fine," MacGregor said. He reached up suddenly with his left hand, almost as if he were reaching up for a light cord. At the same time he grasped Davis's shoulder with his right hand and spun him around, bringing the hand with the gun down in a fast motion, flipping it butt end up.

The walnut stock caught Davis at the base of his skull. He stumbled forward, his hands grasping the sink in front of him. He felt the second blow at the back of his head, and then his hands dropped from the sink, and the aluminum deck of the plane came up to meet him suddenly, all too fast.

Someone said, "He's coming around now," and he idly thought, Coming around where?

"How do you feel, Mr. Davis?" a second voice asked.

He looked up at the ring of faces. He did not recognize any of them. "Where am I?" he asked.

"San Francisco," the second voice said. The voice belonged to a tall man with a salt-and-pepper mustache and friendly blue eyes. MacGregor had owned friendly green eyes, Davis remembered.

"We found you in the men's room after all the passengers had disembarked," the voice went on. "You've had a nasty fall, Mr. Davis. Nothing serious, however. I've dressed the cut, and I'm sure there'll be no complication."

"Thank you," Davis said. "I wonder…did you say all the passengers have already gone?"

"Why, yes."

"I wonder if I might see the passenger list? There was a fel-low aboard I promised to look up, and I'm darned if I haven't forgotten his name."

"I'll ask the stewardess," the man said. "By the way, I'm Dr. Burke."

"How do you do?" Davis said. He reached for a cigarette and lighted it. When the stewardess brought the passenger list, he scanned it hurriedly. There was no MacGregor listed, Charles or otherwise. This fact did not surprise him greatly. He looked down the list to see if there were any names with the initials C. M., knowing that when a person assumes an alias, he will usually choose a name with the same initials as his real name. There were no C. M.s on the list, either.

"Does that help?" the stewardess asked.

"Oh, yes. Thank you. I'll find him now."

The doctor shook Davis's hand, and then asked if he'd sign a release stating he had received medical treatment and ab-solving the airline. Davis felt the back of his head, and then signed the paper.

He walked outside and leaned against the building, puff-ing idly at his cigarette. The night was a nest of lights. He watched the lights and listened to the hum of aircraft all around him. It wasn't until he finished his cigarette that he re-membered he was in San Francisco.

He dropped the cigarette to the concrete and ground it out beneath his heel. Quite curiously, he found himself ignor-ing MacGregor's warning. He was a little surprised at himself, but he was also pleased. Even more curiously, he found him-self wishing that he and MacGregor would meet again.

———

He walked briskly to the cyclone fence that hemmed in the runway area. Quickly, he showed the uniformed guard at the gate his credentials, and then asked where he could find the hangars belonging to Intercoastal Airways. The guard pointed them out.

Davis walked through the gate and toward the hangars the guard had indicated, stopping at the first one. Two mechanics in greasy coveralls were leaning against a work bench, chatting idly. One was smoking and the other tilted a Coke bottle to his lips, draining half of it in one pull. Davis walked over to them.

"I'm looking for the mechanics who serviced the DC-4 that crashed up in Seattle," he said.

They looked at him blankly for a few seconds, and then the one with the Coke bottle asked, "You from the CAB?"

"No," Davis said. "I'm investigating privately."

The mechanic with the bottle was short, with black hair curling over his forehead, and quick brown eyes that silently appraised Davis now. "If you're thinking about that fire warning," he said, "it had nothing to do with the crash. There was a bomb aboard."

"I know," Davis said. "Were you one of the mechanics?"

"I was one of them," he said.

"Good." Davis smiled and said, "I didn't catch your name."

"Jerry," the man said. "Mangione." His black brows pulled together suspiciously. "Who you investigating for?"

"A private client. The father of the girl who was a passenger."

"Oh. Carruthers's wife, huh?"

"Yes. Did you know her?"

"No. I just heard it was his wife. He's chief pilot down Burbank, ain't he?"

"Yes," Davis said.

Mangione paused and studied Davis intently. "What'd you want to know?"

"First, was the fire-warning system okay?"

"Yeah. We checked it out. Just one of those things, you know. False alarm."

"Did you go into the plane?"

"Yeah, sure. I had to check the signal in the cockpit. Why?"

"I'm just asking."

"You don't think I put that damn bomb on the plane, do you?"

"Somebody did," Davis said.

"That's for sure. But not me. There were a lot of people on that plane, mister. Any one of 'em could've done it."

"Be a little silly to bring a bomb onto a plane you were going to fly."

"I guess so. But don't drag me into this. I just checked the fire-warning system, that's all."

"Were you around when Mrs. Carruthers boarded the plane?"

"Yeah, I was there."

"What'd she look like?"

Mangione shrugged. "A broad, just like any other broad. Red hair."

"Was she pretty?"

"The red hair was the only thing gave her any flash. In fact, I was a little surprised."

"Surprised? What about?"

"That Tony would bother, you know."

"Who?"

"Tony Radner."

"Are you sure about that? Sure you know who the man with her was?"

Mangione made an exasperated gesture with his hands. "Hell, ain't I been working here for three years? Don't I know Tony when I see him? He used to sell tickets inside. It was him, all right. He brought her out to the plane and helped her get aboard. Took her right to her seat, in fact. I guess maybe… well, I gotta tell you, I was surprised."

"Why's that?"

"Tony's a good-looking guy. And this Mrs. Carruthers… well, she wasn't much. I'm surprised he went out of his way. But I guess maybe she wasn't feeling so hot. Tony's a gent that way."

"Wasn't feeling so hot?"

"Well, I don't like to talk about anybody's dead, but she looked like she had a snootful to me. Either that, or she was pretty damn sick."

"What makes you say that?"

"Hell, Tony had to help her up the ladder, and he practically carried her to her seat. Yeah, she musta been looped."

"You said Radner used to work here. Has he quit?"

"Yeah, he quit."

"Do you know where I can find him?"

Mangione shrugged. "Maybe you can get his address from the office in the morning. But, mister, I wouldn't bother him right now, if I was you."

"Why not?"

Mangione smiled.

"Because he's on his honeymoon."


When Davis awoke in the morning, the back of his head hardly hurt at all. He shaved and washed quickly, downed a breakfast of orange juice and coffee, and then went to the San Francisco office of Intercoastal Airways.

Radner, they told him, was no longer with them. But they did have his last address, and they parted with it willingly. Davis grabbed a cab, and then sat back while the driver fought the California traffic. When he reached Radner's address, he paid and tipped the cabbie, and listed the expenditure in his book.

The rooming house was not in a good section of the city. It was red brick, with a brown front stoop. There was an old-fashioned bellpull set in the wide, wooden doorjamb. He pulled this and heard the sound inside, and then he waited for footsteps. They came sooner than he expected.

The woman who opened the door couldn't have been more than fifty. Her face was still greasy with cold cream, and her hair was tied up in rags.

"Yes?" she said.

"I'm looking for Tony Radner," Davis said. "I'm an old friend of his, knew him in the Army. I went out to Intercoastal, but they told me he doesn't work for them anymore. I wonder if you know where I can reach him."

The landlady regarded him suspiciously for a moment. "He doesn't live here anymore," she said.

"Darn," Davis said. He shook his head and assumed a false

smile. "Isn't that always the way? I came all the way from New York, and now I can't locate him."

"That's too bad," the landlady agreed.

"Did he leave any forwarding address?" Davis asked.

"No. He left because he was getting married."

"Married!" Davis said. "Well, I'll be darned! Old Tony getting married!"

The landlady continued to watch Davis, her small eyes staring fixedly.

"You wouldn't know who he married, would you?"

"Yes," she said guardedly. "I guess I would."

"Who?" he asked.

"Trimble," the landlady said. "A girl named Alice Trimble."

"Alice Trimble," Davis said reflectively. "You wouldn't have her phone number, would you?"

"Come on in," the landlady said, finally accepting Davis at face value. She led him into the foyer of the house, and Davis followed her to the pay phone on the wall.

"They all scribble numbers here," she said. "I keep washing them off, but they keep putting them back again."

"Shame," Davis said sympathetically.

"Hers is up there, too. You just wait a second, and I'll tell you which one." She stepped close to the phone and examined the scribbled numbers on the wall. She stood very close to the wall, moving her head whenever she wanted to move her eyes. She stepped back at last and placed a long white finger on one of the numbers. "This one. This is the one he always called."

Davis jotted down the number hastily, and then said, "Well, gee, thanks a million. You don't know how much I appreciate this."

"I hope you find him," the landlady said. "Nice fellow, Mr. Radner."

"One of the best," Davis said.

He called the number from the first pay phone he found. He listened to the phone ring four times on the other end, and then a voice said, "Hello?"

"Hello," he said. "I'm an old friend of Tony Radner's. He asked me to look him up if ever I was in town." He paused and forced himself to laugh in embarrassment. "Trouble is I can't seem to find him. His landlady gave me this number..."

"Oh," the girl said. "You must want my sister. This is *Anne* Trimble."

"Oh," he said. "I'm sorry. I didn't realize..." He paused. "Is your sister there?"

"No, she doesn't live with me anymore. She and Tony got married."

"Well, now, that's wonderful," Davis said. "Know where I can find them?"

"They're still on their honeymoon."

"Oh, that's too bad." He thought for a few seconds, and then said, "I've got to catch a plane back tonight. I wonder if I might come over and...well, you could fill me in on what Tony's been doing and all. Hate like the devil to go back without knowing something about him."

The girl hesitated.

"I promise I'll make it a very short visit. I've still got some business to attend to here. Besides...well, Tony loaned me a little money once, and I thought...well, if you don't mind, I'd like to leave it with you."

"I...I suppose that'd be all right," she said.

"Fine. May I have the address?"

She gave it to him, and he told her he'd be there in about an hour, if that was all right with her. He went to the coffee counter then, ordered coffee and a toasted English, and browsed over them until it was time to go. He bought a plain white envelope on the way out, slipped twenty dollars into it, and sealed it. Then he hailed a cab.

He found the mailbox marked A. Trimble, and realized the initial sufficed for both Alice and Anne. He walked up two flights, stopped outside apartment 22, and thumbed the ivory stud in the doorjamb. A series of chimes floated from beyond the door, and then the peephole flap was thrown back.

"I'm Mr. Davis," he said to the flap. "I called about—"

"Oh, yes," Anne Trimble said. The flap descended, and the door swung wide.

She was a tall brunette, and her costume emphasized her height. She was wearing tightly tailored toreador slacks. A starched white blouse with a wide collar and long sleeves was tucked firmly into the band of the slacks. A bird in flight, captured in sterling, rested on the blouse just below the left breast pocket.

"Come in," she said, "won't you?" She had green eyes and black eyebrows, and she smiled pleasantly now.

Davis stepped into the cool apartment, and she closed the door behind him.

"I'm sorry if I seemed rude when you called," she said. "I'm afraid you woke me."

"Then I should be the one to apologize," Davis said.

He followed her into a sunken living room furnished in Swedish modern. She walked to a long, low coffee table and took a cigarette from a box there, offering the box to him first. Davis shook his head and watched her as she lighted the cigarette. Her hair was cut close to her head, ringing her face with ebony wisps. She wore only lipstick, and Davis reflected that this was the first truly beautiful woman he had ever met. Two large, silver hoop earrings hung from her ears. She lifted her head, and the earrings caught the rays of the sun streaming through the blinds.

"Now," she said. "You're a friend of Tony's, are you?"

"Yes," he answered. He reached into his jacket pocket and took out the sealed envelope. "First, let me get this off my mind. Please tell Tony I sincerely appreciate the loan, won't you?"

She took the envelope without comment, dropping it on the coffee table.

This is a very cool one, Davis thought.

"I was really surprised to learn that Tony was married," he said.

"It was a little sudden, yes," she said.

"Oh? Hadn't he known your sister long?"

"Three months, four months."

Davis shook his head.

"I still can't get over it. How'd he happen to meet her?"

"Like that," Anne said. "How do people meet? A concert, a club, a soda fountain." She shrugged. "You know, people meet."

"Don't you like Tony?" he asked suddenly.

She seemed surprised. "Me? Yes, as a matter of fact, I do. I think he'll be very good for Alice. He has a strong personality, and she needs someone like him. Yes, I like Tony."

"Well, that's good," Davis said.

"When we came to Frisco, you see, Alice was sort of at loose ends. We'd lived in L.A. all our lives, and Alice depended on Mom a good deal, I suppose. When Mom passed away, and this job opening came for me…well, the change affected her. Moving and all. It was a good thing Tony came along."

"You live here alone then, just the two of you?"

Anne Trimble smiled and sucked in a deep cloud of smoke. "Just two little gals from Little Rock," she said.

Davis smiled with her. "L.A., you mean."

"The same thing. We're all alone in the world. Just Alice and me. Dad died when we were both little girls. Now, of course, Alice is married. Don't misunderstand me. I'm very happy for her."

"When were they married?"

"January sixth," she answered. "It's been a long honeymoon."

January sixth, Davis thought. The day the DC-4 crashed. "Where are they now?" he asked.

"Las Vegas."

"Where in Las Vegas?"

Anne Trimble smiled again. "You're not planning on visiting a pair of honeymooners, are you, Mr. Davis?"

"God, no," he said. "I'm just curious."

"Fact is," Anne said, "I don't *know* where they're staying. I've only had a wire from them since they got married. I don't imagine they're thinking much about me. Not on their honeymoon."

"No, I guess not," Davis said, and smiled. "I understand Tony left his job. Is that right?"

# Ed McBain

"Yes. It didn't pay much, and Tony is really a brilliant person. He and Alice said they'd look around after the honeymoon and settle wherever he could get located."

"When did he quit?"

"A few days before they were married, I think. No, wait, it was on New Year's Eve, that's right. He quit then."

"Then he wasn't selling tickets on the day of..."

Anne looked at him strangely.

"The day of what?"

"The day he was married," Davis said quickly.

"No, he wasn't." She continued looking at him, and then asked, "How do you happen to know Tony, Mr. Davis?"

"The Army," Davis said. "The last war."

"That's quite a feat," Anne said.

"Huh?" Davis looked up.

"Tony was in the Navy."

Once again, he felt like a damn fool. He cursed the crashed plane, and he cursed George Ellison, and he cursed the stupidity that had led him to take the job in the first place. He sighed deeply.

"Well," he said. "I guess I didn't meet him in the Army."

"I guess you didn't meet him at all," Anne said. She was staring at him coldly now. "Maybe you'd better get out, Mr. Davis. If that's your name."

"It's my name. Look," he said, "I'm a private eye. I'm investigating the crash for my client. I thought..."

"What crash?"

"A DC-4 took a dive in Seattle. My client's daughter was aboard her when she went down. There was also a bomb aboard."

"Is this another one of your stories?"

160

# Death Flight

Davis lifted his right hand. "God's truth, s'help me. I'm trying to find whoever put the bomb aboard."

"And you think Tony did?"

"No, I didn't say that. But I've got to investigate all the possibilities."

Anne suddenly smiled. "Are you new at this business?"

"No, I've been at it a long time now. This case is a little out of my usual line."

"You called yourself a private eye. Do private eyes really call themselves that? I thought that was just for the paperback trade."

"I'm afraid we really do," Davis said. "Private Investigator, shortened to Private I, and then naturally to private eye."

"It must be exciting."

"Well, I'm afraid it's usually deadly dull." He rose and said, "Thanks very much for your time, Miss Trimble. I'm sorry I got to see you on a ruse, but…"

"You should have just asked. I'm always willing to help the cause of justice." She smiled again. "And I think you'd better take this money back."

"Well, thanks again," he said, taking the envelope.

"Not at all," she said. She led him to the door, and shook his hand. Her grip was firm and warm. "Good luck," she said.

The door whispered shut behind him.

He stood in the hallway for a few moments, sighed, and then made his way down to the courtyard and the street.

The time has come, he thought, to replenish the bank account. If Ellison expects me to chase hither and yon, then Ellison should also realize I'm a poor boy, raised by the side of a railroad car. And if a trip to Vegas is in the offing… the time has come to replenish the bank account.

**161**

He thought no more about it. He hailed a cab for which Ellison would pay, and headed for the old man's estate.

The butler opened the door and announced, "Mr. Davis, sir."

Davis smiled at him and entered the room. It was full of plates and pitchers and cups and saucers and mugs and jugs and platters. For a moment Davis thought he'd wandered into the pantry by error, but then he saw Ellison seated behind a large desk.

Ellison did not look old, even though Davis knew he was somewhere in his seventies. He had led an easy life, and the rich are expert at conserving their youth. The only signs of age on Ellison were in his face. It was perhaps a bit too ruddy for good health, and it reminded him of MacGregor's complexion, but Ellison was not a fat man. He had steel-gray hair cropped close to his head. His brows were black, in direct contrast to the hair on his head, and his eyes were a penetrating pale blue. Davis wondered from whom Janet had inherited her red hair, then let the thought drop when Ellison rose and extended his hand.

"Ah, Davis, come in," he said. "Come in."

Davis walked to the desk, and Ellison took his hand in a tight grip.

"Hope you don't mind talking in here," he said. "I've got a new piece of porcelain, and I wanted to mount it."

"Not at all," Davis said.

"Know anything about porcelain?" Ellison asked.

"Not a thing, sir."

"Pity. Volkstedt wouldn't mean anything to you then, would it?"

"No, sir."

"Or Rudolstadt? It's more generally known as that."

"I'm afraid not, sir," Davis said.

"Here now," Ellison said. "Look at this sauceboat."

Davis looked.

"This dates back to 1783, Davis. Here, look." He turned over the sauceboat, but he did not let it out of his hands. "See the crossed hayforks? That's the mark, you know, shows it's genuine stuff. Funny thing about this. The mark so resembles the Meissen crossed swords..." He seemed suddenly to remember that he was not talking to a fellow connoisseur. He put the sauceboat down swiftly but gently. "Have you learned anything yet, Davis?"

"A little, Mr. Ellison. I'm here mainly for money."

Ellison looked up sharply and then began chuckling. "You're a frank man, aren't you?"

"I try to be," Davis said. "When it concerns money."

"How much will you need?"

"A thousand will do it. I'll probably be flying to Vegas and back, and I may have to spread a little money for information while I'm there."

Ellison nodded briefly. "I'll give you a check before you leave. What progress have you made?"

"Not very much. Do you know anyone named Tony Radner?"

Ellison looked up swiftly. "Why?"

"He put your daughter on that DC-4, sir. Do you know him?"

Ellison's mouth lengthened, and he tightened his fists on the desktop. "Has that son of a bitch got something to do with this?" he asked.

"Do you know him, sir?"

"Of course I do! How do you know he put Janet on that plane?"

"An eyewitness, sir."

"I'll kill that bastard!" Ellison shouted. "If he had anything to do with…"

"How do you know him, Mr. Ellison?"

Ellison's rage subsided for a moment. "Janet was seeing him," he said.

"What do you mean, seeing him?"

"She fancied herself to be in love with him."

"You mean she knew him before she met Carruthers?"

"No, that's not what I mean. I mean she was seeing him *after* she and Nick were married. She…she had the supreme gall to tell me she wanted a divorce from Nick." Ellison clenched his hands and then relaxed them again. "You don't know Nick, Davis. He's a fine boy, one of the best. I feel toward him the way I'd feel toward my own son. I never had any boys, Davis, and Janet wasn't much of a daughter." He paused. "I'm grateful I've still got Nick," he said.

"Did Carruthers know she wanted to divorce him?"

"No," Ellison said. "When she told me, I said I'd cut her off without a penny if she did any such damn-fool thing. She changed her mind mighty fast after that. Janet was used to money, Davis. The idea of marrying a ticket seller didn't appeal to her when she knew she'd have to do without it."

"So she broke off with him?"

"On the spot."

"When was this?"

"About six months ago," Ellison said. "I thought it was over and done with. Now you tell me he put her on that plane. I don't know what to think."

Davis nodded.

"It is a little confusing."

"You don't suppose they were going to be together in Washington, do you? Damn it, I wouldn't put it past her!"

"I don't think so. At least...well, wouldn't they have flown together if that were the case?"

"Not if she didn't want to be seen. She was traveling on a company pass, you know."

"That seems odd," Davis said. "I mean—"

"You mean, with all the money I gave them both, why was she traveling on a pass?" Ellison smiled. "Nick's a proud boy. Getting Janet her ticket was one of the things that kept his pride going."

"You gave them money, huh?"

"I still give Nick money. He's all I've got now."

"I see," Davis said, and washed his hand over his face. "Well, I'll talk to Radner. Did you know he was married now?"

"No, I didn't."

"Yes. On the day of the crash."

"On the day...then what on earth was he doing with Janet?"

"That's a good question," Davis said. He paused, and then added, "Can I have that check now?"

It was not until after dinner that evening that Nicholas Carruthers showed up. Davis had eaten lightly, and after a hasty cigarette had begun packing a small bag for the Vegas trip. When the knock sounded on the door to his apartment, he dropped a pair of shorts into the suitcase and called, "Who is it?"

"Me. Carruthers."

"Second," Davis said. He went to the door rapidly, wondering what had occasioned this visit from the pilot. He threw back the night latch and then unlocked the door.

Carruthers was in uniform this time. He wore a white shirt and black tie, together with the pale blue trousers and jacket of the airline. A peaked cap was tilted rakishly on his head.

"Surprised to see you," Davis said. "Come on in."

"Thanks," Carruthers said. He glanced around the simply furnished apartment noncommittally, then stepped inside and took off his cap, keeping it in his hands.

"Something to drink?" Davis asked. "Scotch okay?"

"Please," Carruthers replied.

"What's on your mind?" Davis asked.

Carruthers looked into the depths of his glass, sipped a bit of the scotch, and then looked up.

"Janet," he said.

"What about her?"

"Let it lie. Tell the old man you're dropping it. Let it lie."

"Why?"

"How much is the old man paying you?" Carruthers asked, avoiding Davis's question.

"That's between the old man and myself."

"I'll match it," Carruthers said. "And then some. Just let's drop the whole damn thing."

Davis thought back to the genial Mr. MacGregor. "You remind me of someone else I know," he said.

Carruthers did not seem interested. "Look, Davis, what does this mean to you, anyway? Nothing. You're getting paid for a job. All right, I'm willing to pay you what you would have made. So why are you being difficult?"

"Am I being difficult? I didn't say I wouldn't drop it, did I?"

"Will you?"

"It depends. I'd like to know why you want it dropped."

"Let's just say I'd like it better if the whole thing were forgotten."

"A lot of people would like it better that way. Including the person who put that bomb on the plane."

Carruthers opened his eyes wide. "You don't think I did that, do you?"

"You were aboard the plane. You could have."

"Why would I do a thing like that?"

"I can think of several reasons," Davis said.

"Like what?" Carruthers said, and sipped at the scotch again.

"Maybe you found out Janet was playing around with Tony Radner."

Carruthers laughed a short, brittle laugh. "You think that bothered me? That two-bit punk? Don't be ridiculous."

"You mean you knew about it?"

Carruthers nodded, sipped some more scotch, and then said, "I was used to Janet's little excursions. Radner didn't bother me at all. Janet collected men the way the old man collects porcelain. A hobby, you know."

"Did the old man know this?"

"I doubt it. He knew his daughter was a bitch, but I think Radner was the first time it came out in the open. He squelched that pretty darn fast, you can bet."

"But you knew about it? And it didn't bother you?"

"Not in the least. I'm no angel myself, Davis. If Janet wanted to roam, fine. If she thought of leaving me, that was another thing."

"That you didn't like," Davis said.

"That I didn't like at all." Carruthers paused. "Look, Davis, I like money. The old man has a lot of it. Janet was my wife, and the old man saw to it that we lived in style. I could have left the airline any time I wanted to, and he'd have set me up for life. Fact is, I like flying so I stayed on. But I sure as hell wasn't going to let my meal ticket walk out."

"That's not the way I heard it," Davis said.

"What do you mean?"

"Janet's gone, and the old man is *still* making sure you live in style."

"Sure, but I didn't know it would work that way."

"Didn't you?"

"I don't get you," Carruthers said, and swallowed the rest of his scotch.

"Look at it this way. Janet's a handy thing to have around. She comes and goes, and you come and go, and the old man sees to it that you come and go in Cadillacs. A smart man may begin wondering why he needs Janet at all. If he can be subsidized even after she's gone, why not get rid of her? Why not give her a bomb to play with?"

"Why not?" Carruthers asked. "But I didn't."

"That's what they all say," Davis told him. "Right up to the gas chamber."

"You're forgetting that I didn't know what the old man's reaction would be. Still don't know. It's early in the game yet, and he's still crossing my palm, but that may change. Look, Davis, when a man takes out accident insurance, it's not because he hopes he'll get into an accident. The same thing with Janet. I needed her. She was my insurance. As long as she was around, my father-in-law saw to it that I wasn't needing."

Carruthers shook his head. "No, Davis, I couldn't take a chance on my insurance lapsing."

"Perhaps not. Why do you want me to drop the case?"

"Because I like the status quo. The memory of Janet is still fresh in the old man's mind. I'm coupled with that memory. That means he keeps my Cadillac full of gas. Suppose you crack this damned thing? Suppose you find out who set that bomb? It becomes something that's resolved. There's a conclusion, and the old man can file it away like a piece of rare porcelain. He loses interest—and maybe my Cadillac stops running."

"You know something, Carruthers? I don't think I like you very much."

Carruthers smiled. "Why? Because I'm trying to protect an investment? Because I don't give a damn that Janet is gone? Look, Davis, let's get this thing straight. We hated each other's guts. I stayed with her because I like the old man's money. And she stayed with me because she knew she'd be cut off penniless if she didn't. A very simple arrangement." He paused. "What do you say?"

"I say get the hell out of here."

"Be sensible, Davis. Look at it…"

"Take a walk, Carruthers. Take a long walk and don't come back."

Carruthers stared at Davis for a long time. He said nothing, and there was no enmity in his eyes. At last he rose and settled his cap on his head. At the door, he turned and said, "You're not being smart, Davis."

Davis didn't answer him.

Maybe he wasn't being smart. Maybe Carruthers was right. It would have been so much easier to have said no, right from the start. No, Mr. Ellison, I'm sorry. I won't take the case. Sorry.

That would have been the easy way. He had not taken the easy way. The money had appealed to him, yes, and so he'd stepped into something that was really far too big for him, something that still made very little sense to him. A bomb seemed an awfully elaborate way of killing someone, assuming the death of Janet Carruthers was, in fact, the reason for the bomb. It would have been so much easier to have used a knife, or a gun, or a rope, or even poison.

Unless the destruction of the plane was an important factor in the killing.

Did the killer have a grudge against the airline as well?

Carruthers worked for the airline, but he was apparently well-satisfied with his job. Liked flying, he'd said. Besides, to hear him tell it, he'd never even considered killing his wife. Sort of killing the goose, you know. She was too valuable to him. She was—what had he alluded to? Insurance. Yes, insurance.

Which, in a way, was true.

Carruthers had no way of knowing how Ellison would react to his daughter's death. He could just as easily have washed his hands of Carruthers, and a man couldn't take a chance on—

"I'll be goddamned!" Davis said aloud.

He glanced at his watch. It was too late now. He would have to wait until morning.

"I'll be goddamned," he said again.

It would be a long night.


Arthur Schlemmer was a balding man in his early fifties. A pair of rimless glasses perched on his nose, and his blue eyes were genial behind them.

"I can only speak for Aircraft Insurance Association of America, you understand," he said. "Other companies may operate on a different basis, though I think it unlikely."

"I understand," Davis said.

"First, you wanted to know how much insurance can be obtained from our machines at the San Francisco airport." Schlemmer paused. "We sell it at fifty cents for twenty-five thousand dollars' worth. Costs you two quarters in the machine."

"And what's the maximum insurance for any one person?"

"Two hundred thousand," Schlemmer said. "The premium is four dollars."

"Is there anything in your policy that excludes a woman traveling on a company pass?" Davis asked.

"No," Schlemmer said. "Our airline trip policy states 'traveling on ticket or pass.' No, this woman would not be excluded."

"Suppose the plane's accident occurred because of a bomb explosion aboard the plane while it was in flight? Would that invalidate a beneficiary's claim?"

"I should hardly think so. Just a moment, I'll read you the exclusions." He dug into his desk drawer and came out with a policy that he placed on the desktop, leafing through it rapidly. "No," he said. "The exclusions are disease, suicide, war, and, of course, we will not insure the pilot or any active member of the crew."

"I see," Davis said. "Can I get down to brass tacks now?"

"By all means, do," Schlemmer said.

"How long does it take to pay?"

"Well, the claim must be filed within twenty days after the occurrence. Upon receipt of the claim, and within fifteen days, we must supply proof-of-loss forms to the claimant. As soon as these are completed and presented to us, we pay. We've paid within hours on some occasions. Sometimes it takes days, and sometimes weeks. It depends on how rapidly the claim is made, the proof of loss submitted, and all that. You understand."

"Yes," Davis said. He took a deep breath. "A DC-4 crashed near Seattle on January sixth. Was anyone on that plane insured with your company?"

Schlemmer smiled, and a knowing look crossed his face. "I had a suspicion you were driving at that, Mr. Davis. That was the reason for your 'bomb' question, wasn't it?"

"Yes. Was anyone insured?"

"There was only one passenger," Schlemmer said. "We would not, of course, insure the crew."

"The passenger was Janet Carruthers," Davis said. "Was she insured?"

"Yes."

"For how much?"

Schlemmer paused. "Two hundred thousand dollars, Mr. Davis. The maximum." He wiped his lips and said, "You know how it works, of course. You purchase your insurance from a machine at the airport. An envelope is supplied for the policy, and you mail this directly to your beneficiary or beneficiaries as the case may be, before you board the flight."

"Yes, I've taken insurance," Davis said.

"A simple matter," Schlemmer assured him, "and well worth the investment. In this case, the beneficiaries have already received a check for two hundred thousand dollars."

"They have?"

"Yes. The claim was made almost instantly, proof of loss filed, the entire works. We paid at once."

"I see," Davis said. "I wonder...could you tell me...you mentioned suicide in your excluding clause. Was there any thought about Mrs. Carruthers's death being suicide?"

"We considered it," Schlemmer said. "But quite frankly, it seemed a bit absurd. An accident like this one is hardly conceivable as suicide. I mean, a person would have to be seriously unbalanced to take a plane and its crew with her when she chose to kill herself. Mrs. Carruthers's medical history showed no signs of mental instability. In fact, she was in amazingly good health all through her life. No, suicide was out. We paid."

Davis nodded. "Can you tell me who the beneficiaries were?" he asked.

"Certainly," Schlemmer said. "A Mr. and Mrs. Anthony Radner."

He asked her to meet him in front of DiAngelo's and they lingered on the wharf a while, watching the small boats before entering the restaurant. When they were seated, Anne Trimble asked, "Have you ever been here before?"

"I followed a delinquent husband as far as the door once," Davis answered.

"Then it's your first time."

"Yes."

"Mine, too." She rounded her mouth in mock surprise. "Goodness, we're sharing a first."

"That calls for a drink," he said.

She ordered a daiquiri, and he settled for scotch on the rocks. As he sipped at the drink, he wished he didn't suspect her sister of complicity in murder.

They made small talk while they ate. Davis felt he'd known her for a long time, and that made his job even harder. When they were on their coffee, she said, "I'm a silly girl, I know. But not silly enough to believe this is strictly social."

"I'm an honest man," he said. "It isn't."

She laughed. "Well, what is it then?"

"I want to know more about your sister."

"Alice? For heaven's sake, why?" Her brow furrowed, and she said, "I really should be offended, you know. You take me out and then want to know more about my sister."

"You've no cause for worry," he said very softly. He was not even sure she heard him. She lifted her coffee cup. Her eyes were wide over the rim.

"Will you tell me about her?" he asked.

"Do you think she put the bomb on that plane?"

He was not prepared for the question. He blinked his eyes.

"Do you?" she repeated. "Remember, you're an honest man."

"Maybe she did," he said.

Anne considered this, and then took another sip of coffee. "What'd you want to know?" she asked.

"I want to…"

"Understand, Mr. Davis…"

"Milt," he corrected.

"All right. Understand that I don't go along with you, not at all. Not knowing my sister. But I'll answer any of your questions because that's the only way you'll see she had nothing to do with it."

"That's fair enough," he said.

"All right, fire away."

"First, what kind of a girl is she?"

"A simple girl. Shy, often awkward. Honest, Milt, very honest. Innocent. I think Tony Radner is the first man she ever
kissed."

"Do you come from a wealthy family, Anne?"

"No."

"How does your sister feel about—"

"About not having a tremendous amount of money?"
Anne shrugged. "All right, I suppose. We weren't destitute,
even after Dad died. We always got along very nicely, and I
don't think she ever yearned for anything. What are you driving at, Milt?"

"Would two hundred thousand dollars seem like a lot of
money to Alice?"

"Yes," Anne answered without hesitation. "Two hundred
thousand would seem like a lot of money to anyone."

"Is she easily persuaded? Can she be talked into doing
things?"

"Perhaps. I know damn well she couldn't be talked into
putting a bomb on a plane, though."

"No. But could she be talked into sharing two hundred
thousand that was come by through devious means?"

"Why all this concentration on two hundred thousand
dollars? Is that an arbitrary sum, or has a bank been robbed in
addition to the plane crash?"

"Could she be talked," Davis persisted, "into drugging another woman?"

"No," Anne said firmly.

"Could she be talked into forging another woman's signature on an insurance policy?"

"Alice wouldn't do anything like that. Not in a million
years."

"But she married Radner. A man without money, a man without a job. Doesn't that seem like a shaky foundation upon which to build a marriage?"

"Not if the two people are in love."

"Or unless the two people were going to come into a lot of money shortly."

Anne said, "You're making me angry. And just when I was beginning to like you."

"Then please don't be angry. I'm just digging, believe me."

"Well, dig a little more gently, please."

"What does your sister look like?"

"Fairly pretty, I suppose. Well, not really. Actually, I don't know if she is or not. I never appraised her looks."

"Do you have a picture of her?"

"Yes, I do."

She put her purse on the table and unclasped it. She pulled out a leather wallet, unsnapped it, and then removed one of the pictures from the gatefold. "It's not a good picture," she apologized.

The girl was not what Davis would have termed pretty at all. He was surprised, in fact, that she could be Anne's sister. He studied the black-and-white photograph of a fair-haired girl with a wide forehead, her nose a bit too long, her lips thin. He studied the eyes, but they had the vacuous smile common to all posed snapshots.

"She doesn't look like your sister," he said.

"Don't you think so?"

"No, not at all. You're much prettier."

"No, I'm not."

"Yes, you are."

"It's all fake," Anne said. "I visit a remarkable magician known as Antoine. He operates a beauty salon and fender repair shop. He is responsible for the midnight of my hair and the ripe apple of my lips. He made me what I am today, and now you won't love me anymore." She brushed away an imaginary tear.

"I'd love you if you were bald and had green lips," he said, hoping his voice sounded light enough.

"Goodness!" she said, and then she laughed suddenly, a rich, full laugh he enjoyed hearing. "I may very *well* be bald after a few more tinting sessions with Antoine."

"May I keep the picture?" he asked.

"Certainly," she said. "Why?"

"I'm going up to Vegas. I want to find your sister and Radner."

"Then you're serious about all this," she said softly.

"Yes, I am. At least, until I'm convinced otherwise. Anne..."

"Yes?"

"It's just a job. I..."

"I'm not really worried, you understand. I know you're wrong about Alice. And Tony, too. So I won't worry."

"Good," he said. "I hope I am wrong."

"Will you call me when you get back?" she asked.

"Yes," he said. "Definitely."

"If I'm out when you call, you can try my next-door neighbor. Her name is Freida, she'll take a message." She scribbled the number on a sheet of paper. "You will call, won't you, Milt?"

He covered her hand with his and said, "Try and stop me."

———

He went to City Hall right after he left her. He checked on marriage certificates issued on January 6, and was not surprised to find that one had been issued to Anthony Louis Radner and Alice May Trimble. He left there and went directly to the airport, making a reservation on the next plane for Las Vegas. Then he headed back for his apartment to pick up his bag.

The door was locked, just as he'd left it.

He put his key into the lock, twisted it, and then swung the door wide.

"Close it," MacGregor said.

He was sitting in the armchair to the left of the door. One hand rested across his wide middle and the other held the familiar .38, and this time it was pointed at Davis's head. Davis closed the door, and MacGregor said, "Better lock it, Miltie."

"You're a bad penny, MacGregor," Davis said, locking the door.

MacGregor chuckled. "Ain't it the truth, Miltie?"

"Why are you back, MacGregor? Three strikes and I'm out, is that it?"

"Three…" MacGregor cut himself short, and then grinned broadly. "So you figured the mountain, huh, Miltie?"

"I figured it."

"I wasn't aiming at you, you know. I just wanted to scare you off. You don't scare too easy, Miltie."

"Who's paying you, MacGregor?"

"Now, now," MacGregor said chidingly, waving the gun like an extended forefinger. "That's a secret now, ain't it?" Davis watched the way MacGregor moved the gun, and wondered if he'd repeat the gesture again.

"So what do we do?" he asked.

"We take a little ride, Miltie."

"Like in the movies, huh? Real melodrama."

MacGregor scratched his head. "Is a pleasant little ride melodrama?"

"Come on, MacGregor, who hired you?" He poised himself on the balls of his feet, ready to jump the moment MacGregor started wagging the gun again. MacGregor's hand did not move.

"Don't let's be silly, Miltie boy," he said.

"Do you know *why* you were hired?"

"I was told to see that you dropped the case. That's enough instructions for me."

"Do you know that two hundred grand is involved? How much are you getting for handling the sloppy end of the stick?"

MacGregor raised his eyebrows and then nodded his head. "Two hundred grand, huh?"

"Sure. Do you know there's a murder involved, MacGregor? Five murders, if you want to get technical. Do you know what it means to be an accessory after?"

"Can it, Davis. I've been in the game longer than you're walking."

"Then you know the score. And you know I can go down to R and I, and identify you from a mug shot. Think about that, MacGregor. It adds up to rock-chopping."

"Maybe you'll never get to see a mug shot."

"Maybe not. But that adds another murder to it. Are they paying you enough for a homicide rap?"

"Little Miltie, we've talked enough."

"Maybe we haven't talked enough yet. Maybe you don't know that the Feds are in on this thing, and that the Army..."

"Oh, come on, Miltie. Come on now, boy. You're reaching."

"Am I? Check around, MacGregor. Find out what happens when sabotage is suspected, especially on a plane headed to pick up military personnel. Find out if the Feds aren't on the scene. And find out what happens when a big-time fools with the government."

"I never done a state pen," MacGregor said, seemingly hurt. "Don't call me a big-time."

"Then why are you juggling a potato as hot as this one? Do you yearn for Quentin, MacGregor? Wise up, friend. You've been conned. The gravy is all on the other end of the line. You're getting all the cold beans, and when it comes time to hang a frame, guess who'll be it? Give a good guess, MacGregor."

MacGregor said seriously, "You're a fast talker."

"What do you say, MacGregor? How do you feel, playing the boob in a big ante deal? How much are you getting?"

"Four G's," MacGregor said. "Plus."

"Plus what?"

MacGregor smiled the age-old smile of a man who has known a woman and is reluctant to admit it. "Just plus," he said.

"All right, keep the dough and forget you were hired. You've already had the 'plus,' and you can keep that as a memory."

"I've only been paid half the dough," MacGregor said.

"When's the rest due?"

"When you drop the case."

"I can't match it, MacGregor, but I'll give you a thou for your trouble. You're getting off easy, believe me. If I don't crack this, the Feds will, and then you'll really be in hot water."

"Yeah," MacGregor said, nodding.

"Does that mean you'll forget it?"

"Where's the G-note?"

Davis reached for his wallet on the dresser.

"Who hired you, MacGregor?"

He looked up.

MacGregor's smile had widened now.

"I'll take it all, Miltie."

"Huh?"

"All of it." MacGregor waved the gun. "Everything in the wallet. Come on."

"You *are* a jackass, aren't you?" Davis said.

He fanned out the money in the wallet, and held it out to MacGregor. MacGregor reached for it, and Davis loosened his grip, and the bills began fluttering toward the floor. Mac-Gregor grabbed for them with his free hand, turning sideways at the same time, taking the gun off Davis.

It had to be then, and it had to be right, because the talking game was over and MacGregor wasn't buying anything.

Davis leaped, ramming his shoulder against the fat man's chest. MacGregor staggered back, and then swung his arm around just as Davis's fingers clamped on his wrist. They staggered across the room in a clumsy embrace, like partners at a dance school for beginners. Davis had both hands on Mac-Gregor's gun wrist now. They didn't speak or curse. MacGregor grunted loudly each time he swung his arm, and Davis's breath was audible as it rushed through his parted lips. He did not loosen his grip. He forced MacGregor across the room, and when the fat man's back was against the wall Davis began methodically smashing the gun hand against the plaster.

"Drop it," he said through clenched teeth. "Drop it."

He hit the wall with MacGregor's hand again, and this time the fat man's fingers opened and the gun clattered to the floor. Davis stepped back for just an instant, kicking the gun across the room, and then rushed forward and sank his clenched fist into the fat man's middle.

MacGregor's face went white. Clutching his belly, he lurched backward, slamming into the wall, knocking a picture to the floor. Davis hit him once more, on the point of the jaw, and MacGregor pitched forward onto his face. He wriggled once, and was still.

Davis stood over him, breathing hard. He waited until he caught his breath, and then he glanced at his watch. Quickly, he picked up the .38 from where it lay on the floor. He broke it open, checked the load, and then brought it to his suitcase and placed it on top of his shirts.

He snapped the suitcase shut, called the police to tell them he'd just subdued a burglar in his apartment, and then left to catch his Las Vegas plane.

He started with the biggest hotels first.

"Mr. and Mrs. Anthony Radner," he said. "Are they registered here?"

The clerks all looked the same.

"Radner, Radner. The name doesn't sound familiar, but I'll check, sir."

Then the shifting of the ledger, the turning of pages, the signature largely scrawled, and usually illegible.

"No, sir, I'm sorry. No Radner."

"Perhaps you'd recognize the woman, if I showed you her picture?"

"Well…" The apologetic cough. "Well, we get an awful lot of guests, sir."

And the fair-haired girl emerging from the wallet. The black-and-white, stereotyped snapshot of Alice Trimble, and the explanation, "She's a newlywed with her husband."

"We get a lot of newlyweds, sir." The careful scrutiny of the head shot, the tilting of one eyebrow, the picture held at arm's length, then closer.

"No, I'm sorry. I don't recognize her. Why don't you try…?"

He tried them all, all the hotels, and then all the rooming houses and then all the motor courts. They were all very sorry. They had no Radners registered, and couldn't identify the photograph.

So he started making the rounds then.

He lingered at the machines, feeding quarters into the slots, watching the oranges and lemons and cherries whirl before his eyes, but never watching them too closely, always watching the place instead, looking for the elusive woman named Alice Trimble Radner.

Or he sat at the bars, nursing endless scotches, his eyes fastened to the mirrors that commanded the entrance doorways. He was bored, and he was tired, but he kept watching, and he began making the rounds again as dusk tinted the sky, and the lights of the city flicked their siren song on the air.

He picked up the local newspaper in the hotel lobby.

In his room, drinking a scotch from the minibar, he flipped through the paper idly, and almost missed the story.

The headline read: FATAL ACCIDENT. The subhead read: FATE CHEATS BRIDE.

The article told of a Pontiac crashing through a highway

guardrail, instantly killing its occupant. Initial inspection indicated defective brakes. The occupant's name was Anthony Radner. There was a picture of Alice Trimble Radner leaving the coroner's office. She was raising her hand to cover her face when the picture was taken. It was a good shot, close up, clear. The caption read: *Tearful Alice Trimble Radner, leaving the coroner's office after identifying the body of her husband, Anthony Radner.*

Davis did not notice any tears on Alice's face.

Little Alice Trimble, he thought.

Shy, often awkward.

Honest.

A simple girl.

Well, murder is a simple thing, he thought. All it involves is killing another person or persons. You can be shy and awkward, and even honest—but that doesn't mean you can't be a murderer besides. So what is it that takes a simple girl like Alice Trimble and transforms her into a murderess?

Figure it this way. Figure a louse named Tony Radner who sees a way of striking back at the girl who jilted him and coming in to a goodly chunk of dough besides. Figure a lot of secret conversation, a pile of carefully planned moves. Figure a wedding, planned to coincide with the day of the plotted murder, so the murderers can be far away when the bomb they planted explodes.

Radner gets to see Janet Carruthers on some pretext, perhaps a farewell drink to show there are no hard feelings. This is his wedding day, and he introduces her to his bride, Alice Trimble. They share a drink, perhaps, but the drink is loaded and Janet suddenly feels very woozy. They help her to the airport, and they stow the bomb in her valise. None of the pilots know Radner. The only bad piece of luck is the fact that the fire-warning system is acting up, and a mechanic named Mangione recognizes him. But, hey, those are the breaks.

Radner helps her aboard and then goes back to his loving wife, Alice. They hop the next plane for Vegas, and when the bomb explodes they're far, far away. They get the news from the papers, file claim, and come into two hundred thousand bucks.

Just like falling off Pier 8.

Except that it begins to go sour about there. Except that maybe Alice Trimble likes the big time now. Two hundred G's is a nice little pile. Why share it?

So Tony Radner meets with an accident. If he's not insured, the two hundred grand is still Alice's. If he is insured, there's more for her.

The little girl has made her debut. The shy, awkward thing has emerged.

Portrait of a killer.

The easy part was over, of course. The hard part was still ahead. He still had to tell Anne about it, and he'd give his right arm not to have that task ahead of him. Alice Trimble? The police would find her. She probably left Vegas the moment Radner piled up the Pontiac. She was an amateur, and it wouldn't be too hard to find her. But telling Anne, that was the difficult thing.

He looked at the newspaper photograph again.

He sat erect all at once, and swallowed a long gulp of his scotch, and then he took the snapshot of Alice Trimble from his wallet and compared it with the newspaper photo of the woman named Alice Trimble Radner, and said aloud, "Oh no," and went immediately to the phone.

He asked long distance for Anne's number, and then let the phone ring for five minutes before he gave up. He remembered the alternate number she'd given him then, the one belonging to Freida, the girl next door. He fished the scrap of paper out of his wallet, studying the number in Anne's handwriting, recalling their conversation in the restaurant. He got long distance to work again, and the phone was picked up on the fourth ring.

"Hello?"

"Hello, Freida?"

"Yes?"

"My name is Milt Davis. You don't know me, but Anne said I could leave a message here if…"

"Oh, yes. Anne's told me all about you, Mr. Davis."

"Well, good, good. I just tried to phone her, and there was no answer. I wonder if you know where I can reach her?"

"Why, yes," Freida said. "She's in Las Vegas."

"What!"

"Yes. Her brother-in-law was killed in a car crash there. She…"

"You mean she's here in Vegas? Now?"

"Well, I suppose so. She caught a plane early this evening. Yes, I'm sure she's there by now. Her sister called, you see. Alice. She called and asked me to tell Anne to come right away. Terrible thing, her husband getting killed like…"

"Oh, Christ!" Davis said. He thought for a moment and then asked, "Did she tell you where she'd be staying?"

"Yes, with her sister."

"Yes, where?"

"Just outside of Las Vegas. A rooming house. Alice and Tony were lucky to find a nice…"

"Please, the address!"

"Well, all *right*," Freida said, a little miffed. She read off the address and Davis scribbled it quickly. He said good-bye, and hung up immediately. There was no time for checking plane schedules now. No time for finding out which plane Anne had caught out of Frisco, nor for finding out what time it had arrived in Vegas.

There was only time to tuck MacGregor's .38 into the waistband of his trousers and then run like hell down to the street. He caught a cab and reeled off the address, and then sat on the edge of his seat while the lights of Vegas dimmed behind him.


When the cabbie pulled up in front of the clapboard structure, he gave him ten dollars and then leaped out of the taxi. He ran up the front steps, rang the doorbell, and heard footsteps approaching inside. A white-haired woman opened the door.

"Alice Radner," Davis said. "Where?"

"Upstairs, but who…?"

Davis brushed past the woman and started up the flight of steps, not looking back. There was a door at the top of the stairwell. He rapped on it loudly. When he received no answer, he shouted, "I know you're in there! Open the goddamn door!"

The door opened instantly.

"Come in," a woman's voice said.

She was tall, and redheaded, and beautiful, with a pale complexion and blue eyes set against the ivory of her skin. She stared at Davis solemnly. A .22 caliber pistol was steady in her hand.

"Where is she?" Davis asked, and stepped into the room. Anne was lying on the bed, her hands tied behind her, a gag in her mouth. He made a move toward her just as a voice came from outside the closed door.

"Mrs. Radner?"

The landlady.

"Are you all right?"

"Yes, I'm fine, Mrs. Mulready. He's a friend of mine. Everything's all right, thanks."

He heard her footsteps retreating. He turned to the redhead again. The .22 was still steady in her hand.

"It all seemed out of whack," he said, "but I didn't know just where. It all pointed to Tony Radner and Alice Trimble, but I couldn't conceive of her as a murderess. Sure, I figured Tony led her into it. A woman in love can be talked into anything. But when I learned about Tony's accident here, a new Alice Trimble took shape. Not the woman who was talked into anything, and not the woman who'd do anything for love. This new Alice Trimble was a cold-blooded killer."

Davis saw Anne's eyes widen.

"Tell me," he said. "Was your sister a redhead?"

Anne nodded.

"I never thought to ask," he said. "About her hair. I had her picture and I thought that was all I needed."

There was a puzzled, apprehensive look of recognition in Anne's eyes now. All at once, Davis realized he'd said, "Was your sister a redhead?" Past tense. Was.

"I'm sorry," he said, and drew a deep breath. "Alice is dead."

She flinched as if he's struck her.

"Believe me," he said, "I'm sorry. I..." He wiped his hand across his lips and then said, again, "I'm sorry, Anne."

Tears sprang into her eyes. He went to her in spite of the .22 that was still pointed at him, ripped the gag from her mouth, and said again, "I'm sorry."

She was shaking her head now. "I don't understand," she said.

"Alice left you on the sixth," he said, "to meet Tony Radner, allegedly to marry him. She didn't know about the trap that had been planned by Tony and Janet Carruthers, who wanted to be free of her husband more than anything else in the world. But not at the expense of cutting herself off without a cent." He turned to the redheaded woman holding the gun. "Am I right so far, Janet? Or should I call you Mrs. Radner now?"

"Be my guest," Janet said. "You're doing fine so far."

"Alice met Tony as scheduled on the day they were to be married. He probably suggested a drink in celebration, drugged her, and then took her directly to the airport. You met him there because she was being insured as Janet Carruthers, and your signature was necessary on the insurance policy. The beneficiaries were Mr. and Mrs. Anthony Radner. That's who you are now, am I right?"

"Ever since the afternoon of the crash," Janet said. "You've got it all right except for the drug, Mr. Davis. That would have been overdoing it a bit."

"What'd Tony do, just get her too damned drunk to know what was going on?"

"Exactly. Her wedding day, you know. It wasn't difficult."

A sob caught in Anne's throat. Davis glanced at her briefly and then said to Janet, "Did Tony know he was going to be driving into a pile of rocks?"

Janet smiled. "Poor Tony. No, I'm afraid he didn't know. That part was all my idea. Even down to stripping the brakes. Tony never knew what hit him."

"Neither did all the people on that DC-4. It was a long way to go for a lousy hunk of cash," Davis said. "Was Tony insured, too?"

"Yes," Janet said, "but not for much." She smiled. "Enough, though."

"I still don't know how you hoped to swing it. You obviously sent for Anne because you were afraid someone would recognize you in Frisco. Hell, someone would have recognized you sooner or later, anyway."

"In Mexico?" Janet asked. "Or South America? I doubt it. Two hundred thousand can buy a lot outside of this country, Mr. Davis. Plus what I'll get on Tony's death. I'll manage nicely, don't you worry," she said, and smiled pleasantly, and leveled the gun at his head.

Davis smiled back.

"Go ahead," he said. "Shoot. And then try to explain the shots to your landlady."

"Oh, is that what you think?" Janet said, and walked to the dresser. She opened a drawer and came out with a long, narrow cylinder. The cylinder had holes punched into its sides, and Davis knew a silencer when he saw one. He saw her fitting the silencer to the end of the .22 and he saw the dull gleam in her eyes and knew it was time to move. He threw back his coat and reached for the .38 in his waistband.

The .22 went off with a sharp *pouff* and he felt instant pain when the small bullet ripped into his shoulder. But he'd already squeezed the trigger of the .38 and Janet's arm jerked as his larger bullet tore into flesh and bone. Her fingers opened, and the silenced gun fell to the floor. He kicked it out of her reach.

Footsteps were rushing up the stairs. Outside the door, the landlady shouted, "What is it, Mrs. Radner? What *is* it?"

"Call the police!" Davis yelled through the closed door. "Now!"

"You don't know what you're doing," Janet said. "This will kill my father."

"Your father still has Nick," Davis said. "And his porcelain." He paused and looked directly into Janet's eyes. "That's all he ever had."

When you start writing parodies of private eye stories, it's time to stop writing them. By the time this story was published, in January of 1955, I had written the last of the Matt Cordell stories and was ready to give up on the subgenre. Not only was I finding it increasingly more difficult to justify a private citizen investigating murders, but Cordell presented the added problem of an investigator who wasn't even licensed! Manhunt published this story under the Hunt Collins byline. It was a kiss-off to private eyes in general and Matt Cordell in particular.

# Kiss Me, Dudley

SHE WAS CLEANING FISH BY THE KITCHEN SINK WHEN I climbed through the window, my .45 in my hand. She wore a low-cut apron, shadowed near the frilly top. When she saw me, her eyes went wide, and her lips parted, moist and full. I walked to the sink, and I picked up the fish by the tail, and I batted her over the eye with it.

"Darling," she murmured.

I gave her another shot with the fish, this time right over her nose. She came into my arms, and there was ecstasy in her eyes, and her breath rushed against my throat. I shoved her away, and I swatted her full on the mouth. She shivered and came to me again. I held her close, and there was the odor of fish and seaweed about her. I inhaled deeply, savoring the taste. My father had been a sea captain.

"They're outside," I said, "all of them. And they're all after me. The whole stinking, dirty, rotten, crawling, filthy, obscene, disgusting mess of them. Me. Dudley Sledge. They've all got guns in their maggoty fists, and murder in their grimy eyes."

"They're rats," she said.

"And all because of you. They want me because I'm helping you."

"There's the money, too," she reminded me.

"Money?" I asked. "You think money means anything to them? You think they came all the way from Washington Heights for a lousy ten million bucks? Don't make me laugh." I laughed.

"What are we going to do, Dudley?"

"Do? Do? I'm going to go out there and cut them down like the unholy rats they are. When I get done, there'll be twenty-six less rats in the world, and the streets will be a cleaner place for our kids to play in."

"Oh, Dudley," she said.

"But first..."

The pulse in her throat began beating wildly. There was a hungry animal look in her eyes. She sucked in a deep breath and ran her hands over her hips, smoothing the apron. I went to her, and cupped her chin in the palm of my left hand.

"Baby," I said.

Then I drew back my right fist and hit her on the mouth. She fell back against the sink, and I followed with a quick chop to the gut, and a fast uppercut to the jaw. She went down on the floor and she rolled around in the fish scales, and I thought of my sea captain father, and my mother who was a nice little lass from New England. And then I didn't think of anything but the blonde in my arms, and the .45 in my fist, and the twenty-six men outside, and the four shares of Consolidated I'd bought that afternoon, and the bet I'd made on the fight with One-Lamp Louie, and the defective brake lining on my Olds, and the bottle of rye in the bottom drawer of my file cabinet back at Dudley Sledge, Investigations.

I enjoyed it.

———

She had come to me less than a week ago.

Giselle, my pretty redheaded secretary, had swiveled into the office and said, "Dud, there's a woman to see you."

"Another one?" I asked.

"She looks distraught."

"Show her in."

She had walked into the office then, and my whole life had changed. I took one look at the blonde hair piled high on her head. My eyes dropped to the clean sweep of her throat, to the figure filling out the green silk dress. When she lifted her green eyes to meet mine, I almost drowned in their fathomless depths. I gripped the desktop and asked, "Yes?"

"Mr. Sledge?"

"Yes."

"My name is Melinda Jones," she said.

"Yes, Miss Jones."

"Oh, please call me Agnes."

"Agnes?"

"Yes. All my friends call me Agnes. I…I was hoping we could be friends."

"What's your problem, Agnes?" I asked.

"My husband."

"He's giving you trouble?"

"Well, yes, in a way."

"Stepping out on you?"

"Well, no."

"What then?"

"Well, he's dead."

I sighed in relief. "Good," I said. "What's the problem?"

"He left me ten million dollars. Some of his friends think

the money belongs to them. It's not fair, really. Just because they were in on the bank job. Percy..."

"Percy?"

"My husband. Percy *did* kill the bank guards, and it was he who crashed through the roadblock, injuring twelve policemen. The money *was* rightfully his."

"Of course," I said. "No doubt about it. And these scum want it?"

"Yes. Oh, Mr. Sledge, I need help so desperately. Please say you'll help me. Please, please. I beg you. I'll do anything, anything."

"Anything?"

Her eyes narrowed, and she wet her lips with a sharp, pink tongue. Her voice dropped to a husky whisper. "Anything," she said.

I belted her over the left eye.


That was the beginning, and now they were all outside, all twenty-six of them, waiting to close in, waiting to drop down like the venomous vultures they were. But they hadn't counted on the .45 in my fist, and they hadn't counted on the slow anger that had been building up inside me, boiling over like a black brew, filling my mind, filling my body, poisoning my liver and my bile, quickening my heart, putting a throb in my appendix, tightening the pectoral muscles on my chest, girding my loins. They hadn't counted on the kill lust that raged through my veins. They hadn't counted on the hammer that kept pounding one word over and over again in my skull: kill, kill, *kill.*

They were all outside waiting, and I had to get them. We were inside, and they knew it, so I did the only thing any sensible person would have done under the circumstances.

I set fire to the house.

I piled rags and empty crates and furniture and fish in the basement and then I soaked them with gasoline. I touched a match, and the flames leaped up, lapping at the wooden crossbeams, eating away at the undersides of the first-floor boards.

Melinda was close to me. I cupped her chin in one hand, and then tapped her lightly with the .45, just bruising her. We listened to the flames crackling in the basement, and I whispered, "That fish smells good." And then all hell broke loose, just the way I had planned it. They stormed the house, twenty-six strong. I threw open the front door and I stood there with the .45 in my mitt, and I shouted, "Come on, you rats. Come and get it!" Three men appeared on the walk and I fired low, and I fired fast. The first man took two in the stomach, and he bent over and died. The second man took two in the stomach, and he bent over and died, too. I hit the third man in the chest, and I swore as he died peacefully.

"Agnes," I yelled, "there's a submachine gun in the closet. Get it! And bring the hand grenades and the mortar shells."

"Yes, Dud," she murmured.

I kept firing. Three down, four down, five down. I reloaded, and they kept coming up the walk and I kept cutting them down. And then Melinda came back with the ammunition. I gathered up a batch of hand grenades, stuck four of them in my mouth, and pulled the pins. I grabbed two in each hand and lobbed them out on the walk and six more of the rats were blown to their reward. I watched the bodies come down to the pavement, and I took a quick count of arms and legs. It had been seven of the rats.

"Seven and five is thirteen," I told Melinda. "That leaves eleven more."

Melinda did some quick arithmetic. "Twelve more," she said.

I cut loose with the submachine gun. Kill, kill, my brain screamed. I swung it back and forth over the lawn, and they dropped like flies. Fourteen, fifteen, sixteen. Nine more to go. Seventeen, eighteen, and they kept dying, and the blood ran red on the grass, and the flames licked at my back. They all ran for cover, and there was nothing to cut down, so I concentrated on a clump of weeds near the barn, shooting fast bursts into it. Pretty soon there were no more weeds, and the barn was a skeleton against the deepening dusk. I grabbed a mortar and tossed it into the yard, just for kicks. Pretty soon, there was no more barn. Behind me, I heard Melinda scream. I whirled. Her clothes were aflame, and I seized her roughly and threw her to the floor. I almost lost my mind, and I almost forgot all about the nine guys still out there. I tore myself away from her, and I ran into the yard with two mortar shells in my mouth, the submachine gun in my right hand, and the .45 in my left. I shook my head, and the mortar shells flew, and three more of the rats were dead and gone. I fired a burst with the machine gun, and another two dropped. There were four or five left now, and I picked them off one by one with the .45. The yard ran red with blood, and the bodies lay like twisted sticks. I sighed heavily and walked back to the house because the worst part still lay ahead of me.

I found her in the bedroom.

# Kiss Me, Dudley

She had taken a quick sponge bath, and her body gleamed like dull ivory in the gathering darkness.

"All right, Agnes," I said. "It's all over."

"What do you mean, Dud?"

"The whole mess, Agnes. Everything, from start to finish. A big hoax. A big plot to sucker Dudley Sledge. Well, no one suckers Sledge. No one."

"I don't know what you mean, Dud."

"You don't know, huh? You don't know what I mean? I mean the phony story about the bank job, and the ten million dollars your husband left you."

"He did leave it to me, Dudley."

"No, Agnes. That was all a lie. Every bit of it. I'm only sorry I had to kill twenty-six bird-watchers before I realized the truth."

"You're wrong, Dudley," she said. "Dead wrong."

"No, baby. I'm right, and that's the pity of it because I love you, and I know what I have to do now."

"Dudley..." she started.

"No, Agnes. Don't try to sway me. I know you stole that ten million from the Washington Avenue Bird Watchers Society. You invented that other story because you wanted someone with a gun, someone who would keep them away from you. Well, twenty-six people have paid...and now one more has to pay."

She clipped two earrings to her delicate ears, snapped a bracelet onto her wrist, dabbed some lipstick onto her wide mouth. She was fully dressed now, dressed the way she'd been that first time in my office, the first time I'd slugged her, the time I knew I was hopelessly in love with her.

She took a step toward me, and I raised the .45.

"Kiss me, Dudley," she said.

I kissed her, all right. I shot her right in the stomach.

She fell to the floor, a look of incredible ecstasy in her eyes, and when I turned around I realized she wasn't reaching for the mortar shell on the table behind me. Nor was she reaching for the submachine gun that rested in a corner near the table. She was reaching for the ten million bucks.

There were tears in my eyes.

"I guess that's the least I can do for you, Agnes," I said. "It was what you wanted, even in death."

So I took the ten million bucks, and I bought a case of Irish whiskey.

# COPS AND ROBBERS

*The four cop stories that follow were all published in Man-hunt. The first three were published in 1953, the last one in 1954. The first two were by Evan Hunter, the next two by Richard Marsten. Go figure.*

*When I wrote these stories, Ed McBain hadn't been born yet, and I knew nothing about cops or police routine except what I had learned from* Dragnet *on radio and television. I forget what* Manhunt *used to pay, but it couldn't have been more than two or three cents a word, and that wasn't enough to allow research. Whatever verisimilitude exists in these stories is entirely due to sleight of hand—and the fact that I once sold lobsters by telephone. They follow now in chronological order, no further commercial breaks.*

# Small Homicide

HER FACE WAS SMALL AND CHUBBY, THE EYES BLUE AND innocently rounded, but seeing nothing. Her body rested on the seat of the wooden bench, one arm twisted awkwardly beneath her soft little body.

The candles near the altar flickered and cast their dancing shadows on her face. There was a faded pink blanket wrapped around her, and against the whiteness of her throat were the purple bruises that told us she'd been strangled.

Her mouth was open, exposing two small teeth and the beginnings of a third.

She was no more than eight months old.

The church was quiet and immense, with early morning sunlight lighting the stained glass windows. Dust motes filtered down the long, slanting columns of sunlight, and Father Barron stood tall and darkly somber at the end of the pew.

"This is the way you found her, Father?" I asked.

"Yes. Just that way." The priest's eyes were a deep brown against the chalky whiteness of his face. "I didn't touch her."

Pat Travers scratched his jaw and stood up, reaching for the pad in his back pocket. His mouth was set in a tight, angry line. Pat had three children of his own. "What time was this, Father?"

"At about five thirty. We have a six o'clock mass, and I came out to see that the altar was prepared. Our altar boys go to school, you understand, and they usually arrive at the last minute. I generally attend to the altar myself."

"No sexton?" Pat asked.

"Yes, we have a sexton, but he doesn't arrive until about eight every morning. He comes earlier on Sunday mornings."

I nodded while Pat jotted the information in his pad.

"How did you happen to see her, Father?"

"I was walking to the back of the church to open the doors. I saw something in the pew, and I...well, at first I thought it was just a package someone had forgotten. When I came closer, I saw it was...was a baby." He sighed deeply and shook his head.

"The doors were locked, Father?"

"No. No, they're never locked. This is God's house, you know. They were simply closed. I was walking back to open them. I usually open them before the first mass in the morning."

"They were unlocked all night?"

"Yes, of course."

"I see." I looked down at the baby again. "You wouldn't know who she is, would you, Father?"

Father Barron shook his head again. "I'm afraid not. She may have been baptized here, but infants all look alike, you know. It would be different if I saw her every Sunday. But..." He spread his hands wide in a helpless gesture.

Pat nodded, and kept looking at the dead child.

"We'll have to send some of the boys to take pictures and

prints, Father. I hope you don't mind. And we'll have to chalk up the pew. It shouldn't take too long, and we'll have the body out as soon as possible."

Father Barron looked down at the dead baby. He crossed himself and said, "God have mercy on her soul."

We filed a report back at headquarters, and then sent out for some coffee. Pat had already detailed the powder and flash-bulb boys, and there wasn't much we could do until they were through and the body had been autopsied.

I was sipping at my hot coffee when the buzzer on my desk sounded. I pushed down the toggle and said, "Levine here."

"Dave, want to come into my office a minute? This is the lieutenant."

"Sure thing," I told him. I put down the cup, said, "Be right back" to Pat, and headed for the Old Man's office.

He was sitting behind his desk with our report in his hands. He glanced up when I came in and said, "Sit down, Dave. Hell of a thing, isn't it?"

"Yes," I said.

"I'm holding it back from the papers, Dave. If this breaks, we'll have every mother in the city telephoning us. You know what that means."

"You want it fast."

"I want it damned fast. I'm pulling six men from other jobs to help you and Pat. I don't want to go to another precinct for help because the bigger this gets, the better its chances of breaking into print. I want it quiet and small, and I want it fast." He stopped and shook his head, and then muttered, "Goddamn thing."

"We're waiting for the body to come in now," I said. "As soon as we get some reports, we may be able to learn something."

"What did it look like to you?"

"Strangulation. It's there in the report."

The lieutenant glanced at the typewritten sheet in his hands, mumbled "Uhm," and then said, "While you're waiting, you'd better start checking the missing persons calls."

"Pat's doing that now, sir."

"Good, good. You know what to do, Dave. Just get me an answer to it fast."

"We'll do our best, sir."

He leaned back in his leather chair. "A little girl, huh?" He shook his head. "Damn shame. Damn shame." He kept shaking his head and looking at the report, and then he dropped the report on his desk and said, "Here're the boys you've got to work with." He handed me a typewritten list of names. "All good, Dave. Get me results."

"I'll try, sir," I said.

Pat had a list of calls on his desk when I went outside again. I picked it up and glanced through it rapidly. A few older kids were lost, and there had been the usual frantic pleas from mothers who should have watched their kids more carefully in the first place.

"What's this?" I asked. I put my forefinger alongside a call clocked in at eight fifteen. A Mrs. Wilkes had phoned to say she'd left her baby outside in the carriage and the carriage was gone.

"They found the kid," Pat said. "Her older daughter had taken the kid for a walk. There's nothing there, Dave."

"The Old Man wants action, Pat. The photos come in yet?"

"Over there." He indicated the pile of glossy photographs on his desk. I picked up the stack and thumbed through it. They'd shot the baby from every conceivable angle, and there were two good close-ups of her face. I fanned the pictures out on my desktop and buzzed the lab. I recognized Caputo's voice at once.

"Any luck, Cappy?"

"That you, Dave?"

"Yep."

"You mean on the baby?"

"Yeah."

"The boys brought in a whole slew of stuff. A pew collects a lot of prints, Dave."

"Anything we can use?"

"I'm running them through now. If we get anything, I'll let you know."

"Fine. I want the baby's footprints taken, and a stat sent to every hospital in the state."

"Okay. It's going to be tough if the baby was born outside, though."

"Maybe we'll be lucky. Put the stat on the machine, will you? And tell them we want immediate replies."

"I'll have it taken care of, Dave."

"Good. Cappy, we're going to need all the help we can get. So…"

"I'll do all I can."

"Thanks. Let me know if you get anything."

"I will. So long, Dave, I've got work."

He clicked off, and I leaned back and lit a cigarette. Pat picked up one of the baby's photos and studied it glumly.

"When they get him, they should cut off his…"

"He'll get the chair," I said. "That's for sure."

"I'll pull the switch. Personally. Just ask me. Just ask me and I'll do it."

I nodded. "Except one thing, Pat."

"What's that?"

"We got to catch him first."

The baby was stretched out on the big white table when I went down to see Doc Edwards. A sheet covered the corpse, and Doc was busy filling out a report. I looked over his shoulder:

POLICE DEPARTMENT
City of New York

DATE: June 12, 1953
FROM: Commanding Officer Charles R. Brandon, 37th Precinct
TO: Chief Medical Examiner
SUBJECT: DEATH OF Baby girl (unidentified)
Please furnish information on items checked below in connection of death of the above named.
Body was found on June 12, 1953, at Church of the Holy Mother, 1220 Benson Avenue, Bronx, New York.
AUTOPSY PERFORMED? Examination made? Yes.
BY: Dr. James L. Edwards, Fordham Hospital Mortuary
DATE: June 12, 1953
WHERE? Bronx County
CAUSE OF DEATH: Broken neck.

Doc Edwards looked up from the typewriter.

"Not nice, Dave."

"No, not nice at all."

I saw that he was ready to type in the "Result of chemical analysis" space.

"Anything else on her?"

"Not much. Dried tears on her face. Urine on her abdomen, buttocks, and genitals. Traces of a zinc oxide ointment, and petroleum jelly there, too. That's about it."

"Time of death?"

"I'd put it at about three A.M. last night."

"Uh-huh."

"You want a guess?"

"Sure."

"Somebody doesn't like his sleep to be disturbed by a crying kid. That's my guess."

I said, "Nobody likes his sleep disturbed, Doc. What's the zinc oxide and petroleum jelly for? That normal?"

"Yeah, sure. Lots of mothers use it. Mostly for minor irritations. Urine burn, diaper rash, that sort of thing."

"I see."

"This shouldn't be too tough, Dave. You know who the kid is yet?"

"We're working on that now."

"Well, good luck."

"Thanks."

I turned to go, and Doc Edwards began pecking at the typewriter again, completing the autopsy report.


There was good news waiting for me back at the precinct. Pat came over with a smile on his face, and a thick sheet of paper in his hands.

"Here's the ticket," he said.

I took the paper, and looked at it. It was the photostat of a birth certificate.

## U.S. NAVAL HOSPITAL
### St. Albans, N.Y.
### *Birth Certificate*

This certifies that Louise Ann Dreiser was born to Alice Dreiser in this hospital at 4:15 P.M. on the tenth day of November, 1952. Weight 7 lbs. 6 ozs. In witness whereof, the said hospital has caused this certificate to be issued, properly signed and the seal of the hospital hereunto affixed.

Gregory Freeman, LTJG MC USN,
attending physician
Frederick L. Mann, CAPTAIN MC
commanding officer USN

"Here's how they got it," Pat said, handing me another stat. I looked at it quickly. It was the reverse side of the birth certificate. There were two tiny footprints on it, a left foot and a right foot. Beneath those:

Sex of child: <u>Female</u>
Weight at birth: <u>7 lbs. 6 ozs.</u>

Certificate of birth should be carefully preserved as record of value for future use.

1– To identify relationship
2– To establish age to enter school

There were several more good reasons why a birth certificate should be kept in the sugar bowl, and then below that the address where the official registration was filed.

"Alice Dreiser," I said.

"That's the mother. Prints and all. I've already sent a copy down to Cappy to check against the ones they lifted from the pew."

"Fine. Pick one of the boys from the list the Old Man gave us, Pat. Tell him to get whatever he can on Alice Dreiser and her husband. They have to be sailors or relations to get admitted to a naval hospital, don't they?"

"Yeah. You've got to prove dependency."

"Fine. Get the guy's last address and we'll try to run down the woman, or him, or both. Get whoever you pick to call right away, will you?"

"Right. Why pick anyone? I'll make the call myself."

"No, I want you to check the phone book for Alice Dreisers. In the meantime, I'll be looking over the baby's garments."

"You'll be in the lab?"

"Yeah. Buzz me, Pat."

"Right."

Caputo had the garments separated and tagged when I got there.

"You're not going to get much out of these," he told me. "No luck, huh?"

He held out the pink blanket. "Black River Mills. A big trade name. You can probably buy it in any retail shop in the city." He picked up the small pink sweater with the pearl buttons. "Toddler's Inc. Ditto. The socks have no markings at all. The undershirt came from Gilman's here in the city. It's the largest department store in the world, so you can imagine how many of these they sell every day. The cotton pajamas were bought there, too."

"No shoes?"

"No shoes."

"What about the diaper?"

"What about it? It's a plain diaper. No label. You got any kids, Dave?"

"One."

"You ever see a diaper with a label?"

"I don't recall seeing any."

"If you did, it wasn't in it long. Diapers take a hell of a beating, Dave."

"Maybe this one came from a diaper service."

"Maybe. You can check that."

"Safety pins?"

"Two. No identifying marks. Look like five-and-dime stuff."

"Any prints?"

"Yeah. There are smudged prints on the pins, but there's a good thumbprint on one of the pajama snaps."

"Whose?"

"It matches the right thumbprint on the stat you sent down. Mrs. Dreiser's."

"Uh-huh. Did you check her prints against the ones from the pew?"

"Nothing, Dave. None are hers anyway."

"Okay, Cappy. Thanks a lot."

Cappy shrugged. "I get paid," he said. He grinned and

waved as I walked out and headed upstairs again. I met Pat in the hallway, coming down to the lab after me.

"What's up?" I asked.

"I called the Naval Hospital. They gave me the last address they had for the guy. His name is Carl Dreiser, lived at 831 East 217th Street, Bronx, when the baby was born."

"How come?"

"He was a yeoman, working downtown on Church Street. Lived with his wife uptown, got an allotment, you know the story."

"Yeah. So?"

"I sent Artie to check at that address. He should be calling in soon now."

"What about the sailor?"

"I called the Church Street office, spoke to the Commanding Officer, Captain..." He consulted a slip of paper. "Captain Thibot. This Dreiser was working there back in November. He got orders in January, reported aboard the USS *Hanfield*, DD 981 at the Brooklyn Navy Yard on January fifth of this year."

"Where is he now?"

"That's the problem, Dave."

"What kind of problem?"

"The *Hanfield* was sunk off Pyongyang in March."

"Oh."

"Dreiser is listed as killed in action."

I didn't say anything. I nodded, and waited.

"A telegram was sent to Mrs. Dreiser at the Bronx address. The War Department says the telegram was delivered and signed for by Alice Dreiser."

"Let's wait for Artie to call in," I said.

We ordered more coffee and waited. Pat had checked the phone book and there'd been no listing for either Carl or Alice Dreiser. He'd had a list typed of every Dreiser in the city. It ran longer than my arm.

"Why didn't you ask the Navy what his parents' names are?" I said.

"I did. Both parents are dead."

"Who does he list as next of kin?"

"His wife. Alice Dreiser."

"Great."

In a half hour, Artie called in. There was no Alice Dreiser living at the Bronx address. The landlady said she'd lived there until April and had left without giving a forwarding address. Yes, she'd had a baby daughter. I told Artie to keep the place staked out, and then buzzed George Tabin and told him to check the Post Office Department for any forwarding address.

When he buzzed back in twenty minutes, he said, "Nothing, Dave. Nothing at all."


We split the available force of men, and I managed to wangle four more men from the lieutenant. Half of us began checking on the Dreisers listed in the phone directories, and the rest of us began checking the diaper services.

The first diaper place I called on had a manager who needed only a beard to look like Santa Claus. He greeted me affably and offered all his assistance. Unfortunately, they'd never had a customer named Alice Dreiser.

At my fourth stop, I got what looked like a lead.

I spoke directly to the vice president, and he listened intently.

"Perhaps," he said, "perhaps." He was a big man, with a wide waist, a gold watch chain straddling it. He leaned over and pushed down on his intercom buzzer.

"Yes, sir?"

"Bring in a list of our customers. Starting with November of 1952."

"Sir?"

"Starting with November of 1952."

"Yes, sir."

We talked about the diaper business in general until the list came, and then he handed it to me and I began checking off the names. There were a hell of a lot of names on it. For the month of December, I found a listing for Alice Dreiser. The address given was the one we'd checked in the Bronx.

"Here she is," I said. "Can you get her records?"

The vice president looked at the name. "Certainly, just a moment." He buzzed his secretary again, told her what he wanted, and she brought the yellow file cards in a few moments later. The cards told me that Alice Dreiser had continued the diaper service through February. She'd been late on her February payment, and had canceled service in March. She'd had the diapers delivered for the first week in March, but had not paid for them. She did not notify the company that she was moving. She had not returned the diapers they'd sent her that first week in March. The company did not know where she was.

"If you find her," the vice president told me, "I'd like to know. She owes us money."

"I'll keep that in mind," I said.

The reports on the Dreisers were waiting for me back at the precinct. George had found a couple who claimed to be

Carl's aunt and uncle. They knew he was married. They gave Alice's maiden name as Grant. They said she lived somewhere on Walton Avenue in the Bronx, or she had lived there when Carl first met her. No, they hadn't seen either Alice or Carl for months. Yes, they knew the Dreisers had had a daughter. They'd received an announcement card. They had never seen the baby.

Pat and I looked up the Grants on Walton Avenue, found a listing for Peter Grant, and went there together.

A bald man in his undershirt, his suspenders hanging over his trousers, opened the door.

"What is it?" he asked.

"Police officers," I said. "We'd like to ask a few questions."

"What about? Let me see your badges."

Pat and I flashed our buzzers and the bald man studied them.

"What kind of questions do you want to ask?"

"Are you Peter Grant?"

"Yeah, that's right. What's this all about?"

"May we come in?"

"Sure, come on in." We followed him into the apartment, and he motioned us to chairs in the small living room. "Now, what is it?" he asked.

"Your daughter is Alice Dreiser?"

"Yes," he said, his face unchanged.

"Do you know where she lives?"

"No."

"Come on, mister," Pat said. "You know where your daughter lives."

"I don't," Grant said, "and I don't give a damn, either."

"Why? What's wrong, mister?"

"Nothing. Nothing's wrong. It's none of your business, anyway."

"Her daughter had her neck broken," I said. "It's our business."

"I don't give a…" he started to say. He stopped then and looked straight ahead of him, his brows pulled together into a tight frown. "I'm sorry. I still don't know where she lives."

"Did you know she was married?"

"To that sailor. Yes, I knew."

"And you knew she had a daughter?"

"Don't make me laugh," Grant said.

"What's funny, mister?" Pat said.

"Did I know she had a daughter? Why the hell do you think she married the sailor? Don't make me laugh!"

"When was your daughter married, Mr. Grant?"

"Last September." He saw the look on my face, and added, "Go ahead, you count it. The kid was born in November."

"Have you seen her since the marriage?"

"No."

"Have you ever seen the baby?"

"No."

"Do you have a picture of your daughter?"

"I think so. Is she in trouble? Do you think she did it?"

"We don't know who did it yet."

"Maybe she did," Grant said softly. "She just maybe did. I'll get you the picture."

He came back in a few minutes with the picture of a plain girl wearing a cap and gown. She had light eyes and straight hair, and her face was intently serious.

"She favors her mother," Grant said. "God rest her soul."

"Your wife is dead?"

"Yes. That picture was taken when Alice graduated from high school."

"May we have it?"

He hesitated and said, "It's the only one I've got. She… she didn't take many pictures. She wasn't a very…pretty girl."

"We'll return it."

"All right," he said. His eyes were troubled. "She…if she's in trouble, you'll let me know, won't you?"

"We'll let you know."

"A girl…makes mistakes sometimes." He stood up abruptly. "Let me know."

We had copies of the photo made, and then we staked out every church in the neighborhood where the baby was found. Pat and I covered the Church of the Holy Mother, because we figured the woman was most likely to come back there.

We didn't talk much. There is something about a church of any denomination that makes a man think rather than talk. Pat and I knocked off at about seven every night, and the night boys took over then. We were back on the job at seven in the morning.

It was a week before she came in.

She stopped at the font in the rear of the church, dipped her hand in the holy water, and crossed herself. Then she walked to the altar, stopping before a statue of the Virgin Mary, lit a candle, and kneeled down before it.

"That's her," I said.

"Let's go," Pat answered.

"Not here. Outside."

Pat's eyes locked with mine for an instant. "Sure," he said.

She kneeled before the statue for a long time, and then got to her feet slowly, drying her eyes. She walked up the aisle, stopped at the font, crossed herself, and then walked outside.

We followed her out, catching up with her at the corner. I walked over on one side of her, and Pat on the other.

"Mrs. Dreiser?" I asked.

She stopped walking. "Yes?"

I showed my buzzer. "Police officers," I said. "We'd like to ask some questions."

She stared at my face for a long time. She drew a trembling breath then, and said, "I killed her. I…Carl was dead, you see. I…I guess that was it. It wasn't right…his getting killed, I mean. And she was crying."

"Want to tell it downtown, ma'am?" I asked.

She nodded blankly. "Yes, that was it. She just cried all the time, not knowing that I was crying inside. You don't know how I cried inside. Carl…he was all I had. I…I couldn't stand it anymore. I told her to shut up and when she didn't, I…I…"

"Come on along, ma'am," I said.

"I brought her to the church."

She nodded, remembering it all now.

"She was innocent, you know. So I brought her to the church. Did you find her there?"

"Yes, ma'am," I said. "That's where we found her."

She seemed pleased. A small smile covered her mouth and she said, "I'm glad you found her."

She told the story again to the lieutenant.

Pat and I checked out, and on the way to the subway, I asked him, "Do you still want to pull the switch, Pat?"

He didn't answer.

223

# Still Life

It was two in the morning, raining to beat all hell outside, and it felt good to be sitting opposite Johnny Knowles sipping hot coffee. Johnny had his jacket off, with his sleeves rolled up and the .38 Police Special hanging in its shoulder clip. He had a deck of cards spread in front of him at the table, and he was looking for a black queen to put on his king of diamonds. I was sitting there looking past Johnny at the rain streaming down the barred window. It had been a dull night, and I was half dozing, the hot steam from the coffee cup haloing my head. When the phone began ringing, Johnny looked up from his solitaire.

"I'll get it," I said.

I put down the cup, swung my legs out from under the table, and picked up the receiver.

"Hannigan," I said.

Johnny watched me as I listened.

"Yep," I said, "I've got it, Barney. Right away."

I hung up and Johnny looked at me quizzically.

"Young girl," I said. "Gun Hill Road and Bronxwood Avenue. Looks bad, Johnny."

224

Johnny stood up quickly and began shrugging into his jacket.

"Some guy found her lying on the sidewalk, and he called in. Barney took it."

"Hurt bad?" Johnny asked.

"The guy who called in thinks she's dead."

We checked out a car and headed for Gun Hill Road. Johnny was quiet as he drove, and I listened to the *swick-swack* of the windshield wipers, staring through the rain-streaked glass at the glistening wet asphalt outside. When we turned off White Plains Avenue, Johnny said, "Hell of a night."

"Yeah."

He drove past the Catholic church, past the ball field belonging to the high school, and then slowed down as we cruised up to the school itself.

"There he is," Johnny said.

He motioned with his head, and I saw a thin man standing on the sidewalk, flagging us down. He stood hunched against the rain, his fedora pulled down over his ears. Johnny pulled up alongside him, and I opened the door on my side. A sheet of rain washed into the car and the guy stuck in his head.

"Right around the corner," he said.

"Get in," I told him. I moved over to make room, and he squeezed onto the seat, bringing the clinging wetness of the rain with him. Johnny turned the corner, and the old man pointed through the windshield. "There," he said. "Right there."

We pulled the car over to the curb, and Johnny got out from behind the wheel before the man next to me had moved.

The man shrugged, sighed, and stepped out into the rain. I followed close behind him.

The girl was sprawled against the iron bar fence that surrounded the school. She'd been wearing a raincoat, but it had been forcibly ripped down the front, pulling all the buttons loose. Her blouse had been torn down the center, her bra cruelly ripped from her breasts. Johnny played his flash over her, and we saw the ugly welts covering her wet skin. Her skirt and underclothing had been shredded, too, and she lay grotesque in death, her legs twisted at a curious widespread angle.

"Better get a blanket, Mike," Johnny said.

I nodded and walked to the car. I took a blanket from the back, and when I walked over to the girl again, Johnny was getting the man's name and address.

"The ambulance should be along soon," I said.

"Yeah." Johnny closed his pad, took the blanket and draped it over the girl. The rain thudded at it, turning it into a sodden, black mass on the pavement.

"How'd you find her?" I asked the man.

"I been workin' the four to twelve at my plant," he said, "out on Long Island. I usually get home about this time when I got that shift. I live right off Bronxwood, get off the train at Gun Hill."

"You were walking home when you found the girl?"

"Yes, sir."

"What'd you do then?"

"I walked clear back to White Plains Avenue, found an open candy store, and called you fellows. Then I came back to wait for you."

"What'd you tell the man who answered the phone?"

"All about the girl. That I'd found her. That's all."

"Did you say she was dead?"

"Well, yes. Yes, I did." He stared down at the girl. "My guess is she was raped." He looked at me for confirmation, but I said nothing.

"I think you can go home now, sir," Johnny said. "Thanks a lot for reporting this. We'll call you if you're needed."

"Glad to help," the old man said. He nodded at us briefly, and then glanced down at the girl under the blanket again. He shook his head, and started off down Bronxwood Avenue. We watched him go, the rain slicing at the pavement around us. Johnny looked off down the street, watching for the ambulance.

"Might be rape at that," he said.

I pulled my collar up against the rain.

"Yeah."

We got the autopsy report at six that morning. We'd already found a wallet in the dead girl's coat pocket, asking anyone to call a Mrs. Iris Ferroni in case of accident. We called Mrs. Ferroni, assuming her to be the girl's mother, and she'd identified the body as that of her daughter, Jean Ferroni. She'd almost collapsed after that, and we were holding off questioning her until she pulled herself together.

Johnny brought the report in and put it next to my coffee cup on the table.

I scanned it quickly, my eyes skimming to the cause of death space. In neat typescript, it read: SHARP INSTRUMENT ENTERING HEART FROM BELOW LEFT BREAST.

I flipped the page and looked at the attached detailed report. The girl had been raped, all right, consecutively, brutally.

I turned back to the first page and looked at it once more. My eyes lingered on one item.

Burial Permit No. 63-7501-H

"Now she's just a number," I said. "Sixteen-year-old kid with a grave number."

"She was seventeen," Johnny said.

"That makes a big difference."

"I think we can talk to her mother now," Johnny said.

I rubbed my forehead and said, "Sure. Why don't you bring her in?"

Johnny nodded and went out, to return in a few minutes with a small, dark woman in a plain black coat. The woman's eyes were red, and her lips trembled with her grief. She still looked dazed from the shock of having seen her daughter with the life torn from her.

"This is Detective-Sergeant Hannigan," Johnny said, "and I'm his partner, Detective-Sergeant Knowles. We'd like to ask you a few questions, if you don't mind."

Mrs. Ferroni nodded, but said nothing.

"What time did your daughter leave the house last night, Mrs. Ferroni?" I asked.

The woman sighed and touched her forehead. "Eight o'clock, I think," she said. There was the faintest trace of an accent in her voice.

"Did she leave with anyone?"

"Yes."

"Who?"

"A boy. He takes her out sometimes. Ricky. Ricky Tocca."

"Do you know the boy well?"

"He's from the neighborhood. He's a good boy."

"Did they say where they were going?"

"To a movie. I think they go up to Mount Vernon a lot. That's where they were going."

"Does this Tocca have a car?"

"Yes."

"Would you know the year and make, Mrs. Ferroni?"

"A Plymouth," she said. "Or a Chevy, I think. I don't know. It's a new car." She paused and bit her lip. "He wouldn't hurt my daughter. He's a nice boy."

"We're not saying he would," Johnny said gently. "We're just trying to get some sort of a lead, Mrs. Ferroni."

"I understand."

"They left the house at eight, you say?"

"About that time."

"What time does your daughter usually come home?"

"One, two. On weekends. During the week...well, I like her to come home early..."

"But she didn't, is that it?"

"You know how it is with a young girl. They think they know everything. She stayed out late every night. I told her to be careful...I *told* her...I *told* her..."

She bit her lip, and I expected tears again, but there were none. Johnny cleared his throat and asked, "Weren't you worried when she didn't show up this morning? I mean, we didn't call you until about four A.M."

Mrs. Ferroni shook her head. "She comes in very late sometimes. I worry...but she always comes home. This time..."

There was a strained, painful silence. "I think you can go, Mrs. Ferroni," I said. "We'll have one of our men drive you home. Thank you very much."

"You'll…you'll find who did it, won't you?" she asked.

"We'll sure as hell try," I told her.

We picked up Richard Tocca, age twenty, as he was leaving for work. He stepped out of a two-story frame on Burke Avenue, looked up at the overcast sky, and then began walking quickly to a blue Nash parked at the curb. Johnny collared him as he was opening the door on the driver's side.

"Richard Tocca?" he asked.

The kid looked up suspiciously. "Yeah." He looked at Johnny's fist tightened in his coat sleeve and said, "What is this?"

I pulled up and flashed my buzzer. "Police officers, Tocca. Mind answering a few questions?"

"What's the matter?" he asked. "What did *I* do?"

"Routine," Johnny said. "Come on over to our car, won't you?"

"All right," Tocca said. He glanced at his watch. "I hope this won't take long. I got to be at work at nine."

"It may not take long," I said.

We walked over to the car and I held the door for him. He climbed in, and Johnny and I sat on either side of him. He was a thin-faced kid with straight blond hair and pale blue eyes. Clear complexioned, clean shaven. Slightly protruding teeth. Dressed neatly and conservatively, for a kid his age.

"Now what's this all about?" he asked.

"You date Jean Ferroni last night?" Johnny asked.

"Yes. Jesus, don't tell me she's in some kind of trouble."

"What time'd you pick her up?"

"About eight fifteen, I guess. Listen, is she…"

"Where'd you go?"

"Well, that's just it. We were supposed to have a date, and she told me it was off, just like that. She made me drive her to Gun Hill and then she got out of the car. If she's in any trouble, I didn't have anything to do with it."

"She's in big trouble," Johnny said. "The biggest trouble."

"Yeah, well, I didn't have..."

"She's dead," I said.

The kid stopped talking, and his jaw hung slack for a minute. He blinked his eyes rapidly two or three times and then said, "Jesus, Jesus."

"You date her often, Ricky?"

"Huh?" He still seemed shocked, which was just what we wanted.

"Yeah, yeah, pretty often."

"How often?"

"Two, three times a week. No, less."

"When'd you see her last?"

"Last night."

"Before that."

"Last...Wednesday, I guess it was. Yeah."

"Why'd you date her?"

"I don't know. Why do you date girls?"

"We don't care why you date girls! Why'd you date *this* girl? Why'd you date Jean Ferroni?"

"I don't know. You know, she's...she was a nice kid. That's all."

"You serious about her?" Johnny snapped.

"Well..."

"You sleeping with her?"

"What?"

"You heard me!"

"No. No. I mean…well no, I wasn't."

"Yes or no, goddamn it!"

"No."

"Then why'd you date her? You planning on marrying her?"

"No."

"What time did you pick her up last night?"

"Eight fifteen. I told you…"

"Where'd you drop her off?"

"Gun Hill and White Plains."

"What time was this?"

"About eight thirty."

"Why'd you date her so much?"

"I heard she was…hell, I don't like to say this. I mean, the girl's dead…"

"You heard what?"

"I heard she was…hot stuff."

"Where'd you hear that?"

"Around. You know how the word spreads."

"Who'd you hear it from?"

"Just around, that's all."

"And you believed it?"

"Well, yeah. You see, I…" He stopped short, catching himself and his tongue.

"You what?"

"Nothing."

"Look, sonny," Johnny said. "The girl was raped and stabbed. That's murder. We'll get the truth if we have to…"

"I'm telling the truth!"

"But not all of it. Come on, sonny, give."

"All right, all right." He fell into a surly silence. Johnny and I waited. Finally, he said, "I saw pictures."

"What kind of pictures?"

"You know. Pictures. Her and a guy. You know."

"You mean pornographic pictures?"

"Yeah."

"Then say what you mean. Where'd you see these pictures?"

"A guy had them."

"Have you got any?"

"No."

"We can get a search warrant. We can take you with us and slap you in the cooler and..."

"I got one," the kid admitted. "Just one."

"Let's see it."

He fished into his wallet and said, "I feel awful funny about this. You know, Jean is dead and all."

"Let's see the picture."

He handed a worn photograph to Johnny, and Johnny studied it briefly and passed it to me. It was Jean Ferroni, all right, and I couldn't very much blame the Tocca kid for his assumption about her.

"Know the guy in this picture?" I asked.

"No."

"Never seen him around?"

"No."

"All right, kid," Johnny said. "Go to work. And keep your nose clean because we may be back."

Richard Tocca looked at the picture in my hand longingly, reluctant to leave it. He glanced up at me hopefully, saw my eyes, and changed his mind about the question he was ready to ask. I got out of the car to let him out, and he walked to his

Nash without looking back at us. The questioning had taken exactly seven minutes.

Johnny started the car, threw it into gear.

"Want me to drive?" I asked.

"No, that's okay."

"This puts a different light on it, huh?"

Johnny nodded. "I'm sleepy as hell," he said.

We drove back to the precinct, checked out, and then walked to the subway together.

"This may be a tough one," he said.

"*May* be?"

Johnny yawned.

We staked out every candy store and ice cream parlor in the Gun Hill Road to 219th Street area, figuring we might pick up someone passing the pornos there. We also set up four police-women in apartments, thinking there was an off chance some-one might contact them for lewd posing. The policewomen circulated at the local dances, visited the local bars, bowling alleys, movies. We didn't get a rumble.

The Skipper kept us on the case, but it seemed to have bogged down temporarily.

We'd already gone over the dead girl's belongings at her home. She'd had an address book, but we'd checked on every-one in it, and they were all apparently only casual acquain-tances with a few high school chums tossed in for flavoring. We'd checked the wallet the girl was carrying on the night of her murder. Aside from the in-case-of card, a Social Security card, and some pictures taken outside the high school with her girlfriends, there was nothing.

Under questioning, most of her high school friends said that Jean Ferroni didn't hang around with them much anymore. They said she'd gone snooty and was circulating with an older crowd. None of them knew who the people in the older crowd were.

Her teachers at school insisted she was a nice girl, a little subdued and quiet in class, but intelligent enough. Several of them complained that she'd been delinquent in homework assignments. None of them knew anything about her outside life.

We got our first real break when Mrs. Ferroni showed up with the key. She placed it on the desk in front of Johnny and said, "I was cleaning out her things. I found this. It doesn't fit any of the doors in the house. I don't know what it's for."

"Maybe her gym locker at school," I said.

"No. She had a combination lock. I remember she had to buy one when she first started high school."

Johnny took the key, looked at it, and passed it to me. "Post office box?" he asked.

"Maybe." I turned the key over in my hands. The numerals 894 were stamped into its head.

"Thanks, Mrs. Ferroni," Johnny said. "We'll look into it right away."

We started at the Williamsbridge Post Office right on Gun Hill Road. The mailmen were very cooperative, but the fact remained it wasn't a key to any of their boxes. In fact, it didn't look like a post office key at all. We tried the Wakefield Branch, up the line a bit, and got the same answer.

We started on the banks then.

Luckily, we hit it on the first try. The bank was on 220th Street, and the manager was cordial and helpful. He took one look at the key and said, "Yes, that's one of ours."

"Who owns the box?" we asked.

He looked at the key again. "Safety deposit 894. Just a moment, and I'll have that checked."

We stood on either side of his polished desk while he picked up a phone, asked for a Miss Delaney, and then questioned her about the key. "Yes," he said. "I see. Yes. Thank you." He cradled the phone, put the key on the desk and said, "Jo Ann Ferris. Does that help you, gentlemen?"

"Jo Ann Ferris," Johnny said. "Jean Ferroni. That's close enough." He looked directly at the manager. "We'll be back in a little while with a court order to open that box. We'll ask for you."

In a little over two hours, we were back, and we followed the manager past the barred gate at the rear of the bank, stepped into the vault, and walked back to the rows of safe deposit boxes.

"894," he said. "Yes, here it is."

He opened the box, pulled out a slab, and rested the box on it. Johnny lifted the lid.

"Anything?" I asked.

He pulled out what looked like several rolled sheets of stiff white paper. They were secured with rubber bands, and Johnny slid the bands off quickly. When he unrolled them, they turned out to be eight-by-ten glossy prints. I took one of the prints and looked at Jean Ferroni's contorted body. Beside me, the manager's mouth fell open and he began sputtering wildly.

"Well," I said, "this gives us something."

"We'll just take the contents of this box," Johnny said to the manager. "Make out a receipt for it, will you, Mike?"

I made out the receipt and we took the bundle of porno-graphic photos back to the lab with us. Whatever else Jean Ferroni had done, she had certainly posed in a variety of com-promising positions. She'd owned a ripe young body, and the pictures left nothing whatever to the imagination. But we weren't looking for kicks. We were looking for clues.

Dave Alger, one of the lab men, didn't hold out much hope.

"Nothing," he said. "What did you expect? Ordinary print paper. You can get the same stuff in any home developing kit."

"What about fingerprints?"

"The girl's mostly. A few others, but all smeared. You want me to track down the rubber bands?"

"Comedian," Johnny said.

"You guys expect miracles, that's all. You forget this is sci-ence and not witchcraft."

I was looking at the pictures spread out on the lab counter. They were all apparently taken in the same room, on the same bed. The bed had brass posts and railings at the head and foot. Behind the bed was an open window, with a murky city display of buildings outside. The pictures had evidently been taken at night, and probably recently because the window was wide open. Alongside the window on the wall was a picture of an In-dian sitting on a black horse. A wide strip of wallpaper had been torn almost from ceiling to floor, leaving a white path on the wall. The room did not have the feel of a private apartment. It looked like any third-rate hotel. I kept looking at the pictures and at the open window with the buildings beyond.

"Hey!" I said.

"...you think all we do is wave a rattle and shake some feathers and wham, we got your goddamned murderer. Well, it ain't that simple. We put in a lot of time on..."

"Shut the hell up, Dave!"

Dave sank into a frowning silence. I lifted one of the pictures and said, "Blow this one up, will you?"

"Why? You looking for tattoo marks?"

"No. I want to look through that window."

Dave suddenly brightened. "How big you want it, Mike?"

"Big enough to read those neon signs across the street."

"Can do," he said. He scooped up all the pictures and ran off, his heels clicking against the asphalt tile floor.

"Think we got something?" Johnny asked.

"Maybe. We sure as hell can't lose anything."

"Besides, you'll have something to hang over your couch," Johnny cracked.

"Another comedian," I said, but I was beginning to feel better already. I smoked three cigarettes down to butts, and then Dave came back.

"One Rheingold beer ad," he said.

"Yeah?"

"And one Hotel Mason. That help?"

I didn't answer. I was busy racing Johnny to the door.

The Hotel Mason was a dingy, gray-faced building on West Forty-seventh. We weren't interested in it. We were interested in the building directly across the way, an equally dingy, gray-faced edifice that claimed the fancy title of Allistair Arms.

We walked directly to the desk and flashed our buzzers, and the desk clerk looked hastily to the elevator bank.

"Relax, buster," Johnny said.

He pulled one of the pictures from under his jacket. The lab had whitened out the figures of Jean Ferroni and her male companion, leaving only the bed, the picture on the wall, and the open window. Johnny showed the picture to the desk clerk.

"What room is this?"

"I...I don't know."

"Look hard."

"I tell you I don't know. Maybe one of the bellhops."

He pounded a bell on the desk, and an old man in a bellhop's rig hobbled over. Johnny showed him the picture and repeated his question.

"Damned if I know," the old man said. "All these rooms look alike." He stared at the picture again, shaking his head. Then his eyes narrowed and he bent closer and looked harder. "Oh," he said, "that's 305. That picture of the Injun and the ripped wallpaper there. Yep, that's 305." He paused. "Why?"

I turned. "Who's in 305?"

The desk clerk made a show of looking at the register. "Mr. Adams. Harley Adams."

"Let's go, Johnny," I said.

We started up the steps, and I saw Johnny's hand flick to his shoulder holster. When it came out from under his coat, it was holding a cocked .38. I took out my own gun and we padded up noiselessly.

We stopped outside room 305, flattening ourselves against the walls on either side of the door. Johnny reached out and rapped the butt of his gun against the door.

"Who is it?" a voice asked.

"Open up!"

"Who is it?"

"Police officers. Open up!"

"Wha…"

There was a short silence inside, and then we heard the frantic slap of leather on the floor. "Hit it, Johnny!" I shouted.

Johnny backed off against the opposite wall, put the sole of his shoe against it, and shoved off toward the door. His shoulder hit the wood, and the door splintered inward.

Adams was in his undershirt and trousers and he had one leg over the windowsill, heading for the fire escape, when we came in. I swung my .38 in his direction and yelled, "You better hold it, Adams."

He looked at the gun, and then slowly lowered his leg to the floor.

"Sure," he said. "I wasn't going anyplace."

We found piles of pictures in the room, all bundled neatly. Some of them were of Jean Ferroni. But there were other girls and other men. We found an expensive camera in the closet, and a darkroom setup in the bathroom. We also found a switch knife with a six-inch blade in the top drawer of his dresser.

"I don't know anything about it," Adams insisted.

He kept insisting that for a long time, even after we showed him the pictures we'd taken from Jean Ferroni's safe-deposit box. He kept insisting until we told him his knife would go down to the lab and they'd sure as hell find some trace of the dead girl on it, no matter how careful he'd been. We were stretching the truth a little, because a knife can be washed as clean as anything else. But Adams took the hook and told us everything.

He'd given the kid a come-on, getting her to pose alone at first, in the nude. From there, it had been simple to get her to pose for the big stuff, the stuff that paid off.

"She was getting classy," Adams said. "A cheap tramp like that getting classy. Wanted a percentage of the net. I gave her a percentage, all right. I arranged a nice little party right in my hotel room. Six guys. They fixed her good, one after the other. Then I drove her up to her own neighborhood and left her the way you found her—so it would look like a rape kill."

He paused and shifted in his chair, making himself comfortable.

"Imagine that broad," he continued. "Wanting to share. Wanting to share with me. I showed her."

"You showed her, all right," Johnny said tightly.

That was when I swung out with my closed fist, catching Adams on the side of his jaw. He fell backward, knocking the chair over, sprawling onto the floor.

He scrambled to his feet, crouched low, and said, "Hey, what the hell? Are you crazy?"

I didn't answer him. I left the interrogation room, walking past the patrolman at the door. Johnny caught up with me in the corridor, clamped his hand onto my shoulder.

"Why'd you hit him, Mike?" he asked.

"I wanted to. I just wanted to."

Johnny's eyes met mine for a moment, held them. His hand tightened on my shoulder, and his head nodded almost imperceptibly.

We walked down the corridor together, our heels clicking noisily on the hard floor.

# Accident Report

THERE WAS A BLANKET THROWN OVER THE PATROLMAN by the time we got there. The ambulance was waiting, and a white-clad intern was standing near the step of the ambulance, puffing on a cigarette. He looked up as I walked over to him, and then flicked his cigarette away.

"Detective-Sergeant Jonas," I said.

"How do you do?" the intern answered. "Dr. Mallaby."

"What's the story?"

"Broken neck. It must have been a big car. His chest is caved in where he was first hit. I figure he was knocked down, and then run over. The bumper probably broke his neck. That's the cause of death, anyway."

Andy Larson walked over to where we were standing. He shook his head and said, "A real bloody one, Mike."

"Yeah." I turned to the intern. "When was he hit?"

"Hard to say. No more than a half hour ago, I'd guess offhand. An autopsy will tell."

"That checks, Mike," Andy said. "Patrolman on the beat called it in about twenty-five minutes ago."

"A big car, huh?"

"I'd say so," the intern answered.

"I wonder how many big cars there are in this city?"

Andy nodded. "You can cart him away, Doc," he said. "The boys are through with their pictures."

The intern fired another cigarette, and we watched while he and an attendant put the dead patrolman on a stretcher and then into the ambulance. The intern and the attendant climbed aboard, and the ambulance pulled off down the street. They didn't use the siren. There was no rush now.


A cop gets it, and you say, "Well, gee, that's tough. But that was his trade." Sure. Except that being a cop doesn't mean you don't have a wife, and maybe a few kids. It doesn't hurt any less, being a cop. You're just as dead.

I went over the accident report with Andy.

> ACCIDENT NUMBER: 46A-3
> SURNAME: Benson
> FIRST NAME AND INITIALS: James C.
> PRECINCT NO.: 032
> AIDED NUMBER: 67-4
> ADDRESS: 1812 Crescent Ave.
> SEX: M      AGE: 28

My eyes skipped down the length of the card, noting the date, time, place of occurrence. Then

> NATURE OF ILLNESS OR INJURY:
> Hit and run
> FATAL ✓
> SERIOUS

SLIGHT
UNKNOWN

I kept reading, down to the circled items on the card that told me the body had been taken to the morgue and claimed already. The rest would have been routine in any other case, but it was slightly ironic here:

TRAFFIC CONTROLLED BY OFFICER? ✓
NAME: Ptm. James C. Benson
SHIELD NO: 3685
TRAFFIC CONTROLLED BY LIGHTS? ✓
COMMAND: Traffic Division
LIGHTS IN OPERATION? ✓

I read the rest of the technical information about the direction of the traffic moving on the lights, the police action taken, the city involved, and then flipped the card over.

Under NAMES AND ADDRESSES OF WITNESSES (IF NONE, SO STATE) the single word "None" was scribbled. The officer who'd reported the hit and run was Patrolman P. Margolis. He'd been making the rounds, stopped for his usual afternoon chat with Benson, and had found the traffic cop dead in the gutter. There were skid marks on the asphalt street, but there hadn't been a soul in sight.

"How do you figure it, Andy?" I asked.

"A few ideas."

"Let's hear them."

"The guy may have done something wrong. Benson may have hailed him for something entirely different. The guy panicked and cut him down."

"Something wrong like what?"

"Who knows? Hot furs in the trunk. Dead man in the backseat. You know."

"And you figure Benson hailed him because he was speeding, or his windshield wiper was crooked? Something like that?"

"Yeah, you know."

"I don't buy it, Andy."

"Well, I got another idea."

"What's that? Drunk?"

Andy nodded.

"That's what I was thinking. Where do we start?"

"I've already had a check put in on stolen cars, and the lab boys are going over the skid marks. Why don't we go back and see if we can scare up any witnesses?"

I picked my jacket off the back of the chair, buttoned it on, and then adjusted my shoulder clip.

"Come on," I said.


The scene of the accident was at the intersection of two narrow streets. There was a two-family stucco house on one corner, and empty lots on the other three corners. It was a quiet intersection, and the only reason it warranted a light was the high school two blocks away. A traffic cop was used to supplement the light in the morning and afternoon when the kids were going to and coming from school. Benson had been hit about ten minutes before classes broke. It was a shame, because a bunch of homebound kids might have saved his life — or at least provided some witnesses.

"There's not much choice," Andy said.

I looked at the stucco house. "No, I guess not. Let's go."

We climbed the flat, brick steps at the front of the house, and Andy pushed the bell button. We waited for a few moments, and then the door opened a crack, and a voice asked, "Yes?"

I flashed my buzzer. "Police officers," I said. "We'd like to ask a few questions."

The door stayed closed, with the voice coming from behind the small crack. "What about?"

"Accident here yesterday. Won't you open the door?"

The door swung wide, and a thin young kid in his undershirt peered out at us. His brows pulled together in a hostile frown.

"You got a search warrant?" he asked.

"What have you got to hide, kid?" Andy asked.

"Nothing. I just don't like cops barging in like storm troopers."

"Nobody's barging in on you," Andy said. "We want to ask a few questions, that's all. You want to get snotty about it, we'll go get a goddamn search warrant, and then you'd better hold on to your head."

"All right, what do you want?"

"You changed your song, huh, kid?"

"Leave it be, Andy," I said.

"Were you home this afternoon?"

"Yeah."

"All afternoon?"

"Yeah."

"You hear any noise out here on the street?"

"What kind of noise?"

"You tell me."

"I didn't hear any noise."

"A car skidding, maybe? Something like that?"

"No."

"Did you *see* anything unusual?"

"I didn't see anything. You're here about the cop who was run over, ain't you?"

"That's right."

"Well, I didn't see anything."

"You live here alone?"

"No. With my mother."

"Where is she?"

"She ain't feeling too good. That's why I've been staying home from school. She's been sick in bed. She didn't hear anything, either. She's in a fog."

"Have you had the doctor?"

"Yeah, she'll be all right."

"Where's your mother's room?"

"In the back of the house. She couldn't have seen anything out here even if she was able to. You're barking up the wrong tree."

"How long you been out of school, kid?"

"Why?"

"How long?"

"A month."

"Your mother been sick that long?"

"Yeah."

"How old are you?"

"Fifteen."

"You better get back to school," Andy said. "Damn fast. Tell the city about your mother, and they'll do something for her. You hear that?"

"I hear it."

"We'll send someone around to check tomorrow. Remember that, kid."

"I'll remember it," the kid said, a surly look on his face.

"Anybody else live here with you?"

"Yeah. My dog. You want to ask him some questions, maybe?"

I saw Andy clench his fists, so I said, "That'll be all, son. Thanks."

"For what?" the kid asked, and then he slammed the door.

"That lousy snot nose," Andy said. "That little son of a..."

"Come on," I said.

We started down, and I looked at the empty lots on the other corners. Then I turned back to take a last look at the house. "There's nothing more here," I said. "We better get back."

There were thirty-nine cars stolen in New York City that day. Of the bigger cars, two were Buicks, four Chryslers, and one Cadillac. One of the Chryslers was stolen from a neighborhood about two miles from the scene of the accident.

"How about that?" Andy asked.

"How about it?"

"The guy stole the buggy and when Benson hailed him he knew he was in hot water. He cut him down."

"*If* Benson hailed him."

"Maybe Benson only stuck up his hand to stop traffic. The guy misunderstood, and crashed through."

"We'll see," I said.

# Accident Report

We checked with the owner of the Chrysler. She was a fluttery woman who was obviously impressed with the fact that two policemen were calling on her personally about her missing car.

"Well, I never expected such quick action," she said. "I mean, really."

"The car was a Chrysler, ma'am?" I asked.

"Oh, yes," she said, nodding her head emphatically. "We've never owned anything but a Chrysler."

"What was the year, ma'am?"

"I gave all this information on the phone," she said.

"I know, ma'am. We're just checking it again."

"A new car. 1953."

"The color?"

"Blue. A sort of robin's egg blue, do you know? I told that to the man who answered the phone."

"License number?"

"Oh, again? Well, just a moment." She stood up and walked to the kitchen, returning with her purse. She fished into the purse, came up with a wallet, and then rummaged through that for her registration. "Here it is," she said.

"What, ma'am?"

"7T 8458."

Andy looked up. "That's a Nassau County plate, ma'am."

"Yes, yes, I know."

"In the Bronx? How come?"

"Well...oh, you'll think this is silly."

"Let's hear it, ma'am."

"Well, a Long Island plate is so much more impressive. I mean, well, we plan on moving there soon anyway."

"And you went all the way to Nassau to get a plate?"

"Yes."

Andy coughed politely. "Well, maybe that'll make it easier."

"Do you think you'll find the car?"

"We certainly hope so, ma'am."

We found the car that afternoon. It was parked on a side street in Brooklyn. It was in perfect condition, no damage to the front end, no blood anywhere on the grille or bumper. The lab checked the tires against the skid marks. Negative. This, coupled with the fact that the murder car would undoubtedly have sustained injuries after such a violent smash, told us we'd drawn a blank. We returned the car to the owner.

She was very happy.

By the end of the week, we'd recovered all but one of the stolen cars. None of them checked with what we had. The only missing car was the Cadillac. It had been swiped from a parking lot in Queens, with the thief presenting the attendant with a claim ticket for the car. The m.o. sounded professional, whereas the kill looked like a fool stunt. When another Caddy was stolen from a lot in Jamaica, with the thief using the same modus operandi, we figured it for a ring, and left it to the Automobile Squad.

In the meantime, we'd begun checking all auto body and fender repair shops in the city. We had just about ruled out a stolen car by this time, and if the car was privately owned, the person who'd run down Benson would undoubtedly try to have the damage to his car repaired.

The lab had reported finding glass slivers from a sealbeam imbedded in Benson's shirt, together with chips of black paint.

# Accident Report

From the position of the skid marks, they estimated that he'd been hit by the right side of the car, and they figured the broken light would be on that side, together with the heaviest damage to the grille.

Because Andy still clung to the theory that the driver had been involved in something fishy just before he hit Benson, we checked with the local precinct squads for any possibly related robberies or burglaries, and we also checked with the Safe, Loft, and Truck Squad. There'd been a grocery store holdup in the neighboring vicinity on the day of the hit and run but the thief had already been apprehended, and he was driving a '37 Ford. Both headlights were intact, and any damage to the grille had been sustained years ago.

We continued to check on repair shops.

When the Complaint Report came in, we leaped on it at once. We glossed over the usual garbage in the heading and skipped down to the DETAILS:

Telephone message from one Mrs. James Dalley, owner and resident of private dwelling at 2389 Barnes Avenue. Dispatched Radio Motor Patrol #761. Mrs. Dalley returned from two-week vacation to find picket fence around house smashed in on northwest corner. Tire marks in bed of irises in front yard indicate heavy automobile or light truck responsible for damage. Black paint discovered on damaged pickets. Good tire marks in wet mud of iris bed, casts made. Tire size 7.60-15, 4-ply. Estimated weight 28 pounds. Further investigation of tread marks disclosed tire to be Sears, Roebuck and Company, registered trademark Allstate Tires. Catalog number 95K 01227K. Case still active pending receipt of reports and further investigation.

"You can damn well bet it's still active," Andy said. "This may be it, Mike."

"Maybe," I said.

It wasn't.

The tire was a very popular seller, and the mail order house sold thousands of them every year, both through the mails and over the counter. It was impossible to check over-the-counter sales, and a check of mail order receipts revealed that no purchases had been made within a two-mile radius of the hit and run. We extended the radius, checked on all the purchasers, and found no suspicious-looking automobiles, although all of the cars were big ones. There was one black car in the batch—and there wasn't a scratch on it.

But Mrs. Dalley's house was about ten blocks from the scene of the killing, and that was too close for coincidence. We checked out a car and drove over.

She was a woman in her late thirties, and she greeted us at the door in a loose housecoat, her hair up in curlers.

"Police officers," I said.

Her hand went to her hair, and she said, "Oh, my goodness." She fretted a little more about her appearance, belted the housecoat tighter around her waist, and then said, "Come in, come in."

We questioned her a little about the fence and the iris bed, got substantially what was in the Complaint Report, and then went out to look at the damage. She stayed in the house, and when she joined us later, she was wearing tight black slacks and a chartreuse sweater. She'd also tied a scarf around her hair, hiding the curlers.

The house was situated on a corner with a side street intersecting Barnes Avenue, and then a gravel road cutting into another intersection. The tire marks seemed to indicate the car had come down the gravel road, and then backed up the side street, knocking over the picket fence when it did. It all pointed to a drunken driver.

"How does it look?" she asked.

"We're working on it," Andy said. "Any of your neighbors witness this?"

"No. I asked around. No one saw the car. They heard the crash, came out and saw the damaged fence, but the car had gone already."

"Was anything missing from your house or yard?"

"No. It was locked up tight. We were on vacation, you know."

"What kind of a car does your husband drive, ma'am?"

"A '48 Olds. Why?"

"Just wondering."

"Let's amble up the street, Mike," Andy said. "Thank you very much, ma'am."

We got into the car, and Mrs. Dalley watched us go, striking a pretty pose in the doorway of her house. I looked back and saw her wave at one of her neighbors, and then she went inside.

"Where to?" I asked Andy.

"There's a service station at the end of that gravel road, on the intersection. If the car came up that road, maybe he stopped at the station for gas. We've got nothing to lose."

We had nothing to gain, either. They'd gassed up a hundred big black cars every day. They didn't remember anything that looked out of line. We thanked them, and stopped at the nearest diner for some coffee. The coffee was hot, but the case sure as hell wasn't.


It really griped us. It really griped us.

Some son of a bitch had a black car stashed away in his garage. The car had a damaged front end, and it may still have had bloodstains on it. If he'd been a drunken driver, he'd sure as hell sobered up fast enough — and long enough — to realize he had to keep that car out of sight. We mulled it over, and we squatted on it, and we were going over all the angles again when the phone rang.

I picked it up. "Jonas here."

"Mike, this is Charlie on the desk. I was going to turn this over to Complaint, but I thought you might like to sit in on it."

"Tie in with the Benson kill?"

"Maybe."

"I'll be right down." I hung up quickly. "Come on, Andy."

We went downstairs to the desk, and Charlie introduced us to a Mr. George Sullivan and his daughter Grace, a young kid of about sixteen. We took them into an empty office, leaving Charlie at the desk.

"What is it, Mr. Sullivan?" I asked.

"I want better protection," he said.

"Of what, sir?"

"My child. Grace here. All the kids at the high school, in fact."

"What happened, sir?"

"You tell him, Grace."

The kid was a pretty blonde, fresh and clean-looking in a sweater and skirt. She wet her lips and said, "Daddy, can't…"

"Go on, Grace, it's for your own good."

"What is it, miss?" Andy asked gently.

"Well…"

"Go on, Grace. Just the way you told it to me. Go on."

"Well, it was last week. I…"

"Where was this, miss?"

"Outside the high school. I cut my last period, a study hour. I wanted to do some shopping downtown, and anyway a study hour is nowhere. You know, they're not so strict if you cut one."

"Yes, miss."

"I got out early, about a half hour before most of the kids start home. I was crossing the street when this car came around the corner. I got onto the sidewalk, and the car slowed down and started following me."

"What kind of a car, miss?"

"A big black one."

"Did you notice the year and make?"

"No. I'm not so good at cars."

"All right, what happened?"

"Well, the man driving kept following me, and I started walking faster, and he kept the car even with me all the time. He leaned over toward the window near the curb and said, 'Come on, sweetheart, let's go for a ride.'" She paused. "Daddy, do I have to…"

"Tell them all of it, Grace."

She swallowed hard, and then stared down at her saddle shoes.

"I didn't answer him. I kept walking, and he pulled up about ten feet ahead of me, and sat waiting there. When I came up alongside the car, he opened the door and got out. He...he...made a grab for me and...and I screamed."

"What happened then?"

"He got scared. He jumped into the car and pulled away from the curb. He was going very fast. I stopped screaming after he'd gone because...because I didn't want to attract any attention."

"When was this, miss?"

"Last week."

"What day?"

"It was Wednesday," Mr. Sullivan put in. "She came home looking like hell, and I asked her what was wrong, and she said, 'Nothing.' I didn't get the story out of her until today."

"You should have reported this earlier, miss," Andy said.

"I...I was too embarrassed."

"Did you notice the license plate on the car?"

"Yes."

"Did you get the number?"

"No, it was a funny plate."

"What do you mean, funny?"

"Well, it was a New York plate, but it had a lot of lettering on it."

"A lot of lettering? Was it a suburban plate? Was the car a station wagon?"

"No, it wasn't."

"A delivery truck?"

"No, it was a regular car. A new one."

"A new car," I repeated.

"Are you going to do something about this?" Mr. Sullivan asked.

"We're going to try, sir. Did you get a good look at the man, miss?"

"Yes. He was old, and fat. He wore a brown suit."

"How old would you say, miss?"

"At least forty."

Mr. Sullivan smiled, and then the smile dropped from his face. "There should be a cop around there. There definitely should be."

"Would you be able to identify the man if we showed him to you?"

"Yes, but...do I have to? I mean, I don't want any trouble. I don't want the other kids to find out."

"No one will find out, miss."

"This wouldn't have happened if there was a cop around," Mr. Sullivan said.

"There was a cop," I told him. "He's dead."


When they left, we got some coffee and mulled it over a bit more.

"A new car," Andy said.

"With a funny plate. What the hell did she mean by a funny plate?"

"On a new car."

I stood up suddenly. "I'll be dipped!" I said.

"What?"

"A new car, Andy. A funny plate. A New York plate with lettering on it. For Christ's sake, it was a *dealer's* plate!"

Andy snapped his fingers. "Sure. That explains how the bastard kept the car hidden so well. It's probably on some goddamn garage floor, hidden behind the other cars in the showroom."

"Let's go, Andy," I said.

It wasn't difficult. It's tough to get a dealer's franchise, and there aren't very many dealers in any specific neighborhood. We tried two, and then we hit the jackpot on the third try.

We spotted the car in one corner of the big garage. We walked over to it, and there was a mechanic in grease-stained coveralls working on the right headlight.

"Police," I told him. "What's wrong there?"

He continued working, apparently used to periodic checks from the Automobile Squad. "Sealbeam is broken. Just replacing it."

"What happened to the grille?"

"Oh, a small accident. Damn shame, too. A new car."

Andy walked around to the back and saw the paint scratches on the trunk. He nodded when he came around to me again.

"Back's all scratched, too," he said to the mechanic.

"Yeah, this goddamn car's been a jinx ever since we got it in."

"How so?"

"Got a headache with this one. The day we took it out for a test, the fool driver ran it into a ditch. Sliced hell out of both rear tires, and we had to replace them. All this in the first week we had this pig."

"Did you replace with Allstate?" I asked.

The mechanic looked up in surprise. "Why, yeah. Say, how did you know?"

"Where's your boss?" Andy asked.

"In the front office." The mechanic got up. "Hey, what's this all about?"

"Nothing that concerns you, Mac. Fix your car."

We went to the front office, a small cubicle that held two desks and two leather customer chairs. A stout man was sitting at one desk, a telephone to his ear. I estimated his age at about forty-two, forty-three. He looked up and smiled when we came in, nodded at us, and then continued talking.

"Yes...well, okay, if you say so. Well look, Sam, I can't sell cars if I haven't got them...You just do your best, that's all. Okay, fine." He hung up without saying good-bye, got out of his chair, and walked over to us.

"Can I help you, gentlemen?"

"Yes," Andy said. "We're interested in a car. Are you the owner of this place?"

"I am."

"With whom are we doing business?"

"Fred Whitaker," he said. "Did you have any particular car in mind?"

"Yes. The black Buick on the floor."

"A beautiful car," Whitaker said, smiling.

"The one with the smashed grille and headlight," I added.

The smile froze on his face, and he went white. "Wh... what?"

"Did you smash that car up?"

Whitaker swallowed hard. "No...no. One of my mechanics did."

"Who?"

"I've...I've fired him. He..."

"We can check this, Whitaker."

"Are...are you policemen?"

"We are. Come on, let's have it all. We've got a girl to identify you."

Whitaker's face crumbled. "I...I guess that's best, isn't it?"

"It's best," Andy said.

"I didn't mean to run him down. But the girl screamed, you know, and I thought he'd heard it. He stuck up his hand, and I...I got scared, I suppose, and there was no one around, so I...I knocked him...I knocked him down. Is he all right? I mean..."

"He's dead," I said.

"Dead?" Whitaker's eyes went wide. "Dead..."

"Was it you who smashed that picket fence?" Andy asked. Whitaker was still dazed.

"Wh...what?" he said.

"The picket fence. On Barnes."

"Oh. Yes, yes. That was afterwards. I was still scared. I...I made a wrong turn, and I saw a police car, and I wanted to get away fast. I...I backed into the fence."

"Why'd you bother that little girl, Whitaker?"

He collapsed into a chair. "I don't know," he said. "I don't know."

"You're in a jam," Andy said. "You'd better come along with us."

"Yes, yes." He stood up, took his hat from a rack in the corner, and then started for the door. At the door, he stopped and said, "I'd better tell my mechanics. I'd better tell them I'll be gone for the day."

I looked at Whitaker, and I thought of Benson. My eyes met Andy's, and I put it into words for both of us.

"You'll be gone a lot longer than that," I said.

# Chinese Puzzle

THE GIRL SLUMPED AT THE DESK JUST INSIDE THE ENtrance doorway of the small office. The phone lay uncradled, just the way she'd dropped it. An open pad of telephone numbers rested just beyond reach of her lifeless left hand.

The legend on the frosted glass door read GOTHAM LOBSTER COMPANY. The same legend was repeated on the long row of windows facing Columbus Avenue, and the sun glared hotly through those windows, casting the name of the company onto the wooden floor in shadowed black.

Mr. Godrow, President of Gotham Lobster, stood before those windows now. He was a big man with rounded shoulders and a heavy paunch. He wore a gray linen jacket over his suit pants, and the pocket of the jacket was stitched with the word *Gotham*. He tried to keep his meaty hands from fluttering, but he wasn't good at pretending. The hands wandered restlessly, and then exploded in a gesture of impatience.

"Well, aren't you going to do something?" he demanded.

"We just got here, Mr. Godrow," I said. "Give us a little..."

"The police are supposed to be so good," he said petulantly. "This girl drops dead in my office and all you do is stand around and look. Is this supposed to be a sightseeing tour?"

I didn't answer him. I looked at Donny, and Donny looked back at me, and then we turned our attention to the dead girl. Her left arm was stretched out across the top of the small desk, and her body was arched crookedly, with her head resting on the arm. Long black hair spilled over her face, but it could not hide the contorted, hideously locked grin on her mouth. She wore a tight silk dress, slit on either side in the Oriental fashion, buttoned to the throat. The dress had pulled back over a portion of her right thigh, revealing a roll-gartered stocking. The tight line of her panties was clearly visible through the thin silk of her dress. The dead girl was Chinese, but her lips and face were blue.

"Suppose you tell us what happened, Mr. Godrow," I said.

"Freddie can tell you," Godrow answered. "Freddie was sitting closer to her."

"Who's Freddie?"

"My boy," Godrow said.

"Your son?"

"No, I haven't any children. My boy. He works for me."

"Where is he now, sir?"

"I sent him down for some coffee. After I called you." Godrow paused, and then reluctantly said, "I didn't think you'd get here so quickly."

"Score one for the Police Department," Donny murmured.

"Well, you fill us in until he gets back, will you?" I said.

"All right," Godrow answered. He said everything grudgingly, as if he resented our presence in his office, as if this whole business of dead bodies lying around should never have been allowed to happen in his office. "What do you want to know?"

"What did the girl do here?" Donny asked.

"She made telephone calls."

"Is that all?"

"Yes. Freddie does that, too, but he also runs the addressing machine. Freddie…"

"Maybe you'd better explain your operation a little," I said.

"I sell lobsters," Godrow said.

"From this office?" Donny asked skeptically.

"We take the orders from this office," Godrow explained, warming up a little. It was amazing the way they always warmed up when they began discussing their work. "My plant is in Boothbay Harbor, Maine."

"I see."

"We take the orders here, and then the lobsters are shipped down from Maine, alive of course."

"I like lobsters," Donny said. "Especially lobster tails."

"Those are not lobsters," Godrow said indignantly. "Those are crawfish. African rock lobster. There's a big difference."

"Who do you sell to, Mr. Godrow?" I asked.

"Restaurants. That's why Mary worked for me."

"Is that the girl's name? Mary?"

"Yes, Mary Chang. You see, we do a lot of business with Chinese restaurants. Lobster Cantonese, you know, like that. They buy small lobsters usually, and in half-barrel quantities for the most part, but they're good steady customers."

"And Miss Chang called these Chinese restaurants, is that right?"

"Yes. I found it more effective that way. She spoke several Chinese dialects, and she inspired confidence, I suppose. At any rate, she got me more orders than any Occidental who ever held the job."

"And Freddie? What does he do?"

"He calls the American restaurants. We call them every morning. Not all of them each morning, of course, but those we feel are ready to reorder. We give them quotations, and we hope they'll place orders. We try to keep our quotes low. For example, our jumbos today were going for..."

"How much did Miss Chang receive for her duties, Mr. Godrow?"

"She got a good salary."

"How much?"

"Why? What difference does it make?"

"It might be important, Mr. Godrow. How much?"

"Forty-five a week, plus a dollar-fifty commission on each barrel order from a new customer." Godrow paused. "Those are good wages, Mr...."

"Parker. Detective-Sergeant Ralph Parker."

"Those are good wages, Sergeant Parker." He paused again. "Much more than my competitors are paying."

"I wouldn't know about that, Mr. Godrow, but I'll take your word for it. Now..."

A shadow fell across the floor, and Godrow looked up and said, "Ah, Freddie, it's about time."

I turned to the door, expecting to find a sixteen-year-old kid maybe. Freddie was not sixteen, nor was he twenty-six. He was closer to thirty-six, and he was a thin man with sparse hair and a narrow mouth. He wore a rumpled tweed suit and a stained knitted tie.

"This is my boy," Godrow said. "Freddie, this is Detective-Sergeant Parker and..."

"Katz," Donny said. "Donald Katz."

"How do you do?" Freddie said.

"Now that you're here," I said, "suppose you tell us what happened this morning, Freddie."

"Mr. Godrow's coffee..." Freddie started apologetically.

"Yes, yes, my coffee," Godrow said. Freddie brought it to his desk, put it down, and then fished into his pocket for some silver, which he deposited alongside the paper container. Godrow counted the change meticulously, and then took the lid from the container and dropped one lump of sugar into it. He opened his top drawer and put the remaining lump of sugar into a small jar there.

"What happened this morning, Freddie?" I asked.

"Well, I got in at about nine, or a little before," he said.

"Were you here then, Mr. Godrow?"

"No. I didn't come in until nine thirty or so."

"I see. Go on, Freddie."

"Mary...Miss Chang was here. I said good morning to her, and then we got down to work."

"I like my people to start work right away," Godrow said. "No nonsense."

"Was Miss Chang all right when you came in, Freddie?"

"Yes. Well, that is...she was complaining of a stiff neck, and she seemed to be very jumpy, but she started making her phone calls, so I guess she was all right."

"Was she drinking anything?"

"Sir?"

"Was she drinking anything?"

"No, sir."

"Did she drink anything all the while you were here?"

"No, sir. I didn't see her, at least."

"I see." I looked around the office and said, "Three phones here, is that right?"

"Yes," Godrow answered. "One extension for each of us. You know how they work. You push a button on the face of the instrument, and that's the line you're on. We can all talk simultaneously that way, on different lines."

"I know how it works," I said. "What happened then, Freddie?"

"We kept calling, that's all. Mr. Godrow came in about nine thirty, like he said, and we kept on calling while he changed to his office jacket."

"I like to wear this jacket in the office," Godrow explained. "Makes me feel as if I'm ready for the day's work, you know."

"Also saves wear and tear on your suit jacket," Donny said.

Godrow seemed about to say something, but I beat him to the punch. "Did you notice anything unusual about Miss Chang's behavior, Mr. Godrow?"

"Well, yes, as a matter of fact. As Freddie told you, she was quite jumpy. I dropped a book at one point, and she almost leaped out of her chair."

"Did you see her drink anything?"

"No."

"All right, Freddie, what happened after Mr. Godrow came in?"

"Well, Mary started making another phone call. This was at about nine thirty-five. She was behaving very peculiar by this time. She was twitching and well...she was having... well, like spasms. I asked her if she was all right, and she flinched when I spoke, and then she went right on with her call. I remember the time because I started a call at about the same time. You see, we have to get our orders in the morning if Boothbay is to deliver the next morning. That means we're racing against the clock, sort of, so you learn to keep your eye on it. Well, I picked up my phone and started dialing, and then Mary started talking Chinese to someone on her phone. She sits at the desk right next to mine, you see, and I can hear everything she says."

"Do you know who she was calling?"

"No. She always dials...dialed...the numbers and then started talking right off in Chinese. She called all the Chinese restau..."

"Yes, I know. Go on."

"Well, she was talking on her phone, and I was talking on mine, and all of a sudden she said in English, 'No, why?'"

"She said this in English?"

"Yes."

"Did you hear this, Mr. Godrow?"

"No. My desk is rather far away, over here near the windows. But I heard what she said next. I couldn't miss hearing that. She yelled it out loud."

"What was that, sir?"

"She said, 'Kill me? No! No!'"

"What happened then?"

"Well," Freddie said, "I was still on the phone. I looked up, and I didn't know what was going on. Mary started to shove her chair back, and then she began...shaking all over... like...like..."

"The girl had a convulsion," Godrow put in. "If I'd known she was predisposed toward..."

"Did she pass out?"

"Yes," Freddie said.

"What did you do then?"

"I didn't know what to do."

"Why didn't you call a doctor?"

"Well, we did, after the second convulsion."

"When was that?"

"About...oh, I don't know...ten, fifteen minutes later. I really don't know."

"And when the doctor came, what did he say?"

"Well, he didn't come," Freddie said apologetically.

"Why not? I thought you called him."

"The girl died after the second convulsion," Godrow said. "Good Lord, man, she turned blue, you saw her. Why should I pay a doctor for a visit when the girl was dead? I canceled the call."

"I see."

"It's obvious she was predisposed toward convulsions, and whoever spoke to her on the phone frightened her, bringing one on," Godrow said. "He obviously told her he was going to kill her or something."

"This is all very obvious, is it, Mr. Godrow?" I asked.

"Well, of course. You can see the girl is blue. What else..."

"Lots of things," I said. "Lots of things could have caused her coloration. But only one thing would put that grin on her face."

"What's that?" Godrow asked.

"Strychnine poisoning," I said.

When we got back to Homicide I put a call through to Mike Reilly. The coroner had already confirmed my suspicions, but I wanted the official autopsy report on it. Mike picked up the phone on the third ring and said, "Reilly here."

"This is Ralph," I said. "What've you got on the Chinese girl?"

"Oh. Like you figured, Ralph. It's strychnine, all right."

"No question?"

"None at all. She sure took enough of the stuff. Any witnesses around when she went under?"

"Yes, two."

"She complain of a stiff neck, twitching, spasms?"

"Yes."

"Convulsions?"

"Yes."

"Sure, that's all strychnine. Yeah, Ralph. And her jaws locked the way they are, that grin. And the cyanotic coloring of lips and face. Oh, no question. Hell, I could have diagnosed this without taking a test."

"What else did you find, Mike?"

"She didn't have a very big breakfast, Ralph. Coffee and an English muffin."

"Have any idea when she got the strychnine?"

"Hard to say. Around breakfast, I suppose. You're gonna have a tough nut with strychnine, Ralph."

"How so?"

"Tracing it, I mean. Hell, Ralph, they sell it by the can. For getting rid of animal pests."

"Yeah. Well, thanks, Mike."

"No trouble at all. Drop in anytime."

He hung up, and I turned to Donny who had already started on a cup of coffee.

"Strychnine, all right."

"What'd you expect?" he said. "Malted milk?"

"So where now?"

"Got a check on the contents of the girl's purse from the lab. Nothing important. Lipstick. Some change. Five-dollar bill, and three singles. Theater stubs."

"For where?"

"Chinese theater in Chinatown."

"Anything else?"

"Letter to a sister in Hong Kong."

"In Chinese?"

"Yes."

"And?"

"That's it. Oh yes, a program card. She was a transfer student at Columbia. Went there nights."

"So what do you figure, Donny?"

"I figure some bastard slipped the strychnine to her this morning before she came to work. Maybe a lover, how do I know? She called him later to say hello. She talks Chinese on the phone, so who can tell whether she's calling a restaurant or her uncle in Singapore? The guy all at once says, 'You know why you're feeling so punk, honey?' So she is feeling punk. She's got a stiff neck, and her reflexes are hypersensitive, and she's beginning to shake a little. She forgets she's supposed to be talking to a Chinese restaurant owner. She drops the pose for a minute and says 'No, why?' in English. The boyfriend on the other end says, 'Here's why, honey. I gave you a dose of strychnine when I saw you this morning. It's going to kill you in about zero minutes flat.' The kid jumps up and screams 'Kill me? No! No!' Curtain. The poison's already hit her."

"Sounds good," I said. "Except for one thing."

"Yeah?"

"Would the poisoner take a chance like that? Tipping her off on the phone?"

"Why not? He probably knew how long it would take for the poison to kill her."

"But why would she call him?"

"Assuming it was a him. How do I know? Maybe she didn't call anybody special. Maybe the joker works at one of the Chinese restaurants she always called. Maybe she met him every morning for chop suey, and then he went his way and she went hers. Or maybe she called...Ralph, she could have called anyone."

"No. Someone who spoke Chinese. She spoke Chinese to the party in the beginning."

"Lots of Chinese in this city, Ralph."

"Why don't we start with the restaurants? This book was open on her desk. Two pages showing. She could have been talking to someone at any one of the restaurants listed on those pages, assuming she opened the book to refer to a number. If she called a sweetheart, we're up the creek."

"Not necessarily," Donny said. "It'll just take longer, that's all."

There were a lot of Chinese restaurants listed on those two pages. They were not listed in any geographical order. Apparently, Mary Chang knew the best times to call each of the owners, and she'd listed the restaurant numbers in a system all her own. So where the first number on the list was in Chinatown, the second was up on Fordham Road in the Bronx. We had a typist rearrange the list according to location, and then we asked the Skipper for two extra men to help with the legwork. He gave us Belloni and Hicks, yanking them off a case that was ready for the DA anyway. Since they were our guests, so to speak, we gave them the easy half of the list, the portion in Chinatown where all the restaurants were clustered together and there wouldn't be as much hoofing to do. Donny and I took the half that covered Upper Manhattan and the Bronx.

A Chinese restaurant in the early afternoon is something like a bar at that time. There are few diners. Everyone looks bleary-eyed. The dim lights somehow clash with the bright sunshine outside. It's like stepping out of reality into something unreal and vague. Besides, a lot of the doors were locked solid, and when a man can't speak English it's a little difficult to make him understand what a police shield means.

It took a lot of time. We pounded on the doors first, and then we talked to whoever's face appeared behind the plate glass. We showed shields, we gestured, we waited for someone who spoke English. When the doors opened, we told them who we were and what we wanted. There was distrust, a natural distrust of cops, and another natural distrust of Westerners.

"Did Gotham Lobster call you this morning?"

"No."

"When did Gotham call you?"

"Yes'day. We take one ba'l. One ba'l small."

"Who did you speak to at Gotham?"

"Ma'y Chang."

And on to the next place, and the same round of questions, and always no luck, always no call from Gotham or Mary Chang. And then we hit a place on the Grand Concourse where the waiter opened the door promptly. We told him what we wanted, and he hurried off to the back of the restaurant while we waited by the cash register. A young Chinese in an impeccable blue suit came out to us in about five minutes. He smiled and shook hands and then said, "I'm David Loo. My father owns the restaurant. May I help you?"

He was a good-looking boy of about twenty, I would say. He spoke English without a trace of singsong. He was wearing a white button-down shirt with a blue and silver striped silk tie. A small Drama Masks tie clasp held the tie to the shirt.

"I'm Detective-Sergeant Parker, and this is my partner, Detective-Sergeant Katz. Do you know Mary Chang?"

"Chang? Mary Chang? Why, no, I...oh, do you mean the girl who calls from Gotham Lobster?"

"Yes, that's her. Do you know her?"

"Oh yes, certainly."

"When did you see her last?"

"See her?" David Loo smiled. "I'm afraid I've never seen her. I spoke to her on the phone occasionally, but that was the extent of our relationship."

"I see. When did you speak to her last?"

"This morning."

"What time was this?"

"Oh, I don't know. Early this morning."

"Can you try to pinpoint the time?"

David Loo shrugged. "Nine, nine fifteen, nine thirty. I really don't know." He paused. "Has Miss Chang done something?"

"Can you give us a closer time than that, Mr. Loo? Mary Chang was poisoned this morning, and it might be..."

"Poisoned? My God!"

"Yes. So you see, any help you can give us would be appreciated."

"Yes, yes, I can understand that. Well, let me see. I came to the restaurant at about...nine ten it was, I suppose. So she couldn't have called at nine, could she?" David Loo smiled graciously, as if he were immensely enjoying this game of murder. "I had some coffee, and I listened to the radio back in the kitchen, and..." Loo snapped his fingers. "Of course," he said. "She called right after that."

"Right after what?"

"Well, I listen to swing a lot. WNEW is a good station for music, you know. Do you follow bop?"

"No. Go on."

"Well, WNEW has a newsbreak every hour on the half hour. I remember the news coming on at nine thirty, and then as the newscaster signed off, the phone rang. That must have been at nine thirty-five. The news takes five minutes, you see. As a matter of fact, I always resent that intrusion on the music. If a person likes music, it seems unfair..."

"And the phone rang at nine thirty-five, is that right?"

"Yes, sir, I'm positive."

"Who answered the phone?"

"I did. I'd finished my coffee."

"Was it Mary Chang calling?"

"Yes."

"What did she say?"

"She said, 'Gotham Lobster, good morning.' I said good morning back to her—she's always very pleasant on the phone—and..."

"Wasn't she pleasant *off* the phone?"

"Well, I wouldn't know. I only spoke to her on the phone."

"Go on."

"She gave me a quotation then and asked if I'd like some nice lobster."

"Was this in Chinese?"

"Yes. I don't know why she spoke Chinese. Perhaps she thought I was the chef."

"What did you do then?"

"I asked her to hold on, and then I went to find the chef. I asked the chef if he needed any lobster, and he said we should take a half barrel. So I went back to the phone. But Miss Chang was gone by that time." Loo shrugged. "We had to order our lobsters from another outfit. Shame, too, because Gotham has some good stuff."

"Did you speak to her in English at all?"

"No. All Chinese."

"I see. Is that customary? I mean, do you usually check with the chef after she gives her quotation?"

"Yes, of course. The chef is the only one who'd know. Sometimes, of course, the chef himself answers the phone. But if he doesn't, we always leave the phone to check with him."

"And you didn't speak to her in English at all?"

"No, sir."

"And you didn't know her, other than through these phone conversations?"

"No, sir."

"Ever have breakfast with her?" Donny asked.

"Sir?"

"Did you ever…"

"No, of course not. I told you, I didn't know her personally."

"All right, Mr. Loo, thank you very much. We may be back."

"Please feel free to return," he said a little coldly.

We left the restaurant, and outside Donny said, "So?"

"So now we know who she was speaking to. What do you think of him?"

"Educated guy. Could conceivably run in the same circles as a Columbia student. And if he did poison her this morning and then tell her about it on the phone, it's a cinch he'd lie his goddamned head off."

"Sure. Let's check Miss Chang's residence. Someone there might know whether or not Loo knew her better than he says he did."


Mary Chang, when she was alive, lived at International House near the Columbia campus, on Riverside Drive. Her roommate was a girl named Frieda who was a transfer student from Vienna. The girl was shocked to learn of Miss Chang's death. She actually wept for several moments, and then she pulled herself together when we started questioning her.

"Did she have any boyfriends?"

"Yes. A few."

"Do you know any of their names?"

"I know all of their names. She always talked about them."

"Would you let us have them, please."

Frieda reeled off a list of names, and Donny and I listened. Then Donny asked, "A David Loo? Did he ever come around?"

"No, I don't think so. She never mentioned a David Loo."

"Never talked about him at all?"

"No."

"That list you gave us—all Chinese names. Did she ever date any American boys?"

"No. Mary was funny that way. She didn't like to go out with Americans. I mean, she liked the country and all, but I

guess she figured there was no future in dating Occidentals."
Frieda paused. "She was a pretty girl, Mary, and a very happy
one, always laughing, always full of life. A lot of American
boys figured her for...an easy mark, I suppose. She...sensed
this. She wouldn't date any of them."

"Did they ask her?"

"Oh, yes, all the time. She was always very angry when an
American asked her for a date. It was sort of an insult to her.
She...knew what they wanted."

"Where'd she eat breakfast?"

"Breakfast?"

"Yes. Where'd she eat? Who'd she eat with?"

"I don't know. I don't remember ever seeing her eat
breakfast."

"She didn't eat breakfast?"

"I don't think so. We always left here together in the morning. I have a job, too, you see. I work at Lord and Taylor's.
I'm..."

"Yes, you left here together?"

"To take the subway. She never stopped to eat."

"Coffee?" I asked. "An English muffin? Something?"

"No, not when I was with her."

"I see. What subway did you take?"

"The Broadway line."

"Where did she get off?"

"At Seventy-second Street."

"What time did she get off the subway usually?"

"At about nine, or maybe a few minutes before. Yes, just
about nine."

"But she didn't stop for breakfast."

"No. Mary was very slim, very well-built. I don't think she ate breakfast in the morning."

"She ate breakfast this morning," I said. "Thank you, miss. Come on, Donny."

There was an Automat on West 72nd Street, a few doors from Broadway. Mary Chang wouldn't have gone to the Automat because Mary Chang had to be at work at nine, and she got off the train at nine. We walked down the street, all the way up to the building that housed the offices of Gotham Lobster, close to Columbus Avenue. There was a luncheonette on the ground floor of that building. Donny and I went inside and took seats at the counter, and then we ordered coffee. When our coffee came, we showed the counterman our buzzers. He got scared all at once, the way some people will get scared when a cop shows his shield.

"Just a few questions," we told him.

"Sure. Sure," he said. He gulped. "I don't know why..."

"You know any of the people who work in this building?"

"Sure, most of 'em. But..."

"Did you know Mary Chang?"

He seemed immensely relieved. "Oh, her. There's some trouble with her, ain't there? She got shot, or stabbed, or something, didn't she?"

"Did you know her?"

"I seen her around, yeah. Quite a piece, you know? With them tight silk dresses, slit up there on the side." He smiled. "You ever seen her? Man, I go for them Chinese broads."

"Did she ever eat here?"

"No."

"Breakfast?"

"No."

"She never stopped here in the morning for coffee?"

"No, why should she do that?"

"I don't know. You tell me."

"Well, what I mean, he always come down for the coffee, you know."

I felt Donny tense beside me.

"Who?" I asked. "Who came down for the coffee?"

"Why, Freddie. From the lobster joint. Every morning like clockwork, before he went upstairs. Two coffees, one heavy on the sugar. That Chinese broad liked it sweet. Also a jelly doughnut and a toasted English. Sure, every morning."

"You're sure about this?"

"Oh yes, sure. The boss didn't know nothing about it, you know. Mr. Godrow. He don't go for that junk. They always had their coffee before he come in in the morning."

"Thanks," I said. "Did Freddie come down for the coffee this morning?"

"Sure, every morning."


We left the luncheonette and went upstairs. Freddie was working the addressing machine when we came in. The machine made a hell of a clatter as the metal address plates fed through it. We said hello to Mr. Godrow and then walked right to the machine. Freddie fed postcards and stepped on the foot lever and the address plates banged onto the cards and then dropped into the tray below.

"We've got an idea, Freddie," I said.

He didn't look up. He kept feeding postcards into the machine. The cards read MAINE LIVE LOBSTERS AT FANTASTIC PRICES!

"We figure a guy who kept asking Mary Chang out, Freddie. A guy who constantly got refused."

Freddie said nothing.

"You ever ask her out, Freddie?"

"Yes," he said under the roar of the machine.

"We figure she drove the guy nuts, sitting there in her tight dresses, drinking coffee with him, being friendly, but never anything more, never what he wanted. We figured he got sore at all the Chinese boys who could date her just because they were Chinese. We figure he decided to do something about it. Want to hear more, Freddie?"

"What is this?" Godrow asked. "This is a place of business, you know. Those cards have to..."

"You went down for your customary coffee this morning, Freddie."

"Coffee?" Godrow asked. "What coffee? Have you been..."

"Only this time you dumped strychnine into Mary Chang's. She took her coffee very sweet, and that probably helped to hide the bitter taste. Or maybe you made some comment about the coffee being very bitter this morning, anything to hide the fact that you were poisoning her."

"No..." Freddie said.

"She drank her coffee and ate her English muffin, and then—the way you did every morning—you gathered up the cups and the napkins and the crumbs and whatever, and you rushed out with them before Mr. Godrow arrived. Only this time, you were disposing of evidence. Where'd you take them? The garbage cans on Columbus Avenue? Do they collect the garbage early, Freddie?"

"I...I..."

"You knew the symptoms. You watched, and when you thought the time was ripe, you couldn't resist boasting about what you'd done. Mary was making a call. You also knew how these calls worked because you made them yourself. There was usually a pause in the conversation while someone checked with the chef. You waited for that pause, and then you asked Mary if she knew why she was feeling so ill. You asked her because you weren't making a call, Freddie, you were plugged in on her extension, listening to her conversation. She recognized your voice, and so she answered you in English. You told her then, and she jumped up, but it was too late, the convulsion came. Am I right, Freddie?"

Freddie nodded.

"You'd better come with us," I said.

"I...I still have to stamp the quotations on these," Freddie said.

"Mr. Godrow will get along without you, Freddie," I said. "He'll get himself a new boy."

"I...I'm sorry," Freddie said.

"This is terrible," Godrow said.

"Think how Mary Chang must have felt," I told him, and we left.

$A$ *continuing character in the 87th Precinct novels is a villain known as the Deaf Man, Carella's nemesis, even as Moriarty was Sherlock Holmes's. Whenever the Deaf Man is on the scene, the cops of the 87th behave like Keystone Kops. He made his first appearance in 1960, in a novel titled* The Heckler. *Since then, there have been five other novels in which the Deaf Man has wreaked havoc in the old Eight-Seven, the most recent of which was* Hark! *Traditionally, the Deaf Man will concoct a brilliant caper that is foiled not by any clever deduction on the part of the Eight-Seven's stalwarts, but instead by pure chance or misfortune.*

*But think about this:*

*Five years before the Deaf Man made his first appearance, I wrote the following story about some guys planning to rob a bank. It appeared under the Richard Marsten byline, in the September 1955 issue of* Manhunt.

# The Big Day

"FRIDAY IS OUR BIG DAY," THE GIRL SAID.

She drained the remains of her Manhattan, and then fished for the cherry at the bottom of the glass. Anson Grubb watched her, no sign of interest on his face.

The girl popped the cherry into her mouth and then touched her fingers lightly to the napkin in her lap. The gesture was a completely feminine one, turned gross and somehow ugly by the girl herself. She was a big girl, her hair inexpertly tinted blonde, her lipstick badly applied. Anson had never liked cheap merchandise, and he winced inwardly as the girl munched on the cherry, her mouth working like a garbage disposal unit.

"The first and the fifteenth," the girl said around the shredded remnants of the cherry, "and Friday is the fifteenth."

"Payday, huh?" Anson asked, sipping at his scotch, apparently bored with all this shoptalk, but with his ears keyed to every syllable that came from her mouth.

"The steel mill and the airplane factory both," she said, nodding. "Can't we have another round, Anse?"

"Sure," Anson said. He signaled the waiter and then added, "Well, it's only twice a month, so that isn't too bad."

"That twice a month is enough to break our backs, Anse," the girl said, impatiently looking over her shoulder for the waiter. "On those paydays, we must handle close to $500,000, cashing checks for the plants."

"That right?" Anson said.

"Sure. You'd never think our little bank handled so much money, would you?" The girl gave a pleased little wiggle. "We don't, usually, except on the first and the fifteenth."

"That's when the plants send over their payrolls, huh?" Anson asked. The waiter appeared at his elbow. "Two of the same, please," he said. The waiter nodded and silently vanished.

"This is a nice place," the girl said.

"I figured you needed a little relaxation," Anson said. "Enjoy yourself before the mad rush on Friday, you know…"

"God, when I think of it," the girl said. "It's enough to drive you nuts."

"I can imagine," Anson said. "First those payrolls arriving early in the morning, and then the employees coming to cash their checks later in the day. That must be very trying."

"Well, the payrolls don't come on Friday," the girl said. The waiter reappeared, depositing their drinks on the table. The girl lifted her Manhattan, said, "Here's how," and drank.

"Oh, they don't come on Friday?" Anson said.

"No, they'll reach us Thursday afternoon."

"Well, that's sensible, at least," Anson said. He paused and lifted his drink. "Probably after you close those big bronze doors to the public, huh?"

"No, we don't close until three. The payrolls get there at about two."

"Oh, that's good. Then the payrolls are safe in the vault before three."

"Oh, sure. We've got a good vault."

"I'll bet you do. Do you want to dance, honey?"

"I'd love to," the girl said. She shoved her chair back with all the grace of a bus laboring uphill. She went into Anson's arms, and he maneuvered her onto the floor skillfully, feeling the roll of fat under his fingers, his mouth curled into a distasteful smile over her shoulder.

"Yep," the girl said, "Friday is our big day."

No, Anson thought. *Thursday* is our big day.

Jeremy Thorpe stood at the far end of the counter, the ballpoint pen in his hand. He took out his passbook, opened it before him, and then drew a deposit slip from one of the cubbyholes beneath the counter. He flipped the deposit slip over so that he could write on the blank yellow surface, and then he knotted his brow as if he were trying to work out a tricky problem in arithmetic.

He drew a large rectangle on the back of the deposit slip. On the north side of the rectangle, he drew two lines which intersected the side, and between the lines he scribbled the word "doors." In the right-hand corner of the rectangle, he drew a small square resembling a desk, and he labeled it "mgr." Across the entire south side of the rectangle, opposite his "doors," he drew a line representing the half wall dividing the tellers' cages from the remainder of the bank. He jotted four lines onto this to show the approximate position of the cages, and another line to indicate the locked doorway that led to the back of the bank and the vault. In the left-hand corner of his plan, the east and north sides intersected in a right angle which he labeled "counter."

He folded the deposit slip in half, slipped it into his coat pocket, took a new deposit slip from the cubbyhole, and filled it in for a deposit of five dollars. In the space that asked for his name, he did not write Jeremy Thorpe. He carefully lettered in the words "Arthur Samuels." He brought the deposit slip and a five-dollar bill to one of the cages, waiting behind a small man in a dark suit.

This was the third time he'd been inside the bank. He'd opened an account close to a month ago with fifty dollars. He'd added twenty dollars to it last week. He was adding five dollars to it now. He'd used different tellers for each deposit. The teller who took his passbook and money now had never seen Jeremy Thorpe before, and he certainly didn't know his name wasn't really Arthur Samuels. The teller stamped the book, put the money and deposit slip into his drawer, and handed the book back to Jeremy. Jeremy put the passbook into its protective case, and then walked directly to the doors, glancing once at the manager's desk which was on his left behind a short wooden railing. The big bronze doors were folded back against the wall, and the uniformed bank guard was chatting with a white-haired woman. Jeremy pushed open one of the glass doors and walked down the stairs into the sunshine. This was Tuesday.

From the soda fountain across the way from the bank, Carl Semmer could see the bank very clearly. There was a driveway to the right of the bank, and a door was at the end of that driveway, and the payroll trucks would roll up that driveway on Thursday. The guards would step out and enter through the door at the end of the driveway, and the payrolls for American Steel and Tartogue Aircraft would be carried back to the vault, awaiting the demands of the employees' checks next day. He had sat at the soda fountain counter on two payroll delivery days thus far. On both those days, the American Steel payroll had arrived in an armored car bearing the shield of International Armored Car Corp. On the fourteenth of last month, it had arrived at 2:01 P.M. On the thirty-first of last month, it had arrived at 2:07 P.M. On both occasions it had taken the guards approximately six minutes to deliver the payroll and back the truck out into the street. They had then turned left around the corner and been out of sight before an additional minute had expired.

On the fourteenth, the Safeguard Company's truck bearing the second payroll had arrived at 2:10, several minutes after the first truck departed. On the thirty-first, the Safeguard Company's truck arrived while the first truck was still in the driveway. It waited in front of the A&P alongside the bank's driveway, and when the first truck swung out into the street and around the corner, it pulled up to the rear door at 2:15. On both occasions, each truck was gone and out of sight by 2:22 P.M.

Carl had watched these operations with careful scrutiny. He was now watching an equally important operation.

The big clock on the outside wall of the bank read 2:59. He glanced at his own wristwatch to check the time, and then his eyes moved to the front steps where he saw Anson Grubb starting for the doors. Anson entered the glass doors and moved into the bank. Carl's eyes fled to the clock again. The big hand was moving slowly, almost imperceptibly.

Three o'clock.

Jeremy Thorpe started up the front steps of the bank. From behind the glass doors, the uniformed guard shook his head, smiled a sad smile at Jeremy, and then began closing the big bronze doors. Jeremy snapped his fingers, turned, and walked down the steps again and turned left toward the A&P. Carl studied his watch. It took thirty seconds to close the big bronze doors.

He kept watching the front of the bank. At 3:05, one of the bronze doors opened, and an old lady started down the steps. The door closed behind her. At 3:07, the door opened again, and two more people left the bank. At 3:10, four people left. At 3:17, two people left. At 3:21, Anson Grubb left the bank. Carl knew he would be the last person to leave. He paid for his coffee and went back to the furnished room at the other end of town.

This was Wednesday.

"The payroll trucks should be gone by 2:25," Anson said that night. "We'll give ourselves leeway and say they'll be gone by 2:30. Add another five minutes to that in case there are any foul-ups inside the bank, and we can figure the money'll be safe in the vault by 2:35."

He scratched his chin thoughtfully. He was a tall man with wild black hair. His eyes were blue, and his nose was long and thin. He wore an immaculate blue suit, and a black homburg rested on the chair beside him. One knee was raised as he leaned onto the chair, the trouser leg pulled back in a crease-preserving manner.

"Where's the plan, Jerry?" he said.

Jeremy Thorpe rose and walked to the dresser. He opened

the top drawer and removed an eight-by-eleven enlargement of the plan he'd sketched onto the deposit slip. He brought this to the table, put it in the center under the hanging lightbulb and said, "I'm no Michelangelo."

The other men studied the plan once more. They had seen it often enough since Jeremy had drawn it up, but they studied it again, coupling it with their own memories of what they'd seen inside the bank, giving the two-dimensional drawing a three-dimensional reality.

"What do you think?" Anson said.

"Looks good," Carl answered. He was a short man with a pug nose and bad teeth. He was smoking now, and the gray smoke of his cigarette drifted up past the cooler gray of his eyes. He wore his brown hair in a crew cut.

"Jerry?"

"I like it," Jeremy said. He blinked his eyes. Now that the time was close, he was getting a little nervous. The nervousness showed in his pale features. He tweaked his feminine nose, and his lids blinked again, like short flesh curtains spasmodically closing and opening over his brown eyes.

"Only two of us are going in, you understand that, don't you?" Anson said.

Carl nodded.

"Jerry?"

"I understand."

"You think we can knock it over with just two inside?" Carl asked. "Maybe we all ought to go in."

"We can do it," Anson said.

"There's just one weak spot in the plan," Jeremy said, blinking.

"What's that?"

"The last guy to leave."

"How do you figure that to be a weak spot?"

"Suppose the timing is off? What happens then?"

"The timing won't be off," Anson said. "Look, you want me to run through this again?"

"Yeah, I'd feel better if you did," Jeremy said.

"Okay. The trucks are gone by 2:30, we're figuring. The money is in the vault by 2:35. Carl is across the street in the soda fountain, watching all the time. If anything happens to delay the trucks, he gives us a buzz before we leave here, and we postpone the thing to the first of next month. So there's no chance of a slipup there, right?"

"Right," Jeremy said.

"Okay. At 2:45, assuming we get no call from Carl, you and I leave here. It takes us five minutes to drive from here to the parking lot on Main and West Davis. That's a public parking lot, so we don't have to worry about attendants or anything. We just pull the car in, and leave it. Time: 2:50. We walk to the bank. It takes only four minutes to walk to the bank, we've timed that a dozen times already. That would put us in the bank at 2:54, but that's a little too early, so we dally a bit, getting to the bank at 2:58. We've entered as late as 2:59 with no trouble from the guard at the door, so there shouldn't be any trouble at 2:58. I go straight to the manager's desk. At three o'clock, four things are going to happen."

"Go ahead," Jeremy said.

"One: the bank guard is going to close those big bronze doors so nobody else can come into the bank."

"Yeah."

"Two: you're going over to the bank guard, Jerry. You're

telling him a holdup is in progress, and that he is to behave normally, letting no one into the bank and letting anyone out who wants to go out. You got that?"

"Yes."

"Three: I'm going to sit down at the manager's desk and tell him I have a gun in my pocket and I want him to take me back to the vault. Four: Carl leaves the soda fountain and heads for the parking lot the second he sees the bronze doors closing."

"Well, it's okay so far," Jeremy said. "It's what comes later that bothers me."

"This is perfect," Anson said. "There's nothing to worry about. The time is now 3:00 P.M. The doors are closed, you and I are inside the bank, Carl is on his way to the car. There are only two people inside that bank who know there's a holdup going on. And they're the only two people who'll know about it until it's all over and we're gone. It takes Carl four minutes to walk to the car. Time: 3:04. By 3:04, the bank manager and I will have left his desk, gone through the locked door to the right of the tellers' cages, and be at the door to the vault. You're still at the entrance with the bank guard, Jerry. Some people will be leaving, but that's all right. We let them go. By 3:05, the vault door is open, and the manager and I are inside."

"The light on the corner of Main and West Davis turns red at 3:06," Carl said. "It's a one-minute light, turning green again at 3:07. It takes two minutes to drive from that corner to the bank driveway. Time: 3:09."

"I've been in the vault for four minutes already," Anson said. "I figure I can clean it out in six minutes. We've practiced stuffing that suitcase already, and I've always done it in less than five. But we'll figure six minutes to play it safe. In other words, at 3:11 I'm ready to leave the vault with the money, and Carl is parked in the driveway at the rear door."

"And I'm still with the bank guard," Jeremy said.

"Correct," Anson replied. "At 3:11, I leave the vault and close the door. The manager is still inside. If he starts yelling, no one's going to hear him through that thick steel. So we don't have to worry about the manager after 3:11. I walk to my left and to the rear door. It's approximately ten feet to that door. I open it, step into the rear of the car, and Carl pulls out of the driveway. It shouldn't take us longer than a minute to clear the driveway and turn toward the front of the bank. We'll play it safe. Give us two minutes from the time I leave the vault to the time the car will be waiting for you at the front of the bank, Jerry. In other words: 3:13."

"That's the part that bothers me," Jeremy said. "I don't like leaving last."

"There's nothing to worry about," Anson said. "At 3:13 by the bank's clock, you tell the guard to open the door. You walk out and down to the car. It'll take you twenty seconds to cross the sidewalk to the car. It'll take the guard at least thirty seconds to get over his shock and open those doors again. That gives us a ten-second start. By that time, we're around the corner and away. We'll be on the highway before the cops even know about this. The guard'll probably rush out and start yelling and then remember he ought to pull the alarm. That's all the lead we'll need."

"I don't like leaving last," Jeremy said.

"Why not? I'm the only one who'll be carrying any money," Anson said. "When you leave, you'll look just like any other depositor who got caught inside when the doors closed. You're not allowed to park in front of the bank, which means there'll be a space for our car guaranteed. We'll be in it just as you come out of the bank. Believe me, we can't miss."

"I hope so," Jeremy said, blinking.


On Thursday, the fourteenth, the sun rose over the town and splashed the streets with gold. There was a pale blue sky behind the sun, and the natives of the town talked about spring coming early this year. It was a warm sun, and it dispelled harsh thoughts of winter, and the people of the town responded to the sun and quickened their steps, and walked with the collars of their coats open, walked with their heads high. It was good to be alive on a day like this. The people in the bank, the tellers, the clerks, the manager, the guard looked through the glass entrance doors and up at the high windows on the walls, seeing the golden splash of the sun and wishing for their lunch hours so they could get outside and soak up some fresh air.

The three men ate lunch in a diner. They did not sit together. They did not talk to each other. They ate their lunches quietly and then separately went back to their furnished room to prepare for the business that lay ahead of them.

Anson was in a holiday mood. He took the theatrical makeup kit from the bottom drawer of the dresser, and then he went to the closet for the suitcase bearing the wigs, and there was a perky spring in his step, and a smile on his face.

"It isn't enough to be merely unrecognizable," Anson said, like a professor delivering a lecture to his students. "To begin with, we can't wear masks because we're allegedly just customers entering the bank. We have to look like normal, everyday people." He tapped the makeup kit. "That's the beauty of this."

"I'll feel strange," Jeremy said.

"Of course you will," Anson replied. "But when the time comes for descriptions, you'll feel a whole lot better. Come on, let's get started."

They began with the spirit gum. Carl had a pug nose, but he sat before the mirror and diligently wadded spirit gum onto it until the nose took a definite downward curve. Jeremy used a heavy hand with the gum, adding to his own slender, feminine nose until the nose was gross and wide. Anson built a hook into the center of his nose, so that the nose appeared to have been broken at one time. They tinted the spirit gum to match the color of their complexions, and then they started with the theatrical hair. Carefully, painstakingly, they snipped patches of hair from the long strands they held in their hands. Carl built up his eyebrows so that they were shaggy and unkempt. Anson, bit by careful bit, built a red mustache under his false broken nose. Jeremy put a hairline mustache under his.

They powdered their noses to take the shine of the makeup off them, and then they took the wigs out of the suitcase. Anson put the red wig over his own wild black hair. Jeremy, in character with the thin mustache, donned a black wig and then plastered the hair down with petroleum jelly. Carl put on a shaggy wig which matched his eyebrows. They glued the wigs tight at their temples, combing the hair so that it fell naturally. The time was 1:30.

At 1:32, the International Armored Car Corp. truck pulled up at the offices of American Steel and two armed guards transported the payroll into the steel-plated truck. At 1:35, the truck from the Safeguard Company arrived at Tartogue Aircraft to pick up its payroll load.

At 1:37, Anson Grubb said, "You'd better hurry, Carl."

"I'm hurrying," Carl answered. He was wearing a pale yellow sports shirt, and he stood before the mirror now, knotting a tie. He did not put either a sports jacket or a suit jacket over the shirt. He wore, instead, a red plaid lumber jacket. The other men would follow the same sartorial plan. Over the lumber jackets would go overcoats. Once they were in the car and away from the bank after the holdup, the overcoats, the wigs, the false hair and the built-up noses, the neckties, all would be dumped into a suitcase in the backseat of the car. Anyone who'd seen them in the bank would remember men in overcoats, wearing neckties. Once they left that bank, their physical appearances would be completely changed. The three men in the car would be wearing lumber jackets and sports shirts. They would be of different hair coloring than the men who'd robbed the bank. Their faces would look different. They would all be clean shaven, whereas the two men who'd robbed the bank had worn mustaches. Only the driver of the car — if anyone happened to see him — had sported a hairless face.

But the escape precautions did not end at this point. Three men traveling alone, no matter what their description, would certainly be suspect after a bank had been looted by three strangers. Two drop-off points had been marked along the escape route. Jeremy would be dropped off first, carrying the suitcase with the overcoats and the rest of the junk. He would run around to the back of the car and — in the event anyone had caught the license number as they'd driven from the bank — he would take off the phony plate that was taped onto the car's original plate.

Anson would be dropped off two miles later, carrying the suitcase with the money, and also carrying Carl's gun as well as his own. If Carl were stopped after the two men had been dropped off, he'd be clean as a whistle. He was unarmed. There was no loot in the car. There was nothing in the car which could tie him to the holdup. There was no reason to assume he would be stopped, but if he were, he would be a workman in a lumber jacket, returning to the city after a hard day. A rendezvous point, some thousand miles and two weeks away, had been arranged. It looked perfect.

"I'm going to enjoy this money," Carl said.

"Mmmm," Anson said, grinning.

"What will you do with it, Carl?" Jeremy asked, stepping close to the mirror and admiring his masquerade handiwork.

"Spend it," Carl said.

"On what?"

"Women."

"He's a ladies' man," Jeremy said to Anson.

"Damn right, I'm a ladies' man. There isn't anybody in the world who couldn't be a ladies' man with one-third of $500,000."

"That's a mean hunk of cabbage," Anson said.

"I'm getting out of the country with my share," Jeremy said. "Down to Mexico."

"What the hell're you gonna do there?" Anson wanted to know.

"He'll open up a chain of houses."

"The hell I am. I'll just sit around in the sun and have myself a ball, that's all. Nothing to do but soak up sun for the rest of my life."

"I can't go to Mexico," Carl said.

"Why not?"

"I once cooled a Mexican cop. We were running some weed out of Tijuana, and he stepped in and began making noise."

"There are other places besides Tijuana," Anson said.

"Sure, but my face is in every police station in Mexico," Carl said.

"I've got no worries there," Jeremy said.

"Just so you stay out of Kansas City," Anson said.

"I'm not wanted in Kansas City."

"Not by the cops, no," Anson said.

"You talking about Harry Kale?"

"Harry Kale is who I'm talking about."

"Kale doesn't bother me," Jeremy said.

"No, huh?"

"No. He made up all that business. He invented all that statutory rape junk so he could get me out of K.C."

"He did, huh? That sounds screwy, considering it brought the bulls down around his ears."

"He made it all up."

"Well, just stay clear of Kansas City, and you're all right."

"I'm not going anywhere near K.C.," Jeremy said, "but not because Harry Kale scares me. He doesn't scare me at all."

"I once did a job for Harry," Anson said. "In the old days, when we were still running booze. He pays well."

"He doesn't pay the way this job is going to pay," Carl said.

"*Nobody* pays the way this job is going to pay."

"You think we should run through it again?" Jeremy asked.

"Sure," Anson said. "Once more before Carl leaves. We've still got a few minutes, haven't we?"

They ran through the job again, committing it to their separate memories, and then they synchronized their watches with Anson's, which had been set with the bank's clock that morning.

At 1:50, Carl left the room.


The man behind the soda fountain did not recognize him, and he considered that a good omen. He had been secretly afraid that his disguise could be penetrated, but the man behind the counter hadn't given him a second look. To complete the transition of character, and to completely disassociate himself from the Carl Semmer who'd sat at this same counter yesterday and ordered coffee, Carl ordered a cherry Coke. He paid for the Coke when he was served, eliminating any possible delay later when it would be time to leave for the car. He sat sipping his Coke and watching the driveway across the street.

At 2:02, the International Armored Car Corp. truck arrived. He watched the guards as they entered the rear door with the American Steel payroll. At 2:08, they entered the truck, backed it out of the driveway, and drove off. At 2:10, the second armored car appeared. They finished their delivery, and drove off at 2:16. Carl glanced at his watch, checking it against the time on the bank clock, and then relaxed.

"Let me have a newspaper," he said to the man behind the counter.

The man gave him a paper, and Carl paid for it, and then began reading it, glancing across the street every few minutes. Not many people were going into the bank. That was good. Everything was running very smoothly. He was tempted to

call Anson and Jeremy, tell them the loot was there, just waiting to be picked up, but he didn't want to throw them into a
panic. He bided his time instead, aware of the crawling hands
of the clock. At 2:45, he knew Anson and Jeremy were leaving
the room. Carl waited, folding his newspaper, sipping at his
Coke.

At 2:57, he saw them coming down the street. He rose and
walked to the plate-glass door, looking out.

"Hey, mister," the man behind the counter said. Carl
whirled.

"What?"

"You forgot your newspaper."

"Thanks, you can keep it."

He watched Anson and Jeremy as they walked past the
A&P, past the bank driveway, up the flat steps leading to
the entrance doors. The bank guard smiled as they entered the
bank. The clock above the doors read 2:58. Everything was
moving according to schedule. At 3:00 P.M., the guard closed
the big bronze doors. Carl walked out of the shop, turned
right, and headed for the parking lot and the waiting automobile.

"A holdup is in progress," Jeremy said to the bank guard.

"What?" the guard said as he turned away from the doors.
"What are you...?"

"This is a gun in my pocket. Keep quiet and no one will
get hurt. Open your mouth, and the whole place gets shot up."

The guard blinked his eyes and then looked down to the
menacing bulge in Jeremy's pocket. He was tempted for a moment to begin yelling, and then his eyes took in the slicked-
down hair and the pencil-thin mustache, and something
warned him to keep his silence. This man was a killer.

"Don't let anyone else in," Jeremy said. "If anyone wants to go out, let them out. Act the way you always do. No funny business. We'll just stand here and chat as if nothing's happening. Have you got that?"

The bank guard nodded.


"Good afternoon, sir," the bank manager said to Anson. "What can I do for you?"

"I'm carrying a gun," Anson whispered, "and I know how to use it. Get up from that desk and walk back to the vault with me. If anyone looks at you curiously, smile back at them. When we get to the vault, you'll open the door, and we'll go in together. If you so much as look crooked at anybody, you're a dead man. You understand?"

"I…understand," the manager said. He estimated the distance between his foot and the alarm buzzer set in the floor under his desk, and then he estimated the distance between his heart and the gun the redheaded, mustached man held in his pocket. "I…I'll do what you say," he murmured, and he rose from the desk. Anson walked with him to the locked door. The manager signaled to the teller nearest the door, and the teller pushed a button and the door clicked open. The manager and Anson walked back to the vault door. One of the tellers turned to look at the manager, but he smiled and nodded, and the teller went back to his work.

"Open it," Anson whispered.

The manager nodded weakly and began twisting the dials in the face of the huge steel door.

At 3:05, he swung back the door, and he and Anson stepped into the vault. The bank guard, the only other member of the bank's staff who knew that the bank was being held up, watched the manager and the redheaded man enter the vault, and he sighed deeply, and then smiled as he let a customer out of the bank.


Carl sat at the wheel of the car and glanced at his watch.

3:06.

He looked up at the light on the corner of Main and West Davis, and then he watched the sweep hand of his watch as it swung through sixty seconds. At 3:07, the light changed to green and Carl turned the corner and headed for the bank driveway at the end of the street. In four minutes, Anson would be coming out of that door with $500,000 worth of cabbage. In six minutes, Jeremy would be leaving the front of the bank. They'd be gone before anybody inside had sense enough to know what had hit them.

He drove leisurely down the street. There was a line of traffic on the other side of the two-lane street, but there was only one car behind him. He could see the A&P ahead, the driveway on its left. He threw the directional signal shaft up, saw the little light on the dashboard begin blinking intermittently as he prepared for his right turn. He saw the A&P truck then.

The truck had just pulled into the area in front of the driveway, ready to back into a space in front of the supermarket. Anson cursed silently and jammed on the brakes. The truck driver was taking all his damn sweet time, maneuvering the big lumbering machine into position against the curb, its nose jutting out so that it blocked the entrance to the driveway. Carl looked at his watch. 3:09. He had two minutes to get that damned car into the driveway. The man in the car behind him began honking his horn.

"Shut up, you damn fool," Carl said angrily.

It suddenly occurred to him that the man honking his horn behind him was attracting attention. And if anyone looked at Carl's car, they'd automatically figure he was getting ready to turn into the driveway. Where else could he be going? Why else was he waiting for the truck to back up in front of the supermarket?

He stepped on the gas at once, driving to the corner and making a U-turn against the stream of oncoming traffic. He drove down the street again, signaled for a left turn, and headed for the driveway as the truck backed into position in front of the supermarket. It was almost 3:11. Anson would be coming out of that rear door in a few seconds.

"Well, for Christ's sake, move it up a little," he heard the voice at the end of the driveway say.

"Move it where, you damn fool!" a second voice answered.

"Can't you see the driveway?"

"The hell with the driveway. You're backed up too close to this car. I can't get your doors open."

"Oh, hell!" Carl heard the second voice reply, and then his heart lurched into his throat when he heard the truck's motor whine into action again.

Anson stuffed the suitcase rapidly. Bills, more bills than he'd seen in his life. Crisp and green, and smelling of big cars and women and liquor and anything a man wanted.

"Get over there in the corner," he said to the manager.

The manager moved swiftly. Anson kept piling the stacked

and bound bills into the suitcase. His hands moved rapidly, the gun dangling on his forefinger from its trigger guard. He slammed the suitcase shut and glanced at his watch. 3:10.

"Don't start yelling," he said to the manager. "Now that I've got the money, I'm more likely to kill for it."

He stepped quickly to the vault door, put the gun into his coat pocket, slammed the door and whirled the dials, and then walked rapidly to the rear door of the bank, not turning to look behind him.

Jeremy, at the entrance doors, saw Anson come out of the vault and head out of the building. He looked up at the clock on the wall over the tellers' cages. 3:11. Two minutes to go. Two minutes and he would be out of here.

Anson stepped into the driveway, closed the door behind him, and reached for the rear door handle of the car. He opened the door, tossed the suitcase onto the backseat, climbed in after it, and said, "Go, Carl."

"Go where? There's a truck at the other end of the drive!"

Anson whirled on the seat. He spotted the truck. Sweat broke out on his forehead. "Back up," he said. "As far as you can go. I'll get rid of the truck."

"How? What can you...?"

"I don't know! Move! Jerry's comin' out that front door in a minute and a half!"

Carl threw the car into reverse and backed down the driveway.

"More," Anson said.

"I can't go no more. We don't want to block the sidewalk."

"Okay." Anson was already opening the door. "I'll move

the truck. As soon as you're clear, back into the street and over to the front of the bank. I'll catch you."

"How will you...?"

"Go!" Anson snapped, and left the car. He ran directly to the truck, around the front end, and then he climbed into the cab and threw the gears into reverse. He rammed his foot down onto the accelerator, felt the truck lurch backward, heard screams behind him, and then heard the sullen crunch of metal as the truck's doors struck the car parked behind. As he leaped out of the cab, he saw one of the bronze bank doors open, saw Jeremy starting down the steps, heading for the curb. Jeremy's face went pale and his eyes popped wide when he saw the empty space at the curb. He looked back at the bronze doors, and then he wet his lips, his eyes blinking furiously. The car! Where the hell was the goddamn car!

Anson's feet struck the pavement. He heard the car in the driveway grind into gear an instant before Carl stepped on the gas. Jeremy was about to panic, he could see that.

"Jerry!" he yelled. "This way! Quick!"

Jeremy's eyes darted to the street. He saw Anson, and he began to run instantly, and at the same moment the bronze doors swung open and the bank guard shouted, "Stop, thief!"

Jeremy turned blindly, his gun leaping into his hand. He fired at the guard, his head turned, his body moving forward on churning legs.

Anson's eyes widened.

"Jerry! For Christ's sake, watch..."

The car lunged out of the driveway, catching Jeremy on the run. Jeremy screamed, the gun in his hand bucking as his finger closed around the trigger again. He screamed again when the car knocked him to the pavement, and the wheels crushed his body flat.

The bank guard was down the steps now, his gun in his hand. Anson reached the car and pulled open the rear door. The guard sighted carefully, and then he squeezed the trigger as Anson climbed into the car. The shots erupted into the quiet of the small street. Two spurts of dust rose on Anson's back, and then the dust gave way before two rivers of blood. He fell backward, clinging to the center post as the car wheeled into the street and backed for its turn. He lost his grip then, toppling out of the car to fall facedown on the pavement, his back running blood.

*The money,* Carl thought. *The money's still here in the car.* Then the windshield was shattering and he had only a second to realize those were bullet holes before his face crumbled and he lurched forward onto the wheel.

The big day was over.

Tomorrow was payday.

# INNOCENT
# BYSTANDERS

*L*et me tell you how I happened to change my name.

It wasn't that I got irritated by bosun's mates in the Navy stumbling over "Lombino" even before they got to the first vowel. It wasn't even editors calling the agency to ask for "that Italian guy up there." It was a novel titled Don't Crowd Me, and an editor named Charlie Heckelman at a paperback house called Popular Library.

Early in 1952, I had finished, and the agency was marketing, a mystery novel in which an advertising man on vacation in Lake George comes upon a dead body in his cabin and is subsequently blamed for the murder. This was a sort of Innocent Bystander story that became a sort of Man on the Run story, and the byline on it was one of my then still-pseudonyms, Evan Hunter. Well, we sent the book to Popular Library, and Charlie—with whom I'd had business lunches on many an occasion—called to say he liked the book a lot, and would like to buy it, but would like to meet Evan Hunter first to see if he'd agree to some revision suggestions. I ran into Scott's office and told him Charlie Heckelman wanted to meet Evan Hunter! Scott said, "So take Evan Hunter to meet him."

A few days later I went to Charlie's office, and he took one look at me and said, "Where's Evan Hunter?"

"I'm Evan Hunter," I said.

Well, after he got over his surprise, he told me the book was a good one, whoever had written it, and then explained *where he thought it could benefit from a few revisions. He said he thought he could publish it by December of that year if I could get the revisions to him fairly quickly. I told him I thought I could, and then I suggested—since the cat was now out of the bag—that we use the byline S. A. Lombino on it, which was the name I'd used in college on my weekly column for the school newspaper.*

*Charlie looked at me long and hard.*

*"Well," he said, "it's your book, and you can put whatever name you like on it. But I have to tell you...Evan Hunter will sell a lot more tickets."*

*So that's what it's all about, I thought. Never mind Grandpa traipsing all the way from Ruvo del Monte to Naples to get on a ship and sail steerage to America, never mind him getting his "first papers" here and later his citizenship, never mind all those bonfires celebrating freedom on election night, never mind all that Land of the Free and Home of the Brave oratory; if I put S. A. Lombino on a novel, everyone will think it was written in crayon by a ditch digger or a gangster.*

*The very next week, I went downtown with a lawyer and got a court order that legally changed my name. I've been Evan Hunter since May of 1952, longer than I ever was Salvatore Lombino, longer than most of my readers have ever been on this earth. A sure affirmation of the correctness of my decision is that the Internet has never allowed me to forget that once upon a time, long long ago, in a galaxy far far away, I was "that Italian guy" named Salvatore Lombino.*

*Which brings us to the story that follows.*

*By February of 1954, when "Runaway" was first published in Manhunt, the neighborhood I'd lived in until I was twelve had changed drastically enough so that I could use it as the setting for the tale of an Innocent Bystander who becomes a Man on the Run. But even before the story was published, I had already changed the hero's name from Johnny Trachetti to Johnny Lane, radically changed the setting from Italian Harlem to what was then called Negro Harlem, expanded the story into a novel, and submitted it to Gold Medal Books, who published the longer version in July as Runaway Black, the new title I'd given the novel. I was enormously pleased when one reviewer thought the Harlem background rang so true because Richard Marsten was undoubtedly a black man!*

*But the tale does not end there.*

*Years later, when a new paperback edition of the book was being planned by a publisher who shall go unnamed, I received a proof of the cover, and was shocked to see that the word "Black" had been dropped from the title. The book was now simply called Runaway, even though the lead character was now black and the setting was now black Harlem. I thought I'd entered a time warp. So I asked them how come. They told me that Runaway Black was a "racist" title. Racist! I told them that I had proved my credentials forever with The Blackboard Jungle, wherein Gregory Miller, a black kid (later played brilliantly on the screen by Sidney Poitier) was the god-damn hero, and if they didn't want to use my title on the book, they could have their money back and forget publishing it altogether! Guess what? They took back their money.*

*This, then, is my first run at "Runaway," with its original title and its original setting (the neighborhood I grew up in) and its original Johnny Trachetti—an innocent bystander if ever I saw one.*

# Runaway

BECAUSE THE NEIGHBORHOOD HAD INGRAINED FEAR SO deeply inside him, he ran the instant he heard the shots.

He did not stop to wonder where the shots had come from. Shots meant trouble, and trouble meant cops, and in this neighborhood you ran when the cops came.

He cut down First Avenue, past the coal yards, past the corner bar, and then turned left on 119th Street, heading for Pleasant Avenue and then down toward the river. He didn't stop running until he reached a bench on the Drive, and then he sat and looked uptown to where the Triboro arched its silvery sleek back against the sky. There was a football game today at Randall's Island. He had seen the college girls, nubby-looking in their tweeds, and the men with pipes and porkpie hats, walking across the bridge earlier that day. They were like invaders from another world. They did not belong in the neighborhood, and he resented them.

He had been sitting on the bench for ten minutes when Snow White and the two cops pulled up. The white top of the squad car reflected the brilliant October sun, and it struck the old panic within him, but there was no place to go except the river, so he sat still and bulled it through. He heard the car

315

doors slam shut with the solidity of bank vault doors, heard the empty, hollow clatter of the cops' shoes on the pavement, and then saw shadows, long and thin in the afternoon sun, fall across the bench.

"Watching the water?" one cop asked.

He looked up, trying to feign surprise.

"Yeah," he said, his voice trembling a little. "I've been watching the water."

"We got a dead man," the second cop said drily.

He blinked up at the cop, condemning himself for feeling guilty when he was completely innocent.

"A dead man?" he said. "Yeah?"

"This is all news to you, huh?" the first cop said.

"Yeah. Yeah, it is."

"He got it with a zip gun, this guy," the cop went on. "You ever own a zip gun?"

"No," he lied. He had owned a zip gun once, before the cops had begun giving the gangs a lot of trouble. He had ditched the gun then, together with a knife that was over the legal limit in blade size.

"You never owned one, huh?" the cop said drily.

"No, never," he lied again.

"You know a guy called Angelo?" He knew instantly that it was Angelo Brancusi they were speaking of. He wet his lips. "Lots of guys named Angelo," he said.

"Only one guy named Angelo Brancusi. You know him?"

"I know him," he said. "Sure. Everybody knows him."

"But you particularly, huh?"

"Why me, particularly?"

"Maybe because your name is Johnny Trachetti."

"That's my name," he said. "What's this all about?"

"Maybe because Angelo tried to rape your kid sister, say two or three weeks ago. Maybe, let's say, you and Angelo had a big tangle outside the RKO on 125th, with Angelo pulling homemade brass knucks and trying to rip your face apart with them. Maybe that's why you know him particularly, huh, boy?"

"Angelo tried to work over lots of guys. Everybody knows his brass knucks. He made 'em from a garbage can handle. Besides, he stayed away from me since that time near the RKO. Angelo don't bother me or my sister anymore."

"You're right there, boy," the first cop said.

"What do you mean?"

"Angelo ain't bothering anybody anymore," the cop said. "It was Angelo who got zip-gunned."

He wet his lips again. Out on the river a tug sent a blast to the sky, high and strident. The blast hung on the silence of the October air, and he could almost taste the brackishness of the river.

"I didn't shoot him," he said.

"I know," the first cop told him. "That's why you ran like a rat when we came on the scene."

"Look," he said, appealing to their common sense now, "I didn't shoot him. I didn't like him, but there was lots of guys didn't like him. Look, why should I shoot him? Hey, come on, you don't really think..."

He saw the look in the first cop's eyes. That same look was mirrored on the second cop's face. He saw, too, the irrefutable logic there. Angelo had been gunned down. Angelo was scum, but he was a citizen of this fair city. Someone had gunned him, and it was like tagging someone for a parking violation. Some big boy upstairs would raise six kinds of hell if this sort of thing went on, people cluttering up the streets with worthless garbage like Angelo. There was only one way to handle a case of this exceptional caliber. Pull in the nearest sucker. Take Johnny because he was as neat a patsy as the next guy, all made to order with an attempted rape on his sister, and a knock-down-drag-out right on 125th, where Angelo had done his best to kill him.

Whatever you do, avoid trouble on your beat. Squelch trouble on your beat. Step on trouble.

Step on Johnny Trachetti.

He read the logic. You can't fight logic. He didn't try to.

He brought his knee up into the groin of the first cop, and then clobbered him on the back of the head with both hands squeezed together like the head of a mallet. The cop fell to the pavement like a pile of manure, and his buddy unsnapped the Police Special hanging in the holster near his right buttock. The shot rang out on the crisp autumn air, but Johnny was already behind the squad car, ducking around the grille, heading for the door near the driver's seat. He knew it was crazy, and he knew you didn't go around driving cops' cars, but taking the rap for Angelo's kill was just as nuts, and he had nothing to lose now, not after the logic he had read.

He heard the second shot, and the third one, but he was already behind the wheel, his head ducked low, his hand releasing the emergency brake, his foot on the accelerator. The car leaped ahead, and then the shots came like bursts from a tommy gun, fast and sharp, pinging against the sides of the car.

He heard the first cop banging his nightstick against the pavement, and the pounding was as loud and as frightening as the bark of the other cop's gun. The last bullet found one of the rear tires, and the car lurched crazily, but he held on to the wheel and kept his foot pressed to the floor, and the rubber flapped and beat the asphalt as he headed for 116th. The cop had stopped to reload, and by the time the next shots came, he couldn't have hit him if he'd been using a bazooka. He drove down to the York Avenue exit, wondering whether or not he should turn on the siren, a little excited about all of it now, a little reckless-feeling.

He ditched the car, and then ran like a thief up to First Avenue, cutting back uptown. He reached 116th Street, wondered where he should go then. Back home? That was the first place they'd look.

He stood on the corner, looking up toward the Third Avenue El, wondering. When he saw the squad car pull around Second Avenue, he made up his mind, and he made it up fast.

He didn't run this time. He walked casually, his head turned toward the shop windows that lined the wide street. The corset shop was in the middle of the street, between Second and Third. The plate-glass window carried the fancy legend FOUNDATION GARMENTS, but everybody knew this was the corset shop, and everybody knew it was run by Gussie the Corset Lady.

He walked into the shop quickly. The front room was stacked with dummies wearing brassieres and girdles and corsets and contraptions he couldn't name. He'd worked for Gussie a long time ago, when he was fifteen, delivering the garments to fat women who should have ordered pants with zippers instead. He heard the hum of the sewing machine in the back room, and he looked out at the street once and then parted the flowered curtains and stepped out of sight.

Gussie looked up from the machine. She was a tall woman in her early fifties, with large brown eyes and full, sensuous lips. She wore her own foundation garments, and she was wearing one now that bunched her full breasts up into the low yoke of her neckline, like the heroine on the jacket of a historical novel.

"Well!" she said. "Who's after you?"

"The cops," Johnny said quickly.

She'd been smiling, but the smile dropped from her face now. "What do you mean, the cops? What for?"

"They say I killed Angelo Brancusi."

"He's dead?" Gussie asked. She nodded her head emphatically. "Good. He deserved it."

"Yeah, but I didn't do it."

"I didn't say you did. No matter who did it, he deserved it."

Johnny glanced through the curtains and out at the street again. "I ran away from them," he said. "They were planning a run-through. I don't like working on a railroad."

"You shouldn't have run. That was stupid."

"All right, it was stupid. You didn't see their eyes."

Gussie stared at him contemplatively for a few moments. "Why'd you come to me?" she asked.

"Just to get off the streets. You don't have to worry, I'm leaving."

Gussie's face was worried now.

"What are you going to do?" she asked.

"I don't know. How do I know? Just stay away from them for now, that's all."

"And then what?"

"Somebody killed Angelo," he said. "That's for sure."

"They'll catch you," she said. "And it'll be worse because you ran away."

"I also slugged a cop and stole a squad car. I got nothin' to lose now."

"Stay until dark," Gussie said suddenly. "Stay here in the back."

"Thanks," he said.

"I'm only saving my own skin. If the cops think..."

"Don't spoil it," Johnny said. "I was beginning to think you were human."

"Go to hell, you snot nose," Gussie said, but she was smiling.


He saw the lights come on in the church across the street, saw the streetlamps throw their dim rays into the gathering October darkness. The clock on the wall in Gussie's front room read five ten. The lights all along the street came on, warm yellow lights that built a solid, cozy front against the crisp near-winter blackness.

"You'd better get started," she said. "We're lucky they haven't been here yet."

"I ditched the car on York," he told her. "They probably figure I headed downtown."

"Go through the back way," Gussie said. "You can cut through the yard and climb the fence. That way you'll come out on a Hun' fifteenth. Less lights."

"All right," he said. He hesitated, biting his lip. "You got money?"

"A little."

Gussie walked to a chair and unhooked a black leather purse from where it hung. "This'll help a little. Things haven't been too good lately."

She handed him the sawbuck, and he hesitated before taking it. "You don't have to…"

"Angelo broke my window once," she said simply.

"Well, thanks a lot."

She nodded and he left by the back door, cutting into the concrete alleyway behind the apartment building. He knew there would be steps now leading to the sidewalk. He remembered the times when he and the other kids used to duck down behind the steps like this on his own block, whenever they were too busy or too rushed to look for a toilet.

He passed the garbage cans and the familiar sharp stench. It was dark there where the steps dropped down into the bowels of the tenement. He saw the iron railing up ahead of him on the sidewalk, and the dangling chain that was supposed to stop kids from parading up and down the steps, but which only served as an impromptu swing. He started up the steps, and when he collided with the other man he almost shrieked in terror.

He heard a dull clatter as something dropped to the steps and then rolled away into the blackness near the garbage cans. His fists balled immediately and he waited, hearing the other man's hoarse breathing. He figured the guy for a wino or a stumblebum, or maybe a degenerate.

"You damn fool," the man said. He still could not see his face. He heard only the hoarse breathing, saw only the dim outline of the man in the feeble glow of the streetlight which filtered down onto the steps below the building.

"Where'd it go?" the man asked.

"Where'd what go?" he heard himself answer.

"You damn fool," the man cursed again. He pushed back past Johnny, dropped to his hands and knees, and began scrambling around near the garbage cans. Johnny looked at him for a moment, and then wondered, What the hell am I standing around for? He started up the steps, heard the movement behind him, and then felt the wiry fingers clamp onto his shoulder.

"Just a second, punk," the man said. "If you broke that syringe, then you're going to pay for it." He pulled Johnny back down the steps and Johnny stumbled.

"You think syringes grow on trees? I had to swipe this one from a doctor's bag."

Johnny got up and moved toward the steps again, and the man slammed him back against the wall. He was a big man, with arms like oaks and a head like a bullet. His eyes gleamed dully in the darkness. "I said stay where you are," he said.

He shoved Johnny back into the alley, blocking him from the steps, and then he reached down for something that glittered near one of the garbage cans.

"You did it, punk," he said. "You broke the damn thing."

Johnny saw the jagged shards of the syringe in the man's open hand. And then the fingers of the hand closed around the syringe, hefting it like a knife, with the glass ends crooked and sharp.

"You shouldn't have been shooting up down here," Johnny said lamely. "I didn't even see you. I..."

"How much money you got, punk?" the man said.

"Nothing," Johnny lied.

"Suppose we see," the man said, advancing with the broken shards of the syringe ahead of him.

"Suppose we don't?" Johnny answered, planting his feet, and tightening his fists.

"A smart guy, huh? Break the damn syringe, and then pull a wise-o. I don't like smart guys. If you done something you pay for it, that's my motto."

He stepped closer, reaching for Johnny, and Johnny lashed out with his right fist catching the man solidly on his chest. The man staggered back, raising the hand with the syringe high. The streetlight caught the syringe, gave it up to the darkness again as it slashed downward and up. Johnny felt the ragged glass ends when they struck his wrist. He tried to pull his hand back, but the biting glass followed his arm, ripping the thin sleeve of his Eisenhower jacket, the jacket his brother had brought home in the last war. The glass ripped skin clear to his elbow and he felt the blood begin pouring down his arm and he cursed the addict, and brought back his left hand balled at the same time, throwing it at the addict's head.

He felt his knuckles collide with the bridge of the man's nose, felt bone crush inward and then the face fell away and back, slamming down against the concrete with the syringe shattering into a thousand brittle pieces now. Now that it was too late. He stepped around the man, and the man moved, and Johnny kicked him in the temple, wanting to knock his head off.

There was pain in his arm, and the blood had soaked through the thin sleeve of his jacket. He touched the arm and felt the blood, and when his hand came away sticky he felt a twinge of panic.

He stood at the base of the steps, wanting to kill the addict, wanting to really kill him.

He kicked him again, happy when he heard the sound of his shoe thudding against bone.

What do I do now? he wondered.

He needed a doctor, but a doctor was out. What about a druggist? What about Frankie Shea who worked for Old Man Sinisi? What about him? Did Frankie owe him a favor?

No, Frankie did not owe him a favor, Frankie did not owe him the sweat from his armpits. But they'd grown up together, had lighted bonfires together on election eve, had thrown snowballs together, had roasted spuds together when there used to be the empty lot behind Grandoso's Grocery. You figure maybe a guy will do you a favor when your arm is running off into the gutter.

He waited until the drugstore was empty. He knew Old Man Sinisi left the store to Frankie every night after supper, leaving him just enough cash in the register to handle the few sales that piddled in before closing time. So there was no danger there. When the store was empty he walked in, and the bell over the door sounded loudly in the warm, antiseptic stillness. He walked straight behind the counter, running into Frankie as he started to come around front.

"Let's stay back here," he whispered.

"Johnny! The cops are..."

"It's around already, huh?"

"Johnny, you should never have come here. Why'd you come here? Want to get me in trouble?"

"I want my arm bandaged. And something to stop the pain."

Frankie looked at the bleeding arm and his face went white. "How'd that happen? You...you kill somebody else, Johnny? You..."

"I ain't killed nobody yet. Look, Frankie, fix it for me, will you? You work in a drugstore, you know the ropes. Just a bandage, and something smeared on the cut, that's all."

"I ain't a doctor, Johnny. Hell, I just work here."

"You can fix it. I'll rip your eyes out if you don't."

Frankie stared at him levelly. "Come on in back," he said.

They were in the back of the shop now, in the darkened corner where the retorts and measures rested on a long brown table. Johnny sat and took off his jacket. The cut was worse than he'd thought it was. It spread on his arm in a jagged red streak. He looked at it, and was almost sick, and the pale cast to Frankie's face told him he was almost sick, too.

"I...I got to go...go get some bandages," he said. "Out front. I...I'll be right back, Johnny."

"Hurry up," Johnny said.

Frankie went and he sat and looked at the wall of the back room, at the bottles of pills and powder with the strange, dangerous-sounding names.

He sat waiting, and it wasn't until five minutes had passed that he realized Frankie Shea was taking a damned long time to get a roll of bandage from the shelves out front. A damned long time, and then he remembered there were phone booths just inside the entrance doorway, and he also remembered the time Frankie Shea had ducked out on him, the time the cops had caught them sticking NRA tags on the fenders and bodies of parked cars, gluing them to the metal surface.

Frankie had left him to talk to the cops that time, and whereas that was a long time ago, guys don't usually change a hell of a lot.

Hastily, Johnny slipped into his soggy jacket.

When Frankie came to the back of the store ten minutes later, the cops behind him with drawn guns, Johnny was already gone. There was only a pool of blood on the table to testify to the fact that he'd been there at all.

The Grand was on 125th Street, just between Lexington and Third avenues. It showed the movies the RKO Proctor's didn't run, and it was there that Johnny went, taking a seat near the back, favoring his right arm by leaning over to the left and cradling the gashed wrist and forearm in his lap. The 3-D glasses they had given him were lying useless on his lap, alongside his cradled arm. Without the glasses, the screen was a distorted hodgepodge of color, but Johnny hadn't come here to catch up on the latest Hollywood attempt. He'd come to get a breather.

"You ain't even watching the picture," the girl said.

He turned abruptly, startled, ready to run. The girl was no more than twenty. She wore a white sweater that was filled to capacity. He could see that even in the dark. She was blonde and pretty, he supposed, in a brassy, hard way. He couldn't make out her features too clearly, except for the vivid slash of lipstick across her mouth, and the glow on the whites of her eyes reflected from the screen.

"No, I ain't," he said. He hadn't even noticed the girl sitting there, and he wondered now when she'd come in. She reeked of cheap perfume but there was something exciting about the perfume and her nearness.

"These 3-D things are good," she said, taking the glasses from his lap, her hand long and tapering, brushing against his arm. "Supposed to put these Hollywood women right in your arms. Don't you go for Hollywood women right in your arms?"

"I...look, I'm busy," he said.

"Too busy to watch the picture?"

He felt an instant panic. Had she heard about him? Did she know he was the one the cops wanted?

"Yes," he said slowly, "too busy."

"Too busy for other things, too?"

He caught the pitch then, and an idea began kicking around in the back of his mind. "Things like what?" he asked.

"Things like a way to kill the night. Better than doing eye muscle tricks in a movie."

"How?" he asked.

"A room on Lex. Not the Waldorf but clean sheets. A bottle, if you can afford it. And a price that's right."

"Like?" His mind was racing ahead now. A room on Lex, away from the eyes of the cops, more time to think, more time to work it out.

"Like seven-fifty for all night. Plus the bottle. You got seven-fifty?" she asked.

"I've got seven-fifty," he whispered.

"Don't let the price fool you. It's quality merchandise, germ-free. I'm feeling generous."

"You're on," he said, making up his mind.

He saw her grin in the darkness. "I knew you was an intellectual," she said. "Come on."

They moved out of the row into the aisle, and she started for the rear of the theater.

"This way," he said. "We'll use the exit down front."

"You ashamed or something?" she asked, her hands on her hips.

He decided to give it to her straight. "I got in a fight. My arm is bleeding. I don't want to attract attention."

She stared at him for a few moments, and then said, "Okay. Come on. Down front."

He gave her money for a jug and then he waited in the darkness of a hallway while she bought it in a brilliantly lighted liquor store. When she came back, she walked on the side of his wounded arm, blocking it effectively from inquisitive eyes.

They walked in silence to a brownstone set next to a delicatessen. She led him up the steps then, and opened the wooden door to her room. It was a small room with a bare bulb hanging overhead and a dresser in one corner. A bed occupied most of the room, and there was a table with an enamel washbasin on a stand alongside the bed.

"Like I said," she told him, "it ain't the Waldorf."

She was not as big as he'd thought she was in the movies. She was, in fact, almost small, except for the breasts that crowded the woolen sweater.

"Which shall we treat first? The arm or the gullet?"

"Have a drink, if you want," he said. "I can wait."

"Yeah, but you're bleeding on my imported Persian rug." She grinned and went to the dresser, taking out a bottle of peroxide and a roll of gauze. She brought him to the basin, rolled up his sleeve, and then said, "You run into a buzz saw?"

"No, a hophead."

"Same thing," she said pouring the peroxide onto the wound.

He winced, holding back the scream that bubbled onto his lips.

"You got glass in there," she said.

"Pull it out, if you can."

She looked at him curiously. "Sure," she said. She wrapped absorbent cotton around a toothpick and then began fishing for the glass splinters. Each time she got one, he clamped down on his teeth hard, and finally it was all over. She drenched the arm in peroxide again, and then wrapped the gauze around it, so tight that he could feel the veins throbbing against the thin material.

"That rates a swallow," she said. She broke the seal on the fifth, poured whiskey for them both into water glasses, and handed him one. "Here's to the hophead," she said.

"May he drop dead," Johnny answered, tossing off the drink. It burned a hole clear down to his stomach and he remembered abruptly that he hadn't eaten for a good long while.

The girl took another drink, and then put the glass and the bottle on the dresser top again. "Well, now," she said. "Let's try and forget that arm, shall we?"

She moved closer to him, and he thought, The hell with the cops, the hell with Angelo, the hell with everyone. The sweater moved in on him, warm and high, soft, beating with the soft muted beat of her heart beneath the wool and the flesh. He pulled her to him, his head pressed tight against the wool.

"Easy now," she said, chiding, smiling. "Easy now, boy. Slow and easy."

A knock sounded on the door.

She broke away from him, and he leaped to his feet.

"Who…" he whispered.

More knocking.

"Get in the closet!"

"The clos…?"

"Go on, move," she whispered urgently.

He went to the closet, thinking, Why's she acting like an unfaithful wife? feeling foolish as hell, feeling like the jackass in some low comedy of errors. The closet door closed on him, leaving him in darkness, leaving him with trailing silk dresses flapping around his face, high-heeled shoes crushed under his big feet. He could not stop feeling foolish, and then he heard the outside door open, and the man's voice.

"What took you so long, Bess?"

"Oh, hello, Tony. I was…napping."

Why? Johnny thought. Why that? Why didn't she say, I've got someone with me, Tony. Come back later, come back in the morning. Why the runaround?

"Napping, huh?" The voice was a big voice. It belonged to a big man. It belonged to a suspicious man. Johnny did not like that voice, and the voice was in the room now, moving in from the outside door.

"What's this?" the voice asked.

"What? What's what, Tony?"

"This jacket. You wearing Army jackets now, Bess? That what you doing?"

"Tony…"

"Just shut up! Where is he?"

"Where's who? Tony, I was just taking a nap. The jacket belongs…belongs to…a fellow came to fix the plumbing. He must have left it here. The plumbing leaked. He…"

"Did the plumbing leak blood? Did it leak blood in that basin there?"

"Tony…"

"You're a slut," he shouted. "I'm going to break that guy in two! Where is he?"

"I told you, Tony. There's no one…"

"And I told you! I told you what would happen if I caught you up to your old tricks again. Where is he?"

The footsteps were advancing across the room now, and it was a cinch Tony would look in the closet first. He dropped to his knees quickly, rooting around on the closet floor for a shoe. He found a sturdy-feeling job with a spike heel, and he got to his feet again and waited.

"You got him in the closet?" the voice asked, close now. And then the door opened on Johnny, and the shaft of light spilled onto his face. He didn't hesitate an instant. He brought the shoe up, catching Tony on the bridge of his nose.

Tony was big all right, big and bearded, wearing a leather jacket and corduroy slacks. The shoe caught him on his nose, and the line of blood appeared magically, and then he stumbled backward. Johnny swung out with his left hand, catching Tony in the gut. He hit him again with the shoe, and as Tony went down, he heard the girl screaming, screaming, her voice like an air-raid siren. She dropped to her knees beside Tony, took his head into her lap, and then looked up at Johnny.

"You crumb!" she shrieked. "You filthy crumb! He's my brother! He's my brother!"

Johnny was already halfway to the door.

"My brother!" she kept screaming, and he didn't hang around to listen to the encore. He ran down the steps and out into the street, a little sorry Tony had arrived when he had, and a little sorry he'd left an almost full fifth of good whiskey in the room.

The fifth had cost him close to four bucks. Well, he'd got a bandage for his arm out of it, if nothing else. It didn't seem to matter at the moment that blood was already beginning to seep through the bandage again.

Detective-Sergeant Leo Palazzo lived in the Bronx. He did not particularly like Harlem, even though he'd been a cop there for sixteen years.

He was holding in his hands now a signed confession from a punk they'd had in before on a possessions charge.

The punk's name was Andrew Ryan. They'd picked him up on 117th Street and they'd found him with a zip gun and they'd worked him over hardly fifteen minutes before he'd told them everything they wanted to know.

The only thing they really wanted to know was whether or not he'd put a few holes in the liver and heart of Angelo Brancusi. And whereas Ryan was extremely reticent in the beginning he loosened up almost instantly and seemed almost proud of his shooting prowess. A stenographer had worked up a literate-sounding confession and Ryan had scrawled his signature to it, and that had been that. Except for Johnny Trachetti.

"What about the other guy?" Corporal Davis asked Palazzo.

"What other guy?" Palazzo said.

"The one slugged Brown and swiped the RMP. Him."

"Forget him," Palazzo said. "He's clean, ain't he?"

"Yeah, but I mean..."

"We really ought to drag him in on a resisting arrest charge, not to mention the theft of the car. Teach him a lesson."

"He was probably scared," Davis said. "Hell, you'd have run, too."

"When he knows the heat's off he'll come out in the open again."

"You really going to pull him in?"

"No, the hell with him. We got this Ryan character, that's all we need."

Davis wiped a hand over his face. "What I mean, Leo, shouldn't we wise the kid up? You know, he still thinks he's got a murder rap hanging over his head."

"So what?" Palazzo asked.

"Well, hell, he's out there someplace thinking..."

"Who cares what the hell he's thinking? He probably done something anyway, the way he ran."

"Suppose he does something else? He thinks he's wanted for murder, Leo, don't you understand?"

"He'll live," Palazzo said. "He's healthy, ain't he? He's young. He's sound of mind and body. From the way Brown tells me he ran, he must be a hardy specimen."

"A murder rap..." Davis said.

"Murder rap, shmurder rap. So long as you got your health," Palazzo cracked.

The arm began bleeding in earnest. It started as a slow trickle of blood that oozed its way through the fresh bandage. But the trickle became a stream, and the stream soaked through the bandage and dripped onto Johnny's wrist, and the drops ran into his cupped palm, hung on his fingertips, and then spattered onto the sidewalk in a crimson trail.

It got colder, too, and he missed his jacket, and he cursed himself for not having grabbed it when he'd left the girl's room. With her screaming like that, though, it's a wonder he managed to remember his head even. Still, it was goddamn cold, too cold for October, too cold even for January.

The trail of blood led from Lexington Avenue down to Third Avenue, past the lighted fronts of the furniture stores, past the all-night restaurants and the bakeries that served coffee from big shining urns. He was very conscious of the blood trail, and he wondered if city cops ever used bloodhounds. All he needed was a pack of mutts chasing down Third Avenue after him. He smiled, the picture striking him somehow as amusing. He could almost see his photo in the *Daily News*, Johnny Trachetti up a lamppost, his pants seat torn to shreds while the mutts stood up on their hind legs and barked and snapped. Caption: *Killer at Bay*.

Bay, you know. The hounds baying, you know?

Very funny, he told himself, but you couldn't wrap a joke around your back, and a laugh wouldn't stop the wind, and the wind was sure cold.

Nor could corny humor hold back the flow of blood from his arm.

Right now, he needed a place for the night.

He remembered the warehouse just off Third Avenue, where the furniture store kept all the new goods. There was a window the guys used to sneak in through, where one of the bars was loose and capable of being swung out of position. They'd taken Carmen Diaz there once when they were all around sixteen and they'd had a jolly old time on the mats the movers used to wrap around the furniture. He wouldn't forget that time so easily because it had been his first time. Nor would he forget how they had gotten into the warehouse, because that had been the trickiest part.

He ducked off Third Avenue now, and into the darkness of the side street. There was no one in sight, and he scaled the fence rapidly and then went directly to the window with the loose bar.

He tried all the bars, beginning to lose hope, and then suddenly happy when the fifth one came free under his hands. He moved the bar to one side, jimmied open the window, and then squeezed through the opening. It was a tighter fit than it had been when he was sixteen, but he made it and dropped to the concrete floor, reaching up to close the window behind him.

He found the old iron stairwell and took that up to the third floor where he knew all the mats would be. When he heard the voices, he turned around and was ready to run, but they'd already spotted him.

"Hold it, Mac," one of them said.

A watchman, he thought.

He froze solid because there was no sense in running now. Maybe he could bull it through, and if not he still had a good left arm, and he still knew how to throw a fist.

The man moved closer to him, a big man in the near darkness.

"Whatta you want, Mac?" he asked.

"You the watchman?" Johnny asked.

The big man laughed. "A watchman, huh? A watchman? You on the bum, too, kid?"

He felt immensely relieved all at once, so relieved that he almost smiled. "Yeah," he said, "I'm on the bum."

"Come on in. You want a cup of java?"

"Man, I could use some," he said. The big man laughed again and reached out for Johnny's arm. He tried to pull it away, but he wasn't quick enough, and he winced in pain, and the big man looked at his sticky fingers.

"You hurt, huh, kid?" he asked. There was no sympathy in his voice. There was instead a crafty sound, as if the man had made a very valuable discovery and was hoarding it under the floorboards of his mind.

"Come on," he said, his voice oily now. "We'll get you that java."

He led Johnny to the circle of men huddled in one corner of the huge concrete-floored room. An electric grill was plugged into an outlet, and a battered coffeepot rested on the glowing orange coils. Johnny looked at the circle of bearded faces, four men all told, five counting the big man who'd led him to the group. The men were smiling, but there was no mirth on their faces. His arm dripped blood onto the concrete floor and the eyes calculated the dripping, and then shifted back to his face, the smiles still on the mouths, but never reaching the calculating eyes.

"Who you brung for dinner, Bugs?" one of the men asked.

"A nice young punk," the big man answered. "Hurt his poor little arm, though, didn't you, sonny?"

Johnny wet his lips. "Yeah, I...I got cut."

"Well, now, that's too bad, punk," one of the men in the circle said. "Now that's too bad you got a cut on your arm."

"Maybe we got a nurse here can fix it up," another man said.

"Sure, we got a lot of nurses here, kid. We'll fix you up fine, kid. Here, have some coffee."

He wasn't sure now. He wasn't sure what they meant, and he wasn't sure whether they intended him harm or whether they were giving him sanctuary. He knew only that there were five of them and that he had only one good arm.

One of the men poured the coffee into a tin cup, and the strong aroma reached his nostrils, clung there. He wanted that coffee very badly, he wanted it almost desperately. The man handed the cup to Bugs, and the steam rose in the orange glow of the grill.

Bugs said, facing Johnny squarely now, "You want the coffee, punk?"

"I'd like a cup," Johnny said warily.

"You got money to pay for it, punk?" Bugs asked. Maybe that was it. Maybe all they wanted was money. But suppose...

"No," Johnny lied. "I'm broke."

"Well now, ain't that a shame?" Bugs said, winking again at the other men. "How you 'spect to get any coffee unless you pay for it? Coffee don't grow on trees now, does it?"

"I guess not," Johnny said slowly. "Forget the coffee. I'll do without."

"Now, now," Bugs said, "no need to take that attitude, is there, boys? We're willing to barter. You know how to horse-trade, punk?"

"I don't want the coffee," Johnny said firmly. He was already figuring how he'd make his break because he knew a break was in the cards, and the way the cards were falling he'd have to make the break soon.

Johnny wet his lips and moved closer to the glowing grill.

Bugs kept eyeing him steadily, the vacuous, stupid smile on his face.

"All right," Johnny said nervously. "Give me the cup."

Bugs extended the steaming tin cup. "That's a good little punk," he said. "That's the way we like it. No fuss and no muss. Now go ahead and drink your coffee, punk. Drink it all down fine. Go ahead, punk."

He handed the cup to Johnny, and Johnny felt the hot liquid through the tin of the container and then he moved. He threw the coffee into Bugs's face, lashing out with his left hand. He heard Bugs scream as the hot liquid scalded him and then Johnny's foot lashed out for the grill, kicking wildly at it, hooking the metal under the glowing coils. The grill leaped into the air like a flashing comet, hung suspended hot at the end of its wire, and then the wire pulled free of the outlet, and the grill glowed for an instant and then began to dwindle, its coils turning pale.

He was already running. Bugs was screaming wildly behind him, and he heard footsteps, and he heard another scream and knew that the wildly kicked grill had burned someone else. He headed for the steps, with the sounds angry behind him, the footsteps thudding against the bare floor. His own feet hit the iron rungs of the stairs, the echoes clattering up the stairwell, down, down to the main floor and then across the darkened room with the piled, dusty furniture, the shouts and cries behind him all the way. He leaped up for the window, jimmied it open, and then shoved the loose bar aside.

"I'll kill the louse!" he heard Bugs shout but he was already outside and sprinting for the fence. He jumped up, forced to use both arms, with the blood smearing across the fence in a wild streak. And then he was over, just as Bugs squeezed through the bars and ran for the fence. He was tired, very tired. His arm hurt like hell, and his heart exploded against his rib cage, and he knew he couldn't risk a prolonged chase because Bugs would surely catch him.

He was at the corner now and Bugs still hadn't reached the fence. He spotted the manhole and he ran for it quickly, stooping down and expertly prying open the lid with his fingers. He'd been down manholes before. He'd been down them when the kids used to play stickball and a ball rolled down the sewer and the only way to get it was by prying open the manhole cover and catching it before it got washed away to the river. He was in the manhole now, and he slid the cover back in place, hearing it wedge firmly in the caked dirt, soundlessly settling back into position. He clung to the iron brackets set into the wall of the sewer, and he could hear the rush of water far below where the sewer elbowed into the pipes. There was noise above him, the noise of feet trampling on the iron lid of the manhole. He held his breath because there was no place to go from here, no place at all. The footsteps clattered overhead and the iron lid rattled and then the footsteps were gone.

He waited until he heard more footsteps, figured them to belong to Bugs's followers.

He was safe. They didn't realize he'd ducked into the manhole. They were probably scouting Third Avenue for him now and they'd give up when they figured they'd lost him.

To play it doubly sure, he edged his way down deeper into the sewer, holding on to the iron brackets with his good hand. The stench of garbage and filthy water reached up to caress his nostrils. He was tempted to move up close to the lid again but it was darker down below and if someone did lift the lid, chances were he wouldn't be seen if he went deeper.

The walls around him were slimy and wet, and they smelled, too, or at least he thought they did. His nose was no longer capable of determining the direction of the stink. It was all around him, like a soggy vile blanket. He felt nauseous and he didn't know whether the nausea came from his dripping arm or the dripping slime of the sewer.

He only knew that he was safe here, and that Bugs and the boys were upstairs, and so he descended deeper until the elbow of the sewer was just beneath his feet and he could hear the rush of water loud beneath him.

He was very weary, more weary than he'd been in all his life. The weight of the entire city seemed to press down on him, as if all the concrete and steel were concentrated on this one hole in the asphalt, determined to crush it into the core of the earth.

He hooked his left arm into one of the brackets, and he hung there like a Christ with one arm free. The free arm dangled at his right side, the bandage soaked through now, the blood running down and dropping into the rushing water below.

Drop by drop, it hit the slimy surface of the brown water while Johnny hung from the rusted iron bracket praying no one would lift the manhole cover. Drop by drop, it mingled with the brown water, flowed into the elbow where manhole joined sewer pipe, rushed toward the river, bright red on the brown, rushed with the water carrying the smell of fresh blood.

And the rat clinging to the rotted orange crate lodged in the sewer pipe turned glittering bright eyes toward the man-hole opening, and his nostrils twitched as he smelled the blood. His teeth gnashed before he plunged into the water and swam toward the source of the blood.

Marie Trachetti got the news from Hannihan, the cop on the beat. She threw on her high school jacket and went into the streets looking for Johnny.

She had known from the moment Angelo got shot that Johnny would be tagged with it. She had known, and she had sought him then, hoping to warn him, but she had not found him, and the next thing she knew a search was out for him and he was suspected of the killing.

All that was over and done with now. This Ryan fellow had confessed to shooting Angelo, a crime for which he should have been awarded a medal. But Johnny was clear now, and Johnny had to be told, and so Marie took to the streets in search of him.

She did not, in all truth, know where to look for him. Johnny and she did not run in the same circles. She had her friends, and he had his, and except for that run-in with Angelo, their separate social paths hardly ever crossed.

She started looking in the pool parlors and when she had no luck there, she tried the movies. She met some of Johnny's friends but none of them had seen him, and so she tried all the restaurants, walking up 125th Street and then down Lexington Avenue.

From Lexington Avenue, she walked down to Third, frightened because it was very late at night and because she knew she was an attractive girl in a dark, exotic-looking way. Her brush with Angelo had taught her that.

The sidewalks seemed to be darker than the gutter, and so

she stayed in the middle of the street, looking from side to side as she made her way from the corner, hoping to spot Johnny huddled in one of the doorways.

She was wearing high heels, the shoes she wore at her after-school job in the delicatessen. Her heels clattered on the iron top of a manhole cover, sending a loud clicking into the silent night. She did not look down. She continued walking up the street into the blackness.

Johnny did not hear the clicking of his sister's heels on the manhole cover above him. Johnny was at the moment listening to another sound. The sound was a squeak at first. He looked down curiously. And then the sound was a scraping, and when he looked this time he saw the glow of two pinpoints of light, and he knew he was looking into a rat's eyes.

He was scared. He was damned scared. It's one thing tangling with a human, but it's another to tangle with a rodent, and Johnny had always been afraid of rats, ever since he'd been bitten by a mouse when they lived over on First Avenue.

He started up the iron brackets set into the sewer wall. He started up rapidly, but the rat was fast, too. He screamed aloud when it leaped onto his foot. He could feel it clinging to his shoe. He shook his foot, climbing up closer to the manhole lid all the time, but the rat clung, and it seemed as if every nerve ending in his body had suddenly moved into his foot. He forgot the pain in his arm, and he forgot the rusted rough edges of the brackets as he climbed closer to the lid. He was aware only of the rat's weight on his foot, of those glittering, pinpointed eyes down below him.

And then the rat began climbing up the tweed of his

trousers, and Johnny screamed again, in real fear this time, fear that crackled into his skull. His head banged against the manhole lid, and he rushed up against it frantically, wedging his shoulders against the flat iron surface, trying to move it. He could not budge the cover. He tried it again, and he felt the rat's claws digging into his trousers, scraping against his flesh.

He tried to scream, but no sound came from his mouth. He pushed upward with his shoulders again, and this time the lid moved a little, and a fine sifting of dirt trickled down onto the back of his neck. He shoved again, and then tried to brush the rat off his leg. The rat clung, snapping at his hand, drawing fresh blood. Johnny's breath came fast now, crowding into his throat. He shoved at the cover and it moved aside, and the light from the street splashed down into the manhole, illuminating the rat.

It was a big animal, nine inches or so not counting the tail. It was covered with matted, filthy fur and the sight of the rat made Johnny's flesh crawl. But the manhole cover was off now and he thrust his head above the surface of the street, not caring about Bugs or his friends, not caring about anything now, wanting only to get away.

The rat pounced onto his arm, its teeth sinking into the sodden bandage. Johnny flipped up onto the asphalt and the rat clung, only now Johnny didn't have to worry about clinging to an iron bracket. He balled his left fist, terror shrieking inside him, and brought it down on the rat's head. The rat clung fiercely.

He got to his feet and ran across the street, stopping alongside the brick wall of a building. And then he began battering the bleeding arm against the brick, over and over again, slamming the tenacious rat against the wall.

And at last the rat's jaws loosened and it fell away to the pavement, a whimpering ball of fur with a long, twitching tail. He did not look down at the rat. He was crying now, crying as he'd never cried in his life. He ran up the street, sobbing and wondering why he'd had to run all his life, all his damn life.

And then he stopped running and fell to the pavement, and blackness closed in on him.

It was Marie who found him ten minutes later as she made her way down the street. It was she who carried him home, half dragging him, half pulling him. It was she who sent for the doctor.

The doctor treated and bandaged his arm, and Johnny slept all that night and through the next day.

Marie and Johnny's parents were by his bedside when he awoke, and the first thing he said was, "Why do I have to keep running? Why?"

And because they thought he was referring to Angelo's death, they said, "The police found the killer, Johnny. It's all right now. It's all right."

Only Johnny Trachetti knew that it wasn't all right, and that maybe it would never be.

*This Richard Marsten story was first published as "Murder on the Keys" in the February 1956 issue of* Argosy. *I don't know why editors—especially magazine editors—insist on changing good titles to invariably lousy ones. I have always liked this story, and I have always liked my original title for it, which is what appears on it now.*

# Downpour

THE STATE OF FLORIDA IS A LUGER.

You think of it as a broad beaver's tail jutting out into the Atlantic but it isn't that at all. There's a perpendicular bar of real estate on the northern end, spreading west to form the muzzle of a pistol, and the muzzle is narrow and thin in comparison to the broad grip of the gun, the way a Luger tapers down to a narrow, lethal grace. You'll find Sun City curling down like the trigger of the gun, and if you travel down the western side of the notched grip, you'll find the Gulf beaches. One of those beaches is called Pass-A-Grille, and it's as much a part of the Luger as the slide mechanism and the clip.

In Pass-A-Grille that week, they talked of nothing but the weather.

The snowstorm had swept through Ontario and Quebec, rampaged into New York State, and then ripped southward. In Tallahassee, Florida, a surprised citizenry awoke to find sleet and snow and a low temperature of thirty-four degrees—and in Pass-A-Grille, there was a cold, steady rain together with high winds.

People came into the diner with the collars of their coats high, their eyes watery from the angry winds that blew raw off the bay. It was a cold March in Florida, and people looked at the skies and said, "It'll break tomorrow"—but tomorrow never came.

David Coe watched the skies, too.

David owned a boat. It was a thirty-six-footer and not a yacht, but it had a good engine and it managed to earn its keep. When the weather was good, David carried fishing parties. He could usually get up a good party in Pass-A-Grille. His rates were reasonable and he got all kinds of fishermen— when the weather was good. The weather was not good. The weather was lousy, and he was contemplating a pretty lean week when Leslie Grew came down to the docks.

Grew was a thin man with gold-rimmed spectacles, no more than thirty-eight but with the tired look of a man of seventy. His shoulders were hunched, and he took tentative, birdlike steps as he came down onto the wood planking. He glanced over his shoulder every now and then, almost as if he had a nervous tic. He had thin, sandy-brown hair, and it danced on top of his head, rising and falling with the fresh gusts of wind that whipped off the water. He seemed not to notice the rain. He walked directly to where David was squatting on the deck of the *Helen*, cleaning out the bait well.

"Mr. Coe?" Grew asked. He had a deep voice, surprising because it came up from such a narrow chest.

"Yes?"

"I want to rent your boat."

David squinted up at him. He was surprised by the unexpected windfall, but he was also suspicious of a man who wanted to go out in this kind of weather.

"How many in your party, Mr. —"

"Grew," he supplied, and he looked at David long and hard, as if trying to see whether or not the name meant anything to him. "Leslie Grew," he added and he kept looking, and David simply nodded because the name meant nothing.

"How many in the party?" David asked again.

"Two," Grew answered.

"How long do you expect to be out?"

"That depends. I'd say a week or so."

"You and your friend must be hardy fellows," David said.

"My friend is a woman," Grew answered. "My secretary."

"This is a fishing boat. Does your secretary fish?"

"Is the boat for hire or isn't it?" Grew asked impatiently. "I haven't the time to argue."

"I didn't say I was renting."

"I'm a friend of Sam Friedman," Grew said.

"Yeah?"

"Yes. He suggested I try you. He said you would rent us the boat for a week or so. It's really quite urgent."

"How well do you know Sam?"

"Not too well," Grew admitted. "He told me you were in the Army together. He said you were a man to be trusted. Are you?"

"It depends on what I'm entrusted with." David looked at his watch. "Come back at noon. I want to call Sam first."

"Certainly," Grew said. He paused and then added, "We'd like to get under way as soon as possible. We'll bring our stuff with us when we come."

"I'm not sure you're going yet," David said.

Grew allowed a tiny smile to briefly appear on his face. "I'm willing to gamble, Mr. Coe," he said.

———

David walked over to the diner and crowded himself into a phone booth. Sam Friedman worked on the Sun City afternoon daily, and David had known him for a long time. Sam knew the way David felt about things in general, and it sounded strange that he'd recommend Grew and his "secretary."

When Sam came on, David said, "Hi. David Coe. Sam, who's Leslie Grew? He wants to rent a boat. He's also got a girl with him. Why'd you send him to me?"

"I'd like you to take him aboard. I'd appreciate it a lot. It'll just be for a week or so. The secretary—it's not what you think it is."

"Is he in trouble with the law?"

"No."

"What then? Look, Sam, give it to me. All of it."

There was a long silence on the line. Sam sighed then and said, "I can't, David. Not even a part of it. If you take them aboard, you'll be doing a lot of people a favor. But I won't try to influence you. I don't want to be responsible for getting you involved."

"What's there to get involved in?"

"I can't say another word, David."

"I just wasted a dime," David said. He paused, sighing. "I'll think it over. In the meantime, have you got any other interesting business for me? Like smuggling in some Cubans, or heroin?"

"Go to hell," Sam said, a smile in his voice.

David hung up and went out of the booth and over to the counter. He ordered a cup of hot coffee, and Charlie went over to draw it while David mulled over Leslie Grew and Company. He was still mulling when the coffee came. The diner was empty except for him and Charlie. When the door opened, David didn't look around.

The fellow who sat down at the end of the counter didn't leave room for much else. He was at least six-two in his bare soles, and he probably tipped the scales at two-twenty, bone-dry. He was wearing a camel's hair polo coat and a brown porkpie hat. He had a thick, beefy-looking face with a lot of meat between the ears, and a nose that looked like a segment of corrugated tin roof. His eyes were almost black, set deep into his head. He sat down, and the stool creaked under his weight. He picked up the menu with a hair-shrouded hand.

Charlie ambled over and said, "Morning, sir. See anything you like?"

The man's voice was like the sound of a hacksaw, high and rasping. "Cup of coffee and a French," he said.

"Yes, sir," Charlie answered. "Some weather, huh?"

"Yeah," the man said. When Charlie brought him his coffee and doughnut, he leaned closer to the counter and said, "My name's Williston. Harry Williston."

"Pleased to meet you," Charlie said.

Williston nodded. "You know everybody in town?"

"Almost," Charlie answered.

"I'm looking for a friend of mine," Williston said.

"Yeah?"

"Yeah. Don't know where he's staying, but I'd sure like to find him. Appreciate your help."

"Happy to help, if I can," Charlie said. "What's his name?"

"He's a tall guy," Williston said. "Skinny. Brown hair. Wears gold-rimmed glasses." Williston paused. "There's a girl with him."

David didn't look up. He was raising the coffee cup, and he kept on raising it while he listened.

"What's his name?" Charlie asked again.

"Put it this way," Williston said. "He may be traveling incognito. I wouldn't want to give him away. Have you seen him around?"

Charlie shrugged. "Don't recall."

"Put it this way," Williston said. "It might be worth your while to recall."

"What's the girl look like?"

"Blonde, about five-four, good body, good legs."

"Lots of girls like that in this town."

"Yeah, but put it this way. They ain't all with a skinny guy wearing gold-rimmed glasses."

"Don't recall seeing either of them," Charlie said.

Williston turned on his stool. "How about you?" he asked.

David looked up. "How about me what?"

"You see the people I'm inquiring about?"

"I haven't been listening to your inquiries," David said. He turned on his stool, and he and Williston had a short staring contest, and then Williston's stare turned slightly ugly and he said, "I thought everyone in small towns listened."

"Not everyone," David said, and he turned back to his coffee.

"You mind listening now?" Williston asked, an edge to his voice.

"What do you want?" David said.

"I'm looking for some friends of mine. A tall, skinny guy with glasses, and a blonde girl. You see them around?"

"No," David said. "And I don't intend to."

"Put it this way," Williston said. "You can get too bright for your own good."

"Don't bother me," David said. "I came in here for coffee."

Charlie looked as if he were expecting trouble, and to tell the truth, David was expecting it, too. But people who barged in and started shoving their weight around had always annoyed him. Williston got off his stool and walked over to where David was drinking his coffee. He stood there with his hands on his hips, looking down at David as if he were a spider.

"I didn't know I was bothering you," Williston said.

"Put it this way," David said. "You were, and you are. Go find your friends by yourself. I don't know anything about them."

"This is a real friendly town, ain't it?" Williston said.

"As friendly as most."

"If you're an example of—"

David got off the stool and Williston stopped talking. David saw him clench his fists, so he guessed Williston expected him to take a swing. Instead, he reached into his pocket for some change to pay for the coffee. He saw Williston's hand move unconsciously toward the opening of his coat and linger there until he realized David was only reaching for money. David put his change on the counter. He was heading for the door when Williston put his hand on his arm and turned him around.

"Where you going?" he asked, smiling pleasantly.

"Outside. Take your hand off my arm."

"You're the sensitive type, ain't you?"

"Take your hand back while you've still got fingers, mister."

"Tough, too," Williston said mockingly, but he pulled back his hand.

David walked to the door and stepped outside.

Leslie Grew and the blonde were waiting on the dock, standing there with the rain coming down around them. The blonde was wearing a dark blue trench coat, the collar turned up against the wind. Her hair was in a long ponytail, and the wind whipped it over her shoulder and occasionally lashed it against her cheek. Her face was wet, a good face with strong cheekbones and a generous mouth. She was wearing black-rimmed eyeglasses.

David walked over to them.

"I guess you're in trouble," he said.

"Who told you that?" Grew wanted to know.

"Nobody. Sam's a clam. But there was a heavy inquiring about you in the diner. He wasn't the type you take home to Mother."

Grew and the girl exchanged a hasty glance.

"Are you taking us aboard?" the girl asked. Her voice was surprisingly husky.

"I want a hundred and a quarter for the week," David said. "If you do any fishing, the bait and tackle are extra." He paused. "I don't imagine we'll be doing much fishing, will we?"

The girl smiled, her gray eyes crinkling at the edges. "I don't imagine so."

"Have you got your baggage?"

"Yes," the girl said. "On the dock."

"I don't think I know your name," David said.

Again, the pair exchanged glances. David caught the

quick flicker of their eyes and then Grew said, "David Coe, Miss Meadows." He paused, as if he were testing the name. "Wanda Meadows."

"How do you do," David said. "Come on, I'll help you with your baggage. We can shove off as soon as I get some provisions."

There were two valises and what looked like a typewriter case on the dock alongside the boat. David picked up one of the bags, and it almost pulled him back down to the dock. "What've you got in here?" he asked. "An anvil?"

Wanda stared at him levelly. "A Luger, among other things," she said, and walked past him to the gangplank. Grew picked up the typewriter case and followed her. They went down into the cabin, and David put down the bags.

"The dinette on your port forms into a double berth," he said. "Galley's over here on the starboard. I've got two transom berths up forward, where the john is. You can take the double, Miss Meadows. Mr. Grew and I will sleep up forward."

"Thank you," she said. "And please make it Wanda."

"I will. Have you given any thought to where you want to go?"

"Anywhere, it doesn't matter," Grew said. "Just so we're away from shore."

David considered this. "Well, I can carry meat for about three days in my icebox. I don't think she'll hold more than that. If we're going to be out for longer than that, we'll have to put in some place. I'll need some money in advance if I'm going to stock up."

"I'll have to cash a traveler's check," Grew said. "I'll go with you." He turned to Wanda anxiously. "Will you be all right?"

"I have a gun," Wanda said. "And I know how to use it."

Grew nodded to himself, sighed, and patted her hand. "Very well then. Shall we go, Mr. Coe?"

The rain had a cutting edge to it.

They ducked their heads and went off the dock and onto Pass-A-Grille Way. They walked up to Eighth Street, then crossed the boulevard. Grew didn't say anything. He kept walking with his head bent against the rain, and every now and then he'd raise it and look around.

"Who's after you?" David asked suddenly. "Man named Williston?"

Grew looked up sharply. "So he's the one who was asking questions."

"Is there going to be any gunplay on this little voyage?"

"I don't know."

"Why's the girl carrying a Luger?"

"For protection."

"Against what?"

Grew didn't answer that question. Instead, he said, "If you'd rather not carry us, Mr. Coe…"

"I frankly would rather not carry you, Mr. Grew. But the question is whether I should let the *Helen* lie idle for the rest of this blow, or take her out and earn myself some eating money. I also didn't like the looks of your friend Harry Williston. You don't seem like a match for him."

"And you are a match for him, Mr. Coe?"

"I don't intend to find out. But if I have to use a gun, I'm going to charge you for the service."

They went into the grocery and loaded up with meat and

canned goods. They carried the food out in three shopping bags, David carrying two and Grew carrying the remaining one. They were passing the post office when Grew stopped dead in his tracks.

"Let's cross over," he whispered.

David followed Grew's glance. Harry Williston was leaning against the wall to the right of the post office entrance, and David figured he'd stationed himself there on the assumption that anyone wanting his mail in this general delivery town would have to come here for it. David took Grew's elbow, and they started across the street against the rain.

Williston looked up and spotted Grew. He walked out into the gutter.

"Get going," David told Grew. "Head for the boat!"

"No," Grew said firmly, and David glanced at him curiously, then shifted his attention back to Williston. Williston was walking across the gutter in an apparent collision course. He stopped about a foot from them, his big feet planted in a wide, wet puddle. They started to walk around him, but he moved over again, blocking their path.

"You're in our way," David said. Williston ignored him. He looked straight at Grew and said, "Well. Hello there. Long time no see."

Grew pulled back his shoulders. "Get out of our way," he said.

"Have you started it yet?" Williston asked.

"That's none of your business," Grew answered.

"Put it this way," Williston said. "It *is* my business."

"We're driving out of here," Grew said. "We've hired a car and we're leaving this afternoon and you can't stop us. I wouldn't try if I were you."

"Where's the girl?" Williston asked.

"She's going with us," Grew said.

Williston indicated David. "This your chauffeur?" he asked, smiling.

"Yes," David answered. "I'm his chauffeur."

"I should have broke your arm back in the diner."

"You should have," David told him. "Now you'll never get the chance."

"You know who you're chauffeuring around, mister?" Williston asked.

"Yes, I do. Get out of our way, Harry. We're in a hurry."

"Mr. Williston to you," he corrected.

"Gee, I'm so sorry," David said, and then turned to Grew and said, "Come on." Together they walked away from Williston who stood in the center of the street, in the rain, watching them.

"Away from the docks," David whispered.

They began walking back toward the center of town.

"You accomplished nothing," Grew said breathlessly. "There are others. He isn't alone. They'll find Sam Friedman, and he'll tell them about you, and then they'll know we're on a boat. Wanda and I were senseless to run. We should have stayed put."

"This way," David said, and ducked into an alley.

They walked for a while in silence, circling back toward the docks. Williston was nowhere behind them.

"They don't know you're on a boat," David said at last. "If they look up Sam, he won't breathe a word to them. You have nothing to worry about. This'll all blow over."

"Will it?" Grew said. "Will it?"

And he gave a short, hollow laugh that ran the length of David's spine.

The gentleman stood against the sink with his hands up over his head. He was wearing Army khakis and a tan windbreaker and he was a slim man with a shock of fiery-red hair. Wanda Meadows sat on the port side of the cabin on one of the dinette seats, and the Luger was in her fist and pointed at the gentleman's back. Her legs were crossed demurely, and she held the gun as steadily as if it were a cup of tea.

Grew and David came down into the cabin, and the first thing they saw was the slim gentleman, and the next thing they saw was Wanda with the gun. David looked at Wanda. Her eyes were cold and the coldness had turned the gray two shades darker. Her full lips were taut across her teeth.

"Who is he?" David asked.

The man didn't turn. "Tell the dame to put up the gun, will you?"

"Put it up, Wanda."

Wanda lowered the gun. The man against the sink made a motion to turn —

"Stay where you are," she snapped. "If you turn around, I'll shoot you."

"The dame's nuts," he said, shaking his head. "I come aboard and she pulls a gun on me."

"Who invited you?" David asked.

"I come aboard to see if I could rent her. She's a fishing boat, ain't she? I heard they was bitin' like crazy. I figured the owner of the boat wouldn't mind making a fast buck."

"I'm the owner," David said. "I've already got a party."

"Then I'll be goin'," the man said. He turned around, and Wanda brought the Luger up and pointed it at his navel.

"What's your name?" she asked.

"Frank Reardon."

"Where are you from?"

"Tampa."

"Why'd you come all the way down here to fish?"

"I heard they was bitin'. Hell, they ain't even *swimmin'* in Tampa Bay."

"How'd you find the boat?" David asked.

"What do you mean, how'd I find it? I come looking for a good boat, so I come down to the docks. I spot this one, and she looks clean, so I come aboard. What the hell did I stumble into, anyway? A Russian spy ring?"

"Okay," David said. "Get ashore. And don't come back."

"Don't worry," Reardon said. He looked tentatively toward Wanda and the Luger. "Okay, sister?"

"Go on," she said lowering the gun. Reardon looked at her queerly, shook his head, and mounted the steps. David walked up after him, watching him until he was ashore, then went below again.

"Is someone about ready to tell me what the hell's going on?" he said.

Neither Grew nor Wanda answered.

"Why are they after you?"

Wanda smiled a bit tremulously.

David stared into the silence. "One thing I hate," he said, "is talkative fishing parties. Come on, we'd better get under way."

--------

He gassed her up and then took her out past the rocks. He had no real idea where he should go, no real idea where he should take the fugitives. He vaguely surmised, however, that any chase party would assume they'd head into the Gulf, and so he chose Boca Ciega Bay as the place least likely to encourage pursuit.

He still could not understand his own reasons for having taken them aboard. But there'd been something pathetically appealing about the underweight Grew, and he could not deny the obvious attractiveness of Wanda Meadows. It wasn't every woman who could handle Pitman and a Luger with equal ease.

He opened the throttle a little wider, and the *Helen* rushed past Villa del Mar in a burst of flying green and gray and white spray. He kept her nosed into the channel, past the shallow flats and the grass, past Mud Key Point and Mud Key Cutoff and Big McPherson Bayou, heading for the open waters of the bay.

He looked back toward the seat aft near the fishing boxes. There was a locker under that seat, and there was a rifle in the locker, and there was also an Army .45 there, and the .45 had a fresh clip in it. He'd once shot the head off a barracuda with that .45 after a careless fisherman had lost two toes dangling his feet in the water. The way things were going, he surmised there might be more to shoot than barracuda this trip.

He heard a clicking from below, and for a moment he couldn't place the sound. Then he realized it was a typewriter, and he silently congratulated Grew on his capacity for concentration. Even in the midst of headlong flight, the man could find time to dictate letters to his secretary. He wondered what type of business Grew was in. He didn't look like a man who got entangled with people like Harry Williston. The typing stopped abruptly. Grew was coming up the steps from the cabin.

"Nasty up here," Grew said.

"Yes," David replied.

"How fast will she go?"

"Twenty, twenty-five knots."

"No faster?"

"This isn't a destroyer, Mr. Grew."

"More's the pity," Grew answered.

"Getting off some correspondence?"

"What?"

"The typewriter," David said.

"Oh." Grew hesitated. "Yes."

"What line are you in, Mr. Grew?"

Grew hesitated for another moment. He smiled broadly then, as though pleased with the answer he had formulated. "Communications," he said.

David pulled the throttle out a notch, realizing at the same instant that the typewriter below had stopped when Grew came up on deck.

"Your secretary's goofing off," he said.

"Eh? Oh, is she?" Grew seemed to remember something. "I'd better get below."

He went below and in a moment the typewriter started again. A gull swooped low over the boat, decided it was not carrying any fish, and went screaming off.

Suddenly David felt Wanda's presence beside him.

"How does it feel?" she asked.

"How does what feel?"

"Being a sailor."

"Like being a millionaire," David said, smiling. "Minus the million bucks."

Wanda sucked in a deep breath and threw back her head, the ponytail trailing down her back. "It smells good," she said. "The water. You can smell the salt and the fish." Suddenly she pointed off the starboard bow and said, "Look!"

David followed her finger, picking out the yellow speck in the sky. "Coast Guard helicopter," he said.

Wanda took off her glasses, squinted, reached for a handkerchief in the pocket of her trench coat, began wiping off the lenses of her glasses. He studied her eyes. They were slightly tilted, almost Oriental, a deep gray reflecting the somber water, flecked with chips of white.

"You're prettier without them," he said.

"Thanks," she answered. "I'm also blind as a bat without them." She put the glasses on again, peered out over the water to where the helicopter was closer now, its roar filling the sky. David watched the craft as it dropped closer to his boat. He saw an enlisted man in the cockpit toss out a rope ladder, and then an officer in grays climbed over him and started down toward the boat. The enlisted man wrestled with the controls, trying to keep the plane hovering over the boat. The officer was a lieutenant j.g. He clung to the last rung of the ladder for an instant, then dropped to the *Helen*'s deck.

"You David Coe?" he asked.

"Yes," David said.

The j.g.'s eyes flicked Wanda briefly. "Hate to break up your party," he said.

"What is it, Lieutenant?" David asked, miffed by the j.g.'s implication.

"The Sun City Police would like to see you, pal. Seems

you talked to a Sam Friedman this morning on the telephone?"

"What about it?"

"You were the last guy to talk to him. He was shot to death about an hour ago. They found him with eight bullets in his head and chest." The lieutenant paused long enough to see the shock spread across David's face. "You better pull into Madeira Beach," he said. "The cops sounded kind of impatient."

The room could have been a broom closet. There was a square, scarred desk with a chair behind it. There was a bulletin board and a battery of green metal filing cases. There was a shaded lightbulb hanging over the desk and there was a window with dust-covered venetian blinds hiding it. There was a door with a frosted-glass panel, and on the other side of the frosted glass were lettered the words DETECTIVE DIVISION. A narrow wooden plaque on the desk read: LIEUTENANT MAUROW.

Maurow was a big man with a thatch of red hair. His eyes were pale blue, as cold as a swimming pool in January. He had thick lips and a mole close to the deep cleft in his chin. He studied David and his eyes said nothing and his mouth said nothing. He picked up a pencil and tapped it on the desk.

"What do you do, Coe?" he asked.

"I own a boat."

"Why'd you call Sam Friedman this morning?"

"I just called him socially," David said. "Sam was one of my best friends."

"You know anybody named Leslie Grew?" Maurow asked.

David hesitated. "No," he said.

"Friedman's secretary tells us you called about eleven thirty or so."

"Yes. I guess it was about then."

"What'd you talk about?"

"The weather," David said.

"Don't get wise, Coe. I've got a jail full of wise guys downstairs. Did you discuss Leslie Grew with him?"

"I don't know any Leslie Grew."

"I hope you're leveling with me, Coe."

"Why should I lie?"

"Maybe you're just a natural liar. Maybe you'd lie if I asked you your own name."

"Maybe. Why don't you ask me?"

Maurow looked at him steadily, narrowly.

"You don't know Leslie Grew, huh?"

"No."

"A certain police department up north a ways is looking for him." Maurow smiled. "You still never heard of him?"

"No," David said.

"Grew and Meadows," Maurow said. "Meadows is the secretary. Funny, too." He shrugged massive shoulders. "I guess work is hard to find."

"What do you mean?"

"I mean Grew and Meadows are both wanted. They're wanted bad. That police department is in a small town, a very small town. That doesn't mean we don't cooperate with them, though. We got a teletype just a little while after Friedman's body turned up. Told us they might try to contact him. We got the teletype just a little too late."

"What are they wanted for?" David asked.

"Grand theft," Maurow said. "Your pals are heeled, too."

"Guns?"

"A gun. A souvenir Luger, missing from Grew's desk. You see any suspicious-looking Lugers lately?"

"I wouldn't know a Luger if I did see one," David lied.

"You're a pretty ignorant fellow for somebody who went through the Italian campaign, ain't you?"

"Sometimes," David said.

"Is it true Friedman pulled you away from a grenade once in Italy and maybe saved you from being a splash on the Italian countryside?"

"Yes."

"Then why are you protecting his murderers?"

"I'm not."

"You're protecting Grew and Meadows, aren't you? You called about Grew this morning, didn't you? That's what your conversation with Friedman was about. Isn't that right?"

"No." David paused. "I don't know anyone by those names."

"You couldn't miss this babe, Coe. She's a blonde, and she has it all in the right places. She's also wearing glasses. What do you say?"

"I don't know any blondes who wear glasses."

"I don't think very kindly of you for making things tough for us." Maurow paused. "Don't spit on the sidewalk, Coe. And don't speed, and don't do a lot of things you may not even know about. This city has a lot of ordinances, and we'll be waiting for you, Coe. Now get out of here."

David headed for the deserted dock alongside which he'd berthed the boat, thinking of Sam Friedman and allowing his murder to build a cold, festering rage inside him. He knew that neither Wanda nor Grew could have committed the murder. He'd spoken to Sam on the telephone and then gone directly to the dock to find Grew and the girl waiting for him. After that neither had been much out of his sight.

The boat bobbed gently on the waterline. The dock was very silent, the rain pressing drearily against the wooden planking. David jumped onto the deck, then headed below into the cabin.

The cabin reeked of cordite. The room was filled with smoke that hung in unshifting layers on the still air. He peered through the smoke. The typewriter rested on the dinette table, a sheet of paper in the roller. One suitcase lay on the deck, unopened. The Luger was nowhere in sight. Neither was the girl.

Leslie Grew was on the deck. There was a bullet hole between his eyes. David knelt down. Grew was dead.

"Wanda!" David called, standing up quickly. He walked to the galley side of the cabin and shoved open the door there. "Wanda!"

He went forward and checked both transom berths. He went into the head and checked there. Wanda Meadows was not aboard. He went back into the cabin and looked down at Grew's body. The man's spectacles lay on the deck several feet from his outstretched hand. One of the lenses was smashed, as if someone had stepped on it.

He went to the suitcase that lay on the deck. He lifted it. This was not the heavy suitcase. The heavy suitcase was gone. He put the bag on the dinette table alongside the typewriter, and snapped it open. Quickly he went through it. Lingerie, mostly. Very lacy. Very feminine. He looked through the pocket of the bag. A pair of toothbrushes, toothpaste, shaving cream, a safety razor, a packet of bobby pins, lipstick. He closed the bag. He swung the typewriter around. There were two lines typed on the otherwise blank page. In the right-hand corner was the number "14." Beneath that, in heavy black type, were the words: "men like Harry Williston, who poses as the innocuous proprietor of a pool parlor. Men like the late and vociferously lamented Geo5"

Harry Williston again.

And somebody who was dead and apparently named George something-or-other. David looked at the keyboard. The "5" was directly above the "r." A simple typo, except for the fact that the typo and the end of the typewritten matter happened to coincide. Had something happened to cause Wanda Meadows to stop in the middle of the thought—and with an error?

He moved away from the typewriter and began scanning the deck. He found the shoe first. A blue calf, high-heeled pump. It matched the color of the dark blue raincoat she'd been wearing. He looked around the cabin again, wondering if the raincoat was gone, too. Then he saw it sprawled across the seat of the dinette. She had left without her raincoat, and she had left in enough haste to drop her shoe at the foot of the ladder leading above decks. He put the shoe alongside the typewriter, then studied the deck again.

Glistening metal lay several feet from Grew's body. He bent down and picked it up, recognizing it instantly as an ejected cartridge case. He turned it over in his fingers, seeing the indentation where the firing pin had struck. Lettered onto the back of the case in a semicircle were the letters REM.UMC.

Beneath that, and coming up to form the lower half of the circle: 9-MM LUGER.

Harry Williston had been carrying a snub-nosed .38, a gun that looked like a Banker's Special. But Banker's Special or not, it had been a revolver, and revolvers don't eject cartridges, and the cartridge David held was unmistakably stamped LUGER.

He had seen only one Luger since all this started.

That Luger had been in the fist of Wanda Meadows. He looked down at the bullet hole in Grew's face, wondering if it had been made by Wanda's Luger.

When he heard the creak above him, and he looked up at once. Someone was onboard.

"Hello?" a voice called. "Anybody aboard?"

For an instant, David panicked. He looked at the body on the deck, then hurriedly went toward the ladder. Two men were waiting above. They both wore trench coats and gray fedoras. He closed the door to the cabin and walked toward them.

"What can I do for you?"

"Sun City Police," one of the men said. "I'm Detective-Sergeant Sloane. My partner, Detective Belgrave."

Belgrave nodded briefly. His eyes were on the closed cabin door.

"Maurow didn't waste any time, did he?" David said.

"Maurow can move fast when he has to," Sloane said.

"We've got a search warrant," Belgrave said. "Let's get to work." He was a big man with a pinched face and hooded brown eyes. "Anybody else aboard this tub?"

"No," David said.

"What's your name, anyway?" Belgrave asked.

"David Coe."

"He's the one spoke to Friedman last," Sloane said.

"Yeah," Belgrave said. "He a friend of yours, Coe?"

"Yes."

"Shame. Somebody must have sure hated that poor bastard."

"How do you mean?"

"Emptied a whole damn magazine into him. That don't betoken brotherly love, pal."

"A whole magazine?"

He thought back to what the lieutenant j.g. had said. *They found him with eight bullet holes in his head and chest.* A whole magazine. A .45 carried seven or nine cartridges. A .22 usually carried ten cartridges. A .38 carried nine. A .32 carried eight.

"He was killed with a .32?" David asked.

Belgrave snorted. "Hell no. A Luger. Come on, let's take a look belowdecks."

He moved toward the cabin door, and David stepped around him quickly.

"What do you expect to find down there?" he asked.

"Happens we're looking for a dame," Belgrave said, and he shoved past David and was reaching for the latch on the door when David clawed at his shoulder and spun him around and hit him. Belgrave slammed back against the cabin door, and was reaching under his coat when David hit him again, and he crumpled to the deck. Behind him, David heard Sloane shout, "Hey! *Hey!*" He whirled and shot his fist at Sloane's stomach.

"Hey!" Sloane shouted again, and then there was a surprised look on his face and David hit the surprised look, and Sloane hit the deck and was still. David looked off up the dock. There was no one in sight. Quickly, he went to the seat aft near the fishing boxes. He opened the locker under the seat, reached in, and took out the .45 in its Army holster. He removed the gun from the holster, and put the holster back into the locker. He closed the locker and slid the gun's magazine onto the palm of his hand. It was a full clip. He slapped the clip home and then worked a cartridge into the firing chamber. He tucked the gun into his waistband, took a last look at the quiet detectives, and left the boat.

Maurow's going to love this, he thought. This will absolutely delight Maurow. But the alternative had been to let the cops go belowdecks and find Grew's body, after which they'd have put the arm on David for sure. The important thing now was to find a young lady running around somewhere in the rain, a secretary with a very heavy suitcase and a Luger—but without a typewriter.

There were nine typewriter-rental places listed in the Gulf Beaches telephone directory. The fourth one he called told him a woman in Madeira Beach had phoned to rent a typewriter that afternoon.

"What's her name?" he asked.

"Name? Just a second." The man paused, obviously checking some papers. "Rebecca Jones," he said. "At the Sunbright Motel. You know where that is?"

"I'll find it," David said.

"Who is this, anyway?" the man asked, but David had already hung up.

The Sunbright Motel was a plush, luxurious, wood-and-glass structure that hugged the beach. Doggedly, David pushed through the rain and into the lobby. The front desk was set along a solid wooden wall that faced the glass entrance wall. There were a good many people in the lobby, seated in the comfortable, modern easy chairs, staring glumly through the rain. David was starting for the desk when he saw Williston. The big man saw him at the same instant. His eyes sparked angrily, then flicked over the crowded lobby. The anger fled. He smiled genially, extended his hand, and walked over toward David.

"Hello," he said, almost cheerfully.

David didn't answer. Williston pulled back his hand, the smile still on his face. "We were looking for you," he said.

"What do you want, Williston?"

"Put it this way," Williston said. "We ain't stopping till we get it, so there's no use playing cute."

"How's your pool parlor coming along?" David asked.

The smile dropped from Williston's mouth. "How do you know about that?"

"I get around," David said.

Williston scowled. "Where's Leslie Grew?"

"Leslie Grew is dead."

"Since when?"

"You don't know anything about it, huh?" David said.

"Nothing at all."

"You're as innocent as —"

"Cut it!" Williston whispered sharply. "I know Grew's alive, so just cut it! Just tell me *where*."

"Try looking on my boat," David said.

"We already tried, pal. Don't worry, we'll get what we want."

"What is it you —?"

He stopped suddenly.

Wanda had just entered the lobby through a door to the left of the desk.

Williston hadn't seen her because his back was to her, but she had seen him and she had seen David, and she hesitated now, watching them. She had managed to pick up a pair of flats somewhere, but she was still coatless. She carried the heavy valise.

"If you told me what you're looking for," David went on softly, "I might be able to help you."

"You're a card," Williston said. "Put it this way. You're such a card I'd like to break your nose."

Wanda turned and moved toward the writing desk along one of the glass walls.

"I'll tell you what, Williston," David said, stalling. "You've been talking about 'it' and about how badly you want 'it,' but talk is talk, and talk is cheap." He saw Wanda pick up a pen and hastily scribble something on a sheet of motel stationery.

"Who's got it?" Williston asked. "You?"

"Maybe," David said.

Williston scratched the side of his jaw. Behind him, Wanda held up the folded piece of stationery so that David could see it. Then she tucked the folded page into one of the cubbyholes at the rear of the writing desk and crossed the lobby.

"What would you say it's worth?" Williston asked.

"Plenty," David said. She was walking out into the rain now, a slim figure in sweater and skirt, crossing the gravel parking lot, her skirt whipping around her bare legs, the ponytail sweeping back over her shoulders. She stood near the concrete oval surrounding a young palm tree. The rain was lashing down in sheets.

"How much is that?" Williston asked.

Wanda raised her arm and a taxi pulled to a stop beside the palm. The rear door opened. She climbed in, and the door closed. The cab sped off.

David sighed. "Not for sale," he said. "And there's nothing more to say."

"There's a lot to say. We're willing to be sensible, so long as your price is right. Why spill any more blood?"

David pulled away from Williston and went across the lobby. Williston stared after him, puzzled, considering. David reached in and removed the note from the cubbyhole. She had a clear, firm hand. The note read:

> Get my typewriter. Meet me Passe-A-Grille on beach
> at 26th Street, eight o'clock tonight. Please be careful.
> I didn't do it.

The note was unsigned.

David glanced at his watch. Three thirty. That left a lot of hours to kill. He smiled at Williston, waved, walked past the bellhop at the cigar counter, and stepped through the glass door and out into the rain. He saw the Sun City squad car too late. The policemen had already seen him, and there was no place to run.

Maurow was in an ugly mood.

"All right, Coe," he said. "I'm listening."

"What do you want me to say?"

"I want it all. Every bit of it. Right from the beginning. And you'd better give it to me straight."

"If I knew anything, I'd tell it to you," David said. "All I know is that a couple of people wanted to charter my boat. I called Sam Friedman, and he told me they didn't have any law trouble. So I took them aboard. The next thing I know, Sam is dead."

"These people," Maurow interrupted. "Grew and Meadows?"

"Yes," David said.

"What about them?"

"That's all I know. Except that a rough character named Harry Williston is throwing his weight around. He runs a pool parlor someplace."

"Where?"

"I don't know. There's somebody named George in this, too, but he's dead. Williston is after something, I don't know what it is, but he wants it badly enough to pay for it—or possibly to kill for it."

"George who?"

"I don't know. I saw his name in a typewriter." Maurow went to his desk and opened a drawer. He took out a sheet of paper that had once been crumpled, but which had been pressed smooth. He handed the sheet to David.

"What do you make of this?" he asked.

"What am I supposed to make of it? It's shorthand, isn't it?"

"Yes. But it's not Gregg and it's not Pitman, and it's not Speedwriting. Our experts don't know what the hell it is."

David stared at the jumble of letters on the sheet. There was something familiar about the handwriting, and it took him several seconds to realize it was Wanda's. He said nothing.

"We figure it's some kind of personal shorthand," Maurow said.

"Where'd you find it?"

"In the trash basket aboard your boat. We also got a sheet of paper from the typewriter, probably transcribed from some other notes. We tried cracking this with what we had in English, but it doesn't match up. Is that where you got the George stuff?"

"Yes," David said.

"Where did Grew and Meadows want you to take them?"

"They didn't care."

"Why'd they contact you?"

"Sam recommended me."

"How'd they know him?"

"I don't know. He was a newspaperman. I guess he got to meet a lot of people."

"And he suggested they try you, huh?"

"Yes."

"And that's your stake in this, that right? That's why you've been sticking your neck out right from when this started, huh? You know something, Coe? I think you're full of shit."

"I've told you all I know," David said.

"You haven't told me where Leslie Grew is."

David blinked.

"What?"

"You heard me. For all I know, you're in this, too. Until you prove otherwise to me, you're in it. Right up to your navel. What were you doing with a .45, Coe?"

"It's an Army souvenir."

"That doesn't answer my question. Do you own a Luger, too?"

"No," David mumbled.

"Does Grew?"

"I don't know."

"You *do* know because the teletype we got said Grew was carrying a Luger. Now how about that?"

"If you say so."

"Where's Grew now?"

"Where do you think? Who the hell are you trying to kid?"

"You'd better get out of here before I do something we'll both regret, Coe. I'm still itching to tie you in to this. I'm itching so much, I can't stand still. So you'd better get out. Now! While you can still walk."

David got out.


He did not go back to the boat. He did not go back for one reason alone, and that reason was a simple one. He did not believe Maurow knew there was a dead man in the cabin. It sounded crazy as hell, he knew, especially since Maurow had reeled off every other object in the cabin, down to Wanda's panties and the page of shorthand that had been in the trash basket. But from the line of Maurow's questioning, David assumed the Sun City Police did not know about Grew's murder.

Now he stood in the grass where the sidewalk ended at the beach's edge. There was no moon, and no stars, and the rain swept the gutter and the sidewalk and the tall grass. On his left, a gray weather-beaten beach house faced the Gulf. On his right, the white-studded walls of a small hotel peered bleakly through the rain. He could hear the sullen rush of the surf, could feel the rain's sharp silvery needles on his face. The beach was usually moon-drenched, the water placid. Tonight, there was only the rain and an angry surf. He pulled his collar high and cut through the grass, walking on the narrow path.

He heard the grass swishing, and he dropped to his knees in the sand. The footsteps were light. She came onto the beach, and looked quickly right and left.

"Wanda," he whispered.

"David?"

She ran across the beach, and he held out his arms to her, surprising himself when he did, and somehow not surprised when she came into them. She put her head against his shoulder, dropping the heavy valise to the sand.

"I'm so damned tired," she said.

He held her close. Her clothes were soaked through. He pulled off his windbreaker and wrapped it around her shoulders.

"What happened?" he asked.

"When you left the boat...to go to the police, remember? You told us to stay out of sight in the cabin, so we did. Then— it couldn't have been more than twenty minutes after you left—we heard footsteps above us. I guess we panicked."

"Who was it?"

"We didn't know at first. We stopped working, and I slammed the suitcase shut, and then I went to stand near the steps coming down into the cabin, out of sight. I had the Luger in my hand. I still have the gun. It's in the valise."

"Go ahead."

"A man came down into the cabin. He didn't see me. He saw...only..."

She could not continue for a moment and then her eyes flooded with the memory of the thin, bespectacled man with whom she had worked.

"He was very brave. He stood there and said, 'What do you want? Who are you?' The man didn't say anything. He just brought up his gun and fired."

"Was it a Luger?"

"No. No, I don't think so. I don't remember. Everything happened so quickly, David, it was difficult to..."

"What happened then?"

"I stood there frozen. I had a gun in my hand. The man turned to me, and I...I just fired. I hit him in the right shoulder, and ran for the steps. He was an ugly man, David, with a scar on his face. He reached for me, and he caught my ankle, and I gripped the railings on both sides and kicked back at him. I know I kicked him in the face but I didn't turn to look. That's when my shoe came off—when I kicked him. I didn't look back. I just ran off the boat." She shook her head. "So much trouble," she said. "So much trouble, David."

"Maybe you ought to tell me about this trouble," he said. "What are they after?"

"They want the notes in this valise," Wanda said. "All in shorthand—my own personal shorthand."

"I don't understand," David said. "What kind of notes? Why would anyone want to kill—"

"It's a book manuscript," Wanda said. "It's set for magazine serialization, too."

"Fiction?"

Wanda gave a short laugh. "Hell, no!"

"And Leslie Grew wrote this book?"

"Yes," she said. "Leslie Grew wrote it. David, there's something you—"

"Shh!" he said.

She stopped talking, and they listened together. From the sidewalk came the sound of heavy footsteps.

"They've seen us," David said. "Run!"

She was off instantly, one hand tight around the handle of the valise.

"Through the grass," he yelled. "Go on!"

She didn't look back at him. She slithered into the grass and then broke into a fast run as the men came onto the beach.

There were three of them.

Williston and two others.

"Hold it!" Williston shouted, and then a gun was in his hand. One of the men with him was wearing his right arm in a sling. A gun was in his left hand, and he was pointing it at David.

"The broad shot Freddie this afternoon," Williston said. "Be careful, his temper ain't exactly even."

There was a third man, and a third gun. The third gun was a Luger. The man behind it was short and squat.

"This the one who shot Sam?" David asked.

"Yep," Williston said pleasantly, and smiled. "Meet Ralphie. Come on, let's find that broad."

They walked through the grass almost leisurely. On Pass-A-Grille Way, they stopped beside a black Cadillac. Freddie and Ralphie climbed into the front seat, Williston into the back beside David.

"Cruise, Ralphie."

Ralphie nodded, started the car.

"Why'd you kill Sam?" David asked him.

He didn't turn from the wheel. He drove hunched over it, peering through the windshield. "He wouldn't tell me what I wanted to know," he said.

"So you emptied a Luger into him?"

"He was helping them," Williston said. "That's good enough for me." He leaned forward. "You see her, Ralphie?"

"Not yet."

"Helping them to do what?" David asked.

"Helping them get away."

"From what?"

"From *us!*" Williston said sharply. "There's a town a little ways north of here, Coe. A nice town. A real nice town. It's our town. You know what I mean? *Our* town. Put it this way. We got it sewed up real tight. There ain't nothing goes on in that town, we ain't got our finger in it. It's wide open in a quiet way. That means you can get any kind of action you want there, without having the cops crawling all over you, because the cops is in our pocket, too. You can cool off in our town, you can do anything you want in our town because we control it, and we like the way it's run. Put it this way, Coe. We don't like anybody coming in and fouling up the china closet."

"So?"

"So okay, we're doing what we always do. We're respectable businessmen. I run a pool parlor. Ralphie here owns a candy store. Freddie's a tailor. All respectable. The rest of the boys, too. We learned all that from Georgie Phelps, who was one of the best guys alive. Some jerk from Kansas City come down with a grudge, though, and cooled Georgie. We took care of him, all right. But what I'm saying, when Georgie was alive, and even now, we do things right. Put it this way. The local cops get paid plenty to look the other way. What the state cops don't know ain't gonna hurt them. Right?"

"I'm still listening."

"Sure, listen hard. So there's maybe a little gambling, and maybe a little dope, and maybe a little woman business, and maybe the poor slob ain't getting a fair shake, but we're making dough, and that's the way we want it. So we get a tip from New York. From New York, a guy we know makes a phone call. He tells us we're sittin', we're sittin' on a volcano and the lid is about to blow off. You see her yet, Ralphie?"

"No. This damn rain..."

"Keep lookin'. She couldn't of vanished. This guy in New York tells us there's a big-shot writer in our town. Tells us the writer's been snooping for close to six months, and has enough stuff to blow the town wide open. That's no good, Coe. In six months, you can learn a lot of dangerous things. So we ask our New York friend what the writer's name is, and he tells us Leslie Grew. And he tells us Grew is in our town with a secretary, writing this book, which is gonna break in a national magazine."

"So you started looking for Grew?"

"Sure. Our town ain't exactly a chicken coop, Coe. It took us a while to find what we were looking for. Only trouble is, Grew took off first. Carrying enough notes to fill ten books. Enough notes to bring in not only the state cops, but the Feds as well. That ain't good, Coe. Put it this way. Grew and friend had to go."

"And that's why you came here."

"Why else? But when we come down, there was a few things we didn't know. We didn't know, first of all, that Grew knew a newspaperman named Sam Friedman. We found that out later. By that time, our cops were getting to work, too. We figured if we could get those two back to our town on some phony charge, the rest would be easy. Our cops teletyped the Sun City Police. I sent Ralphie over to see Mr. Friedman. But their wire told me something else, too. All the while we was looking for Grew, we thought—"

"There she is!" Ralphie yelled.

The Cadillac was a more powerful car than the taxi Wanda was in. But the cabdriver knew the roads well, and Ralphie didn't. The cab kept a comfortable lead as they sped out of Pass-A-Grille and through Don Ce-Sar Place, and Belle Vista Beach, and Blind Pass, and Sunset Beach, and Treasure Island, and Sunshine Beach. The big Caddy went over the bridge at John's Pass, made the turn, and then squealed into Madeira Beach.

"There she goes!" Freddie yelled. "Into that joint!"

Ralphie pulled the car over and screeched to a stop.

"Come on, Coe!" Williston yelled, reaching into the backseat and pulling David out into the rain with him. Up ahead, David saw Wanda duck into the aquarium exhibit.

The building was a two-story affair. Upstairs was where the two porpoises were fed every day while spectators goggled and cheered. The downstairs level was a dimly lit stone-and-concrete dungeon, where lighted glass walls showed the other big fish.

A porpoise was in the closest tank. The downstairs level ran for a hundred feet and angled off in an L showing the other side of the second tank, the tank in which a giant turtle, a sand shark, and a giant grouper were kept. The aquarium was dead silent. The fish drifted past silently and eerily. The tortoise pressed against the glass. Behind him the shark flashed into view.

"Upstairs," Williston shouted, pointing to the stairway at the end of the corridor, running for the steps.

Freddie's gun was in his hand. He was standing on David's left, and David could see the wad under his suit jacket near his right shoulder. His wound. As they approached the steps, David gripped the railing and brought both feet up, jackknifing into the air, aiming his heels at the wad on Freddie's right shoulder.

Freddie's scream pierced the air, echoed down the passageway as he dropped to the floor. David charged up the steps. Freddie was still screaming behind him.

"Wanda!" he yelled.

Behind him, Williston leveled the .38 in his fist, and fired. David heard the shot, felt searing pain in his right leg, stumbled forward. Wanda was huddled against the wall at the far end of the aquarium, near the open porpoise tank. A sign behind her read: FEEDING TIME—2:30 AND 7:00 P.M. Two empty buckets lay on the feeding platform. The porpoises kept breaking the surface of water, coming up for air. David started to run toward her, but he felt suddenly dizzy and weak, and he slipped to the floor, close to the railing near the open lip of the first tank.

Wanda dropped the suitcase, and came running toward him. She was still carrying the Luger. He heard Williston's heavy footsteps on the stairs, and then he saw Williston's head appear, and then the hand with the gun came into view.

"Okay," he said, grinning. "End of the road, Miss Grew. Give me those notes!"

"I think not," she said, and fired.

She fired four shots in a row. The first two shots sailed over Williston's head. The third one caught him in the chest, and the fourth one caught him in the stomach. His own gun went off, and then he staggered back toward the railing around the tank. He hung poised over the railing for a moment, and then folded over it into the tank. He was a big man. Water splashed up and over the lid of the tank. In an instant, the grouper darted from one corner, and the sand shark lunged from the other. Both of them made it to Williston's body at about the same time.

Wanda ran to where David lay on the floor.

"Are you all right?" she said.

He was about to lose consciousness. He nodded, shook his head, nodded again.

"Who was the dead man on my boat?" he asked.

"John Meadows, my secretary," she said. "He let them believe they were looking for a man. *I'm—*"

There were footsteps on the stairs.

The aquarium cashier burst into view.

"There they are!" she shouted. "They came in without paying!"

A patrolman was on the stairs behind her.

"There's another one outside," David said. "A man in a black Cadillac. He murdered the Sun City reporter."

"Get the guy in the black Caddy," the patrolman yelled down to his partner. He turned to David. "All right," he said gruffly. "What the hell's going on here? Who's that guy downstairs with his arm in a sling? And who the hell are you, lady?"

"Leslie Grew," David said, and then he relaxed in her arms and hoped she'd still be there when he came to again.

*This story first appeared in 1952, in a magazine called* Verdict. *It was one of the several short short stories I wrote under the Hunt Collins pseudonym. It was probably first submitted to* Manhunt, *and when rejected there—shame on you, Scott!—went to* Verdict, *one of the many detective magazines trying to imitate* Manhunt's *spectacular success. (I still think Scott was editing each and every one of them.)*

*Whereas I later wrote several novels under the Richard Marsten pseudonym, Hunt Collins wrote only one, the book that first attracted the attention of Herb Alexander (remember?) and started the whole 87th Precinct saga.* Cut Me In *was about a murder in a literary agency. (Guess where I got the background for it.) The title referred to the venal practice of taking commissions, and the book was an Innocent Bystander story, like the one that follows.*

# Eye Witness

HE HAD WITNESSED A MURDER, AND THE SIGHT HAD sunken into the brown pits that were his eyes. It had tightened the thin line of his mouth and given him a tic over his left cheekbone.

He sat now with his hat in his hands, his fingers nervously exploring the narrow brim. He was a thin man with a mustache that completely dominated the confined planes of his face.

He was dressed neatly, his trousers carefully raised in a crease-protecting lift that revealed taut socks and the brass clasp of one garter.

"That him?" I asked.

"That's him," Magruder said.

"And he saw the mugging?"

"He says he saw it. He won't talk to anyone but the Chief."

"None of us underlings will do, huh?"

Magruder shrugged. He'd been on the force for a long time now, and he was used to just about every type of taxpayer. I looked over to where the thin man sat on the bench against the wall.

"Well," I said, "let me see what I can get out of him."

Magruder cocked an eyebrow and asked, "You think maybe the old man would like to see him personally?"

"Maybe. If he's got something. If not, we'd be wasting his time. And especially on this case, I don't think..."

"Yeah," Magruder agreed.

I left Magruder and walked over to the little man. He looked up when I approached him, and then blinked.

"Mr. Struthers?" I said. "I'm Detective-Sergeant Cappeli. My partner tells me you have some information about the..."

"You're not the Chief, are you?"

"No," I said, "but I'm working very closely with him on this case."

"I won't talk to anyone but the Chief," he said. His eyes met mine for an instant, and then turned away. He was not being stubborn, I decided. I hadn't seen stubbornness in his eyes. I'd seen fear.

"Why, Mr. Struthers?"

"Why? Why what? Why won't I tell my story to anyone else? Because I won't, that's why."

"Mr. Struthers, withholding information is a serious crime. It makes you an accessory after the fact. We'd hate to have to..."

"I'm not withholding anything. Get the Chief and I'll tell you everything I saw. That's all, get the Chief."

I waited for a moment before trying again. "Are you familiar with the case at all, sir?"

Struthers considered his answer. "Just what I read in the papers. And what I saw."

"You know that it was the Chief's wife who was mugged? That the mugger was after her purse and killed her without getting it?"

"Yes, I know that."

"Can you see then why we don't want to bring the Chief into this until it's absolutely necessary? So far, we've had ten people confessing to the crime, and eight people who claim to have seen the mugging and murder."

"I *did* see it," Struthers protested.

"I'm not saying you didn't, sir. But I'd like to be sure before I bring the Chief in on it."

"I just don't want any slipups," Struthers said. "I...I don't want him coming after me next."

"We'll offer you every possible protection, sir. The Chief, as you can well imagine, has a strong personal interest in this case. He'll certainly see that no harm comes to you."

Struthers looked around him suspiciously. "Well, do we have to talk here?"

"No, sir, you can come into my office."

He deliberated for another moment, and then said, "All right." He stood up abruptly, his fingers still roaming the hat brim.

I led him to the corridor, winking over my shoulder at Magruder as we went out. When we got to my office, I offered him a chair and a cigarette. He took the seat, but declined the smoke.

"Now then, what did you see?"

"I saw the mugger, the man who killed her." Struthers lowered his voice. "But he saw me, too. That's why I want to make absolutely certain that...that I won't get into any trouble over this."

"You won't, sir. I can assure you. Where did you see the killing?"

"On Third and Elm. Right near the old paint factory. I was on my way home from the movies."

"What did you see?"

"Well, the woman, Mrs. Anderson—I didn't know it was her at the time, of course—was standing on a corner waiting for the bus. I was walking down toward her. I walk that way often, especially coming home from the show. It was a nice night and..."

"What happened?"

"Well, it was dark, and I was walking pretty quiet, I guess. I wear gummies—gum sole shoes. The mugger came out of the shadows and grabbed Mrs. Anderson around the throat, from behind her. She threw up her arm, and her purse opened and everything inside fell on the sidewalk. Then the mugger lifted his hand and brought it down, and she screamed, and he yelled, 'Quiet, you witch!' Then he lifted his hand again and brought it down again, all the time yelling, 'Here, you witch, here, here,' while he was stabbing her. He must have lifted the knife at least a dozen times."

"And you saw him? You saw his face?"

"Yes. She dropped to the ground, and he came running up the street toward me. I tried to get against the building, but I was too late. We stood face-to-face, and for a minute I thought he was going to kill me, too. But he gave a kind of a moan and ran up the street."

"Why didn't you come to the police at once?"

"I...I guess I was scared. Mister, I still am. You've got to promise me I won't get into any trouble. I'm a married man, and I got two kids. I can't afford to..."

"Could you pick him out of a lineup? We've already rounded up a lot of men, some with records as muggers. Could you pick the killer?"

"Yes. But not if he can see me. If he sees me, it's all off. I won't go through with it if he can see me."

"He won't see you, sir. We'll put you behind a screen."

"So long as he doesn't see me. He knows what I look like, too, and I got a family. I won't identify him if he knows I'm the one doing it."

"You've got nothing to worry about." I clicked down Magruder's toggle on the intercom, and when he answered, I said, "Looks like we've got something here, Mac. Get the boys ready for a run-through, will you? And set up a screen for the witness."

"Right. I'll let the Chief know."

"Buzz me back," I said, and hung up.

"I won't do it unless I'm behind that screen," Struthers said.

"I've asked for a screen, sir."

I was still waiting for Magruder to get back, when the door opened. A voice lined with anguish and fatigue said, "Mac tells me you've got a witness."

I turned from the window, ready to say, "Yes, sir," and Struthers turned to face the door at the same time.

His eyebrows lifted, and his eyes grew wide.

He stared at the figure in the doorway and I watched both men as their eyes met and locked for an instant.

"No!" Struthers said suddenly. "I...I've changed my mind. I...I can't do it. I have to go. I have to go."

He slammed his hat onto his head and ran out quickly, almost before I'd gotten to my feet.

"Now what the hell got into him all of a sudden?" I asked.

Chief Anderson shrugged wearily.

"I have no idea," he said.

*Two of the major characters in the 87th Precinct novels are Detective Arthur Brown and Deputy Chief Surgeon Sharyn Cooke. They're both black. But long before these two characters were born, I was experimenting with writing from the viewpoint of blacks. In 1954, the same year I tried to become Gregory Miller in* The Blackboard Jungle, *this story by Richard Marsten appeared in* Manhunt.

# Every Morning

HE SANG SOFTLY TO HIMSELF AS HE WORKED ON THE long white beach. He could see the pleasure craft scooting over the deep blue waters, could see the cottony clouds moving leisurely across the wide expanse of sky. There was a mild breeze in the air, and it touched the woolly skullcap that was his hair, caressed his brown skin. He worked with a long rake, pulling at the tangled sea vegetation that the norther had tossed onto the sand. The sun was strong, and the sound of the sea was good, and he was almost happy as he worked.

He watched the muscles ripple on his long brown arms as he pulled at the rake. She would not like it if the beach were dirty. She liked the beach to be sparkling white and clean... the way her skin was.

"Jonas!"

He heard the call, and he turned his head toward the big house. He felt the same panic he'd felt a hundred times before. He could feel the trembling start in his hands, and he turned back to the rake, wanting to stall as long as he could, hoping she would not call again, but knowing she would.

"Jonas! Jo-naaaas!"

The call came from the second floor of the house, and he knew it came from her bedroom, and he knew she was just rising, and he knew exactly what would happen if he went up there. He hated what was about to happen, but at the same time it excited him. He clutched the rake more tightly, telling himself he would not answer her call, lying to himself because he knew he would go if she called one more time.

"Jonas! Where the devil are you?"

"Coming, Mrs. Hicks," he shouted.

He sighed deeply and put down the rake. He climbed the concrete steps leading from the beach, and then he walked past the barbecue pit and the beach house, moving under the Australian pines that lined the beach. The pine needles were soft under his feet, and though he knew the pines were planted to form a covering over the sand, to stop sand from being tracked into the house, he still enjoyed the soft feel under his shoes. For an instant, he wished he were barefoot, and then he scolded himself for having a thought that was strictly "native."

He shook his head and climbed the steps to the screened back porch of the house. The hibiscus climbed the screen in a wild array of color, pinks and reds and orchids. The smaller bougainvillea reached up for the sun where it splashed down through the pines. He closed the door behind him and walked through the dim cool interior of the house, starting up the steps to her bedroom.

When he reached her door, he paused outside, and then he knocked discreetly.

"Is that you, Jonas?"

"Yes, Mrs. Hicks."

"Well, come in."

He opened the door and stepped into the bedroom. She was sitting in bed, the sheet reaching to her waist. Her long blonde hair spilled over her shoulders, trailing down her back. She wore a white nylon gown, and he could see the mounds of her breasts beneath the gown, could see the erect rosebuds of her nipples. Hastily, he lowered his eyes.

"Good morning, Jonas," she said.

"Good morning, Mrs. Hicks."

"My, it's a beautiful morning, isn't it?"

"Yes, Mrs. Hicks."

"Where were you when I called, Jonas?"

"On the beach, Mrs. Hicks."

"Swimming, Jonas?" She lifted one eyebrow archly, and a tiny smile curled her mouth.

"Oh, no, Mrs. Hicks. I was raking up the..."

"Haven't you ever felt like taking a swim at that beach, Jonas?"

He did not answer. He stared at his shoes, and he felt his hands clench at his sides.

"Jonas?"

"Yes, Mrs. Hicks?"

"Haven't you ever felt like taking a swim at that beach?"

"There's lots of places to swim, Mrs. Hicks."

"Yes." The smile expanded. Her green eyes were smiling now, too. She sat in bed like a slender cat, licking her chops. "That's what I like about Nassau. There are lots of places to swim." She continued smiling for a moment, and then she sat up straighter, as if she were ready for business now.

"Well," she said, "what shall we have for breakfast? Has the cook come in, Jonas?"

"Yes, Mrs. Hicks."

"Eggs, I think. Coddled. And some toast and marmalade. And a little juice." He made a movement toward the door, and she stopped him with a wave of her hand. "Oh, there's no rush, Jonas. Stay. I want you to help me."

He swallowed, and he put his hands behind his back to hide the trembling. "Yes...Mrs. Hicks."

She threw back the sheet, and he saw her long legs beneath the hem of the short nightgown. She reached for her slippers on the floor near her bed, squirmed her feet into them, and then stood up. Luxuriantly, she stretched her arms over her head and yawned. The nightgown tightened across her chest, lifting as she raised her arms, showing more of the long curve of her legs. She walked to the window and threw open the blinds, and the sun splashed through the gown, and he saw the full outline of her body, and he thought, Every morning, every morning the same thing.

He could feel the sweat beading his brow, and he wanted to get out of that room, wanted to get far away from her and her body, wanted to escape this labyrinth that led to one exit alone.

"Ahhhhhhhhh."

She let out her breath and then walked across the room to her dressing table. She sat and crossed her legs, and he could see the whiter area on her thigh that the sun never reached. And looking at that whiter stretch of flesh, his own skin felt browner.

"Do you like working for me?" she asked suddenly.

"Yes, Mrs. Hicks," he said quickly.

"You don't really, though, do you?"

"I like it, Mrs. Hicks," he said.

"I like you to work for me, Jonas. I wouldn't have you leave for anything in the world. You know that, don't you, Jonas?"

"Yes, Mrs. Hicks."

There has to be a way out, he thought. There has to be some way. A way other than the one…the one…

"Have you ever thought of quitting this job, Jonas?"

"No, Mrs. Hicks," he lied.

"That's sensible, you know. Not quitting, I mean. It wouldn't be wise for you to quit, would it, Jonas? Aside from the salary, I mean, which is rather handsome, wouldn't you say, Jonas."

"It's a handsome salary," he said.

"Yes. But aside from that, aside from losing the salary if you quit. I wouldn't like you to quit, Jonas. I would let Mr. Hicks know of my displeasure, and my husband is really quite a powerful man, you know that, don't you?"

"Yes, Mrs. Hicks."

"It might be difficult for you to get work afterwards, I mean if you ever decided to leave me. Heaven knows, there's not much work for Bahamians as it is. And Mr. Hicks is quite powerful, knowing the governor and all, isn't that right, Jonas?"

When he did not answer, she giggled suddenly.

"Oh, we're being silly. You like the job, and I like you, so why should we talk of leaving?" She paused. "Has my husband gone to the club?"

"Yes, Mrs. Hicks."

"Good," she said. "Come do my hair, Jonas."

"I…"

"Come do my hair," she said slowly and firmly.

"Y…yes, Mrs. Hicks."

She held out the brush to him, and he took it and then placed himself behind her chair. He could see her face in the mirror of the dressing table, could see the clean sweep of her throat, and beneath that the first rise of her breasts where the neck of the gown ended. She tilted her head back and her eyes met his in the mirror.

"Stroke evenly now, Jonas. And gently. Remember. Gently."

He began stroking her hair. He watched her face as he stroked, not wanting to watch it, but knowing that he was inside the trap now, and knowing that he had to watch her face, had to watch her lips part as he stroked, had to watch the narrowing of those green eyes. Every morning, every morning the same thing, every morning driving him out of his mind with her body and her glances, always daring him, always challenging him, and always reminding him that it could not be. He stroked, and her breath came faster in her throat, and he watched the animal pleasure on her face as the brush bristles searched her scalp.

And as he stroked, he thought again of the only way out, and he wondered if he had the courage to do it, wondered if he could ever muster the courage to stop all this, stop it finally and irrevocably. She counted softly as he stroked, and her voice was a whisper, and he continued to think of what he must do to end it, and he felt the great fear within him, but he knew he could not take much more of this, not every morning, and he knew he could not leave the job because she would make sure there would never be work for him again.

But even knowing all this, the way out was a drastic one, and he wondered what it would be like without her hair to brush every morning, without the sight of her body, without the soft caress of her voice.

Death, he thought.

*Death.*

"That's enough, Jonas," she said.

He handed her the brush. "I'll tell the cook, Mrs. Hicks, to..."

"No, stay."

He looked at her curiously. She always dismissed him after the brushing. Her eyes always turned cold and forbidding then, as if she'd had her day's sport and was then ready to end the farce...until the next morning.

"I think something bit me yesterday. An insect, I think," she said. "I wonder if you'd mind looking. You natives...what I mean, you'd probably be familiar with it."

She stood up and walked toward him, and then she began unbuttoning the yoke neck of her gown. He watched her in panic, not knowing whether to flee or stand, knowing only that he would have to carry out his plan after this, knowing that she would go further and further unless it were ended, and knowing that only he could end it, in the only possible way open for him.

He watched her take the hem of her gown in her fingers and pull it up over her waist. He saw the clean whiteness of her skin, and then she pulled the gown up over her back, turning, her breasts still covered, bending.

"In the center of my back, Jonas, do you see it?"

She came closer to him. He was wet with perspiration now. He stared at her back, the fullness of her buttocks, the impression of her spine against her flesh.

"There's...there's nothing, Mrs. Hicks," he said. "Nothing."

She dropped the gown abruptly, and then turned to face him, the smile on her mouth again, the yoke of the gown open so that he could see her breasts plainly.

"Nothing?" she asked, smiling. "You saw nothing, Jonas?"

"Nothing, Mrs. Hicks," he said, and he turned and left her, still smiling, her hands on her hips.

He slit his wrists with a razor blade the next morning. He watched the blood stain the sand on the beach he'd always kept so clean, and he felt a strange inner peace possess him as the life drained out of him.

The native police did not ask many questions when they arrived, and Mrs. Hicks did not offer to show them her torn and shredded nightgown, or the purple bruises on her breasts and thighs.

She hired a new caretaker that afternoon.

This little story by Richard Marsten appeared in Manhunt in 1953. There is little to say about it except that it is a quintessential Innocent Bystander story—and it still remains one of my favorites.

# The Innocent One

IT WAS THE NEXT POOR BASTARD WHO GOT IT.

You must understand, first, that the sun was very hot on that day and Miguel had been working in it from just after dawn. He had eaten a hearty breakfast, and then had taken to the fields early, remembering what had to be done and wanting to do it quickly.

There were many rocks among the beans that day, and perhaps that is what started it all. When Miguel discovered the first rock, he reached down gingerly and tossed it over his shoulder to the rear of his neat rows of beans. The sun was still not high in the sky and the earth had not yet begun to bake, and so a smile worked its way over his brown features as he heard the rock thud to the soft earth behind. He started hoeing again, thinking of Maria and the night before.

He would never regret having married Maria. *Jesus*, she was a one! There was the passion of the tigress in her, and the energy of the rabbit. He thought again of her, straightening up abruptly, and feeling the ache in his back muscles.

That was when he saw the second rock.

He shrugged, thinking, *Dios*, another one!

He lifted it, threw it over his shoulder, and began hoeing

again. He was surprised when he came across more rocks. At first he thought someone had played a joke on him, and he pulled his black brows together, wondering who it could have been. Juan, that pig? Felipe, that animal with the slobbering lips? Pablo?

Then he remembered that it had rained the night before, and he realized that the waters had washed the soil clean, exposing the rocks, bringing them to the surface.

He cursed himself for not having thought to protect the beans in some way. Then he cursed the rocks. And since the sun was beginning to climb in the sky, he cursed that too, and got to work.

The rocks were not heavy. They were, in fact, rather small.

It was that there were very many of them. He picked them up painstakingly, tossing them over his shoulders. How could a man hoe his beans when the rows were full of rocks? He started to count them, stopping at ten because that was as far as he knew how to count, and then starting with one all over again.

The sun was very hot now. The hoe lay on the ground, the rich earth staining its long handle. He kept picking up the rocks, not looking up now, swearing softly, the sweat pouring down his neck and back. When a long shadow fell over the land before him, he almost didn't notice it.

Then a voice joined the shadow and Miguel straightened his back and rubbed his earth-stained fingers on his white trousers.

"You are busy, Miguel?" the voice asked. The voice came through the speaker's nose rather than his mouth. It whined like the voice of the lamb. It was Felipe.

"No, I am not busy," Miguel said. "I was, at this very moment, lying on my back and counting the stars in the sky."

"But it is morning..." Felipe started. Miguel's subtle humor struck him then, and he slapped his thigh and guffawed like the jackass he was. "Counting the stars!" he bellowed. "Counting the stars!"

Miguel was not amused. "You were perhaps on your way somewhere, *amigo*. If so, don't let me detain you."

"I was going nowhere, Miguel," Felipe said.

Miguel grunted and began picking up rocks again. He forgot how many rocks he had counted thus far, so he started all over again."

"You are picking up rocks, Miguel?"

Miguel did not answer.

"I say you are picking up..."

"Yes!" Miguel said. "Yes, I am picking up rocks." He stood up and kneaded the small of his back, and Felipe grinned knowingly.

"The back, it hurts, eh?"

"Yes," Miguel said. He looked at Felipe. "Why do you nod?"

"Me? Nod? Who, me?"

"Yes, you. Why do you stand here and nod your head like the wise snake who has swallowed the young chicken?"

Felipe grinned and nodded his head. "You must be mistaken, Miguel. I do not nod."

"I am not blind, *amigo*," Miguel said testily. "I say my back hurts, and you begin to nod your head. Why is it funny that my back hurts? Is it funny that there are rocks and stones among my beans?"

"No, Miguel. It is not funny."

"Then why do you nod?"

Felipe grinned. "Maria, eh?"

Miguel clenched his fists. "What about Maria, *amigo*? Maria who is my wife."

Felipe opened his eyes innocently. "Nothing, Miguel. Just...Maria."

"You refer to my back?"

"*Sí!*"

"And you connect this somehow with Maria?"

"*Sí.*"

"How?"

"This Maria...your wife, God bless her...she is a strong one, eh, Miguel?"

Miguel was beginning to get a little angry. He was not used to discussing his wife among the beans. "So? What do you mean she is a strong one?"

"You know. *Muy fuerte*. Like the tigress."

"How do you know this?"

Felipe grinned. "It is known, Miguel."

Miguel's lips tightened into a narrow line. "How is it known?"

"I must go to town, Miguel," Felipe said hastily. "I see you soon."

"Just a moment, Felipe. How is it...?"

"Good-bye, *amigo*."

Felipe turned his back and Miguel stared at him as he walked toward the road. The dust rose about him, and he waved back at Miguel. Miguel did not return the wave. He stood there with the strong sun on his head, and the many rocks and stones at his feet.

How did this animal with the slobbering lips know of Maria's passion? Surely he had never spoken a word about it to any of the men. Then how did Felipe know?

The possibilities annoyed Miguel. He turned back to the rocks, and this time they seemed heavier, and the sun seemed stronger, and his back seemed to ache more.

*How did Felipe know?*

He was pondering this in an ill temper when Juan came to stand beside him. Juan was darkly handsome, his white trousers and shirt bright in the powerful sunlight. Miguel looked up at him sourly and said, "So? Do you wish to pass the time with idle chatter also?"

Juan smiled, his teeth even and white against the ruddy brown of his face. "Did I offend you, Miguel?"

"No!" Miguel snapped.

"Then why do you leap at me like a tiger?"

"Do not mention this animal to me," Miguel said.

"No?"

"No! I have rocks to clear, and I want to clear them before lunch because Maria will be calling me then."

"Ahhhhh," Juan said, grinning.

Miguel stared at him for a moment. The grin was the same one Felipe had worn, except that Felipe was ugly and with slobbering lips and Juan was perhaps the handsomest man in the village.

Miguel stared at him and wondered if it had been *he* who told Felipe of Maria's great passion. And if so, how had Juan known?

"Why do you 'ahhhhh'?" he asked.

"Did I 'ahhhhh'?"

"You did. You did indeed. You made this very sound. Why?"

"I was not aware, *amigo*." Juan said, and smiled again.

"Was it mention of lunch that evoked this sigh?"

"No. No, I do not think so."

"Then there remains only Maria."

Juan grinned and said nothing.

"I said..."

"I heard you, Miguel."

"What about Maria?"

Juan shrugged. "Who said anything about Maria?"

"You are saying it with your eyes," Miguel said heatedly. "What about her?"

"She is your wife, Miguel."

"I know she is my wife. I sleep with her, I..."

Juan was grinning again.

"What's funny about that, Juan? Why do you grin now?"

"I have nothing to say, *amigo*. Maria is your wife. God bless her."

"What does that mean?"

"It means...well, God bless her. She is a good woman."

"How would you know?" Miguel shouted.

"That she is a good woman? Why, Miguel..."

"You know what I mean! Why is my wife the sudden topic of conversation for the whole village? What's going on? Why do you all discuss her so intimately?"

"Intimately?"

"Yes! By God, Juan, if there is something that someone knows..."

Juan smiled again. "But there is nothing, Miguel. Nothing."

"You are sure?"

"I must go to town now, my friend. Is there anything I can do there for you?"

"No!" Miguel snapped.

"Then, *adios, amigo.*"

He turned and walked off, shaking his head, and Miguel could have sworn he heard him mutter the word "tigress."

He went to work on the rocks with a fury. What was all this? Why Felipe? And now Juan?

What was going on with his wife?

He thought of her passion, her gleaming black hair, the way it trailed down the curve of her back, reaching her waist. He thought of the fluid muscles on that back, beneath the soft, firm skin. He thought of the long graceful curve of her legs, the way the firelight played on her lifted breasts, the deep hollow of her navel.

Too passionate, he thought. Far too passionate.

Far too passionate for one man. Far too passionate for simple Miguel who worked the fields picking stones and hoeing beans. Yes, she was a woman who needed many men, many, many men.

Was that why Felipe had laughed with dripping lips? Was that why Juan had smiled that superior handsome smile? Miguel picked up his hoe and swung it at a large rock. The rock chipped, but it did not budge from the earth.

Was that it? Was Maria then making a cuckold of her simple Miguel? Was that why all the men in the village were snickering, smiling, laughing behind their hands? Or was it only the men from this village? Was it the adjoining village, too? Or did it go beyond that?

Did they pass her from hand to hand like a used wine jug? Did they all drink of her, and was that why they laughed at Miguel now? Was that why they laughed behind their hands, laughed aloud with their mouths and their eyes?

The sun was hot, and the bowels of the earth stank, and the rocks and stones were plentiful, and Miguel chopped at them with the hoe, using the sharp blade like an ax.

I shall show them, he thought. I shall teach them to laugh. I shall teach them to make the fool of Miguel de la Piaz!

It was then that Pablo strolled by. He had passed Miguel's house and Maria had asked him to call her husband home for lunch. He was not a bright lad, Pablo. He walked up close to Miguel, who furiously pounded the earth with his hoe, using it like an ax, the sharp blade striking sparks from the rocks. He tapped Miguel on the shoulder, smiled, and started to say, "Maria..."

Miguel whirled like an animal, the hoe raised high.

So you see, it was the next poor bastard who got it.

# LOOSE CANNONS

$N$obody in police work likes to deal with lunatics. There's no predictability to the crimes committed by madmen. Moreover, in most mystery novels, there's a murder to be solved, a puzzle to be unraveled. Loose cannons present no such challenge, so I try to avoid them in the police novels I write today. But back in the fifties, I wrote several stories that...

Well, let me take that back.

Yes, the stories that follow were all published in the fifties. "Chalk" by Evan Hunter in 1953, in a Manhunt imitator called Pursuit; then "Association Test" and "Bedbug," both in Manhunt itself, both in 1954, the first under the Hunt Collins byline, the next under my already-legal name, Evan Hunter; and finally, in 1957 and again in Manhunt, another Evan Hunter story titled "The Merry Merry Christmas." So...er... what is there to take back?

"Chalk."

Although this was finally published in 1953 (under the title "I Killed Jeannie," can you believe it!), I wrote this story in 1945, aboard a destroyer in the middle of the Pacific Ocean. When it circulated among my shipmates, it caused no small degree of apprehension. That's because loose cannons are unpredictable.

Here it is now, followed by the others in uninterrupted chronological order.

# Chalk

HER FACE WAS A PIECE OF UGLY PINK CHALK, AND HER eyes were two little brown mud puddles. Her eyes were mud puddles and they did not fit with the pink chalk. The chalk was ugly, and her eyes were mud puddles, and they made the chalk look uglier.

"Your eyes are mud puddles," I said, and she laughed.

I didn't like her to laugh. I was serious. She shouldn't have laughed when I told her something serious like that.

I hit the pink chalk with my fist but it didn't crumble. I wondered why it didn't crumble. I hit it again and water ran out of the mud puddles. I pushed my hand into one of the mud puddles and it turned all red, and it looked prettier with water coming out of it and red.

I tore the beads from her neck and threw them at the chalk. I felt her nails dig into my skin and I didn't like that. I twisted her arm and she struggled and pushed, and her body felt nice and soft up tight against mine. I wanted to squeeze her and when I began squeezing her she screamed, and the noise reminded me of the Third Avenue El when it stops going, and the noise reminded me of babies crying at night when I'm trying to sleep. So I hit her mouth to stop the noise but instead it got louder.

I ripped her dress in the front and I swore at her and told her to stop the noise, but she wouldn't stop so I kicked her in the leg and she fell. She looked soft and white on the floor. All except her face. It was still pink chalk.

*Ugly pink chalk.*

I stepped on it with all my might and the mud puddles closed and red came from her nose.

I stepped on her again and the pink chalk was getting red all over and it looked good and I kept stepping. And the red got thicker and redder, and then she started to twitch and jerk like she was sick and I bent down and asked, "Are you sick, Jeannie?"

She didn't answer except like a moan, and then she made a noise that sounded like the Third Avenue El again, and I had to hit her again to make her stop.

I kept punching her in the face and the noise stopped.

It was very quiet.

Her eyes weren't mud puddles. Why did I think they were mud puddles? They were two shiny glass marbles and they were looking right at me, only they couldn't see me because they were glass and you can't see out of glass.

The pink chalk was all red now except for white patches here and there. Her mouth was open but there was no noise.

Then I heard the ticking.

It was loud, like an ax splitting wood, and I was afraid it was going to wake her up and then she would make the noise all over again, and I would have to tell her to stop and hit her again. I did not want to hit her again because her eyes were only marbles and you can't see out of marbles, and her face was a pretty red and not made of chalk that would not crumble.

So I stepped on the ticking. I stepped on it twice so that I could be sure. Then I took off her clothes and she looked all red and white and quiet when I put her on the bed. I doused the light and then I left her to sleep. I felt sorry for her.

She couldn't see because her eyes were only marbles.

It was cold in the night. It shouldn't have been cold because the sky was an oil fire, all billowy and black. Why was it cold?

I saw a man coming and I stopped him because I wanted to know why it was so cold when the sky was burning up. He talked funny and he couldn't walk straight and he said it was warm and I was crazy if I thought it was cold. I asked him if he was warm.

He said, "I am warm, and don't bother me because I feel wonderful and I don't want to lose this feeling."

I hit him and I took his coat because he was warm and he didn't need it if he was warm.

I ran fast down the street, and then I knew he was right. It was warm and I didn't need his coat so I went back to take it to him because he might be cold now. He wasn't there so I put the coat on the sidewalk in case he came back for it.

Then I ran down the street because it was nice and warm and it felt like springtime and I wanted to run and leap. I got tired and I began to breathe hard so I sat down on the sidewalk. Then I was tired of sitting and I did not want to run anymore so I began looking at the store windows but they were all dark. I did not like them to be dark because I liked to look at the things in the windows and if they were dark I couldn't see them.

Poor Jeannie.

Her eyes were marbles and she could not see the things in the store windows. Why did God make my eyes out of white jelly and Jeannie's out of glass? I wondered how she knew me if she couldn't see me.

It was getting cold again and I swore at the man who had talked funny and couldn't walk straight. He had lied to me and made me feel warm when it was really cold all along. I lifted my hand up to the light in the street because it was yellow and warm, but I couldn't reach it and I was still cold.

Then the wet fell out of the sky and I began to run so it wouldn't touch me. But it was all around me and the more I ran the more it fell. And the noise in the sky was like a dog growling under his teeth, and the lights that flashed were a pale, scary blue. I ran and ran and I was getting tired of running and the wet was making me wet, and the damp was creeping into my head and the dark was behind it the way the dark always was.

The damp pressed on the inside and it pushed outward, and then the dark creeped up and I screamed, and it sounded like the Third Avenue El when it stops going, and I screamed again and it sounded like babies crying, and I punched myself in the face so I would stop the way Jeannie had. But I screamed again and the damp was all in and over my head. The dark was waiting, too.

I screamed because I didn't want the dark to come in, but I could see it was getting closer and I knew the way the damp always felt just before the dark came in. I hit my face again but the damp was heavy now and it was dripping inside my head and I knew the dark was coming and I ran away from it.

But it was there, and first it was gray like the ocean and then it got deeper like a dense fog and then it turned black and blacker, and the dark came and I knew I was falling, and I couldn't stop because Jeannie's eyes were only marbles.

I am lying on a sidewalk in a strange street.

The sun is just rising and the bustle of the day has not yet begun. There is a severe pain in my head. I know I haven't been drinking, yet where did this terrible pain come from?

I rise and brush off my clothes.

It is then that I notice the blood on my hands and on my shoes. Blood?

Have I been fighting? No, no, I don't remember any fighting. I remember...I remember...calling on Jeannie.

She did not feel like going out, so we decided to sit at home and talk. She made coffee, and we were sitting and drinking and talking.

How do I come to be in this strange street? With blood on my body?

I begin to walk.

There are store windows with various forms of merchandise in them. There is a man's overcoat lying in the street, a ragged overcoat lying in a heap. I pass it rapidly.

It is starting to drizzle now. I walk faster. I must see Jeannie. Perhaps she can clear this up for me.

Anyway, the drizzle is turning into a heavy rain.

And I have never liked the darkness or dampness that come with a storm.

# Association Test

"BOY," THE PSYCHIATRIST SAID.

"Girl," the man answered.

"Black," the psychiatrist said.

"White," the man answered.

"Mmm," the psychiatrist said. He jotted some notes down on a sheet of paper, and then said, "All right, Mr. Bellew, let's go on, shall we?"

Bellew was a thin man with shaggy brown hair.

He twisted his hands nervously and said, "All right, Doctor."

"Now then," the doctor said, consulting his notes. "Bird."

"Free," Bellew said.

"Did you say 'tree'?"

"No. No, I said 'free.' Free."

"Um-huh. Knife."

"Death."

"Um-huh. Red."

"Bl…"

"What did you say?"

"Blue. Blue was what I said."

"I see," the doctor said. "House."

**426**

"Home."

"Home," the doctor said.

"Children," Bellew answered.

"Children."

"Kites."

"Kites," the doctor said.

"Free," Bellew answered.

The doctor made a disinterested note, and then looked up. "According to your letter, Mr. Bellew, you've been disturbed about something, is that right?"

"Yes," Bellew said slowly.

"Um-huh." The doctor reached for the slitted envelope on his desk, and then pulled the letter from it. His free hand picked up a pointed letter opener and idly tapped it on the desk as he read from the sheet of stationery. "It's curious you should write. I mean, most people call, or stop by in person."

"I wanted to do that, but I was afraid to," Bellew said.

"Afraid to?" the doctor asked. He continued tapping the metal letter opener. "Why?"

"I...I don't like doctors," Bellew said nervously.

"Oh, come now. Don't you like me?"

"Well..."

"You *did* come here, didn't you? After I called back to arrange for an appointment, you did come, didn't you? You're here now, aren't you?"

"Yes," Bellew said. "I'm here."

"And it hasn't been so terrible, has it?"

"No, it hasn't."

"Just a few tests, that's all." The doctor chuckled. "Nothing at all to be afraid of."

"I suppose not," Bellew said.

"Then what's been disturbing you?"

"I don't know," Bellew said.

"You don't like doctors, is that it?"

Bellew hesitated. "Yes," he said.

"Well, I'm a doctor, and we're getting along fine, aren't we?" The doctor smiled and dropped the letter opener. "You do like me, don't you, Mr. Bellew?"

"I...I don't know," Bellew said.

"But we're getting along fine, Mr. Bellew," the doctor said enthusiastically. "You must admit that."

"Y...yes," Bellew said.

"There! You see how your dislike is unfounded?"

"I...oh, I..." Bellew wet his lips.

"What is it, Mr. Bellew?"

"I don't know. If I knew, I wouldn't have come to you."

"Now, now. Easy does it," the doctor said. "Quite frankly, Mr. Bellew, the tests we've just taken show no indication of any personality disturbance. I'm speaking off the cuff, you understand, since the tests must still be interpreted. But I can judge fairly accurately from a casual interpretation of your answers, and I'd say you were in the pink of mental health."

"The...the pink," Bellew repeated blankly.

"Yes, the pink. Top shape. Excellent form. Oh, a few anxieties, perhaps, but nothing serious." The doctor chuckled. "Nothing more than all of us are suffering in these nervous times."

"I...I can't believe that," Bellew said.

The doctor lifted his eyebrows. "But the tests..."

"Then the tests must be wrong," Bellew said firmly.

"No, I don't think so," the doctor said patiently. "Really, Mr. Bellew..."

"Are you trying to tell me I'm not disturbed when I know I'm disturbed?"

"There," the doctor said. "Most seriously disturbed persons don't even know they're disturbed. That's the root of all their troubles. When a person seeks the aid of a psychiatrist, seeks the doctor voluntarily, his battle is half won. Don't you see?"

"No. You haven't helped me at all. You've just told me I'm all right when I know I'm not all right."

"I said you may have a few anxieties, but we can clear those up in just a very short time. There's certainly nothing serious to worry about."

"I don't believe it," Bellew said.

"Well…" The doctor spread his hands wide. "I don't see how I can convince you." He paused, a blank expression on his face.

Bellew snorted disgustedly. "You're all the same," he said. "All you damn doctors."

"Now, now, Mr. Bellew…"

"Oh, don't 'now, now' me. All you're after is a fee, just like the rest. I tell you I'm sick, and you won't believe it. What the hell am I supposed to do? You just give me your damn tests and ask me to identify inkblots and associate words and…oh, the hell with it."

"That's all part of your anxiety, Mr. Bellew," the doctor said. "As I said, we can clear that up in no time."

"That's what you say. On the basis of your damn tests," Bellew said, clenching and unclenching his hands.

"The tests are usually valid, Mr. Bellew," the doctor said. He paused, and then an inspired look crossed his face. "Say, look, I'll show you. I mean, I can show you just how normal you are, all right?"

"Go ahead," Bellew said tightly, his fists clenched now.

"Just give me the first word that pops into your mind when I give you a word. The way we just…"

"We did this already," Bellew said, a tic starting at the corner of his mouth.

"I know. But I want to show you one thing. Let's try it, shall we?" He paused and then said, "Boy."

"Girl," Bellew said.

"A perfectly normal response," the doctor said happily. "Girl."

"Woman," Bellew said.

"Again, a normal response. Woman."

"Bed," Bellew said.

"You see, Mr. Bellew, these are normal responses." He rose from his desk and began walking around the room. "Bed."

"Sheet," Bellew answered.

"Fine, fine," the doctor said. "Sheet."

"White."

"White," the doctor said.

"Flesh," Bellew answered.

"Flesh," the doctor said.

"Blood."

"All quite normal," the doctor said, turning his back and examining a picture hanging on the wall. "Flesh and blood, a normal association."

Bellew rose from his seat and stared at the doctor's back.

"Blood," the doctor said, still studying the picture.

"Knife," Bellew answered. His eyes fled to the desktop, and he reached for the letter opener there, grasping it in firm fingers.

"Knife," the doctor said wearily.

"Death," Bellew answered, walking swiftly around the desk and raising the sharp metal letter opener over his head.

"Death," the doctor repeated softly.

The letter opener sped downward with a terrible rush. It sank between the doctor's shoulder blades, and Bellew screamed, "Death, death, death, *death!*" as the doctor sank to the floor.

# Bedbug

MY WIFE WAS WATCHING ME AGAIN. SHE PRETENDED TO be reading her newspaper, but I knew she was watching me. I could feel her eyes boring through the printed page. She was very clever, and so she kept the paper in front of her face, but she wasn't fooling me, not anymore she wasn't.

"What are you reading?" I asked.

I was sitting in the chair opposite her. She had her legs crossed, and I thought what a shame such a pretty girl and with a sickness like that, and the worst kind, the kind they can't fix, even with all their drugs and their shocks.

"The comics," she answered.

"Which? Which comic?"

"Pogo," she said. "Why?"

She was being tricky again. She was always like a defense attorney, always with a comeback, always trying to twist whatever I said. I understand they get clever that way. The minute they get twisted, they start getting clever, too. Only I was just a little bit cleverer than her.

"Why *what*?" I asked.

"I mean, what difference does it make which comic I'm reading?"

"I thought you might be reading something gory," I said. I smiled, and she lowered the paper and looked at me curiously, and maybe she suspected I was on to her in that moment.

"Gory?"

"Yes, gory. Death and violence. Something with blood in it. Gory. Don't you know what gory means, for God's sake?"

"Of course I know what gory means."

"Then why did you say it as if you didn't know what it meant? Were you trying to test me? Were you trying to find out if I knew?"

"Oh, don't be silly. Everybody knows what gory means. I was just surprised that you asked." She shrugged and lifted the paper again, but I could feel her eyes through the page, watching me, always watching me. I stared at the paper until she lowered it again.

"What's the matter with you, Dave?" she asked.

I chuckled a little, and then I narrowed my eyes. "There's nothing the matter with me," I said.

"You've been behaving so...so strangely lately," she said.

"Maybe I'm just beginning to wise up," I said.

"I don't understand you. That's what I mean, the things you say. They don't make sense."

"Does soup make sense?" I asked her.

"What?" She was playing it innocent, as if she didn't know about the soup, as if she had no idea what I was talking about.

"Soup," I said. "Soup. What the hell's wrong with you? Can't you understand English?"

"Well, what about soup? I don't understand."

"The soup last night," I said. I watched her carefully, my eyes slitted.

"Yes, we had soup last night."

"No," I corrected her. "*We* did not have soup last night. *I* had soup last night."

"It was too hot last night," she said, trying to appear tired, trying to pretend she didn't know what I was driving at. "Much too hot to be having soup. I just didn't feel like any, that's all."

"But I did, huh?"

"You said you wanted soup."

"Yes, but that was before I knew you weren't having any."

"What do you mean?"

"Nothing," I said. I paused and waited to see what she'd say next. She didn't say anything, so I prompted her. "Were you surprised I didn't finish the soup?"

"Not particularly. It was a hot night."

"Yes, but I only had two spoonfuls. Weren't you surprised?"

"No," she said.

She was being very cagey now, because we were getting closer to the heart of the matter, and she didn't like that. I had to go on with what I was doing, but I felt sorry for her at the same time. It wasn't her fault, her illness, and it was a shame they wouldn't be able to do anything for her. I felt really sorry.

"But didn't you wonder why I stopped after only two spoonfuls?"

"Are we back to that damned soup again?"

"Yes. Yes, we are back to that damned soup again. It's a good thing I have excellent taste buds."

"What are you talking about?"

"My reasons for not finishing the soup. After I tasted it. That's what I'm talking about."

"Was there something wrong with the soup?"

That I liked. Oh, that I liked. That innocent look on her

face, that little small voice, pretending ignorance, pretending the soup was all right.

"No, nothing," I lied. "Nothing wrong with it at all. There was nothing wrong with the brake lining on the car, either. Nothing that sixty bucks couldn't fix after I discovered it."

"Here we go on the brake lining again," she said.

"You don't like me to talk about it, do you?"

"We've only talked about it for the past three weeks. What the hell is wrong with you anyway, Dave?"

"Nothing's wrong with me, honey," I said. "No, nothing's wrong with me."

"Then why do you keep harping on things? How did I know the brake lining was shot? How could I possibly know that?"

"Oh no, you couldn't know," I said.

"You see? You're implying that I did know."

"I'm not implying anything. Stop trying to twist what I say."

"You had the brakes fixed, didn't you?"

"Yes. Because I discovered them in time. Like the soup. Just in time."

"Dave..."

She stopped talking and shook her head, and I felt sorry for her again, but what could I do about it? How could I continue living with her, knowing what I did about her? And how could I turn her over to people I knew could not help her? I loved her too much for that, far too much. I could not bear seeing her waste away, unhelped, curling into a fetal ball, cutting herself off from reality, escaping the world we both knew. But at the same time, I recognized the danger of having her around, watching me, waiting for her chance.

"You watch me all the time, don't you?" I asked.

"No, I do not watch you all the time. Christ knows I've got better things to do than watch you."

"What's wrong with me?" I asked.

"That's just what I'd like to know, believe me," she said emphatically.

"I didn't mean it that way, and you know it. You're twisting again. You always twist. For Christ's sake, Anne, can't you see that you're all mixed up? These attempts you made on my..."

"Me mixed up? Me?" she said, and sighed heavily.

I got out of my chair and walked toward her.

"Why'd you make those attempts on my life, Anne?" I asked.

"What? What!"

"The poisoned soup, and the..."

"Poisoned soup! Dave, what on earth are you...?"

"...and the brake lining, and that loose step on the basement stairs, and oh, all the other little things. Don't you think I spotted them all? Don't you think I've known for a long time now?"

She stared up at me, bewildered, and I felt immensely sorry for her again, but I could not see turning her over to people who could not help her, I could not see committing her.

I reached down for her throat and pulled her out of the chair, and her eyes opened wide in fright, and she tried to scream "Dave!" but my hands tightened on her windpipe.

She kept watching me all the while, watching me, her eyes bulging, watching, watching, always watching me while

# Bedbug

I squeezed all the twisted rottenness out of her head until she went limp at the end of my arms.

I dropped her to the floor and looked at her, and in death she did not look as crazy as a bedbug, but I knew she was, and now she would not be watching me anymore, but at the same time I couldn't keep myself from crying.

# The Merry Merry Christmas

Sitting at the bar, Pete Charpens looked at his own reflection in the mirror, grinned, and said, "Merry Christmas."

It was not yet Christmas, true enough, but he said it anyway, and the words sounded good, and he grinned foolishly and lifted his drink and sipped a little of it and said again, "Merry Christmas," feeling very good, feeling very warm, feeling in excellent high spirits.

Tonight, the city was his. Tonight, for the first time since he'd arrived from Whiting Center eight months ago, he felt like a part of the city. Tonight, the city enveloped him like a warm bath, and he lounged back and allowed the undulating waters to cover him. It was Christmas Eve, and all was right with the world, and Pete Charpens loved every mother's son who roamed the face of the earth because he felt as if he'd finally come home, finally found the place, finally found himself.

It was a good feeling.

This afternoon, as soon as the office party was over, he'd gone into the streets. The shop windows had gleamed like potbellied stoves, cherry hot against the sharp bite of the air. There was a promise of snow in the sky, and Pete had walked the tinseled streets of New York with his tweed coat collar against the back of his neck, and he had felt warm and happy. There were shoppers in the streets, and Santa Clauses with bells, and giant wreaths and giant trees, and music coming from speakers, the timeless carols of the holiday season. But more than that, for the first time in eight months, he had felt the pulse beat of the city, the people, the noise, the clutter, the rush, and, above all, the warmth. The warmth had engulfed him, surprising him. He had watched it with the foolish smile of a spectator and then, with sudden realization, he had known he was a part of it. In the short space of eight months, he had become a part of the city — and the city had become a part of him.

He had found a home.

"Bartender," he said.

The bartender ambled over. He was a big redheaded man with freckles all over his face. He moved with economy and grace. He seemed like a very nice guy who probably had a very nice wife and family decorating a Christmas tree somewhere in Queens.

"Yes, sir?" he asked.

"Pete. Call me Pete."

"Okay, Pete."

"I'm not drunk," Pete said, "believe me. I know all drunks say that, but I mean it. I'm just so damn happy I could bust. Did you ever feel that way?"

"Sure," the bartender said, smiling.

"Let me buy you a drink."

"I don't drink."

"Bartenders never drink, I know, but let me buy you one. Please. Look, I want to thank people, you know? I want to thank everybody in this city. I want to thank them for being here, for making it a city. Do I sound nuts?"

"Yes," the bartender said.

"Okay. Okay then, I'm nuts. But I'm a hick, do you know? I came here from Whiting Center eight months ago. Straw sticking out of my ears. The confusion here almost killed me. But I got a job, a good job, and I met a lot of wonderful people, and I learned how to dress, and I…I found a home. That's corny. I know it. That's the hick in me talking. But I love this damn city, I love it. I want to go around kissing girls in the streets. I want to shake hands with every guy I meet. I want to tell them I feel like a person, a human being, I'm alive, alive! For Christ's sake, I'm alive!"

"That's a good way to be," the bartender agreed.

"I know it. Oh, my friend, do I know it! I was dead in Whiting Center, and now I'm here and alive and…look, let me buy you a drink, huh?"

"I don't drink," the bartender insisted.

"Okay. Okay, I won't argue. I wouldn't argue with anyone tonight. Gee, it's gonna be a great Christmas, do you know? Gee, I'm so damn happy I could bust." He laughed aloud, and the bartender laughed with him. The laugh trailed off into a chuckle, and then a smile. Pete looked into the mirror, lifted his glass again, and again said, "Merry Christmas. Merry Christmas."

He was still smiling when the man came into the bar and sat down next to him. The man was very tall, his body bulging with power beneath the suit he wore. Coatless, hatless, he came into the bar and sat alongside Pete, signaling for the bartender with a slight flick of his hand. The bartender walked over.

"Rye neat," the man said.

The bartender nodded and walked away. The man reached for his wallet.

"Let me pay for it," Pete said.

The man turned. He had a wide face with a thick nose and small brown eyes. The eyes came as a surprise in his otherwise large body. He studied Pete for a moment and then said, "You a queer or something?"

Pete laughed. "Hell, no," he said. "I'm just happy. It's Christmas Eve, and I feel like buying you a drink."

The man pulled out his wallet, put a five-dollar bill on the bar top, and said, "I'll buy my own drink." He paused. "What's the matter? Don't I look as if I can afford a drink?"

"Sure you do," Pete said. "I just wanted to...look, I'm happy. I want to share it, that's all."

The man grunted and said nothing. The bartender brought his drink. He tossed off the shot and asked for another.

"My name's Pete Charpens," Pete said, extending his hand.

"So what?" the man said.

"Well...what's your name?"

"Frank."

"Glad to know you, Frank." He thrust his hand closer to the man.

"Get lost, Happy," Frank said.

Pete grinned, undismayed. "You ought to relax," he said, "I mean it. You know, you've got to stop..."

"Don't tell me what I've got to stop. Who the hell are you, anyway?"

"Pete Charpens. I told you."

"Take a walk, Pete Charpens. I got worries of my own."

"Want to tell me about them?"

"No, I don't want to tell you about them."

"Why not? Make you feel better."

"Go to hell, and stop bothering me," Frank said.

The bartender brought the second drink. He sipped at it, and then put the shot glass on the bar top.

"Do I look like a hick?" Pete asked.

"You look like a goddamn queer," Frank said.

"No, I mean it."

"You asked me, and I told you."

"What's troubling you, Frank?"

"You a priest or something?"

"No, but I thought..."

"Look, I come in here to have a drink. I didn't come to see the chaplain."

"You an ex-Army man?"

"Yeah."

"I was in the Navy," Pete said. "Glad to be out of that, all right. Glad to be right here where I am, in the most wonderful city in the whole damn world."

"Go down to Union Square and get a soapbox," Frank said.

"Can't I help you, Frank?" Pete asked. "Can't I buy you a drink, lend you an ear, do something? You're so damn sad, I feel like..."

"I'm not sad."

"You sure look sad. What happened? Did you lose your job?"

"No, I didn't lose my job."

"What do you do, Frank?"

"Right now, I'm a truck driver. I used to be a fighter."

"Really? You mean a boxer? No kidding?"

"Why would I kid you?"

"What's your last name?"

"Blake."

"Frank Blake? I don't think I've heard it before. Of course, I didn't follow the fights much."

"Tiger Blake, they called me. That was my ring name."

"Tiger Blake. Well, we didn't have fights in Whiting Center. Had to go over to Waterloo if we wanted to see a bout. I guess that's why I never heard of you."

"Sure," Frank said.

"Why'd you quit fighting?"

"They made me."

"Why?"

"I killed a guy in 1947."

Pete's eyes widened. "In the ring?"

"Of course in the ring. What the hell kind of a moron are you, anyway? You think I'd be walking around if it wasn't in the ring? Jesus!"

"Is that what's troubling you?"

"There ain't nothing troubling me. I'm fine."

"Are you going home for Christmas?"

"I got no home."

"You must have a home," Pete said gently. "*Everybody's* got a home."

"Yeah? Where's your home? Whiting Center or wherever the hell you said?"

"Nope. This is my home now. New York City. New York, New York. The greatest goddamn city in the whole world."

"Sure," Frank said sourly.

"My folks are dead," Pete said. "I'm an only child. Nothing for me in Whiting Center anymore. But in New York,

**443**

well, I get the feeling that I'm here to stay. That I'll meet a nice girl here, and marry her, and raise a family here and...and this'll be home."

"Great," Frank said.

"How'd you happen to kill this fellow?" Pete asked suddenly.

"I hit him."

"And killed him?"

"I hit him on the Adam's apple. Accidentally."

"Were you sore at him?"

"We were in the ring. I already told you that."

"Sure, but were you sore?"

"A fighter don't have to be sore. He's paid to fight."

"Did you like fighting?"

"I loved it," Frank said flatly.

"How about the night you killed that fellow?"

Frank was silent for a long time.

Then he said, "Get lost, huh?"

"I could never fight for money," Pete said. "I got a quick temper, and I get mad as hell, but I could never do it for money. Besides, I'm too happy right now to..."

"Get lost," Frank said again, and he turned his back. Pete sat silently for a moment.

"Frank?" he said at last.

"You back again?"

"I'm sorry. I shouldn't have talked to you about something that's painful to you. Look, it's Christmas Eve. Let's..."

"Forget it."

"Can I buy you a drink?"

"No. I told you no a hundred times. I buy my own damn drinks!"

"This is Christmas E..."

"I don't care what it is. You happy jokers give me the creeps. Get off my back, will you?"

"I'm sorry. I just..."

"Happy, happy, happy. Grinning like a damn fool. What the hell is there to be so happy about? You got an oil well someplace? A gold mine? What is it with you?"

"I'm just..."

"You're just a jerk! I probably pegged you right the minute I laid eyes on you. You're probably a damn queer."

"No, no," Pete said mildly. "You're mistaken, Frank. Honestly, I just feel..."

"Your old man was probably a queer, too. Your old lady probably took on every sailor in town."

The smile left Pete's face, and then tentatively reappeared.

"You don't mean that, Frank," he said.

"I mean everything I ever say," Frank said. There was a strange gleam in his eyes. He studied Pete carefully.

"About my mother, I meant," Pete said.

"I know what you're talking about. And I'll say it again. She probably took on every sailor in town."

"Don't say that, Frank," Pete said, the smile gone now, a perplexed frown teasing his forehead, appearing, vanishing, reappearing.

"You're a queer, and your old lady was a..."

"Stop it, Frank."

"Stop what? If your old lady was..."

Pete leaped off the barstool.

"Cut it out!" he yelled.

From the end of the bar, the bartender turned. Frank caught the movement with the corner of his eye. In a cold whisper, he said, "Your mother was a slut," and Pete swung at him. Frank ducked, and the blow grazed the top of his head. The bartender was coming toward them now. He could not see the strange light in Frank's eyes, nor did he hear Frank whisper again, "A slut, a slut."

Pete pushed himself off the bar wildly. He saw the beer bottle then, picked it up, and lunged at Frank.

The patrolman knelt near his body.

"He's dead, all right," he said. He stood up and dusted off his trousers. "What happened?"

Frank looked bewildered and dazed.

"He went berserk," he said. "We were sitting and talking. Quiet. All of a sudden, he swings at me." He turned to the bartender. "Am I right?"

"He was drinking," the bartender said. "Maybe he was drunk."

"I didn't even swing back," Frank said, "not until he picked up the beer bottle. Hell, this is Christmas Eve. I didn't want no trouble."

"What happened when he picked up the bottle?"

"He swung it at me. So I...I put up my hands to defend myself. I only gave him a push, so help me."

"Where'd you hit him?"

Frank paused. "In...in the throat, I think." He paused again. "It was self-defense, believe me. This guy just went berserk. He musta been a maniac."

"He *was* talking kind of queer," the bartender agreed.

The patrolman nodded sympathetically.

"There's more nuts outside than there is in," he said.

He turned to Frank. "Don't take this so bad, Mac. You'll get off. It looks open and shut to me. Just tell them the story downtown, that's all."

"Berserk," Frank said. "He just went berserk."

"Well..." The patrolman shrugged. "My partner'll take care of the meat wagon when it gets here. You and me better get downtown. I'm sorry I got to ruin your Christmas, but..."

"It's him that ruined it," Frank said, shaking his head and looking down at the body on the floor.

Together, they started out of the bar.

At the door, the patrolman waved to the bartender and said, "Merry Christmas, Mac."

# GANGS

"*First Offense*," the Manhunt *story that opened this collec-*
*tion, was published in 1955. "The Last Spin" was published*
*in that same magazine a year later. "On the Sidewalk, Bleed-*
*ing," which immediately follows, was first published in Man-*
hunt *in 1957. These three stories remain the most anthologized*
*of all the short stories I've ever written.*

# On the Sidewalk, Bleeding

THE BOY LAY BLEEDING IN THE RAIN.

He was sixteen years old, and he wore a bright purple silk jacket, and the lettering across the back of the jacket read THE ROYALS. The boy's name was Andy, and the name was delicately scripted in black thread on the front of the jacket, just over the heart. *Andy.*

He had been stabbed ten minutes ago.

The knife had entered just below his rib cage and had been drawn across his body violently, tearing a wide gap in his flesh. He lay on the sidewalk with the March rain drilling his jacket and drilling his body and washing away the blood that poured from his open wound. He had known excruciating pain when the knife ripped across his body, and then sudden comparative relief when the blade was pulled away. He had heard the voice saying, "That's for you, Royal!" and then the sound of footsteps hurrying into the rain, and then he had fallen to the sidewalk, clutching his stomach, trying to stop the flow of blood.

He tried to yell for help, but he had no voice. He did not know why his voice had deserted him, or why the rain had become so suddenly fierce, or why there was an open hole in his

**453**

body from which his life ran redly, steadily. It was 11:30 P.M., but he did not know the time.

There was another thing he did not know.

He did not know he was dying.

He lay on the sidewalk, bleeding, and he thought only, *That was a fierce rumble, they got me good that time*, but he did not know he was dying. He would have been frightened had he known. In his ignorance, he lay bleeding and wishing he could cry out for help, but there was no voice in his throat. There was only the bubbling of blood from between his lips whenever he opened his mouth to speak. He lay silent in his pain, waiting, waiting for someone to find him. He could hear the sound of automobile tires hushed on the muzzle of rain-swept streets, far away at the other end of the long alley. He lay with his face pressed to the sidewalk, and he could see the splash of neon far away at the other end of the alley, tinting the pavement red and green, slickly brilliant in the rain.

He wondered if Laura would be angry.

He had left the jump to get a package of cigarettes. He had told her he would be back in a few minutes, and then he had gone downstairs and found the candy store closed. He knew that Alfredo's on the next block would be open until at least two, and he had started through the alley, and that was when he'd been ambushed. He could hear the faint sound of music now, coming from a long, long way off, and he wondered if Laura was dancing, wondered if she had missed him yet. Maybe she thought he wasn't coming back. Maybe she thought he'd cut out for good. Maybe she'd already left the jump and gone home. He thought of her face, the brown eyes and the jet-black hair, and thinking of her he forgot his pain a little, forgot that blood was rushing from his body. Someday he would marry Laura. Someday he would marry her, and they would have a lot of kids, and then they would get out of the neighborhood. They would move to a clean project in the Bronx, or maybe they would move to Staten Island. When they were married, when they had kids...

He heard footsteps at the other end of the alley, and he lifted his cheek from the sidewalk and looked into the darkness and tried to cry out, but again there was only a soft hissing bubble of blood on his mouth. The man came down the alley. He had not seen Andy yet. He walked, and then stopped to lean against the brick of the building, and then walked again. He saw Andy then and came toward him, and he stood over him for a long time, the minutes ticking, ticking, watching him and not speaking. Then he said, "What's a matter, buddy?"

Andy could not speak, and he could barely move. He lifted his face slightly and looked up at the man, and in the rain-swept alley he smelled the sickening odor of alcohol and realized the man was drunk. He did not feel any particular panic. He did not know he was dying, and so he felt only mild disappointment that the man who had found him was drunk. The man was smiling.

"Did you fall down, buddy?" he asked. "You mus' be as drunk as I am." He grinned, seemed to remember why he had entered the alley in the first place, and said, "Don' go way. I'll be ri' back."

The man lurched away. Andy heard his footsteps, and then the sound of the man colliding with a garbage can, and some mild swearing, and then the sound of the man urinating, lost in the steady wash of the rain. He waited for the man to come back.

It was 11:39.

When the man returned, he squatted alongside Andy. He studied him with drunken dignity. "You gonna catch cold here," he said. "What's a matter? You like layin' in the wet?"

Andy could not answer. The man tried to focus his eyes on Andy's face. The rain spattered around them.

"You like a drink?"

Andy shook his head. "I gotta bottle. Here," the man said.

He pulled a pint bottle from his inside jacket pocket. He uncapped it and extended it to Andy. Andy tried to move, but pain wrenched him back flat against the sidewalk.

"Take it," the man said. He kept watching Andy. "Take it." When Andy did not move, he said, "Nev' mind, I'll have one m'self." He tilted the bottle to his lips, and then wiped the back of his hand across his mouth. "You too young to be drinkin', anyway. Should be 'shamed of yourself, drunk an' layin' in a alley, all wet. Shame on you. I gotta good minda calla cop."

Andy nodded. Yes, he tried to say. Yes, call a cop. Please. Call one.

"Oh, you don' like that, huh?" the drunk said. "You don' wanna cop to fin' you all drunk an' wet in a alley, huh? Okay, buddy. This time you get off easy." He got to his feet. "This time you lucky," he said. He waved broadly at Andy, and then almost lost his footing. "S'long, buddy," he said.

*Wait,* Andy thought. *Wait, please, I'm bleeding.*

"S'long," the drunk said again, "I see you around," and then he staggered off up the alley.

Andy lay and thought, *Laura, Laura. Are you dancing?*

The couple came into the alley suddenly. They ran into the alley together, running from the rain, the boy holding the girl's elbow, the girl spreading a newspaper over her head to protect her hair. Andy lay crumpled against the pavement, and he watched them run into the alley laughing, and then duck into the doorway not ten feet from him.

"Man, what rain!" the boy said. "You could drown out there."

"I have to get home," the girl said. "It's late, Freddie. I have to get home."

"We got time," Freddie said. "Your people won't raise a fuss if you're a little late. Not with this kind of weather."

"It's dark," the girl said, and she giggled.

"Yeah," the boy answered, his voice very low.

"Freddie...?"

"Um?"

"You're...you're standing very close to me."

"Um."

There was a long silence. Then the girl said, "Oh," only that single word, and Andy knew she'd been kissed, and he suddenly hungered for Laura's mouth. It was then that he wondered if he would ever kiss Laura again. It was then that he wondered if he was dying.

No, he thought, *I can't be dying, not from a little street rumble, not from just getting cut. Guys get cut all the time in rumbles. I can't be dying. No, that's stupid. That don't make any sense at all.*

"You shouldn't," the girl said.

"Why not?"

"I don't know."

"Do you like it?"

"Yes."

"So?"

"I don't know."

"I love you, Angela," the boy said.

"I love you, too, Freddie," the girl said, and Andy listened and thought, *I love you, Laura. Laura, I think maybe I'm dying. Laura, this is stupid but I think maybe I'm dying. Laura, I think I'm dying!* He tried to speak. He tried to move. He tried to crawl toward the doorway where he could see the two figures in embrace. He tried to make a noise, a sound, and a grunt came from his lips, and then he tried again, and another grunt came, a low animal grunt of pain.

"What was that?" the girl said, suddenly alarmed, breaking away from the boy.

"I don't know," he answered.

"Go look, Freddie."

"No. Wait."

Andy moved his lips again. Again the sound came from him.

"Freddie!"

"What?"

"I'm scared."

"I'll go see," the boy said.

He stepped into the alley. He walked over to where Andy lay on the ground. He stood over him, watching him.

"You all right?" he asked.

"What is it?" Angela said from the doorway.

"Somebody's hurt," Freddie said.

"Let's get out of here," Angela said.

"No. Wait a minute."

He knelt down beside Andy. "You cut?" he asked.

Andy nodded.

The boy kept looking at him. He saw the lettering on the jacket then. THE ROYALS. He turned to Angela.

"He's a Royal," he said.

"Let's...what...what do you want to do, Freddie?"

"I don't know. I don't want to get mixed up in this. He's a Royal. We help him, and the Guardians'll be down on our necks. I don't want to get mixed up in this, Angela."

"Is he...is he hurt bad?"

"Yeah, it looks that way."

"What shall we do?"

"I don't know."

"We can't leave him here in the rain." Angela hesitated. "Can we?"

"If we get a cop, the Guardians'll find out who," Freddie said. "I don't know, Angela. I don't know."

Angela hesitated a long time before answering. Then she said, "I have to get home, Freddie. My people will begin to worry."

"Yeah," Freddie said. He looked at Andy again. "You all right?" he asked. Andy lifted his face from the sidewalk, and his eyes said, Please, please help me, and maybe Freddie read what his eyes were saying, and maybe he didn't.

Behind him, Angela said, "Freddie, let's get out of here! Please!"

There was urgency in her voice, urgency bordering on the edge of panic. Freddie stood up. He looked at Andy again, and then mumbled, "I'm sorry," and then he took Angela's arm and together they ran toward the neon splash at the other end of the alley.

*Why, they're afraid of the Guardians*, Andy thought in amazement. *But why should they be? I wasn't afraid of the Guardians. I never turkeyed out of a rumble with the Guardians. I got heart. But I'm bleeding.*

The rain was soothing somehow. It was a cold rain, but his body was hot all over, and the rain helped to cool him. He had always liked rain. He could remember sitting in Laura's house one time, the rain running down the windows, and just looking out over the street, watching the people running from the rain. That was when he'd first joined the Royals. He could remember how happy he was the Royals had taken him. The Royals and the Guardians, two of the biggest. He was a Royal. There had been meaning to the title.

Now, in the alley, with the cold rain washing his hot body, he wondered about the meaning. If he died, he was Andy. He was not a Royal. He was simply Andy, and he was dead. And he wondered suddenly if the Guardians who had ambushed him and knifed him had ever once realized he was Andy. Had they known that he was Andy, or had they simply known that he was a Royal wearing a purple silk jacket? Had they stabbed *him*, Andy, or had they only stabbed the jacket and the title, and what good was the title if you were dying?

*I'm Andy*, he screamed wordlessly. *For Christ's sake, I'm Andy!*

An old lady stopped at the other end of the alley. The garbage cans were stacked there, beating noisily in the rain. The old lady carried an umbrella with broken ribs, carried it with all the dignity of a queen. She stepped into the mouth of the alley, a shopping bag over one arm. She lifted the lids of the garbage cans delicately, and she did not hear Andy grunt because she was a little deaf and because the rain was beating a steady relentless tattoo on the cans. She had been searching and foraging for the better part of the night. She collected her string and her newspapers, and an old hat with a feather on it from one of the garbage cans, and a broken footstool from another of the cans. And then she delicately replaced the lids and lifted her umbrella high and walked out of the alley mouth with queenly dignity. She had worked swiftly and soundlessly, and now she was gone.

The alley looked very long now. He could see people passing at the other end of it, and he wondered who the people were, and he wondered if he would ever get to know them, wondered who it was on the Guardians who had stabbed him, who had plunged the knife into his body. "That's for you, Royal!" the voice had said, and then the footsteps, his arms being released by the others, the fall to the pavement. "That's for you, Royal!" Even in his pain, even as he collapsed, there had been some sort of pride in knowing he was a Royal. Now there was no pride at all. With the rain beginning to chill him, with the blood pouring steadily between his fingers, he knew only a sort of dizziness, and within the giddy dizziness, he could only think, *I want to be Andy.*

It was not very much to ask of the world.

He watched the world passing at the other end of the alley. The world didn't know he was Andy. The world didn't know he was alive. He wanted to say, "Hey, I'm alive! Hey, look at me! I'm alive! Don't you know I'm alive? Don't you know I exist?"

He felt weak and very tired. He felt alone and wet and feverish and chilled, and he knew he was going to die now, and the knowledge made him suddenly sad. He was not frightened. For some reason, he was not frightened. He was only filled with an overwhelming sadness that his life would be over at sixteen. He felt all at once as if he had never done anything, never seen anything, never been anywhere. There were so many things to do, and he wondered why he'd never thought of them before, wondered why the rumbles and the jumps and the purple jacket had always seemed so important to him before, and now they seemed like such small things in a world he was missing, a world that was rushing past at the other end of the alley.

*I don't want to die*, he thought. *I haven't lived yet.*

It seemed very important to him that he take off the purple jacket. He was very close to dying, and when they found him, he did not want them to say, "Oh, it's a Royal." With great effort, he rolled over onto his back. He felt the pain tearing at his stomach when he moved, a pain he did not think was possible. But he wanted to take off the jacket. If he never did another thing, he wanted to take off the jacket. The jacket had only one meaning now, and that was a very simple meaning.

If he had not been wearing the jacket, he would not have been stabbed. The knife had not been plunged in hatred of Andy. The knife hated only the purple jacket. The jacket was a stupid meaningless thing that was robbing him of his life. He wanted the jacket off his back. With an enormous loathing, he wanted the jacket off his back.

He lay struggling with the shiny wet material. His arms were heavy, and pain ripped fire across his body whenever he moved. But he squirmed and fought and twisted until one arm was free and then the other, and then he rolled away from the jacket and lay quite still, breathing heavily, listening to the sound of his breathing and the sound of the rain and thinking, *Rain is sweet, I'm Andy.*

She found him in the alleyway a minute past midnight. She left the dance to look for him, and when she found him she knelt beside him and said, "Andy, it's me, Laura." He did not answer her. She backed away from him, tears springing into her eyes, and then she ran from the alley hysterically and did not stop running until she found the cop. And now, standing with the cop, she looked down at him, and the cop rose and said, "He's dead," and all the crying was out of her now. She stood in the rain and said nothing, looking at the dead boy on the pavement, and looking at the purple jacket that rested a foot away from his body. The cop picked up the jacket and turned it over in his hands.

"A Royal, huh?" he said.

The rain seemed to beat more steadily now, more fiercely.

She looked at the cop and, very quietly, she said, "His name is Andy."

The cop slung the jacket over his arm. He took out his black pad, and he flipped it open to a blank page.

"A Royal," he said.

Then he began writing.

# The Last Spin

THE BOY SITTING OPPOSITE HIM WAS HIS ENEMY.

The boy sitting opposite him was called Tigo, and he wore a green silk jacket with an orange stripe on each sleeve. The jacket told Dave that Tigo was his enemy. The jacket shrieked, "Enemy, enemy!"

"This is a good piece," Tigo said, indicating the gun on the table. "This runs you close to forty-five bucks, you try to buy it in a store. That's a lot of money."

The gun on the table was a Smith & Wesson .38 Police Special.

It rested exactly in the center of the table, its sawed-off, two-inch barrel abruptly terminating the otherwise lethal grace of the weapon. There was a checked walnut stock on the gun, and the gun was finished in a flat blue. Alongside the gun were three .38 Special cartridges.

Dave looked at the gun disinterestedly. He was nervous and apprehensive, but he kept tight control of his face. He could not show Tigo what he was feeling. Tigo was the enemy, and so he presented a mask to the enemy, cocking one eyebrow and saying, "I seen pieces before. There's nothing special about this one."

"Except what we got to do with it," Tigo said.

Tigo was studying him with large brown eyes. The eyes were moist-looking. He was not a bad-looking kid, Tigo, with thick black hair and maybe a nose that was too long, but his mouth and chin were good. You could usually tell a cat by his mouth and his chin. Tigo would not turkey out of this particular rumble. Of that, Dave was sure.

"Why don't we start?" Dave asked. He wet his lips and looked across at Tigo.

"You understand," Tigo said, "I got no bad blood for you."

"I understand."

"This is what the club said. This is how the club said we should settle it. Without a big street diddlebop, you dig? But I want you to know I don't know you from a hole in the wall— except you wear a blue and gold jacket."

"And you wear a green and orange one," Dave said, "and that's enough for me."

"Sure, but what I was tryin to say..."

"We going to sit and talk all night, or we going to get this thing rolling?" Dave asked.

"What I'm tryin to say..." Tigo went on, "is that I just happened to be picked for this, you know? Like to settle this thing that's between the two clubs. I mean, you got to admit your boys shouldn't have come in our territory last night."

"I got to admit nothing," Dave said flatly.

"Well, anyway, they shot at the candy store. That wasn't right. There's supposed to be a truce on."

"Okay, okay," Dave said.

"So like...like this is the way we agreed to settle it. I mean, one of us and...and one of you. Fair and square. Without any street boppin', and without any law trouble."

"Let's get on with it," Dave said.

"I'm tryin to say, I never even seen you on the street before this. So this ain't nothin personal with me. Whichever way it turns out, like…"

"I never seen you neither," Dave said.

Tigo stared at him for a long time. "That's 'cause you're new around here. Where you from originally?"

"My people come down from the Bronx."

"You got a big family?"

"A sister and two brothers, that's all."

"Yeah, I only got a sister." Tigo shrugged. "Well." He sighed. "So." He sighed again. "Let's make it, huh?"

"I'm waitin," Dave said.

Tigo picked up the gun, and then he took one of the cartridges from the tabletop. He broke open the gun, slid the cartridge into the cylinder, and then snapped the gun shut and twirled the cylinder.

"Round and round she goes," he said, "and where she stops, nobody knows. There's six chambers in the cylinder and only one cartridge. That makes the odds five-to-one that the cartridge won't be in firing position when the cylinder stops whirling. You dig?"

"I dig."

"I'll go first," Tigo said.

Dave looked at him suspiciously.

"Why?"

"You want to go first?"

"I don't know."

"I'm giving you a break." Tigo grinned. "I may blow my head off first time out."

"Why you giving me a break?" Dave asked.

Tigo shrugged. "What the hell's the difference?" He gave the cylinder a fast twirl.

"The Russians invented this, huh?" Dave asked.

"Yeah."

"I always said they was crazy bastards."

"Yeah, I always…"

Tigo stopped talking. The cylinder was stopped now. He took a deep breath, put the barrel of the .38 to his temple, and then squeezed the trigger. The firing pin clicked on an empty chamber.

"Well, that was easy, wasn't it?" he asked. He shoved the gun across the table. "Your turn, Dave."

Dave reached for the gun. It was cold in the basement room, but he was sweating now. He pulled the gun toward him, then left it on the table while he dried his palms on his trousers. He picked up the gun then and stared at it.

"It's a nifty piece," Tigo said. "I like a good piece."

"Yeah, I do, too," Dave said. "You can tell a good piece just by the way it feels in your hand."

Tigo looked surprised. "I mentioned that to one of the guys yesterday, and he thought I was nuts."

"Lots of guys don't know about pieces," Dave said, shrugging.

"I was thinking," Tigo said, "when I get old enough, I'll join the Army, you know? I'd like to work around pieces."

"I thought of that, too. I'd join now, only my old lady won't give me permission. She's got to sign if I join now."

"Yeah, they're all the same," Tigo said, smiling. "Your old lady born here or the old country?"

"The old country," Dave said.

"Yeah, well you know they got these old-fashioned ideas."

"I better spin," Dave said.

"Yeah," Tigo agreed.

Dave slapped the cylinder with his left hand. The cylinder whirled, whirled, and then stopped. Slowly, Dave put the gun to his head. He wanted to close his eyes, but he didn't dare. Tigo, the enemy, was watching him. He returned Tigo's stare, and then he squeezed the trigger. His heart skipped a beat, and then over the roar of his blood he heard the empty click. Hastily he put the gun down on the table.

"Makes you sweat, don't it?" Tigo said.

Dave nodded, saying nothing. He watched Tigo. Tigo was looking at the gun.

"Me now, huh?" Tigo said. He took a deep breath, then picked up the .38. He twirled the cylinder, waited for it to stop, and then put the gun to his head.

"Bang!" Tigo said, and then he squeezed the trigger. Again the firing pin clicked on an empty chamber. Tigo let out his breath and put the gun down.

"I thought I was dead that time," he said.

"I could hear the harps," Dave said.

"This is a good way to lose weight, you know that?" Tigo laughed nervously, and then his laugh became honest when he saw Dave was laughing with him.

"Ain't it the truth? You could lose ten pounds this way."

"My old lady's like a house," Dave said laughing. "She ought to try this kind of a diet." He laughed at his own humor, pleased when Tigo joined him.

"That's the trouble," Tigo said. "You see a nice deb in the street, you think it's crazy, you know? Then they get to be our people's age, and they turn to fat." He shook his head.

"You got a chick?" Dave asked.

"Yeah, I got one."

"What's her name?"

"Aw, you don't know her."

"Maybe I do," Dave said.

"Her name is Juana." Tigo watched him. "She's about five-two, got these brown eyes…"

"I think I know her," Dave said. He nodded. "Yeah, I think I know her."

"She's nice, ain't she?" Tigo asked. He leaned forward, as if Dave's answer was of great importance to him.

"Yeah, she's nice," Dave said.

"The guys rib me about her. You know, all they're after—well, you know—they don't understand something like Juana."

"I got a chick, too," Dave said.

"Yeah? Hey, maybe sometime we could…" Tigo cut himself short. He looked down at the gun, and his sudden enthusiasm seemed to ebb completely. "It's your turn," he said.

"Here goes nothing," Dave said. He twirled the cylinder, sucked in his breath, and then fired.

The empty click was loud in the stillness of the room.

"Man!" Dave said.

"We're pretty lucky, you know?" Tigo said.

"So far."

"We better lower the odds. The boys won't like it if we…" He stopped himself again, and then reached for one of the cartridges on the table. He broke open the gun again, and slipped the second cartridge into the cylinder. "Now we got two cartridges in here," he said. "Two cartridges, six chambers. That's four-to-two. Divide it, and you get two-to-one." He paused. "You game?"

"That's...that's what we're here for, ain't it?"

"Sure."

"Okay then."

"Gone," Tigo said, nodding his head. "You got courage, Dave."

"You're the one needs the courage," Dave said gently. "It's your spin."

Tigo lifted the gun. Idly, he began spinning the cylinder.

"You live on the next block, don't you?" Dave asked.

"Yeah." Tigo kept slapping the cylinder. It spun with a gently whirring sound.

"That's how come we never crossed paths, I guess. Also, I'm new on the scene."

"Yeah, well you know, you get hooked up with one club, that's the way it is."

"You like the guys in your club?" Dave asked, wondering why he was asking such a stupid question, listening to the whirring of the cylinder at the same time.

"They're okay." Tigo shrugged. "None of them really send me, but that's the club on my block, so what're you gonna do, huh?" His hand left the cylinder. It stopped spinning. He put the gun to his head.

"Wait!" Dave said.

Tigo looked puzzled. "What's the matter?"

"Nothin. I just wanted to say...I mean..." Dave frowned. "I don't dig too many of the guys in my club, either."

Tigo nodded. For a moment, their eyes locked. Then Tigo shrugged, and fired. The empty click filled the basement room.

"Phew," Tigo said.

"Man, you can say that again."

Tigo slid the gun across the table. Dave hesitated an instant. He did not want to pick up the gun. He felt sure that this time the firing pin would strike the percussion cap of one of the cartridges. He was sure that this time he would shoot himself.

"Sometimes I think I'm turkey," he said to Tigo, surprised that his thoughts had found voice.

"I feel that way sometimes, too," Tigo said.

"I never told that to nobody," Dave said. "The guys in my club would laugh at me, I ever told them that."

"Some things you got to keep to yourself. There ain't nobody you can trust in this world."

"There should be somebody you can trust," Dave said. "Hell, you can't tell nothing to your people. They don't understand."

Tigo laughed. "That's an old story. But that's the way things are. What're you gonna do?"

"Yeah. Still, sometimes I think I'm turkey."

"Sure, sure," Tigo said. "But it ain't only that, though. Like sometimes...well, don't you wonder what you're doing stomping some guy in the street? Like...you know what I mean? Like...who's the guy to you? What you got to beat him up for? 'Cause he messed with somebody else's girl?" Tigo shook his head. "It gets complicated sometimes."

"Yeah, but..." Dave frowned again. "You got to stick with the club. Don't you?"

"Sure, sure...no question."

Again, their eyes locked.

"Well, here goes," Dave said. He lifted the gun. "It's just..." He shook his head, and then twirled the cylinder. The cylinder spun, and then stopped. He studied the gun, wondering if one of the cartridges would roar from the barrel when he squeezed the trigger.

Then he fired.

*Click.*

"I didn't think you was going through with it," Tigo said.

"I didn't neither."

"You got heart, Dave," Tigo said. He looked at the gun. He picked it up and broke it open.

"What you doing?" Dave asked.

"Another cartridge," Tigo said. "Six chambers, three cartridges. That makes it even money. You game?"

"You?"

"The boys said…" Tigo stopped talking. "Yeah, I'm game," he added, his voice curiously low.

"It's your turn, you know."

"I know."

Dave watched as Tigo picked up the gun.

"You ever been rowboating on the lake?"

Tigo looked across the table at Dave, his eyes wide. "Once," he said. "I went with Juana."

"Is it…is it any kicks?"

"Yeah. Yeah, it's grand kicks. You mean you never been?"

"No," Dave said.

"Hey, you got to try it, man," Tigo said excitedly. "You'll like it. Hey, you try it."

"Yeah, I was thinking maybe this Sunday I'd…" He did not complete the sentence.

"My spin," Tigo said wearily. He twirled the cylinder. "Here goes a good man," he said, and he put the revolver to his head and squeezed the trigger.

*Click.*

Dave smiled nervously. "No rest for the weary," he said. "But, Jesus, you got heart, I don't know if I can go through with it."

"Sure, you can," Tigo assured him. "Listen, what's there to be afraid of?" He slid the gun across the table.

"We keep this up all night?" Dave asked.

"They said...you know..."

"Well, it ain't so bad. I mean, hell, we didn't have this operation, we wouldn'ta got a chance to talk, huh?" He grinned feebly.

"Yeah," Tigo said, his face splitting in a wide grin. "It ain't been so bad, huh?"

"No...it's been...well...you know, these guys in the club, who can talk to them?"

He picked up the gun.

"We could..." Tigo started.

"What?"

"We could say...well...like we kept shootin' an' nothin happened, so..." Tigo shrugged. "What the hell! We can't do this all night, can we?"

"I don't know."

"Let's make this the last spin. Listen, they don't like it, they can take a flying leap, you know?"

"I don't think they'll like it. We supposed to settle this for the clubs."

"Screw the clubs!" Tigo said vehemently. "Can't we pick our own..." The word was hard coming. When it came, he said it softly, and his eyes did not leave Dave's face. "...friends?"

"Sure we can," Dave said fervently. "Sure we can! Why not?"

"The last spin," Tigo said. "Come on, the last spin."

"Gone," Dave said. "Hey you know, I'm glad they got this idea. You know that? I'm actually glad!" He twirled the cylinder. "Look, you want to go on the lake this Sunday? I mean with your girl and mine? We could get two boats. Or even one if you want."

"Yeah, one boat," Tigo said. "Hey, your girl'll like Juana, I mean it. She's a swell chick."

The cylinder stopped. Dave put the gun to his head quickly.

"Here's to Sunday," he said. He grinned at Tigo, and Tigo grinned back, and then Dave fired.

The explosion rocked the small basement room, ripping away half of Dave's head, shattering his face. A small cry escaped Tigo's throat, and a look of incredulous shock knifed his eyes. Then he put his head on the table and began weeping.

# Afterword

I was lucky to stumble into a job at a literary agency and to find in Scott Meredith a mentor who recognized my fierce ambition and possible talent, and who offered me opportunities to develop the skills I'd never been taught in all of my college writing courses.

"How would you like to write a novel?" he asked me one day.

"A *novel*?" I said. "No, no, I could *never* write a novel."

I was still learning to write short stories!

But the John C. Winston Company had asked the agency to provide a series of science fiction novels for young adults, and Lester del Rey (he of "Rattlesnake Cave" fame) had written short outlines for each of the novels. Scott offered me the outline for *Find the Feathered Serpent*, which became the first Evan Hunter novel I ever wrote, and then for *Danger, Dinosaurs!* and *Rocket to Luna*, two novels I wrote under the Richard Marsten pseudonym.

It was in *Manhunt*, though, that Scott offered me the greatest opportunities to develop as a writer. I was amazed earlier this year when my Hollywood agent reported that several studios had hoped for more "twists and turns of plot and less *character"* in a novel he'd submitted. Back in the fifties, after decades of plot-driven pulp stories, *Manhunt* was bold enough to explore character—the kids and the women in jeopardy, the loose cannons, the private eyes, the innocent bystanders, the gangs... and yes, the cops and robbers. *Manhunt* and Scott Meredith (and John McCloud, too) offered me the freedom to learn. I shall forever be grateful for the experience. From first offense to last spin, it was a remarkable journey.

Thank you for sharing it with me all over again.

DECEMBER 2004

# Bibliography

1952:

"Eye Witness" — Hunt Collins — *Verdict* (August)


1953:

"Carrera's Woman" — Richard Marsten — *Manhunt* (February)
"Kid Kill" — Evan Hunter — *Manhunt* (April)
"Small Homicide" — Evan Hunter — *Manhunt* (June)
"Good and Dead" — Evan Hunter — *Manhunt* (July)
"Still Life" — Evan Hunter — *Manhunt* (August)
"The Innocent One" — Richard Marsten — *Manhunt* (August)
"The Molested" — Hunt Collins — *Manhunt* (September)
"Accident Report" — Richard Marsten — *Manhunt* (September)
"Chalk," originally published as "I Killed Jeannie" — Evan
     Hunter — *Pursuit* (November)


1954:

"Runaway" — Richard Marsten — *Manhunt* (February)
"Association Test" — Hunt Collins — *Manhunt* (July)

"Chinese Puzzle" — Richard Marsten — *Manhunt* (July)
"Every Morning" — Richard Marsten — *Manhunt* (September)
"Bedbug" — Evan Hunter — *Manhunt* (September)
"Death Flight," originally published as "Ticket to Death" —
    Evan Hunter — *Argosy* (September)


1955:

"Kiss Me, Dudley" — Hunt Collins — *Manhunt* (January)
"Dummy," originally published as "The Big Scream" — Evan
    Hunter — *Real* (June)
"See Him Die" — Evan Hunter — *Manhunt* (July)
"The Big Day" — Richard Marsten — *Manhunt* (September)
"First Offense" — Evan Hunter — *Manhunt* (December)


1956:

"Downpour," originally published as "Murder on the Keys" —
    Richard Marsten — *Argosy* (February)
"The Last Spin" — Evan Hunter — *Manhunt* (September)


1957:

"On the Sidewalk, Bleeding" — Evan Hunter — *Manhunt* (July)
"The Merry Merry Christmas" — Evan Hunter — *Manhunt*
    (December)